James Long

COLLATERAL DAMAGE

VIKING

VIKING

Published by the Penguin Group
Penguin Books Ltd, 27 Wrights Lane, London W8 5TZ, England
Penguin Books USA Inc., 375 Hudson Street, New York, New York 10014, USA
Penguin Books Australia Ltd, Ringwood, Victoria, Australia
Penguin Books Canada Ltd, 10 Alcorn Avenue, Toronto, Ontario, Canada M4V 3B2
Penguin Books (NZ) Ltd, 182–190 Wairau Road, Auckland 10, New Zealand

Penguin Books Ltd, Registered Offices: Harmondsworth, Middlesex, England

First published 1993
10 9 8 7 6 5 4 3 2 1
First edition

Typeset by Datix International Ltd, Bungay, Suffolk
Set in 11/14 pt Lasercomp Photina
Printed in England by Clays Ltd, St Ives plc

A CIP catalogue record for this book is available from the British Library

ISBN 0-670-84157-9

To M.G. and D.G.

for everything they've done

collateral [*kolate*Ral]   *adj*   side by side, parallel, subordinate, secondary

collateral damage   (*US milit*)   accidental injury to civilian population through military action

Author's Note

This book is a work of fiction. Characters, names, companies and incidents are either the product of my imagination or are used fictionally. Bamco and BFSS do not represent real companies. For the background, however, the actual events and atmosphere of the Gulf War have been used as realistically as possible, after much research. Fuel Air Explosives do, unfortunately, exist. The relationships between the press and the military in the Gulf were very much as described here. I am indebted to a number of experts for advice on the current state of the weaponry art. They would rather remain anonymous. I am also indebted to a number of journalists who shared their experiences of the war with me.

The references to Fleet Air Arm operations in World War Two are equally accurate. 899 Squadron was a real squadron. Its 'line book' is in the Fleet Air Arm museum at Yeovilton and I am grateful for the museum's assistance. Quotations from the book, except those referring to Jackie Mainwaring, are accurate. My father, Bill Long, was a Seafire pilot in 899 Squadron and was one of those who contributed to that line book.

James Long
Ashburton, England, 1992

Tuesday July 30th 1991

The last display case was a booby-trap, more dangerous than any of the weapons that filled the floor around it. No one had thought to warn him. He came to it from the side and his eyes almost passed over it. The combat jacket could have been anyone's – just another bit of stained, shredded battlefield rubbish – but then he saw the notebook with its big loopy handwriting, and the anonymous, sterile exhibits behind the glass turned instantly to sharp instruments of personal pain. He moved in horrified slow motion round to the front, and the confirmation kicked him in the guts. Her photo framed in black by some museum worker who had never known her, never held her in his arms, never had to look at her torn body.

His eyes flinched away and skidded down the text below, sampling just a line for fear of the rest. '. . . It is believed she met her death at the hands of a unit of the Republican Guard . . .'

They've got no right, he thought. She's my loss, my own. She's not part of the official history of the war. He slowly raised his eyes to the photo again, and a savage ache constricted his throat and his eyes.

He shouldn't have come. In the dangerous game in which he was now enmeshed, this was time he could not afford, but David Challis had an old-fashioned sense of honour, and an invitation accepted was not something to abandon lightly. He

1

looked round at the celebration, cocktails and canapés among the tanks – the Imperial War Museum in a party frock – and for him it was suddenly a wake.

Chapter One

Thursday August 2nd 1990

Two tom-cats, circling a peach tree in the early morning moonlight, bristled and yowled in a Holland Park back garden. Through an open sash-window, the noise half woke David for a second, interrupting a disturbing and familiar dream in which he was walking along a beach, late for a broadcast, unable to find a studio, a camera or any clothes, and knowing he'd forgotten to write a script.

Three thousand miles away, Fahd Al Ahmad Al Sabah, half-brother to the Emir of Kuwait, was dying a brave death. The extrovert manager of Kuwait's national football team, still holding his gun, lay bleeding his life out on the steps of the Dasman Palace where he had made a last stand against the invading Iraqis as his family fled.

David woke to the sound of the phone ringing. He sat up in the big brass bed and stretched. It was a man's room, spartan and a little old-fashioned in its furnishings, but tidy and airy. He looked out of the open window to the lawn at the back of the house where birds now sang in the old peach tree. It was just before seven-thirty in the morning, and his alarm went as he was picking up the receiver.

'David, it's Angela. Hope I didn't wake you up?' Angela Carver was the editor of his programme *Double Exposure*.

'You did, but that's OK.'

'You won't have heard the news then. Iraq invaded Kuwait at two o'clock this morning.'

David stiffened and his brain raced to life. 'The oilfields?'

'No, the whole lot. They've taken over the whole place, right the way into town. The Al Sabahs have done a runner to Saudi.'

'Many dead?'

'Dunno yet. Not too much resistance, I guess. I don't suppose the Kuwaitis had much chance. Anyway, we ought to get moving. How about meeting here in a couple of hours?'

'I'll be there.'

The first half-hour of the meeting was fine. There were just eight of them, all programme makers, working through the options for what could happen next and making contingency plans to suit any likely out-turn. *Double Exposure* was a unique programme. Co-funded by the BBC in Britain and NBC in America, it did a weekly half-hour which usually consisted of two fifteen-minute films on the same subject, one from the American perspective, the other from Europe. Of its type it was a big-budget show, but not so big-budget that a possible war in the Middle East didn't present huge logistical problems in getting the right people to the right places at the right time.

For all that, they were coming up with good ideas until the door opened and Bertram Glass walked in. He had dressed for the occasion, a mock military jacket covered in epaulettes and extra pockets, with khaki spectacle frames to match, and he had lots of ideas. An ex-BBC mandarin turned independent producer, Glass was the founder and main shareholder of Glass Crystal Productions, and a major crisis always made him forget that his expertise lay in making deals, not programmes.

'Sitrep please, Angela,' he said as he came in through the door.

'Haven't got any, Bertram,' she said with a straight face. 'I don't smoke.'

He didn't get the point. 'Anything fresh?'

'Yes,' she said. 'The Iraqis are still in Kuwait.' She winked at David.

'Right,' he said, not noticing. 'David, I want you on the first plane to Kuwait.'

David sighed. 'Kuwait airport is shut, Bertram, and likely to remain so. We know a British Airways jumbo landed there after the invasion, which probably wasn't a very good idea, but everything else is suspended.'

Glass started drumming his fingers on the table. 'Well then, what about going to, er, Dubai or somewhere, and driving up.'

Angela started to laugh and turned it into a cough. David tossed a map across the table. 'Bertram, the country next to Kuwait is Saudi Arabia, not Dubai. Visas are hard to come by. Anyway, it seems to us that for the moment we should be concentrating on the diplomatic response.' Angela recovered herself and he left it to her, as editor, to continue. She went over the ground they'd covered before the interruption, turning *Double Exposure*'s format neatly on its head by sending David with a British crew to the US and bringing the New York team to Europe to cover the war of words that was bound to start. He looked out of the window at the Charlotte Street traffic as they talked, thinking how many similar meetings he had sat through, reducing it all to words, names and airline tickets. He wondered what was happening on the hot concrete streets of Kuwait, who was dying and how. He looked at the group talking round the table: Bertram, who was getting off on the excitement as though this was the front line itself; Angela, whose reality would be what she saw on the monitors in the cutting-room; and Gwen, their operations manager, caught up in the job of building the logistical bridges to get the crews to the right places. He was the only one there who would have to cross those bridges, see what was on the other side and try to preserve the truth of it through all the distorting mirrors set in his way. Once Glass had left, late (he said) for a big meeting at Channel 4, the business was done quickly. David would leave for Washington on Sunday. Two free days, he thought. If I head north early tomorrow, I needn't lose the whole weekend.

*F*riday *August 3rd 1990*

He was relieved to see the stone gateposts marking the end of his journey. Since Newcastle the temperature gauge had been creeping closer to the red sector and he'd slowed his pace, letting the old Jensen CV-8 amble along. It would be easier to have something more modern, but there were many things about the twenty-five-year-old car which appealed to his nature. The clubland cocoon of the leather interior could be relied on to put him back in a good mood at the worst of times. The six-litre V8 engine normally sufficed to put upstart foreign hatchbacks in their place, even if its Detroit origins took just a little of the shine off the patriotic pride he felt in the rest of the car. Above all, perhaps, the knowledge that every passing year added to its value instead of decreasing it appealed to the Scottish frugality which was his nature, allowing him the illogical luxury of forgetting its sixteen-miles-to-the-gallon thirst.

There was nothing so frugal about his younger brother and that was a source of constant worry to David, reinforced now as he looked around him at the scenery. There were many good reasons for living up here. Well before he had reached Otterburn, David had lowered his window,

6

nostrils flaring to the scent of the heather, letting a small part of his attention drift away from the incessant speculation which had replaced the news on the radio. The turning just before the Percy Arms led to ever smaller roads, until the final lane crossed the beaten track of the Pennine Way and sloped down into a wide moorland bowl of such natural splendour that it took David's breath away. The dark edge of Kielder Forest was the western boundary, the starting-point for an unbroken sprawl of trees stretching all the way to the Scottish border, while to the east stood the ridges leading down to Hareshaw Common. It was magnificent, wild and historic, the land where the Border reivers had gone their marauding way and the Percys had fought hand to hand, steel on steel, to push Douglas and his people back into Scotland.

David frowned because he was sure that wasn't why Duncan had come here. He swung in at the stone gateposts of Chalice Hall, knowing that the coincidence of name, if not of precise spelling, had lain at the heart of his brother's decision to buy the house. He could remember the excited phone call. 'You'll never guess what I've seen in *Country Life*,' Duncan had said. 'Clearly meant for me, wouldn't you say?' He drove down the drive, on this second visit, amazed again at the sight of the house. Three round towers, crowned with slated spires, grew asymmetrically out of a grey stone façade. Mock battlements linked the towers and a giant stone shield hung menacingly over the arched, double front doors. The windows at the left-hand end were freshly painted; to the right of the front door, though, they were still boarded up, testimony to the expenses yet to come in Duncan's quest to restore the house to its former glory.

The house nestled in a grove of trees. A stone wall all around it kept the moorland at bay. A small wood led north to the rest of the property, and its fields to the west played host to a tenant's sheep. Down at heel though the house undoubtedly was, David was quite sure his profligate brother could not afford it and that his purchase had as much to do with his desire to have an impressive address as with any yearning for the wide open spaces after living for so many years on the fringes of London.

It was mid-afternoon, and he could feel the miles in his bones by the time the tyres stopped turning on the gravel and the engine came to a lumpy halt. He sat there for a moment, enjoying the peace, but almost immediately the front door opened and he smiled as he saw Josie come out. Everyone smiled when they saw Duncan's wife. She was an overgrown teenager really, a body that could have looked gawky if it hadn't been so continually and flamboyantly in motion, and an open face which broadcast liveliness and laughter. An American might have called her cute. An Englishman might have called her pretty. Both would have been aware they were somehow missing the point.

He got out of the car and wrapped his arms round her. 'You've cut your hair,' he said, surprised.

'Don't say you don't like it?' she said. He remembered the feel of it when it was really long, running his fingers through it to frame her face in his hands, but he pushed the thought away. That was another time, long ago, when she'd been his – before he had left on a long foreign posting and virtually propelled her into his brother's arms.

'Of course I like it,' he said, and she put an arm round him, smiling up at him, happy to have him there.

'How long have we got you for?'

'Tomorrow afternoon. I'm flying on Sunday.' She made a face. 'So how's Duncan's folly?' he said, looking around him.

'Stop worrying, David,' she said. 'Duncan's a grown-up now. Well, fairly. He's not your responsibility any more.' She opened her arms wide in an expansive gesture that took in the long façade of the house and the moorland beyond. 'I love it. It's far too big, but I never liked being in London. It's so clean up here.'

'Don't you get bored?'

She laughed. 'Maybe in another ten years.'

'What about Dunk?'

'Oh, well, you know your brother. He's in London two or three days a week for the show. He gets his fix of attention then. I'm quite sure he wouldn't be happy if he was up here all the time.'

'Why?'

'Do you need to ask?' she said, and perched cross-legged on the stone steps, patting the step below her for David to sit down. It was warm in the sun. 'I'm allowed to say this to you because I'm his wife and you're his brother, but Duncan only defines himself in bubbles of conversation which start when someone asks him what he does and finish quite a long time later when he's told them. I sometimes think those are the only times he's truly happy.'

'Ouch. That's a little harsh.'

She smiled. 'No, not ouch. It's the way he is. It's just that he knows he's not you.'

'Oh, come on, Josie. I've had a long drive. You're meant to ply me with drink, not give me a hard time for inflicting psychological damage on your husband.'

She jumped up. 'Whoops, sorry. The cooking sherry is at your disposal.'

They went into the house and sat in the comfortable, old-fashioned kitchen with a glass of wine.

'What I meant was –' she started, looking suddenly serious.

9

He held up his hand. 'Don't worry, I know you were joking.'

'No, I wasn't. I've been thinking about this. I don't often see you by yourself, so give me a chance to say it. You've really looked after Duncan ever since your parents died. How old were you?'

'Seventeen,' said David, remembering as if it were yesterday his housemaster's face as he broke the news.

'Seventeen, and Duncan was fifteen, and you've spent the next eighteen years worrying about him.'

'Not without reason. Look what happened. We inherited quite a lot, you know. As soon as he was allowed to get his hands on it, he blew his share.'

'And you didn't, except for bits of it getting him out of trouble. Anyway, the point is, you must know he hero-worships you.'

David snorted, but Josie pressed the point, watching him intently. 'He does. He married me because he'd just spent two years watching me go out with you.' David looked at her sharply, but she looked calmly back at him. 'He went into TV because you were in it. He knows he can never match you. I'm not sure he should be trying.'

'Why?'

'It doesn't come nearly as easily to him as it does to you. He's bought this place to advertise to the world that he's a success. I love it, but I'm not at all sure it was a good idea.'

'Can't you afford it?'

Josie laughed. 'I don't suppose so for a moment. Duncan does things his way. He decided he'd rather have a huge place up here than somewhere smaller down south. That's fine by me, but I haven't the slightest idea how it's financed.'

'Won't he tell you?'

She smiled at him. 'David, my dear, one way in which

10

you and your brother are truly identical is in your built-in genetic chauvinism on the question of finances. I can't get Duncan to even talk about things like that. He's too scared it would all fall to pieces if we looked at it too closely.'

She fell silent then, and David realized there was something serious here, covered up by all the banter.

'Is that bothering you?' he asked gently.

'No, not really. It's not that. Something else. Don't say I said anything, but I think he's drinking a lot too much. See what you think.' She reached over and rested her fingertips on his wrist. 'He might listen to you. He won't take it from me.'

'Oh. I see. Where is he?'

'He's out doing one of his corporate jobs. He rang just before you came. Says he's bringing an unexpected guest to stay the night.'

'That's nice.'

'No, it's not nice at all. I wanted you to myself. We haven't seen you for ages. Now it means I've got to get another bedroom ready. We've only got two in working order. There's two more which are still full of boxes from the move, and the rest have got the sort of floors you see people fall through in Laurel and Hardy films.'

'I'll help. I can move the boxes for you.'

She looked doubtfully at his clean shirt and jeans. 'They'll have to go up in the attic. It's pretty filthy up there.'

'Doesn't matter. It'll brush off. Just as long as I don't have to look smart for dinner.'

'No, I don't think so. It's not somebody from the company. I think it's a cameraman or something. Duncan said he wanted you to meet him.'

'That's a relief. I don't think I could stand having to be nice to one of Duncan's clients.'

Josie sighed. 'Is it so bad?'

'Dunk knows what I think. It's just there are some things you maybe shouldn't mix. Doing a business programme on the box and doing corporate stuff on the side, one day they'll cross over. You'll suddenly find one of your clients pops up in a bad-news story just when you're about to send him a big bill.'

'Duncan's not stupid. He could handle that, couldn't he?'

'No one can handle that.'

Half an hour later David's back was aching. There was a narrow, twisting staircase up to the attic, but Duncan's boxes of books were heavy as hell and a shade too wide to carry up without tipping them at an awkward angle. Old, dried-up electrical flex and broken sockets showed where there had once been lights in the labyrinthine and gloomy attic, but not any more. Duncan had already filled up all the easily accessible bits, so it was a long haul over uneven, loose floorboards into a corner of the roof where the dust lay thick and the rafters were covered in generations of undisturbed cobwebs.

All the same he was quite happy doing it, until he straightened unwarily and knocked the back of his head on a beam, dropping the box he was carrying. For a moment he had visions of it going straight through the lath and plaster ceiling into the room below, but it wasn't as heavy as some and it tipped on its side, spilling its contents into a narrowing gap the far side of a massive joist. He knelt to shovel the books, leaflets and folders back into it again, brushing the dust off them, then reached down into the darkness for a final scrabble around in the cobwebbed corners to check. His fingers touched something right down in the gap between a floorboard and the joist. He pulled it out, a large photo, curled up into a cylinder, stiffened with age and filthy with dust.

12

He took it down into the light and, assuming it must have been there for years, unrolled it with interest. Surprise was his first reaction when he saw what it was, followed by anger that it should have been there at all. Seven young men sat in a line, the sky behind them, legs dangling over the edge of whatever it was they were sitting on. Someone seeing it for the first time might have guessed it was a ship from the naval caps perched on two of the heads, the mixture of clothing that passed as uniforms and the way their shirts were ballooning to one side in a strong breeze. The photo was taken from a lower vantage point, looking up past them and showing no other detail, but it wasn't the first time or even the hundredth time David had looked at it, and he knew a great deal about it.

It was seven young Fleet Air Arm pilots of 899 Squadron, sitting on the edge of the flight-deck of their carrier, HMS *Indomitable*, steaming through the Mediterranean in the summer of 1943, snapped from the catwalk below. They were a scruffy lot in a rag-bag of clothing, looking superficially light-hearted between sorties in their Seafire fighters. Towards the left end, one of them, wearing dark glasses, looked older and tougher than the rest. It was David and Duncan's father, Bill Challis, a twenty-six-year-old among youths five years his junior.

David was deeply irritated by Duncan's lack of care for the photo, an irritation that resurfaced quickly from years of witnessing Duncan's carefree attitude to objects and values that were precious to his older brother. He went downstairs.

'Josie? Look at this, will you. Bloody Duncan. He might have lost it. I just happened to find it because I dropped something. I do wish he'd take a bit more care.'

She took it from him. 'Where was it?'

'Round to the right, in that bay that sticks out.'

'That's funny. We haven't put anything in there yet. I don't think Duncan's even looked in there.'

'Well, that's where it was. It can't have flown there.' Then he saw her expression. 'I'm sorry, Josie, I shouldn't be taking it out on you. It's just that it's a bit special, and I hate it when things like that get spoiled. I'll talk to Duncan when he gets back. I'll put it in my room.'

'Is the other bedroom empty now?'

'Yes. All the boxes are in the attic.'

'I'll just make the bed, then I've got to go to Otterburn. I promised Duncan I'd pick up some wine he ordered, and I forgot.'

'I'll go.'

'You've been driving all day.'

'No, it's OK.'

Now the Jensen had cooled off, it was behaving itself perfectly. Probably just a vapour lock or something, thought David. He enjoyed the short trip into Otterburn, past the tweed mill and on to the general store, a shop which struck an elegant Northumbrian compromise between the basic necessities of life and the little comforts which make it more tolerable. The alcohol was all in one corner, behind the counter, and it didn't look very promising, but Duncan's wine was a special order, waiting in the back room. He pursed his lips at both the exotic vintage and the quantity, then bought a large bunch of flowers for Josie and a book on local history for Duncan, which he wasn't at all sure his brother would read. He drove back fast, enjoying the way the big Chrysler engine growled harder as the kick-down came in on the automatic box. Approaching the turn-off from the A68, he came up behind two slower-moving cars and groaned as they turned into the smaller road ahead of him, slowing his pace. The one immediately in front was a Sierra in primary red with the

14

name of a hire company on a sticker on the back window. In front of it in turn was a big Volvo estate.

The Sierra was driven by a woman. All he could see of her was a mass of hair around the sides of the headrest and an eye-level slice of her face in her rear-view mirror. He saw the eyes move to the mirror to check behind her, meeting his, and he silently awarded her marks for good driving, to be so alert even on this tiny road. In the eight square inches of mirror glass her eyes held the promise of beauty and, seeming aware of him studying her, she looked again in the mirror as if, safe in her moving metal cell, she could risk the thrill of contact with a stranger. He ruminated on the fact that women seen that way are usually so much more attractive than the disappointing reality revealed on overtaking.

The last two miles were slow, but David didn't mind, sharing the occasional eye contact with the woman in front, lost in his own dream world, waiting for the moment when he would turn right into the driveway and she would go on out of his life. It came as something of a shock when both the cars in front turned in through the gates, and he finally, belatedly, realized that the Volvo must be another of Duncan's new toys and the woman in the red Sierra therefore had to be his guest. His first reaction was slight embarrassment at having to meet, face to face, the pair of eyes about which he had been fantasizing.

They all parked, and Duncan climbed out of the Volvo and welcomed David noisily. 'Bro, I didn't see you behind us. Have you just arrived?'

'No, I went to pick up your wine. How are you, Dunk?'

'All the better for seeing you. Thanks for getting the hooch. Just what we need after a hard day.' He swung round to where the door of the Sierra was opening. 'David, come and meet the lovely Yanna.'

15

The girl got out of the Sierra like the sun coming out from behind a cloud and David felt an electric awareness deep inside him. She was a knockout, masses of curly blonde hair cascading over a face whose sculpted cheek-bones and full lips needed no make-up to accentuate them. In that second, when their eyes met directly for the first time, something complicated passed between them. She was annoyed, there was no doubt about that, but it was as if that something had taken the edge off her annoyance.

'Davey. This is Yanna Le Bihan. Yanna, my brother David.'

They shook hands formally. Her grip was firm, but his skin tingled and he suspected hers did too. She looked at him, as if open to any possibility but ready to judge him on his words.

'You are Breton?' he said, and she gave a surprised smile.

'Yes. How did you know?'

'Le Bihan. Isn't that Breton for "small", like Morbihan is the small sea?'

'Very good. Do you know it?'

'I've been there a lot. Where are you from exactly?'

'My family come from Vannes, but these days my mother and I live at Quiberon.'

'Then I envy you,' he said, 'right out on the end of the world with the clean Atlantic on all sides.' He was staring into her bright blue eyes, and some sort of preliminary bargain was sealed between them.

'Yanna, this is my wife, Josie,' said Duncan, and the moment was past. Josie greeted her warmly, then shot a searching glance at David as they all went inside.

Josie showed Yanna to her room. Duncan changed out of his suit and reappeared in a sweater. He poured David a Scotch, took a considerably larger one for himself, and flopped down in an armchair. 'What do you think of Yanna?' he asked, grinning at David with the expression of one who knew there could be only one answer.

David parried it with another question. 'Who is she exactly?'

'She's a photographer. Stills. I thought you'd like to meet her. We've both been working for the same guys today. I don't think she enjoyed it much.'

'Why?'

'Bit above it, Davey, if you ask me. Sordid commerce and all that. Seems she's got quite a name back in France. Takes war pics. Chad and all that Saharan guerrilla stuff. Quite well known apparently. Anyway, she came over here to try it out for a while and that didn't cut too much ice so she's having to soil her hands with a bit of the hard grind.'

'Meaning?'

Duncan's tone was suddenly a little too casual. 'Well, there's this company, Bamco. Have you heard of them?'

'Bamco. Birmingham Ammunition Company or something like that?'

'Well, yes, once upon a time when companies had that sort of name. Been Bamco for a long time now. Anyway, I'm doing a bit of stuff for them and she came along to do some stills for the same shoot.'

David swirled his whisky round the glass as Duncan poured himself another one. 'What sort of stuff are you doing?'

Duncan looked a little evasive. 'Highly technical. All very above-board. Training videos for technicians and that sort of thing.'

'Don't your programme people mind?'

Duncan flushed. 'They don't know. Why should they care anyway? It's never going to overlap.'

'Well, it might. I mean, you are the anchor of a business

programme, after all. Who's to say what might come out of the woodwork about Bamco?'

'Look, don't give me another lecture. Just because you can afford not to –' The door opened and Yanna came in followed by Josie, and David forgot the argument.

Of all the places she might have sat down, she chose the spot on the sofa next to David, and he was pleased. Josie asked Duncan to give her a hand in the kitchen, and David looked at the French girl sitting next to him and counted his blessings.

'Are you still feeling cross?' he said.

'Was it so obvious?' she asked.

'Well, you didn't look very happy when you arrived.'

She made a face. 'Those people,' she said, 'they behave like they own you just because they are paying you. They hire me because I take photographs, then they tell me how to take them. Then the fat one, the boss, he stays close all the time. He rubs himself against me whenever he can.'

'Oh, dear. Are you finished with them?'

'Oh, yes. They are finished with me too, I am sure. They wanted all my films. Maybe they will not pay me.'

David picked up the worry in her voice. 'Have you been finding it difficult?'

'People don't know me here. In France they know my work. I should not have come here. I am going back home next week.'

'Why did you come?'

'To look round. To take pictures. To see how your poor people are different to our poor people. There was an agent who made lots of promises, but this is the only job he could find me.'

'So you don't think much of England?'

She looked directly at him. 'Bits of it are very nice.'

Over dinner, everyone relaxed. David always had a touch

18

of wry humour about him, sometimes more sharp than funny, but occasionally and unpredictably it would blossom into high comedy, and this was one of those nights. Yanna responded to it, laughing with him all the way.

'Now I tell you a story,' she said, 'about this man, Purkiss. This friend of Duncan's. Mr Spencer Purkiss.' She covered the name with layers of artificial pomposity. Duncan looked a little embarrassed. 'You should meet him, David,' she said. 'Spencer Purkiss makes bullets. He calls them rounds. Maybe that is because they make nice round holes in people. But he has this funny trick.'

Duncan interrupted. 'I know he was a bit of a pain, but there's no harm in him really. Let's not talk shop. I –'

David stopped him. 'No, I'd like to hear about it. Go on, Yanna.'

'It would make a subject for a psychiatrist. This big man likes to be shot with his own bullets.'

'What?'

'Just like I say. He puts on this special jacket. Body armour. It makes him look like a tortoise standing on its back legs. Then they put him in a chair and they shoot at him. And he makes us take pictures of him.'

David turned incredulously to Duncan, who was not enjoying this. 'You filmed this?'

'Oh, it's harmless enough for Christ's sake, David. They use half-charged cartridges and Kevlar armour. It's just a bit of fun.'

'You mean that's what they've been paying both of you to shoot today? Sounds weird to me.'

Yanna shook her head. 'No, that was just a sideshow. That was at the factory when we came back from the ranges. No, what we were shooting was far worse. It was –'

'Yanna,' Duncan interrupted, 'that's not really for us to talk about, is it? You signed an agreement.'

There was a jarring silence while Yanna looked angrily at Duncan, then Josie stepped in. 'David, I've been dying to ask you. What do you think is going to happen in Kuwait? The radio says Iraq's hinting it might pull out.'

The expression in her eyes begged him to pick up the change of subject and run with it. 'Well, I wouldn't bank on that,' he said. 'The Iraqis don't mean it. I'd say it looks about as nasty as it can get.'

'They haven't got the guts, surely,' said Duncan, and David noticed his voice was slurred now.

'With Hussein you can never really tell,' said David. 'He'll be probing away, looking to see what sort of signals the Americans send out. We'd better hope Bush lays it on the line for him.'

Yanna had retreated into some kind of shell and Duncan became rather boringly argumentative, so by mutual consent they all encouraged the evening to come to a close.

Yanna and Josie said goodnight, but Duncan insisted on pouring another glass of brandy for David and one for himself. They walked through to his study, which opened into a newly converted editing studio. On a workbench were two Sony editing decks, linked up into a basic hard-cut edit suite with a simple controller. There were racks of videotapes on the wall. One entire section had a cardboard sign stuck on it saying BAMCO.

'You're doing a lot for these guys from the look of it, Dunk.'

'Nothing wrong with that. It's handy. Their head office and design staff are down in Birmingham, but one of their main production facilities is up here, over towards New-castle. Of course, there are all the ranges here, so there's a lot of filming to be done up this way.' He looked challeng-ingly at his older brother. 'It's good money. I need it. Purkiss is all right. Look, I'll show you.'

He took a Beta tape out of its box, switched on the player and the monitor, and pushed it into the slot. The player whirred as it lowered the tape into place and laced it up. Colour bars showed on the monitor, then there was a wide shot of a big man, balding, with dark hair slicked round the sides of his head and glasses which looked too small for the flesh surrounding them. He wore a thick padded jacket, which got in the way of his arms as he sat down in an old leather armchair. A rifle was mounted on a solid stand, and a technician in a white lab coat carefully inserted a round into the chamber, then adjusted the aim precisely. Purkiss gave an exaggerated thumbs up and smile to the camera, then looked towards the gun and nodded. There was a loud bang and he rocked back in the chair.

Duncan stopped the tape and looked at David. 'There, you see. It's just a game. He likes to say he's been shot with every type of small arms ammo they make. Sometimes he gets a bit bruised, but the armour stops the bullet. It's only fun.'

David pondered. 'What was Yanna going to say before you stopped her? What else were you doing, Dunk?'

Suddenly Duncan had on what David thought of as his whisky face – obstinate, staring, his eyes a little too wide, his cheeks a little too red. 'Out of order, bro. She should have known better. Official secrets, commercial confidentiality, the works. She might not want to work for them again, but I do. They're all that stands between us and the mortgage repo men.'

'Is it really that bad?'

'It's a bloody sight worse. It's all right for you, you're the famous David Challis. I'm just his younger brother. All I've got between me and the bailiffs is one weekly TV series, which only runs for thirty weeks a year, plus the occasional documentary and anything else I can scrape up.'

'Dunk, how did you get into this mess?'

'It was all bloody worked out. This place came with some extra property. There's a whole lot of land over the other side. There's a farmhouse and a couple of barns. Big separate barns, well-built. That's quite unusual round here. They're normally either built right on to the end of the house like a longhouse or they're tin shacks. Anyway, I was going to convert them and flog them off. That would have covered us nicely, but it didn't work out.'

'Why not?'

'There's an old tenant in there. I thought I could persuade him to move out if I found him somewhere nice. I saved a bit of money on the conveyancing, but the bloke I got never told me how tightly it was all stitched up. I couldn't get the man out in a month of Sundays.'

As they went upstairs to bed, David remembered the photo in the attic.

'Oh, Dunk, by the way, I have to say I was a little bit hacked off with you earlier. I was shifting some boxes up to the attic for Josie and I found one of Dad's Fleet Air Arm pictures lying in the dirt up there. It could easily have been ruined. I wish you'd be a bit more careful.'

Duncan stared at him. 'I haven't a clue what you're talking about,' he said. 'You've got all Dad's things. You wouldn't let me keep them. You said I'd never look after them.' He laughed. 'If you found it there, you must have dropped it yourself.'

David looked at him and it dawned on him with surprise that Duncan was telling the truth. 'That's odd,' he said. 'Come and see it for yourself.'

In David's room they looked at the photo. Something about it was bugging David. 'This isn't my copy,' he said.

22

'The one I've got has all their signatures on it. This one hasn't.'

Duncan shook his head. 'Beats me.' He yawned. 'Let's talk about it in the morning.'

When he got into bed, David was still puzzling over it.

Saturday August 4th 1990

He woke early from a sleep full of dreams to a silent house. He pulled on a track suit and trainers and set off along the boundary where the fields met the moorland. At the end of the fields he ran down through the heather into a steep valley, jumped across the stream at the bottom and up the far side. Cresting the hill, half a mile behind the house, he saw below him a plantation of conifers and stopped to watch a fox make its way along the edge of the trees. He followed a track leading through it and came to what had once been a small farmyard – two barns and a large, well-kept cottage, somewhat gloomy and overshadowed by the trees. The curtains were closed.

He ran round in a circle and, as he came out of the wood, he saw someone else running, tearing down the slope from his right at great speed. For a brief moment he resented the intrusion on his private, silent morning world, then the resentment was replaced by a thrill of pleasure when he saw it was Yanna. She stopped beside him, hardly out of breath, and there was a moment when it would have felt quite natural to acknowledge the warm electric magnetism linking them by putting his arms round her, but he was too reserved for that and they just gazed at each other.

'That's a nice surprise,' he said.

'Did you see the fox?' she asked. 'There was a badger over the other side.'

'I'm sorry about Duncan last night,' he said. 'I'm afraid he sometimes drinks a bit too much.'

'That does not matter, but he has some bad friends.'

'Yes. I'm afraid he wouldn't listen to me on that subject.'

'You should keep trying. He thinks a lot of you,' she said. 'All the time we were working he talked about you. He told me I had to meet you. That was why he insisted I came to stay.'

'Oh, dear. I hope it was worth it.'

She just smiled, then took off running, and they were nearly back at the house before he caught up with her again.

They stopped on the doorstep, close to each other, flushed with the effort. She reached for the door handle, but his hand closed on hers before she could open it. 'Yanna, wait a moment. I have to leave this afternoon. I'll be in America for a little while. I'd like to see you again.'

'I don't know where I will be. Maybe we will meet when you get back.'

'I'd like that.'

'So would I.'

Chapter Two

Monday August 6th 1990

While the rest of Britain worried about the news from Kuwait, one or two were thinking it just might add up to an early Christmas. On the edge of Dunston, looking across the River Tyne to Newcastle in an area where the Garden Festival had briefly seemed to offer a promise that was never fulfilled, a factory stood isolated by a band of dereliction from other human activity. Whether or not this was accidental, it was a good safety measure bearing in mind what the factory made. Within it was a room of no architectural merit whatsoever, full of men to whom that didn't matter at all.

In the room, inside the featureless factory complex of Bamco's munitions division, a marketing meeting was coming to an end. Spencer Purkiss was rounding off a week-long circuit of the division before returning to his Birmingham head office and, prior to leaving, Purkiss had called a meeting designed to leave an unpleasant taste in the mouths of his staff after his departure. He'd learned his management techniques at his father's knee, and his father had been a wartime sergeant-major who believed that sticking that knee hard into someone's groin was the best way of getting what he wanted. It had certainly got him a long way, and, while the son had never had to go through the same tough upbringing as the father, their basic approach to life had proved remarkably similar.

Sitting next to Purkiss was his right-hand man, Geoff Busby, who divided his time between Newcastle, Birmingham and anywhere else where Purkiss might have a problem which called for an unconventional solution. Purkiss was a hard man who looked soft, a cannon-ball of a head softened to an illusion of marshmallow by the fruits of his labours. Busby was a hard man who looked hard. He'd been out of the army five years now, and he was fond of dropping little references to Hereford and his time there with the Special Air Service, though when asked he always glossed over the circumstances under which he'd left it.

The Divisional Managing Director looked around to bring the meeting to a close with a feeling of relief. He'd been given a rough ride in public on production down-time, absenteeism, reject ratios and machine-tool reliability. It always took him a week or two to get his self-confidence back after one of Purkiss's visits. Now it was pretty much over for three or four months, and he could feel his blood pressure easing back below the danger level again. But then Purkiss's voice stopped him.

'One thing,' Purkiss said, with the overtones of a Birmingham accent which had reasserted itself since his public-school days. 'The sales pack I took on the Gulf trip last month had a little surprise in it I wasn't expecting. Only found it when I got there. A new promo video for the small arms ammo range. Came from someone in your team up here, Jack. Anyone here care to own up to being responsible for it?'

A nervous silence followed as the MD tried unsuccessfully to gauge Purkiss's mood while he strove to remember the genealogy of the video. It sounded like something to disown quickly. 'Yes. I believe, er . . . It was Donaldson. Martin Donaldson.' He watched Purkiss's face nervously.

'Who's he when he's at home then?'

The MD was serving out his time and was wary of Purkiss's sudden tempers and predilection for vendettas. 'He's, um, he's only been with us a few months. Bright lad. Caught on very quick, Why? Has he, er . . .?'

Purkiss was enjoying the moment, stretching it out as he watched the MD wriggle. 'You approved it, of course, Jack?'

'Well. That is, no, not really. I think it went through in a bit of a rush. I do hope . . .'

Purkiss smiled broadly, watching him jump off the fence on the wrong side. 'Pity. It was bloody good. I thought for a moment I might have to congratulate you. Anyway, send this bloke Donaldson up, will you? We'd like to see him, Geoff and me.' He looked around. 'The rest of you can hop it.'

Martin Donaldson was sitting at his desk, gazing into space, when the summons came. He'd been weighing the odds and the call was far from unexpected, though he'd heard enough of Spencer Purkiss's unpredictable reputation to know that the best-laid plans could all too easily fall apart. He went up in the lift, calmly wondering if he was out on his ear or if his shot at attracting attention had hit the mark. He smiled at the MD's secretary. She was a bit older than him, a well-turned-out thirty-five-year-old who wouldn't have been out of place in a TV ad for gravy. She gave him a nervous half-smile back. Women always did that to him in this country. 'Flashy,' she thought. 'Funny. He ought to be quite fanciable. He's just a bit too . . . what's the word . . . reptilian maybe.'

The door of the inner office opened like the curtain lifting on a stage where he knew he had to give the perform-ance of his life. There was Purkiss for the first time close up, face to face. Until now he'd only briefly glimpsed him from afar on his trips round the plant. No surprises. He was just as he looked in the photos. That big, common face at odds with the expensive clothes beneath it.

'Siddown,' Purkiss said. 'You're Donaldson, right?'

'That's right, Mr Purkiss.'

'This is Geoff Busby.' Purkiss indicated the man sitting on the table in the corner. Busby was in an army sweater, complete with leather shoulder-patches. He looked as if he'd been born in it. There was a checked shirt and a brown woollen tie, but no other hint of civilian life. He didn't carry the slightest trace of spare flesh. Below very short, greying hair, there was a chiselled, weathered face whose eyes flicked economically from target to target, weighing up threats, evaluating responses. He was the flick-knife to Purkiss's cosh. Together, they were men to be taken seriously.

Purkiss took his time looking at Donaldson. The flash clothes gave him the creeps, but something in the neutral, self-confident way Donaldson looked back at him made him think his hunch might be right.

'Your video,' said Purkiss. 'I'd like to know where you got the idea that what a bunch of jumped-up ragheads with too much money most wanted to see was the insides of an Argentinian?'

Donaldson decided to go for broke. 'I was put in charge of improving the visual marketing of the small arms ammunition when I joined.' Purkiss marked the slight South African accent and pigeonholed him as probably Cape Town.

'How long ago was that?'

'Eight months. It seemed to me that for some markets we'd got too far away from what the product was all about. In Europe we talk about things like penetration capability of soft targets, right? What do we really mean?'

28

Busby, still perched on his table, swinging a leg, answered him with a chuckle. 'We mean how big a hole do we blow in somebody.'

'That's right. That's what we'd really like to be saying.'

Purkiss broke in. 'You can't use that kind of talk. Not in civilized countries. With the wogs all right, maybe, but you know bloody well there's a whole rack of ways of talking about killing people without having to use the words.'

'Yes. That's exactly my point. It's unacceptable in some markets but not in others. So I decided I'd put together three different versions of the video. One normal version – long shots, graphics, all the fancy euphemisms – and two using the gory bits in different degrees.'

'Where did you get the pictures?'

'Falklands War mostly. Stuff cameramen shot that was too rich to be used. It's amazing what you can find lying around if you twist enough arms.'

'Are you good at twisting arms?' enquired Busby.

Donaldson looked round at him, then insultingly turned back to address Purkiss. 'One of the best,' he said.

Purkiss, hugely amused at his gall, looked at Busby, who didn't seem nearly so amused.

'Those pictures. We didn't have much ammo in the Falklands. How the fuck do you know those were down to us?'

'I didn't. Nor would anyone else. Brains look much the same whatever blew them out.'

This time Purkiss laughed and Donaldson started to relax. 'Well, it went down a treat with the ones we showed it to, though I nearly threw up when those close-ups started.' He looked hard at Donaldson. 'OK, I think you might be in line for a leg-up.'

Donaldson kept a straight face, though inside he was doing a victory dance. 'What sort of leg-up would that be, Mr Purkiss?' he asked.

'Well, Geoff and I have been looking for a bright young man for a while now,' said Purkiss. 'We need a bit of help.' He looked at Donaldson again. 'I expect you know how Bamco's organized? Main board, finance director, divisional MDs, all that shit?'

'More or less.'

'Yeah, exactly. There's more of them and less of us and we're the ones that matter. Forget all that crap. There's two people that make Bamco work and that's Geoff and me, and you won't read all about it in the minutes either. Those guys do their bit to make the meetings look good and sign the papers, but we're the ones pushing, right Geoff? And it's us that keeps the whole bloody lot going in the right direction. We're the inner circle, you might say, and we want a bit more help. Someone like-minded with lots of energy.'

'Sounds good to me.'

'Well, you look good to us so far, son. But looks aren't enough. We got to do a bit of checking and if you check out, well then, you might just win this week's star prize.'

'And that is?'

'Like I say. A leg-up and a trip south. We'll get back to you in an hour or two and I want you ready to move down to Birmingham tomorrow if the answer's yes.'

Donaldson was on the way out, but Purkiss stopped him. 'Hang on, young Martin. You said three versions. That's a clean one for Europe and the US and a nasty one for the Gulf and so on. Who's the middle one for?'

Donaldson smiled a cold smile. 'That was the middle one. Wait until you see the Latin American version. Just don't show it in Argentina.'

He went out leaving Purkiss and Busby shaking their heads in admiring wonder. 'Smart lad,' said Purkiss. 'Get on the phone, Geoff. See if he's clean.'

'Don't like his taste in shirts much,' said Busby. 'A bit artistic if you ask me.' He made it sound like the worst insult possible.

As Busby went out, Purkiss turned to stare intently out of the window across the Tyne to where the Vickers factory dominated Scotswood, envying Vickers its size and strength. He thought about Kuwait and wondered.

The hour passed quickly for Martin Donaldson. He was amused that they thought they could do any serious checking in such a short time. It told him something about their casual attitude. He'd have to fix that. Then he was back in the office again and they were all smiles as he'd known they would be. Purkiss wanted to know more about his track record.

'Did you work for anyone else in South Africa apart from Armscor?'

'Only a little engineering consultancy. That's how I joined Armscor.'

'And you started off on the small arms side?'

'Yes, but I switched to working on the G5 field gun pretty soon. General development stuff.'

Busby interrupted, 'Best gun in the world, isn't it? Gerry Bull's star turn. What did it need development for?'

'Sure, it was brilliant. He should have stuck to that and left the missiles alone. Maybe he'd still be alive. It was mostly the ammo I was working on. Hundred and fifty-five mill base-bleed. Tricky stuff.'

'What do you mean about the missiles? I thought Bull was killed because of the Supergun,' said Purkiss.

'I don't reckon so,' said Donaldson, 'Everyone knew about that. He even went to the trouble of telling most of the main intelligence services about it himself.'

'That was dangerous, wasn't it?'

'No. The thing was a complete joke. You couldn't use it in a war. Bloody great fixed installation. It would get zapped first off. The point about Bull was he was giving the Iraqis a load of help designing their missile nose-cones. That was what did for him.'

The other two nodded, thinking about it. 'So you reckon it was Mossad that did it, do you?' asked Busby.

'Who else?'

'OK, young Martin,' Purkiss said. 'Time for the serious stuff. How much do you know about UK defence procurement?'

'Well, there's an M.o.D. list of approved defence contractors. Bamco's on it, so that's a good start.'

Purkiss broke in. 'Yeah, and so are nine thousand others. Trouble is, we're still small beer. There's fifty-odd companies who get more than ten million quid a year from the M.o.D. and we're not in that league yet.'

'The products are good enough, aren't they?'

Purkiss snorted. 'Course they are. But the bloody M.o.D. doesn't think companies like us are here to design good products. They think that's their business. They just dream up the idea, put the specs out to tender and then we're just one of the gaggle, a long way down the pecking order, scratching around for business.' He put a video in the machine. 'Take a gander at this. This is what might change their mind.'

The video was a Duncan Challis production with his voice-over. It started with a big caption on the screen: RESTRICTED ACCESS. TO BE SHOWN ONLY ON CHAIRMAN'S INSTRUCTION. RETURN TO SAFE STORAGE. It sang the praises of a big black box called Cracksman. Purkiss played only the first minute or so, then switched it off. He looked at Donaldson. 'You don't need to see the rest yet, kid. Give me some guesses from what you've seen.'

Donaldson took a deep breath. It was another hurdle he had to jump. There wasn't much evidence, but then they didn't know just how well he'd been planning for a day like this.

'The Holy Grail of weaponry right now is ballistic analysis,' he said, and he saw from their reaction that he was on the right track. 'If you can plot points on the trajectory of an incoming projectile, you can track back to where it started from and take out the gun, launcher or whatever that fired it.'

Purkiss leaned forward. 'Go on,' he said, 'we all know that.'

Cracksman, thought Donaldson, Cracksman, and then he knew what to say. 'The gear they use for that is all big, heavy, ground-installation stuff. Mainframe computers, stable radar sensors, that sort of thing. Not very mobile. This gismo was being fitted in a chopper. It's lightweight. It doesn't plot points. It looks for the crack, right?' He was talking faster as the ideas came, picking up on their response.

'Clever boy. Go on.'

'The crack is the air closing up into the vacuum the bullet or whatever leaves behind. That's the noise it makes. That's Cracksman's job, right? It looks for the pressure change and backtracks to the source?'

'The kid gets the coconut,' said Busby.

'Only so far,' said Purkiss. 'This is old hat, really. Hush-hush but one step behind. We've had Cracksman for a year, and it more or less works. Now we just need to sell it. Catch-22. M.o.D. have got three sets and they're taking their time. They're sniffy 'cos it wasn't their idea and they reckon we aren't big enough to have clever ideas all of our own. Same time, DESO won't help us sell it overseas. You know about DESO?'

'Defence Export Services Organization. Why won't they help?'

''Cos if M.o.D. aren't buying it yet, why should they be interested? The whole point is to bring the cost down on systems the M.o.D. wants for itself by flogging a few more to other people. Anyway, even if they're not convinced, they don't want any other bugger having it just in case it does do what we say it does.'

The news summary started on the TV in the corner, and he swung round to catch the latest. Bush had ordered troops and fighter aircraft to leave for Saudi Arabia. He turned back. 'Anyway,' he said, 'that's yesterday's problem. We've got ways of dealing with that. All it needs is a nice little war. No, what we're concerned with now is part two. Cracksman countermeasures.'

Donaldson looked blank. Busby laughed. 'Not always so quick off the mark, eh? What do they do in Munitions Division when Protective Equipment send over their latest body armour?'

'Start working on a bullet that will go straight through it.'

'Exactly,' said Purkiss. 'When we get down to Birmingham, we'll introduce you to Dodgem. That's the one that counts. For now, Jean'll sort out your move. You'll need a girl up here and another one down south, and there's a flat somewhere she's booked for you.' He looked Donaldson up and down, and his gaze settled on the shirt. 'One more thing,' he said. 'You're not a poof, are you? Geoff here, he can't stand poofs.'

After he left, Busby and Purkiss looked at each other.

'He'll do nicely, I'd say,' said Purkiss. 'What do you think?'

Busby sniffed. 'A bit flash. Dunno what he'd be like under fire.'

Purkiss shook his head. 'He's not going to war, Geoff. Strictly a fix-it man. Bloody sharp, I'd say.'

'Maybe. Are you going to bring him in all the way?'

'One step at a time. We'll see how he shapes up.'

Busby looked at the TV screen. 'Boss, we might have a bit of a damage limitation problem here. What do you reckon?'

'Only if it turns into a shooting war. Can you really see us going in there? Anyway,' he said, smiling seraphically, 'just think of it as an opportunity. A shooting war's what we need. Something to put the bloody peace dividend on the back burner. I reckon we ought to celebrate. Let's go out on the town. What d'you say I call up that agency and get us a couple of tarts?'

'No, thanks all the same, Spence. I think I'm for an early night.'

Chapter Three

Thursday October 11th 1990

'I don't think there's any question, Bertram. If it's one crew with the Allies and the other one in Baghdad, then it's got to be David with the army.' Angela looked at her boss and wondered why he was still bothering to argue.

'They might not see it that way in New York.'

'Well, you tell them. That's what you're here for. It's got to be David. He has a way with the military. He understands their language. He knows about their machinery, and they like him.'

Glass looked at her, noticed the muscles of her jaw tightening and decided to stop arguing. 'OK. Are you sure he's going to agree to Nielsen?'

'I don't know. I don't think they've met. Chalk and cheese really.'

'As long as it's not acid and water, Angela. Creative tension is all very well, but they might have to share a tent or something. When does David get back?'

'At any second. The flight was early. We had a car for him at Heathrow. He did well, didn't he?'

'Did well? Oh, the film. Yes. I, er ... I haven't had a chance to, er ...'

'You mean you didn't watch your very own show this week? Shame on you, Bertram. For God's sake don't tell David that. Believe me, it was very good. Very good indeed.'

When he arrived, jaded and jet-lagged from the overnight flight, David was weary. His US trip had been extended week by week as the programme demands piled up. Four weeks had stretched out to ten as the White House, the UN and the Pentagon had held centre stage. He'd found a country in turmoil, with a population as yet unconvinced about what they might be asked to fight for and an administration unsure whether to pitch it as a fight against aggression or a necessary move to preserve American jobs from soaring oil prices. He'd found it exasperating, trying to get people on camera to focus their attention on what was to him the central, simple principle that Saddam should be forced to leave.

They had coffee and croissants waiting for him at the office, though Bertram Glass absent-mindedly drank the orange juice Angela had poured. Now Desert Shield was under way, there was no time to waste. They were on the verge of getting David a visa for Saudi, and he was provisionally booked on a flight in a week's time.

'How are you feeling, David?' asked Bertram.

'OK, but I wish they'd ban school kids from business class,' he said. 'They were bouncing around all night, what there was of it.'

'Bertram said he liked the film a lot, David,' said Angela, 'especially the Vietnam vets and the song.' Bertram smiled broadly.

'What did you think of what Paul Tsongas had to say, Bertram?' asked David.

'Tsongas? Oh . . . quite, er . . . sensible, I thought,' said Glass.

'Oh, no, not Tsongas – we didn't use him. I meant Albert Gore,' said David, raising a knowing eyebrow towards Angela.

'Gore, yes, of course,' said Glass. 'Anyway, let's get down

to work, David. It's a question of who goes with you. We're crossing over teams. Rob's going to Baghdad with the New York team as producer. We're sending one of the Americans in with you.'

David thought of Glass Crystal's handful of New York producers and winced. No one had mentioned this while he was over there, and that had been only yesterday. 'They've never been anywhere,' he objected. 'Nice people, but I'll have to wet-nurse them. I mean, those guys think driving through the Bronx is war experience.'

Angela shook her head. 'No, it's not them,' she said. 'I knew you'd need someone with a bit of savvy. It's someone completely different. We've hired him on a contract. I'm sorry, there wasn't really time to consult. He's already here. You might even know him.'

'Who is he?'

She crossed to the door, opened it and called. A man appeared. 'David,' she said, 'meet Nick Nielsen.'

To David's eye Nick Nielsen was an unprepossessing sight. He judged him to be in his early thirties. His swelling gut indicated a long acquaintance with the products of Messrs Budweiser, Michelob or Coors. In every other way he looked like a bear coming out of winter hibernation. He had long, curly, light-brown hair, a frayed walrus moustache and a pair of pale blue eyes. He wore a T-shirt which, if not exactly dirty, looked as though many substances had passed through it over a long period of years, plus jeans and trainers. His face showed twitches of suppressed humour. David looked more closely at the T-shirt. The faded lettering extolled the virtues of the Summerland Hotel. 'When were you in Beirut?' he asked.

'Quite often,' said Nielsen, 'up to the time when they started giving you five years' free board and lodging and a nice length of chain to call your own.'

David weighed him up. He'd heard the name. Tales came back to him of a near-legendary figure, famous for extraordinary generosity with other people's money, drinking bouts of incredible duration and a creative way with problems, but he wanted to make quite sure he wouldn't be carrying any dead weight. 'Beirut, eh? You must have learnt how to stay alive. Tell me about flashes and bangs.'

Nielsen grinned. 'Flashes are when you hit the deck. Wait for the bang and it's all over. TV's killed too many people that way.'

'Would you two start talking English?' said Bertram Glass in an irritated tone.

David turned to him. 'It's the danger of believing it happens the way you see it on the screen, Bertram. A rocket hits a building and you're half a mile away with the camera. That's three and a half seconds of gap you have to close up between the picture and the sound. Like thunder and lightning. Trouble is, too many people who've seen it like that on the screen don't think it's real until they hear the bang. Kills them. They see the flash and they're still standing up when the blast hits them.'

He looked thoughtfully at Nielsen. Nielsen grinned back and scratched the back of his head.

'Nielsen's booked out tomorrow,' said Glass, 'to start putting arrangements in hand. We'd like you to follow next week. The crew should be there by then.'

'Which crew?' asked David.

Glass looked blank. Glass Crystal didn't have many crews, but he left it to others to know who they were. Angela supplied the answer. 'It's Ian and Norman,' she said, and David felt relief. They were a good, tough, fit crew. Cheerful in adversity. Maybe Ian wasn't the most creative cameraman around, but David knew perfectly well that mattered less in these circumstances than the willingness to hack it for maybe twenty hours a day and the ability to field-strip a sand-encrusted camera in the dark.

'Now there's the matter of the subject of the film,' said Glass. 'That requires some thought.'

'Really?' said Nick Nielsen, and he looked impassively around the table, with just a slight twitch of the corner of his mouth under the moustache.

'Yes,' said Glass. 'We want to take the long view. Something which will eclipse the day-to-day news coverage.'

David concealed his irritation. 'Bertram, with respect, none of us has any idea which way this story will go, so I think it's one of those times when you just have to point us in the right direction and see what happens.'

'Whatever happens, David, I want the untold story. The stuff nobody else will get.'

A weary look crossed David's face. He would have left it and gone his own way but Nick Nielsen guffawed, unused to Glass's ways. 'Are you sure about that? Would you have wanted the untold story of the Falklands?'

Glass looked round at him. 'What do you mean?'

Nielsen smiled amiably. 'Just that some of it didn't reflect too well. Let's see, there was the sinking of the *Belgrano*.'

Glass raised an eyebrow. 'Hardly untold, dear boy.'

'No, not the Tam Dalyell stuff. Everyone knows which way it was heading and where it was. I mean the torpedo.'

David looked at him mildly. 'You heard about that?'

'I've made it my special study.'

'What are you talking about?' asked Glass.

'Straight after the *Belgrano* went down, some of the defence correspondents got funny phone calls from their pals in the ministry. Wanted to confide in them that the ship had been sunk with the spanking new all-singing all-dancing Tigerfish torpedo.'

'So?'

'Well, it wasn't. It was sunk with an old-fashioned, low-tech Mark 8. Dime a dozen, discount for two dozen. The Tigerfish costs a zillion bucks a time.'

'So? There must have been good defence reasons at the time.'

'That's what some of the hacks thought. So they played it nice and patriotic, did what the military wanted and wrote the story. I guess they thought maybe the Argentines would wind up looking for the wrong submarine or something. Turned out after the war that wasn't what the whole thing was about at all. It was just the M.o.D. wanted some publicity to help sell a few more of their expensive new toys.'

'Is that true?' Glass demanded from David.

He shrugged. 'I've heard the story. Depends who you listen to.'

'Then there's the one about the first Harrier losses in the Falklands,' Nick went on. 'How the broadcasters knew all about it but the powers that be held up confirming the news all day until the polls closed for some tinpot local elections, in case the voters threw a wobbly.' He looked around at them. Bertram Glass was fidgeting and looking agitated. 'Is that the sort of thing you want?' he said. 'Because there'll be plenty of it. You can be sure of that.'

Glass looked at him with tight lips. 'No, it isn't. I don't think that's what people will want to watch at a time like this. I must say I was thinking more in terms of strategy and gallantry.'

'Ah,' said Nick, 'I see. Just give me a second or two to tune down the cynicism a trifle.'

The meeting over, David picked up a phone. He'd rung Yanna's number a hundred times from Washington, always hoping for an answer, never getting one. His finger raced across the buttons automatically now, going through the motions, knowing the bell would just ring and ring.

She picked it up immediately.

They were both early, as though neither wanted to risk missing a moment. It was a warm evening for October, and they met by chance on the pathway through Holland Park leading to the Belvedere restaurant, where they had arranged the rendezvous. She saw him first and stood watching as he approached. David wasn't mentally ready for her and found himself uncertain how to greet her. A kiss seemed too presumptuous, though it was what his body wanted to do. A handshake would be ridiculous. He settled for holding her hand in both of his for a long moment. It seemed an age since they'd first met, and he had found it harder and harder to preserve the sound of her voice, but now it once again delighted his ear.

'You've been away,' he said, not wanting to admit he'd called her every day.

'All over,' she said, 'pictures everywhere. The same as you. I am back just for two days, talking to embassies.'

'Why?'

'Visas for Saudi Arabia,' she said, as though it should be obvious. 'I have to go there now.'

'Me too, probably,' he said. 'Have you had any luck yet?'

'Saudi is very difficult for a woman,' she said. 'I am trying for Baghdad and maybe I will start in Abu Dhabi or Bahrain or somewhere like that.'

'See you there,' he said. 'I'm going next week. Maybe it will still all come to nothing.'

'It will not come to nothing,' she said.

'How can you be sure?'

'Because oil is oil and presidents are presidents. George Bush worries that people think he is a wimp. If he thinks

42

it will help him win the next election, he will fight a war.'

'Yanna, that's terribly cynical.'

She frowned slightly before replying. 'Is it? I don't think so. I have seen it happen in different ways in many places.'

In the restaurant, they ordered the same food. The waiter brought soup.

'Why did you become a war photographer?' David asked.

'I didn't. There are no tests, no professional qualifications, you know. I just take photographs, but it matters to me that my photographs should affect people, should make them think, so they are often of bad things, that is all.'

'Tell me about your family in France.'

'My father is dead. He was kind of a civil servant, you would say. We travelled a lot. My mother worked with him. Now she sits looking at the sea and says she will never move again.'

'I can understand that. I've been to Quiberon. It's an extraordinary place.'

'You went to see the stones? The stones at Carnac?'

'Yes, I did. It was a long time ago.'

'Maybe you would not like them now. They are caged, wired to keep them safe from the tourists. You have to climb a silly platform to view them.'

David was silent, imagining it and thinking of the last time he'd been there. She looked at him curiously. 'Does that make you so sad?'

He shook his head. 'No, not really. I was just remembering. When I saw the stones, it was the last summer holidays Dunk and I had with my parents. We returned to boarding-school the day after we got back and they were killed about a week later.'

'How did it happen?'

'Just a dumb car accident. My father always drove too fast. He was overtaking when he shouldn't have been. He was a pilot in the Fleet Air Arm.' She raised her eyebrows in interrogation. 'You know, the Navy, flying from aircraft-carriers. I suppose cars seemed pretty tame compared to that. He loved flying so he stayed on after the war.' He took a mouthful of the soup, then looked up at her again. 'The funny thing is, you've just reminded me – for a long time, I used to blame the stones.'

'The Carnac stones?'

'Yes. It was just that they felt so powerful. I never told anyone. It was a way of making myself feel better, I suppose. I had to blame something.'

She touched his hand. 'Well, the poor old stones are behind bars now.'

'Yes.'

'And since then you have been like a father figure to Duncan?'

'I suppose so.'

'He thinks so much of you. He kept telling me.' She stopped for a moment, weighing her words. 'I think he was hoping he could give me to you like a present.'

David looked at her steadily. 'Hardly. You're not his to give.'

They both fell silent, staring at each other, until she flushed slightly and changed the subject. 'If your brother listens to your advice, you should tell him to stop dealing with those men from Bamco.'

'I don't suppose he'd listen, but I'm sure you're right.'

'They are dangerous. I could not follow everything that was happening that time, but they were trying to fake something and Duncan was helping them to do it.'

'What sort of thing?'

'It is not my business, but they flew us to a firing-range in the middle of nowhere. They were shooting some rocket. They were getting very angry. A lot of the time they made me sit where I could not see, but every now and then I had to take some stills.'

'What were they of, exactly?'

The next course arrived and she didn't answer. The food looked beautiful and was served with ceremony, and by the time the waiter left again, the thread was broken.

'Let's talk about something else,' said Yanna. 'It makes me feel angry and, I suppose, a bit ashamed. I have never sold myself like that before. I did not know what they wanted. I will give the money to *Médecins sans Frontières*. That is, if they ever pay me.'

'You really think they might not?'

'They had better. I kept back two rolls of film in case.'

Later, when the meal was done, they walked back through the park in warm darkness, close to each other.

'And you, David? If the shooting starts, what films will you make?'

'Ones that tell the stories I see.'

'I want to know how you see them. Really. In this country you do not see the true face of war. It is always covered. Is that the way you make your films?'

'I think you can suggest violence without shocking people, certainly . . .'

'Shocking people? What is the harm in that?'

'Well, I suppose some people feel putting too much violence on the screen might harden the viewers to it.'

The anger in her reply startled him. 'No, no, no. That is so crazy. Harden them, so they fight more wars? No. Show them what it is really like, then they will not let their politicians do it again.' A squirrel ran across their path and she pointed at it. 'You see that? Suppose I go and beat its head with a rock and you film it. What would you do in your cutting-room? Put your pictures carefully together so they show just the body. No blood, no bits of brain, no mad woman hammering with her stone. That will not save the next little animal from people like me. That will not make people go out to protect them. I believe it is our job to make people sick so that we make them angry.'

'Yanna, I'm sorry. I didn't mean to upset you.'

She walked on in silence and they came out of the park on to the street. She stopped and faced him. 'I am sorry too. Forget it. I have had a lovely evening.'

'Do you want a drink? My flat's just round the corner.'

She put her head on one side and looked at him. 'If I come back to your flat, I will go to bed with you, because that is what my heart wants. But my head knows that if I do I will miss you too much tomorrow when I have to go away, and now I must listen to my head.' She kissed him quickly on the lips, whirled round waving at a cab, and left him stunned on the pavement.

Chapter Four

Friday October 12th 1990

David tossed and turned, wide awake until six in the morning, slept fitfully until lunchtime, then had to fight the jet lag all the way up the motorway, stopping for catnaps and coffee when his eyelids got too heavy. It was the price to pay for a final weekend with Duncan and Josie before he left. When thinking about Yanna became too obsessive, he switched to brooding about Nick Nielsen and trying to decide whether the prospect of an indeterminate amount of time with Nick in the Gulf added up to fun or not.

It was nearly eleven when he finally turned quietly into the drive, but there was a downstairs light on and Josie opened the door before he'd got out of the car.

'Hello, David,' she said, kissing him. 'You must be completely whacked. Come on in.'

'No, I'm all right. I had a quick nap on the way. Did you stay up by yourself?'

She pulled a face. 'Duncan's gone to bed. He'd had a few, I'm afraid.'

'Is it getting worse?'

'I think so. He seems . . . well, less able to cope with it somehow. I know the mortgage is really getting him down, but he just won't talk about it.' She shivered. 'Anyway, let's leave that. I didn't mean to hit you with it as soon as you walked in. He's been trying to do a rough-cut edit all day and I don't think it was going too well, so that's probably part of it.'

'Is he doing the editing himself?' asked David, puzzled, thinking the problems would hardly be surprising if Duncan was trying to bring his amateur skills to bear on a professional job.

'Yes. It's those Bamco people again. He usually does their stuff by himself.' She poured him a cup of tea. 'Enough of that. What about you? Have you seen the gorgeous Yanna again?'

He knew she was watching him closely and wondered why. 'Well, yesterday as it happens. She's heading for the Gulf. We had dinner.'

'Maybe you'll meet up out there.'

'Maybe. Maybe not. It's a big place. Anyway, why the interest?'

She smiled at him ruefully. 'Oh, purely aesthetic. I just thought you two looked quite nice together.'

The bed in David's room left a lot to be desired. Duncan's grand plan hadn't stretched to very much new furniture. It was a single bed and the mattress had an oddly convex top, with a slippery and rather plastic surface so that the undersheet had a less than reassuring hold. The long drive hadn't worked its way out of his system. Headlights flew at him every time he closed his eyes, and the combination of his brief naps on the way and his jet lag made sleep impossible. At half past one he gave up, got out of bed and wandered downstairs.

He made himself a mug of cocoa and strolled round the house drinking it. The sitting-room was under the main bedroom and he didn't want to disturb Josie and Duncan, so he went through to Duncan's office and switched on the light. The tapes Duncan had been working on were still there on his desk. He switched on the player and the monitor, pushed one in at random and twiddled the knob on the edit controller to shuttle through it.

He wondered for just a moment whether he might be prying, but Duncan had showed him lots of his videos in the past and, although curiosity about Bamco was certainly a factor in his mind, his main interest was a professional one. Duncan had been having trouble with the edit and he wondered why.

The monitor came alive. The picture on the screen was quite good quality. It was a long shot of a launcher of some sort, a box on hydraulic rams on the back of a big, blunt truck. It reminded David of pictures of the American MLRS rocket system, but this box was of a different shape, longer and slimmer. There was a flash and a cloud of white smoke as it fired, then the picture went all to pieces. The cameraman started to follow the missile as it rose into the sky, but within a second he was clearly having great difficulty keeping it in the frame. It wasn't until he pulled back to maximum wide-angle that David could see why. The missile had gone crazy. Instead of rising in a smooth trajectory, it was jinking all over the sky. It went higher and higher, still weaving, then seemed to pause and thrash round in rapid, darting, irregular circles high in the air. Then it pounced, arrowing down in a straight line.

David had spent years of his life sitting in darkened edit rooms, watching picture cuts in the finest detail to check that the sequence of shots worked properly. He knew every trick in the book. Now, as he watched, something happened before his eyes that took just the tiniest microsecond, but that microsecond was enough to ring an alarm bell in his experienced head. In the next moment the missile reached the ground, striking a briefly glimpsed dark target and exploding in a small ball of flame. An object now recognizable as a tank turret flipped end over end into the air.

David grabbed the control knob and shuttled the tape backwards to the point where the missile had started to descend, then he pushed the knob in to get precise control and eased the tape forward, bringing it up frame by frame on to the monitor, each frame separated from the next by a diagonal fuzzy line. And there it was, a jump-cut – only visible to the inexperienced eye when brought to a halt. From one frame to the next there was a change in the shot, just a small change in the angle of the missile and the pattern of the flames from its tail. It was two different pieces of video edited together and masquerading as one. He looked at it for a while, considering, then took the tape out. On the label it just said DODGEM. Feeling suddenly very tired, he switched off the gear and went back to bed.

Saturday October 13th 1990

He woke late to find Duncan putting a cup of coffee beside his bed.

'Morning, bro. Sleep OK?'

'Eventually. Thanks, Dunk.'

'Josie's gone shopping. Cooked breakfast downstairs in five minutes if you like?'

'Fine.'

'Bacon, egg, sausage, black pudding?'

'Leave out the black pudding.'

In the kitchen Duncan didn't look like a man who'd tied one on the night before, but then he never did. Maybe that's his problem, David thought. He'd never known Duncan suffer from a hangover in his life. Perhaps what served for most people as aversion therapy simply wasn't part of Duncan's metabolism.

'How's it all going, Dunk?'

'Fine.'

'No, really?'

Duncan looked at him across the table. 'Well, the money side could be better. It's a bit of an uphill struggle.'

'If I can help . . .?'

Duncan smiled at him. 'You've spent your life helping. You've poured quite a lot of money down my drain over the years, haven't you? No, it's a bit beyond that, I'm afraid. It's sink or swim time and I'm not sinking yet.'

David cast around for a way in and couldn't think of anything but the full-frontal approach. 'What about the booze, Dunk? That might sink you.'

Duncan laughed. 'Oh, come *on*, bro. You know me well enough. I know I knock it back a bit, but I can take it.'

'I'm not so sure you can any more, Dunk. I'm a bit worried about it to tell the truth . . .'

But something had changed in Duncan's demeanour. His face hardened and his voice lost its lightness. 'You're not so sure? I think you mean Josie's not so sure. You haven't been around much. How would you know? Has she been going on at you?'

'She's worried, certainly. You were so bad last night, she had to help you to bed. I got here soon after, but I'm not speaking for her, I'm speaking for myself, Dunk. I think you're on the slippery slope.'

Now Duncan was overtly angry. 'Well, you're wrong. Save me the preaching. You're not my father.' He got up from the table, went to the sink and started slamming saucepans around. 'I had a tough job on. I'm trying to get a rough cut ready for viewing. It's got to be approved before we do the on-line edit. I got a bit depressed about it, so I had a few.'

'Was that it really? You managed it. That jump-cut just about works. You did a bloody good job for an amateur. I only just spotted it myself.'

Duncan rounded on him. 'You looked at that tape? What the fuck do you think you're doing? That's totally out of order, David. None of your business.'

'Whoa there. I couldn't sleep, that was all. I didn't mean any harm.'

'Listen, you. That's classified stuff. That's why I'm doing the rough edit and not hiring an editor. I'm shooting it myself, too. It's highly restricted. I should have locked the damned things away last night.'

Duncan was truly upset and it put David in a position of sudden weakness. He apologized, feeling awkward, wanting to ask more questions but unable to. He decided to take a more oblique course. 'I saw Yanna in London a while back. She said I should try to wean you off these guys. I assume it's the same company. She says they're very bad news.'

Duncan looked at him. 'She doesn't know anything. Just drop it, right?'

'I'm sorry, Duncan. I shouldn't have looked at it without asking. I didn't think you'd mind. But that doesn't change what I said before. I can't let the other thing go. I'm worried about you.'

Duncan shook his head in exasperation. 'Don't tell me that. I can handle it. I have never, ever fallen down on the job. I do *not* have a drink problem. You may be my older brother but I'm a grown-up now.'

'OK, Dunk, I'm just trying to help.'

There was a long silence, then Duncan came and sat down opposite him again. 'If you really want to help, there is one thing you might do. It would help take the pressure off.'

'Of course. What?'

'The old bugger that's living in my cottage. Go and talk to him. He might just listen to you.'

52

'You mean where the barns are? In the wood?'

'Yes. George Middleton. He's lived there for ever. He got the house on a peppercorn rent. Buttoned up tight until he dies. I didn't ask enough questions when we bought. I told you, didn't I? We saved money on the conveyancing. The deal was all done before I found out just how protected he is. So much for my barn conversions. The old boy's the wrong side of seventy. I was sure if we offered him a nice little place somewhere, he'd be delighted to move. I think I must have rubbed him up the wrong way.'

'Who is he?'

'Some old family retainer from when the Mainwarings were here. They were the people we bought from, or I should say it was their estate. They'd all snuffed it. Grand old family, been here for generations quietly going to the dogs. I think old Middleton must have been the butler or something. He's quite grand. They installed him in the bloody house ages ago apparently.'

'What's he like?'

'Gentle enough until you cross him. Then he really gets on his high horse.'

'Do I guess you weren't as diplomatic as you might have been?'

'Look, it's my sodding house after all. I was offering him a really good deal.'

Josie walked in then and picked up Duncan's last line. 'Duncan offered him a little pensioner's bungalow in Otterburn. He offered Duncan a boot up the backside. I sympathize with the old man, I'm afraid.'

David winced. 'And now you want me to go and patch it up. Why not leave him in the house? There are two barns. You could convert those, couldn't you?'

'He's got the lease on those too,' said Duncan gloomily. 'Doesn't use them for anything much as far as I can see, but he's got them for all that.' He looked at his elder brother. 'I don't suppose you feel like talking to him, do you?'

Sunday October 14th 1990

It was the following morning, around eleven o'clock, when David drove round to the old man's house. There was a separate driveway from a side-road, stretching for a good quarter of a mile before it dived into the conifer plantation and ended up in the neat farmyard. Wondering just why he'd let himself be talked into it and determined not to be too pushy, he knocked at the door. No one came. The barn opposite the house stuck out of the surrounding trees. It was open-fronted and empty. There were muddy tyre marks on its concrete floor, showing it was used as the garage. The back wall was covered by a huge stack of timber. The other barn was off to one side. It was smaller and its double doors were closed. There was a little door let into one of them. David could see light round the edge of it and he knocked. Again no one came. After some hesitation he pushed the handle down and opened it.

There was no one there and he was about to close it again when his eye settled on something that changed his mind. The barn was mostly empty, but against the right-hand wall there was a bright pool of light from a floodlight left switched on over a workbench. The bench itself was big and spotlessly clean, backed by racks of neatly arranged metalworking and woodworking tools. There was a small but sophisticated lathe next to it and a row of expensive power tools, grinders, pillar drills and a band saw. The floor around the bench was covered with metal swarf and curled wood-shavings, though a broom and a dustpan and brush standing by indicated that cleaning it up was high on the agenda.

It was the object on the end of the bench that caught his eye and led him to forget the normal rules of trespass and courtesy. Standing on a white sheet was a large model, around two feet long, of an aircraft. It was unfinished and it was clear to see that this was no cheap construction kit. Carved wooden formers stood around it with partly shaped sections of copper sheet left, half beaten into shape, over them. Nothing forward of the cockpit had been constructed yet, but from there backwards the fuselage was a skeleton of fine metal frames and girders, some of it clad in a delicately formed skin of thin copper sheet. The wings were still just spiders' webs of ribs and spars, but even without the covering that was still to come, their elliptical shape provided an unmistakable identification.

He was lost in admiration as he stood there, craning all around it for a minute or two, taking in every perfect little detail, so it came as a shock to hear a car draw up outside. He climbed out through the little door, catching a foot on the sill in his haste, to hear an affronted voice, quavering a little with the signs of age, demanding to know what he was doing there.

Standing by an ancient but shiny Riley 1100 was an old man with flowing white hair. He was dressed in a plain tweed suit and David knew immediately that he'd just come back from church. The man's protuberant ears were red with anger.

'What the hell are you doing in my shed?' he demanded in a voice that had the slightly studied, old-fashioned tones of a wartime radio announcer.

'I'm sorry,' he said. 'My name is David Challis and I was . . .' But he got no further.

'I sent that other one off with a flea in his ear, and I'll do

55

the same for you. What the hell do you mean, poking around? It specifically says in the lease that you have no right of access at all. He knows that. I told him I didn't want to see him or anyone else round here.'

David listened to the voice and wondered what he could say to justify his unwelcome intrusion. He felt completely in the wrong.

'I'm sorry, Mr Middleton, I didn't know that. I came to try to be helpful – to make a proposition to you. I know my brother can be a little difficult.'

'What were you doing in my barn?'

'I saw the light on and I thought you might be in there, then I saw the Seafire on the . . .'

'Seafire, you say,' interjected the old man, staring hard at David. 'Most people would have said Spitfire. What makes you say it's a Seafire?'

'I saw the arrester hook. It's the best model of a Seafire I've ever seen. It wasn't difficult. I think I could even tell you which version if you let me have another look.'

The old man stared at him suspiciously, then waved him to follow. Back at the bench, knowing that, to stand any chance of winning the old man's confidence, he had to pass the test he had just set himself, David inspected the model carefully.

'There are no pivots for the wings to fold and you're too good a model-maker to leave them out by accident, so it has to be a Seafire Mark Two, not a Three. I don't see any sign of the engine yet, but I take it that's the correct propeller?' he asked, pointing at a beautifully polished four-bladed creation made from pieces of solid brass.

'Yes,' said the old man, and his voice was more interested than fierce. 'So, what model?'

'Four-bladed Rotol prop. It's got to be an LIIC with a Merlin 32 engine.'

56

The old man gave a little astonished smile and the atmosphere changed just like that. 'A young man of your age, knowing that? Well, I never. I've been making that cab for eight years now.' David was struck by the curious term, then the other man went on. 'It's a lot before your time. How do you happen to know so much?'

'My father was in the Fleet Air Arm in the war and he stayed on afterwards. He flew Seafires. I've been mad about them for years.'

Middleton looked at him with even more interest. 'Was he now? Well, well. What squadron?'

David looked down at the model as he answered. '899. On HMS *Indomitable*, then *Hunter* and *Khedive* after *Indom* was torpedoed. He was at Salerno, then the south of France landings.' He missed the expression on the old man's face, but when he looked up again, Middleton was staring hard at him.

'Challis?'

'Yes, Bill Challis. Were you in the Fleet Air Arm too?'

'No, no,' said Middleton. 'No, I was unfit for service.' He seemed to consider. 'It was their son, up at the house. Young Jackie. He was the one who flew these. You might say I followed everything he did. This one's in memory of him, in a way. Something I've wanted to do for a long time, now all his family are gone.'

'What happened to him?'

The old man sighed. 'He didn't make it. That's all. One of many. Is your father alive?'

'No,' said David. 'I'm afraid not. He was killed in a car crash a long time ago. Almost twenty years now. My mother too.'

'Oh, I'm sorry,' and the old man really looked as though he was. They stood in silence, looking at the model again, until David suddenly thought of the photo in the attic and an extraordinary explanation for its presence suggested itself.

'What squadron was Jackie Mainwaring in?'

The old man nodded his head slowly. 'Well now, that's the strange thing. He was in 899 Squadron too. Like your father.'

Back at the house, Duncan couldn't restrain himself when he heard David's tyres on the gravel. He was at the door of the car before David could open it. 'How was it? Any luck?'

'No joy,' said David, and he saw his brother's face fall. 'You'll never shift him, and I don't think you should even try. He's keeping the memory of the Mainwarings alive in his way. He uses the barns and he likes his peace and quiet and you'll never guess what he told me.'

Chapter Five

Friday October 19th 1990

David had quickly concluded that Dhahran was the pits – blisteringly hot, dirty and depressing. The flight put him in a bad mood. The oilman next to him hailed from Mississippi. He was doing some work with Aramco, who more or less owned Dhahran, and he didn't have a good word for the place. As the plane banked for its final approach, he pointed out the airport hotel. 'See that blue thing, with the domes on the roof? That's where you're staying. Stands out a mile, don't it? I wouldn't like to be you if the Iraqis decide to hit it. See all those metal tanks next to it? That's the airport fuel storage. Be a helluva bang if they hit that.'

'Where do you go to have fun?'

'Europe.'

'Is it really that bad?'

'Well, there's Al Khubar. That's where the restaurants are, if you can call them that, and the beach ain't too good. There's a funfair, but it's full of young Saudi men holding hands and giggling. I don't know if that's your idea of fun, but it ain't mine.'

'What about getting through immigration. Is that going to be a hassle?'

'Hell, no. That's the only easy bit. This is the Eastern Province, oil land. It ain't like the rest of Saudi. It's dirty, it's low-rent and its strictly for the foreigners. Most Saudis wouldn't dream of coming here. There's lots of Pakistanis,

Bangladeshis, all sorts, oil rig workers, tool pushers. The authorities need them. They take the attitude that, if you're mad enough to come here, they should let you in without too much trouble.'

And so it was. The formalities took very little time. There were none of the careful baggage searches for banned products, alcohol or porn magazines which David had experienced in past visits to Jedda or Riyadh. The fact that he had a visa seemed to be enough. He was expecting Nick to meet him, but there was no sign of the man and that irritated him even more. He got a taxi, asked for the airport hotel and was profoundly irritated when the driver took him all of two hundred yards round the corner of the airport concourse, dropped him in front of a building he could have walked to in a couple of minutes, and then demanded an inordinate amount of money.

There was nothing much around the hotel except a few anonymous sheds with a military look to them, interspersed with scrubby palm trees, broken concrete and rough patches of sand. Wide highways led to the other parts of Dhahran, Dammam and Al Khubar, which merged into each other. The roads were busy with traffic, much of it military. Trucks were everywhere. The hotel car park was stuffed full of four-wheel-drive Nissans, Toyotas and Isuzus.

He checked in at the desk, where a Pakistani, in Western dress, gave him a key. He declined the offer of a porter and found his room on the second floor. The door opened to reveal the work of a decorator to whom subtlety had not been a major consideration. The bed had an ornate wooden Arab arch over it. Everything was in shades of blue, mauve or purple. He pulled back the heavy curtains and saw thick smoked glass to keep the sun out. Through it, dimly, he could see a swimming-pool, what looked like a football pitch and, beyond it, palm trees with a C130 transport plane sloping down behind them on its descent to the airport. The weariness of travelling came over him and he sagged on to the bed, but in that moment, when he could have just stretched out and gone straight to sleep, responsibility asserted itself. Out there was a story in the making, maybe the biggest story of his life. In here, he was the latest arrival in a hotel full of competition, all of them more up to speed than him. He sighed, got to his feet and went back down to the desk to get Nick Nielsen's room number, which proved to be right next to his own.

He thanked the man and was turning away when a familiar voice said, 'David?'

Turning, he saw Rory Crosley, a BBC producer he knew well. One familiar face was enough to lift his spirits.

'Rory! How nice to see you.'

'Have you just arrived? Welcome to Boredom House. Come and meet the guys.'

'Thanks. Have you got an office?'

The hotel itself was going through an uneasy metamorphosis. On the ground floor there had once been two aisles of shops and offices. Now they'd mostly been taken over. The BBC were in what had been the catering manager's office. Rory waved at the sign. 'Wait until you experience the catering. I don't know what it was like when it had a manager, but it's not doing too well without him.'

There were piles of aluminium TV-equipment boxes everywhere, and cabling ready to trip any unwary foot. David said hello to the rest of the BBC crew, envying them their degree of support, and went to check out the rest of the place.

The back doors of the hotel were open and walking towards them was like wading into a tide of hot air which the air-conditioning was doing its best to overcome. The doors could no longer close, because a mass of cables, sixty or seventy of them in a two-foot-high heap, were in the way. They led outside, then split. Many went to the left, where what had once been a mini-golf course had been taken over by serried ranks of satellite dishes. The BBC's dish, to David's amusement, was concealed inside a neat white tent, looking fresh from the British Raj. Many of the other dishes were beamed at the Atlantic satellites, low on the horizon. They were set so low that the areas in front of them were cordoned off with marker tapes to prevent any unwary passers-by doing themselves an injury by walking in front of them during transmissions.

To the right, among the palm trees, a couple of men were hammering away, building a wooden stage to add to the four that were already there – live inject points so that the US breakfast shows could two-way their local anchormen, David surmised correctly, looking at the arc lights, the fancy awnings and the camera cabling. He sighed, feeling suddenly discontented with his lot. Another media circus, but for how long? Two days? Six months? He already felt he wouldn't be able to take Dhahran for very long. There was a constant roar of engines from beyond the trees. The airbase was buzzing with one hundred times its normal level of activity, spreading a blanket of vibrating, kerosene-smelling noise across the desert. He glanced wearily around at the flat, featureless buildings. The look of them made him feel alien and uncomfortable. If there was a cultural background here, it wasn't accessible to a visitor. The buildings reflected nothing more than a need to find some cheap way of keeping residents from dehydrating in the baking heat. If traditional bedouin encampments seduced the desert into tolerating human life, here the pourers of concrete had had their way by force. Then the heat really began to get to him and he went back inside.

62

Up on the second floor, he went to Nick's door and knocked. There was a scuffling noise to start with, then Nick's voice inside, asking who was there. Nick opened the door a crack, seemed astonished to see David, then looked up and down the corridor carefully.

'I thought you were coming on Friday,' he said as he let David in.

'It is Friday,' said David coldly as he looked around at a room which already bore the unmistakable scars of Nick's brief stay. 'Am I disturbing you?'

'No,' said Nick. 'Hang in there a minute, I've just got to fix something.'

He went into the bathroom and David looked in through the gap of the half-open door. There was a spirit-lamp balanced in the basin, heating two saucepans, one on top of the other. Nick was carefully lifting the top one off.

'Cooking?' said David, and Nick jumped.

'Er . . . yeah.'

But David was next to him by that time, looking into the bottom pan where a saucer sat on top of a wooden block, surrounded by bubbling clear liquid. The saucer was above the surface of the liquid and had a little puddle of another clear fluid in it. David had seen the set-up before, in a cabin in the woods of Norway outside Stavanger, and it brought to the surface the sudden anger of nerves frayed by the journey.

'It's a still, right, Nick? A bloody still. Here, in the middle of the strictest Muslim country in the world, you're brewing moonshine. Isn't that just the slightest bit dumb? Didn't anyone tell you about the religious police?'

'Whoa there. Listen, I know all about the goddam Metawa or whatever they're called. They don't come round the rooms. Anyway, it's not for me, it's currency. No booze, no pin-ups, no fornication and no Christianity. Two of those bother me. Our Saudi hosts aren't being very nice to their gallant protectors. There's a lot of soldiers out there who are missing their booze. You'd be amazed what a few drops of this will buy.'

On the floor was a big oxygen cylinder. Nick unscrewed the top and poured the contents of the saucer, drop by drop, into it.

'I don't believe this,' said David. 'Is this what you've spent your time doing since you got here?'

Nick looked hurt. 'You wait until you see what this has got me so far. You want to be ahead on this assignment? There's three hundred hacks out there, bored out of their skulls and ready to kill for a story. When they come by one, the military won't let them run it, and the only official information you get is either so dull it would put a shark to sleep or it's lies they happen to want us to tell for their own benefit. This little stash is pure gold. It buys a bit of truth.' He looked at David to see if he was making any impression. 'Anyway, first things first,' he said. 'Let's go get you accredited.'

On the way downstairs he filled David in. He'd got hold of an ancient Toyota Land Cruiser, and he'd sounded out the military. 'The Brits are only just getting their act to-gether,' he said. 'The first tanks are due tomorrow. The Americans and the French have been here for weeks. They won't let them forget it.'

'I'm not surprised. Are the military being helpful?'

Nick blew a raspberry. 'They're already trying to set up a pool system so they can control everything. The plan so far is that each of the Allied forces will choose a few to take with them when they move up towards the Kuwaiti border – one or two written press, a pair of snappers for stills, maybe one TV crew and one radio guy. There's already a whole bunch of hopefuls going to lectures each day on everything from first aid to weapon recognition, hoping they get picked. Saddest sight you ever saw, a bunch of overweight hacks all doing physical exercises with the Marine Corps in the hope they'll suddenly turn into front-line heroes.'

David looked at Nick. 'Maybe you should try it. It wouldn't do you any harm.'

Nielsen gave him a curious look. 'You're not going to turn into one of the gung-ho mob, are you? There's far too many journos round here talking GI gobbledegook without you starting.'

'When in Rome. Anyway, we have a choice. That's the nice thing about being an Anglo-American show. We can choose which side to belong to.'

'Neither, if you ask me,' said Nick. 'Go with the Brits and, if Schwarzkopf has his way, you'll all be left kicking your heels in the desert. Go American and you'll have a minder riding you so hard it'll be like wearing a blindfold.'

'Why do you say that?'

'You know as well as I do,' said Nick. 'Our guys have been working up the plans for years. They don't want to screw it up again. It's the V-word.'

'What?'

'You don't remember? Vietnam? The war every US military commander reckons we only lost on account of letting the media see too much of what was going on, so they could spread alarm and despondency back home. This is their first chance to make up for it.'

'Well, Nick, in a war, maybe they have a point.'

Nick just looked at him with a disbelieving expression, but now they were walking into a large open area at the top of the stairs from the main lobby and there was no time to carry on the argument.

'This is where everyone hangs out,' he said, 'the joint

Allied information bureau.' It was dotted with baize-covered tables piled high with heaps of paper, TV monitors, fax machines and all the impedimenta of modern communications. The people at the tables were mostly Americans. Tucked away in a corner was a table with a Union Jack on it, but no one was there. A group of journalists were looking at a blackboard covered in details of trips on offer: *Bus service of the 7th Airborne. Visit on 23rd. Twenty places only. Sign up now.*

They went and queued at a desk where a harassed-looking officer was searching through files and files of faxes and computer printouts. 'Yeah?' he said when David's turn came.

'David Challis. BBC and NBC.'

'Well, which?'

'Both. It's a programme called *Double Exposure*. We do it for both of them.'

'Gotta put one down here, bud. You're BBC. You sound like a Brit. Gotta photo with you?'

'Yes, but . . .'

'OK, you're down. You gotta go over there and see the nightshirts.'

'Nightshirts?'

The officer sighed. 'Our gallant Saudi friends. Over there.'

On the other side of the room three young men in traditional robes were standing behind another table. They seemed very unsure of themselves and giggled a lot, but they took David's details. It didn't feel either important or reassuring. There was a Kuwaiti table there too, with some graphic and slickly presented posters of mutilated corpses. David paused for a second and a man slid out from behind a desk to buttonhole him. 'This is what they are doing to our country,' he said. 'Come and look at the new photos we have.'

Nick got in between them. 'Later,' he said to the man and pulled David away. 'PR men. They've got some goddam US outfit telling them how to tug our heartstrings. Come on, I'll buy you a drink.'

'Drink?'

'Well, kind of.'

The coffee-shop behind the main stairs was full of American GIs, weapons and all. 'Saudi champagne for my friend,' Nick said to the waiter, 'and a Moussy beer for me.'

David raised his eyebrows.

'Wait and see,' said Nick. 'Now, back to business. The crew's going to be here in two or three days. We can call on NBC and the Beeb, within limits, for technical help so long as we don't get in the way. I've found a few other old friends among the nets. Most of the rest are poncing around trying to get some quick wear and tear into their combat jackets.'

Their drinks arrived. David's was in a champagne glass and it looked quite like champagne except for the lumps of apple floating in it, going quickly brown. Nick's looked like beer. David sipped his. It was sickly sweet and fruity. Nick laughed at his expression. 'Good, eh? Saudi champagne. Perrier and apple juice. I thought I'd hit you with it at the start, just so you didn't let your expectations get too high. Would you rather have a beer instead?'

'Is it really beer?'

'Come on, pal. It's the Swiss chemical industry's answer to the thirst problem. The only resemblance to beer apart from the colour is the hangover it leaves you with. Guaranteed no other side-effects.'

Suddenly, from the entrance to the coffee-shop, came raised voices. The hum of conversation stopped and they swung round to see what was happening. A heavy-set man with long hair and a brightly coloured striped jacket

67

was angrily shaking off the hand of a thin American captain in sharply pressed desert rig and impenetrable sunglasses.

'It's nothing to do with me. Leave me alone,' the man was saying. He sounded French.

'You better be right, scumbag. If I find you ain't, you'll be out of here before you can break wind,' said the captain and walked off.

The Frenchman stared after him, spat and walked into the coffee-shop. Looking around at a sea of hostile GI faces, he focused on the spare chair at David and Nick's table. 'May I sit here?' he said.

'Sure,' said Nick. 'What was all that about?'

'I presume you haven't met Captain Cato, then?'

'Oh, right,' said Nick. 'That was Cato, was it?'

'Who's Cato?' asked David.

The Frenchman glanced at him and grinned mirthlessly. 'Just arrived?'

'Yes, as it happens. I'm David Challis and this is Nick Nielsen, if you haven't already met.'

'Paul Foucault, AFP. Who are you with?'

'BBC and NBC. It's a sort of joint programme.'

'Of course, *Double Exposure*. I've seen you. Well, let me tell you, Cato is the single nastiest thing about the whole US war machine. He has made himself the watchdog for the whole of the media. He thinks his job is to stop any of us doing our job.'

'So what was the fuss about?'

'You haven't heard about the story in *L'Express* today?'

'No. What was it?'

'They gave details of Schwarzkopf's attack plan. Operation Night Camel.'

'Ah.'

'A lot of details.'

'Were they right?'

'Well, the Americans deny it, but when Cato comes trying to break the ass of anyone he can find who talks French, then I find it hard to stop myself wondering.'

Nick laughed. 'Good one. Anything to do with you?'

The Frenchman drew in his breath theatrically. 'No, no. I am just a poor news-agency man, finding my stories where I can.'

David shook his head. 'Well, I suppose Schwarzkopf will have to think up a new plan.'

The Frenchman looked at him. 'Night Camel estimated American losses at twenty thousand minimum. Bush already meant to turn it down.'

'Was that in *L'Express* too?'

The Frenchman winked. 'That's tomorrow's story.'

They wished him luck, signed the bill and went back out to the lobby. 'I've been building up supplies,' said Nick. 'Want to come and see?'

'What for, exactly?'

'For when we have to head out into the desert all by ourselves.'

David stopped and turned to face him. 'Nick, we stand a much better chance of being up near any action if we get into one of the pools, so let's try to curb the excesses just a little bit, right?'

Nick's jaw clenched. 'OK,' he said. 'You're the boss. You know best. Why don't we go and try the desk again on the subject of pools?'

So they did. It was a different officer now, a major, and Cato was sitting within earshot at the next table. The major looked at them impassively.

'Gennlemen, what can I do for you?'

Nick beat David to it. 'NBC. Nielsen and Challis. We're here for *Double Exposure*. My boss here has just flown in and he wants to know about the chances of being picked for one of the pools.'

The major reached for a clipboard, shuffled through it without finding anything useful and, when he'd given himself enough time to think, put it back down.

'*Double Exposure*. That's current affairs, right? Well, it's like this. We haven't shaken the bugs out yet, but first priority is straight news crews. A pool's what it says. Your dispatches are open to any other TV station to use. A show like yours ain't gonna be too useful to the news guys.'

'So what are you saying? Is there a chance?' said David.

'Who am I to say? My advice to you is join in the training and the selection and we'll take a look at it when the time comes. Sure as hell don't stand a chance if you don't make the grade.'

'What does making the grade involve?'

'First aid, physical fitness, battle zone familiarization. NBC countermeasures, that kinda thing.'

'Why do we need to take countermeasures against NBC?' asked David, puzzled.

'You don't if you don't mind ending up dead,' the major retorted. 'I'm not talking TV networks here. NBC means nuclear, biological, chemical. Got it?'

'Suppose we just went on our own?' asked David, and Nick gave him a dirty look.

'Suppose you just get blown up by a mine or hit by an Apache or stomped by Special Forces or just break down and starve to death in the desert, or even, and here's the really unlikely option, get shot by an Iraqi?'

They thanked him and left. 'Satisfied?' said Nick. 'Now come and take a look at the freelance solution.'

They went out of the door into an evening where the heat was just falling to tolerable levels. A voice behind them called. 'Hey. You two.'

They turned. Captain Cato had followed them out. David squinted into the low sun as the wind blew a puff of sand in their faces. Cato's silvered glasses reflected a long line of army trucks grinding past behind them.

'You talking to us?' asked Nick.

'Yeah, Nielsen. I've already been hearing your name. Mine's Cato and I'm assigned to this office. I was listening in there. The major's a nice guy. He gave you a soft ride. I just want you guys to know we ain't here to make life easy for you.' He was up close by now, thrusting his face towards theirs. 'On a need-to-know basis, you guys rank bottom. You step out of line, start doing anything out of order like fishing for information, and I'll come down on you like the pair of cockroaches you are.'

David looked at him calmly. 'Fishing for information sounds like a definition of our job to me. You stick to yours and we'll be fine.'

The captain stopped chewing his gum. 'Listen, you, Gen'l Patton had it about right. He said the British were nothin' but a bunch of spineless ninnies who'd go and drink tea whenever things got too hot for them.'

Nick smiled and spoke with an American accent that was just a bit more pronounced than usual. 'General Patton. Interesting you should mention him. Maybe you don't know too much about him. One of our country's most famous psychotics. Slapped a soldier's face in Sicily in 1943 for feigning illness. The boy happened to be a wounded hero, but he didn't bother to find out. Claimed battle fatigue was an invention of the Jews. Eisenhower told him he'd remove him from his command if he didn't apologize to everyone involved.'

The captain stared at him speechless, then spun on his heel and stalked off. David looked at Nick in surprise. 'Quite a story. Did you just make it up?'

'No,' said Nick, 'it's true.'

'Very good. But look, Nick, I want us to be on the same wavelength. That man's way over the top, but we've got to be prepared to co-operate with the military.'

Nick just looked at him.

A taxi took them to a large concrete garage off Yanbu Street in Al Khubar. Nick unlocked it. Inside was an old red truck.

'What's this?' asked David.

'This is a very fine Toyota Land Cruiser, the modern ship of the desert.'

'Have you rented it?'

Nick looked shifty. 'Well, I kinda bought it. I found this Yemeni who wanted something I had. It's still in his name so it's legal here.'

Piled up behind it were boxes of supplies, rations, tents, even a camouflage net. Nick filled David in on the exchange rates: one box of British tinned compo rations for forty-eight US Army camp-beds.

'Don't they have rations of their own?'

'Ah. You have yet to encounter the fearsome MREs or you wouldn't ask.'

'What are MREs?'

'US Armed Forces meals ready to eat. They're terrible. Freeze-dried cardboard. The grunts call them meals rejected by Ethiopia.'

David looked at the pile and shook his head. 'There's enough here for a full-scale expedition.'

'You will eventually realize, pal, that is exactly what we're going to need.'

'All this was bought with your hooch?'

'Yeah. Everything we need except HRPs. We're going to look real good on our expenses claims. Nielsen vintage '91 is top dollar.'

'HRPs?'

'Yeah. Sorry. New acronym. Body-bags got too familiar so it's HRPs now. Human Remains Pouches.'

Nick was watching David carefully and with hidden trepidation, as he faced up to the fact that it was going to be a rough ride.

'Come on,' he said. 'Let's take the Toyota and go and see some low-life. Wanna see a scorpion fight?'

Chapter Six

Same day

Geoff Busby woke up to the doorbell ringing. He was out of bed in an instant, dressing-gown pulled on before he was completely awake, checking diagonally down through the window. It was only the postman.

'Sorry, mate. Wouldn't fit, this one.' Busby took a bulky brown envelope, went back inside lighting a cigarette and pushed sticky take-away curry cartons to one side to make a clear space on the kitchen table. He should have cleared up last night when he'd got back from the boys' club, but had felt a bit whacked after three hours' non-stop judo. Some of them were coming on quite well, Phil in particular. Promising even.

He pulled it out of the envelope. It was fancy. He'd been expecting a catalogue, but it was more like a loose-leaf folder with big six-by-four glossies in it, black and white. He leafed through. The first few all looked like Filipinos. The advert had said Thailand. He'd heard Thais were the best. Best at keeping their lips buttoned and the house straight. He stopped shuffling through and looked at one of the pictures more closely. Why did they all have to stick their tits out like that? He liked them small and slim, not pretending to be fucking film stars. He sighed, tossed the folder on to the dresser and got dressed to go to work.

Martin Donaldson arrived at Bamco's head office looking forward to the day ahead. He didn't like Birmingham much,

74

but that didn't really matter. He was a big shot now, and with what he had in his briefcase he was about to get even bigger. He parked his car in the third reserved space by the door. Purkiss's Jaguar and Busby's weird machine were already there. He looked at Busby's, not for the first time, with a touch of scorn. It was as near to a battlefield vehicle as you could easily drive on the road, an air-transportable lightweight Land Rover, complete with cutaway wings and brackets once used for weaponry, in drab army green. Inside, though, it had plush seats and all the county gear.

There was a flashing orange light on the bunker over to the right, the warning that they were testing tank ammunition. The old soldier who manned front reception was polishing the display of shells in the case behind his desk, but broke off to wish him a polite good morning. Upstairs, his secretary greeted him with deference. 'Was your flight all right, Mr Donaldson?' she asked. 'I was a bit worried about the hotel.'

'So you should have been,' he said. 'It was a shit-heap. Don't ever do that to me again.'

She blinked. 'The travel agent . . .' But then she thought better of it and went on in a subdued voice, not meeting his eyes. 'Mr Purkiss says would you go through to his office as soon as you get in.'

It was Busby who opened the door to the secretary's knock and ushered Donaldson in, and Donaldson experienced the familiar prickle down his spine. This was his main obstacle. It was the same every time he saw him, the far-away eyes that stared through you to an aiming point on the other side of your skull. The economical movements of the lean body. Such a contrast to the overweight frame and greasy hair of Spencer Purkiss – except in the eyes. But Purkiss and Busby were a bit like two schoolboys together, with an over-readiness to laugh at each other's jokes, a feeling that they'd be quick to gang up on any weaker target. The way he'd planned things, that was just about to change.

'Welcome back, Martin,' said Purkiss. 'Good trip?' He was just a little bit nervous, wondering if the whole idea had been wise.

Donaldson tossed a folder on to his desk. 'I only spent two days in Jersey.' Purkiss looked surprised, but the younger man went on, not bothering to explain yet. 'I've been right through it like you said. You're more or less clean. I'd have trouble tying either of you in to the St Helier company. Jersey company law's got it pretty much buttoned up. Unless you can get at the piece of paper in the vaults that gives the name of the real owners, you can't get behind the local front men.'

Purkiss and Busby both smiled in relief.

Donaldson slammed his fist down on the desk and even Busby jumped. 'It's time you stopped pissing me around,' Donaldson said, standing over them. 'You've told me sod all about what I'm really looking for.'

'What do you mean?'

'You set me running with half-baked information. Then you're pleased when I can't nail you. It's fucking idiotic. It might make you feel good, but it doesn't tell us a damn thing about whether you've really covered your tracks.'

'Stop worrying about it, sonny. We were in this game before you were born,' said Busby, shooting an amused look towards Purkiss.

Got him, thought Donaldson. 'Funny you should say that, Geoff. Personally, I think you must have been born yesterday.'

'What do you mean?' Busby asked, the bantering tone gone.

'Well, I thought I'd go a bit beyond my instructions. Like

I say, I only spent two days in Jersey. After that I spent some time on the phone and then I went to Paris.' He took a sheet out of the folder and put it in front of them. 'Mr G. Busby,' he said. 'American Express bills for the George V Hotel in Paris on two occasions in April and May last year, with accompanying bills for restaurant meals nearby. Geoff, for someone who wasn't born yesterday, you leave a paper trail a mile wide.'

'So?' said Busby defiantly. 'Sales trips.'

'So,' said Donaldson. 'Six hours' legwork and a bit of creative bribery, without even threatening to pull anyone's arms off, and I've already managed to put a leading Iraqi arms procurement official in the same hotel on the same occasion. I've also got a head waiter who will identify you two as dining together.' It was only partly true, but he was sure enough of his ground to make the rest up. 'And that's all by my little self without any sophisticated back-up from MI6, the CIA or whoever. That makes me think that if I was someone else, and that someone else was looking seriously in Jersey, seriously enough to start twisting arms, I might very easily get behind your favourite front company, and who knows what I might find out then.'

'Jesus, Geoff,' exploded Purkiss. 'That wasn't very smart, was it?' Busby looked angry, but before he could say anything the intercom squawked, 'Mr Purkiss. Colonel Unwin is here from the Ministry of Defence.'

'Shit,' said Purkiss. 'OK, we put this one on hold until afterwards. Mustn't keep the colonel waiting.' He got up and shook his head like someone coming up from a dive. Busby was staring at the floor. Donaldson made as if to go out, but Purkiss stopped him. 'No, Martin, you stay. I want you to sit in on this one.'

The colonel was smaller than the title suggested, dressed in a well-cut suit, and he came into the room looking around with interest as if in the presence of an alien culture.

'Michael,' said Purkiss, greeting him. 'You've met Geoff.'

'Many times and in some funny places,' said the colonel in a deep, cultured voice, nodding to Busby, who bared his teeth at him.

'This is Martin Donaldson. He makes up the rest of the team. Fancy a cup of coffee?' They all sat down and, after the small talk was out of the way, Purkiss pushed a video into the player in the corner of the room. 'I wanted to show you Dodgem, Michael. You've only seen it on paper, haven't you?'

'I'd heard you'd been testing. How did it go?'

'Watch this, and you'll see.'

The video rolled. Duncan Challis's logo appeared, then a restricted access warning. A red word suddenly blazed across a black background, DODGEM. The video showed a launcher on the back of a truck in the middle of an expanse of moorland. It elevated, swivelled and locked. A second shot showed a target. It was an old Centurion tank. The video showed the missile firing, jinking crazily around the sky in an apparently random pattern, then streaking down to impact on the target.

A second title came up, DODGEM/CRACKSMAN 1. This time the camera took the viewer in through the back door of another truck. Inside, a man was crouched over a screen surrounded by controls. The video showed the firing sequence again, then cut back to the man and the screen. He was having trouble, fiddling with the controls, trying to do something and clearly failing. There were two big lights next to the screen. A yellow one was lit. It said NO LOCK. The red one next to it had black letters on it spelling out LOCKED ON, but it didn't light up. Again the missile impacted on the target.

'Very good,' said the colonel. 'So you've built a weapon that even Cracksman can't track. Time to let us have a look at it, I think.'

Purkiss drained his coffee and gave a rueful laugh. 'I wish we could, Michael, but you and I both know no one's got time for that while Desert Shield's going on. No, that wasn't really why I invited you over.' He looked hard at the colonel. 'Coming out next year, aren't you?'

'That's right. You're well informed.'

'Oh, I heard it somewhere. I was asking around for a good name or two. Got anything fixed up yet?'

The colonel's voice was cool, but his body language gave him away. He licked his lips and leaned forward. 'Oh, well, not really, but I'll start looking for something in industry somewhere.'

'Man like you would be very valuable to us. It's a tough old world out there. Bloody peace dividend. Thing is, we want someone to head up the Dodgem and Cracksman 2 projects. We all thought you'd be the ideal man. Care to think about it?'

Unwin beamed. 'Most certainly.' Then he looked puzzled. 'Cracksman 2? You haven't told us about that yet, have you?'

Purkiss beamed back. 'No, not yet. You wouldn't expect us to sit on our hands if Dodgem can get past our very own detection system, would you? Cracksman 2 will be designed to track even something like Dodgem. Anyway, it would be splendid to have you aboard. We can discuss details later. Course, that's as long as there *is* a project. I don't have to tell you, Michael, it depends a lot on the first response we get.'

Unwin's smile slipped slightly. 'Well, of course, Spencer, I haven't got much influence on that.'

'No, no, don't get me wrong. I wouldn't dream of putting

any pressure on you. I'm only trying to make the point that the name of the game is track record. It just occurred to me that we could help you out quite a lot. You're sending Cracksman out to the Gulf, aren't you?'

'Two sets only. You know perfectly well it's a bit early and Boscombe Down have been moaning a bit. I think you've seen the report. They think it's much too fragile.'

Purkiss waved dismissively. 'We can sort that. No problem. Those sets were never meant to be the final spec. We've already got a hardened version.' Then he seemed to be struck by a great idea. 'Tell you what, though. Why don't we do our bit for the lads in the Gulf. We'll send out two tech teams to back up Cracksman, free, gratis and for nothing. Bamco's gesture to the nation. How would that be?'

'Greatly appreciated, I should imagine.'

'So if we're doing that, why don't we send out a Dodgem unit as well. All at our expense.'

When Unwin went, there was some mutual back-slapping. Martin Donaldson started it off. 'Brilliant. Do you really want to give him a job?'

'Sure, why not? The big boys do it all the time. Bring 'em in for five years while they've still got some good contacts in the bits that spend the money, then retire 'em early. That way we get the best out of them. Not only that but the word gets round that Bamco is a cushy billet for their twilight years and then they're eager to please while they're still on the inside.'

Busby grunted. 'Pushing it a bit, Spence – promising them Dodgem. It's not exactly in full working order yet.'

Purkiss gave him a sharp look. 'We've got to seize the moment, Geoff. If Saddam stays put and there's a shooting war, you can forget your sales videos and your presentations and your live firing demos. Champagne, free holidays and tarts won't cut the ice with buyers any more. For the next five years the only question anyone will be asking will be "what did you do in the war, weapon?" If you can't put "combat proven" on the bottom line, you're not going to be bringing in customers.'

'Anyway, gentlemen,' said Donaldson, 'if you don't mind, let's get back to business. I want some answers.'

There was silence from the other two as if they had both been trying to put off this moment.

'All you gave me,' Donaldson said, 'was a company name, BFSS, and a location, St Helier. You wanted to know if your tracks were covered. I've already proved they aren't. So it's time to start talking.'

Purkiss had already decided Donaldson was one of them. Now he couldn't think of a reason to hold back, but first he decided to dangle some bait. 'You already know how we work, young Martin. It's all the way or nothing. If you're in, you can have 10 per cent of BFSS for starters.' He saw Busby's head lift suddenly. 'But that means you're all the way in, and you have to decide that right now before I say anything else.'

'What's 10 per cent worth?'

Purkiss laughed. 'I like motives I can understand. Two hundred thou if you play your cards right over the next year.'

'I'm in.' He waited for Purkiss to go on, but faced by the unveiling of the grubby secrets behind his empire, Purkiss suddenly wanted to justify himself.

'My old man wasn't anything grand, you know. He was just a sergeant-major up to the end of the war. Made a bit of money in the occupation of Germany. You can imagine the way it was, satisfying a few needs, matching up buyers and sellers, that kind of thing.'

'Black market,' interjected Busby, and Purkiss sniggered.

'Anyway, when he came back, he used the cash to get into war surplus and scrap. Pulled a few strings and started rebuilding army trucks and that for export. Then a few field guns came his way that needed fixing, and there were plenty of buyers for those. Mind you, he didn't like doing business with some of them. Real patriot he was, my dad. Didn't like black men one bit. Used to give loads of dosh to the National Front. Called me after his hero. Did you know Spencer was Winston Churchill's middle name?'

'Yes,' said Donaldson.

'Anyway, he had high aspirations for me. Bunged me off to a posh school to give me a flying start and all that.'

Donaldson knew this already, but he held his silence.

'Then he bought Bamco. It was on its last legs really, but he knew what he was doing. He knew there was no point in going too far ahead. What this business is all about is staying half a jump ahead, that's all. Sell the kit that just beats the opposition, then everyone will have to re-equip when the Mark 2 comes out. You think it's just the car makers who go in for built-in obsolescence? You take a look at this business. I mean, you should know. There's the late lamented Gerry Bull, brilliant designer, not a clue about business. Goes and builds the best bloody field gun in the world, gives it away for peanuts, and now you've got the South Africans, the Chinese and the Austrians all building it for years to bloody come. Where's the sense in that?'

'I take your point.'

'So the point about BFSS, young Martin, and from here on you're in as deep as a Catholic marriage, is it's all about countermeasures.'

He stopped, but Donaldson said nothing, waiting.

'What I mean is this. We get to know a lot about what

other people are doing in this line of business. I don't just mean the gossip in the trade. We've got technical facilities here that can do things almost nobody else can. So we get a lot of subcontract work. You can find out a lot from subcontract work. Give some of our lads an engineering drawing of one little component and they can work backwards to give you the whole fucking thing. Then of course there's the things we do for our own enlightened self-interest. Gotta get the inside track on the competition. Find out what they're doing one way or another.'

'And BFSS sells the details?'

'Let's say BFSS is in the other half of the weapons trade. Call it our humanitarian arm.' He laughed hugely and Busby joined in with a short bark. 'It's the bit that makes sure no one gets hurt by all these nasty arms sales. Get it? We'll go along and make you bombproof, rocketproof, whatever.'

Donaldson thought back to the earlier conversation. 'So Iraq's been on the customer list?'

Busby drew in his breath sharply. Purkiss shook his huge head, grinning. 'Oh, perish the thought, young Martin, perish the thought. That's where Jersey comes in. It's meant to be squeaky clean. The proceeds go through BFSS, cos I've got all these boring finance directors and accountants and people here, and one day we might just want to go public with Bamco. We wouldn't want a lot of skeletons falling out of the closet when we open the door.'

Donaldson stood up. 'OK, I'm in,' he said, 'but I want details of everywhere you two have been and everyone you've seen.'

'That ain't on,' said Busby, and Donaldson rounded on him.

'There's a good reason for you and an even better one for me. You left a trail a child could follow in Paris.

83

Remember what happened to Gerry Bull in Brussels. Do you think the Israelis are suddenly going to stop minding if people like us deal with the Iraqis? If you two want to end up like Bull, with a Mossad bullet in your head, that's your business, but I don't want them coming after me, nor do I want to be arrested for breaking every export regulation in the book.' He was standing over them, exuding dangerous anger, and though he was the youngest of the three by far, they were watching him like birds watching a snake. 'I've fixed Paris for you,' he said. 'I want to be bloody sure there aren't any other messes like that one lying around.'

Chapter Seven

Sunday October 21st 1990

The Toyota had been backfiring for the last thirty, dusty, stifling miles. Now it was spluttering even worse, kangarooing sickeningly every time the engine momentarily cut out, turning the nerve-racking whine of the transmission into a fusillade of metallic crashes. Nick was driving one-handed through the middle of a giant linear construction project. The US Army Corps of Engineers was reshaping the entire road system of Saudi Arabia's top right-hand corner, doubling the width of the road, scraping a huge, hundred-yard swathe of flattened, compacted desert all along the side of the tarmac. The endless stream of vehicles already thundering along the bits they'd finished showed this was no idle task.

'There's something,' Nick said, swerving off into the hard, stony sand, stopping in a diagonal, plunging lurch that bounced David's head off the side window. He sighed as Nick opened the driver's door and let in a blast of hot air which immediately negated all the good work the tired old air-conditioning had done in the five miles since they had last stopped. This is getting boring, he thought. Nick returned and slung something bulky into the back. 'Looks like another camouflage net,' he said cheerfully.

'It's stealing,' said David.

'It's proffing,' said Nick. 'That's what they call it when you're just picking up stuff from other units. More like borrowing.'

'We're not a unit.'

'I forgot. Anyway, it would only get flattened if we left it.'

There, at least, he had a point. The road to Hafar, like all the roads being used for this vast movement of men and materials, was covered in army equipment which had literally fallen off the backs of the lorries. They'd stopped bothering to pick up boxes of US rations, and any British ration boxes got snapped up before they hit the ground. On one occasion, near the start of the trip, David had stepped in with a heavy-handed veto when Nick had found a bag of grenades, but he couldn't stop his producer picking up anything else that looked halfway useful. The traffic was so bad they would sometimes have to wait two or three minutes to get back into the line.

When they got there, the tiny town of Hafar Al Batin made Dhahran look like the height of sophisticated luxury. Hafar was little more than a few scrubby palm trees and some leprous concrete, a truck stop on the sandy road to nowhere much, a small bedouin trading town with a tenuous grip on the desert. One hundred miles inland west of Khafji, close to the Kuwaiti border, it was one of the places where the first Allied troops had deployed on arrival in Saudi Arabia in the gamble that Saddam would be deterred from pushing past them into the Saudi kingdom.

The French Rapid Reaction Force had been among the earliest arrivals, and now they were a little scornful as the first British forces trailed in weeks late. Nick and David had spent Saturday watching white-skinned Brits dressed in incongruous lightweight jungle gear driving the first Challenger tanks ashore off the transport ship *Sir Bedivere* at the port of Jubayl, their green uniforms showing the depth of their unpreparedness against the universal aching beige of the landscape. Nick and David had decided to drive up to Hafar to take a look at the French Foreign Legion.

They met them in the desert five miles outside Hafar, where the flat sand was broken only by the occasional bedouin tent and the fat-tailed sheep which wandered around them. The French AMX light tanks, running on multiple soft tyres instead of tracks, looked good racing across the sand. They parked next to a tent where a group of officers were watching the manœuvres through field-glasses. They all looked round as they heard the Toyota, and the man at the centre of the group jerked a thumb in their direction and said something to a giant of a man next to him. The giant, cropped fair hair dusted over a skull like a cannon-ball, moved with easy speed to intercept them. David jumped out into the heat.

'Bonjour,' he said, '*je suis journaliste anglais. Je m'appelle David Challis et je me demandais . . .*'

'Fook that then,' said the man, '*je m'appelle* Tom Smith, or that'll do for you, any road, so why don't we speak English?' He had a heavy Yorkshire accent and a face that had probably handed out even more damage than it had received.

'Oh, right,' said David, suddenly at a loss. 'What are you doing with these guys?'

'Long story an' I'm not about to tell it yer. D'yer want to see the colonel?'

The colonel was not a happy man. He was sipping mineral water from a tin mug and peering at a map. He turned a jaundiced eye on them as they came round the corner of the awning. 'English journalists? Come to the ends of the known world just to see us? We should be grateful, I think. Out here in the desert, we have been carefully put where no one will take any notice.'

'You sound as though you think that's deliberate,' said David.

'Deliberate? For sure. Here we are away from the

cameras, from the notebooks. The Americans planned it that way. We have something they want here, a big market. We know these people. We have dealt with them for years. We know more about desert fighting than any American. They say our AMXs are too puny, too delicate.' He gestured at one of the little tanks. 'Poof! They are made for this kind of terrain. You watch the Abrams run out of fuel. You watch the Challengers suck in the sand and destroy their engines. Then we have to come and rescue them. But when this is over, it will be the Abrams pulling in the sales orders, not the Challengers and certainly not our AMXs.'

They talked for a few minutes and made admiring noises about the speed and efficiency of the unit, but they got a strong feeling they were in the way so they made their excuses and left.

'That was a hell of a way to come for a glass of water,' said Nick as they pulled out of the little encampment. He slowed and moved over as a big Nissan Patrol passed them going the other way. They had a brief glimpse of the driver's face turned towards them, nothing much more than a pair of sun-glasses and a helmet. A few seconds later Nick frowned and looked in the mirror again.

'That Nissan,' he said.

'Yes?'

'It did a U-turn. It's coming after us.'

David looked over his shoulder, but he couldn't see much through the dust-covered rear window. 'Coincidence,' he said. 'Must have realized there's nothing much to see. What else could it be?'

There was a fork coming up on the outskirts of Hafar. Nick swung over into the side-road and jolted along the rough track. 'No coincidence,' he said. 'It's still following us.'

'Nick, calm down. Maybe it's someone who collects vintage Toyotas.'

'Maybe it's Captain Cato or one of his merry men.'

'Would that matter? We're not doing anything wrong.'

'You may not be. I've got eight pints of top-quality moonshine in the back.'

'Christ Almighty. Why?'

'It's the next instalment on the Toyota.'

David was speechless. Then Nick swore, and David looked ahead to see that the roadway simply ended in a giant ditch. They stopped.

'Let's go meet the enemy,' said Nick.

It was hard to see back into the glare. The Nissan, much newer and smarter than their shabby old truck, had pulled up a few yards behind them. They climbed down, and David's certainty that this would be something mundane, a request for directions or water or something like that, began to ebb away. The other driver simply got out and stood there watching them, saying nothing.

They walked up close and stopped. 'What do you want?' demanded Nick belligerently.

The driver took off her helmet and shook out a mane of blonde hair. Yanna's soft French voice said, 'Since you ask, I want your friend.'

Chapter Eight

Same day

The meeting-room was a bit on the small side. Everyone had brought so many papers that they were overflowing into their neighbours' spaces, but the Defence Staff brainstorming session had been brought forward at short notice and a few of the details weren't as meticulously prepared as they might normally have been.

The wing commander had made good time from his country cottage near Brize Norton. His children had grumbled at the cancellation of the family game of cricket, but needs must when duty calls, as he was fond of saying, and as they were equally fond of mimicking when he was out of earshot. He was glad he hadn't left his preparation to the last minute, as the frantic activity elsewhere round the table indicated that others had. He'd been pretty certain for days now that the minister would soon have to announce a big reinforcement of the troops and aircraft already sent, so he'd started on the contingency plans well in advance, just in case. A mild throat-clearing from the senior civil servant at the head of the table was enough to call the meeting to order.

The civil servant's voice was a specialized tool, regulated by years of practice to a pitch where his skilful use of nuance could control a delicately phrased argument between colleagues of equal intellectual calibre. In the hierarchy of Whitehall he had achieved a position from which tradition allowed him to deploy his self-consciously clever turns of phrase to mark his seniority and oblige respectful attendance. His humour was so dry it left the smell of old dust in the listeners' sinuses, packaged in a voice hand-polished for delivery from a sitting position behind a table such as this in a room such as this.

Looking around the wing commander could see some who were further from their natural element, happier with a clearer hierarchy of obedience, discipline and responsi-bility, more used to delivering their contributions from a standing position in a command post or flight-line briefing-room.

The civil servant had a high-pitched voice. 'Gentlemen. The first priority is logistics. We know just how much *matériel* the Americans are putting in place.' His languid stress on the final syllable of *matériel* was intended to show the military he was at home with their odd, borrowed words. 'We must be sure that our contribution, while it may be proportionately smaller, will be seen as equally significant.' He cleared his throat. 'It is also necessary to underline that we perceive no incompatibility between the need to provide the most effective weaponry to our armed forces for the duration of this operation and the longer-term aims of making sure our systems are seen in the best light against their competitors, thereby ensuring the con-tinuing ability of our main suppliers to provide for any future conflicts of this nature.' He smiled a humourless smile designed to punctuate the ending of a polite order.

The wing commander saw the sharp-faced lieutenant-colonel next to him scribbling a note. It was pushed towards him. 'What the hell does all that mean?' it read.

The wing commander wrote surreptitiously on the bottom, feeling like a naughty schoolboy, and passed it back. 'Weapons showcase. Think of the foreign sales when the smoke clears.'

The civil servant continued. 'You will by now have read the briefing paper on what our people in Riyadh perceive to be the American attitude to our forces. The Americans question the effectiveness in particular of the Challenger tank in combat, as far as engine reliability goes. They may be planning to relegate it to a minor role. That would mean, according to our latest assessment, that they would intend to use our tank forces only as a backup for the United States Marine Corps rather than as a separate element in the main attack. Do we have a response?'

'Already under way,' said the lieutenant-colonel. 'Civilian teams from Vickers will be on the ground there. Their MD's taking a close personal interest. He's planning to go out there himself. Every power unit they can get their hands on is being shipped, and there's a team of Rolls-Royce tech specialists working on the sand filters.'

The civil servant made a quick note with a look that suggested the blame for any ensuing failure had just been minuted from his own shoulders. 'Now, Air Force matters. It is quite clear from Riyadh that the plans for any air campaign centre on the maximum usage by the Americans of the new generation of what they term, I believe, smart weaponry. We have a clear indication that once such weapons have been used, assuming they perform as intended, there will be maximum publicity given to the results they achieve. This, I need hardly say, will be primarily aimed at showing to other nations that the strikes are being directed with great, indeed surgical, discrimination against military rather than civilian targets.'

The wing commander sat there, trying to come to terms with the idea that public relations had been promoted so far up the chain of command. The PR men used to sweep up after us, he thought to himself. They used to have to make the best of our mistakes, not lay down the rules of

92

how we fight. He became aware, just in time, that he was being asked a question.

'. . . tell us to what extent the RAF is ready to make full play of the more sophisticated resources it can deploy?'

'Yes, indeed,' he said, thinking quickly. 'There is of course Hunting's JP233 airfield deprivation weapon. That's the one delivered by Tornado that scatters bomblets and anti-personnel mines. There is a promotional video of that available for press distribution as and when it is used. Makes it look pretty good. Apart from that, as you know, we are going full speed with the manufacturers trying to get TIALD laser designation gear ready to fit, so we can drop guided weapons from a stand-off position, but that's some way away. The contingency plan is to use the Buccaneers with . . .'

The civil servant's eyebrows shot up and he did something that was rare for him, – he interrupted. 'Forgive me, wing commander, but Buccaneers. That's a design that's, what, thirty years old at least, isn't it?'

'They are at the moment the only aircraft with Pave Spike laser equipment which could go in with the Tornados to guide smart bombs. They're very effective. That's what matters.'

'We'd be laughed out of court.'

The wing commander kept his silence.

'Missiles,' said the civil servant. 'Since our last meeting we have learnt that the Americans have acquired a full ballistic and radar signature profile for both the Al Hussein and the Al Abbas variants of the SS-1 missiles, or the Scud as people seem to be calling them. This clearly gives them a strong advantage in preparing anti-missile defences. Their Patriot system will be brought into play in the event of a missile attack. We should make sure the Navy has every opportunity to deploy Sea Skua against enemy naval

93

forces, and of course Sea Dart against any missile attacks on shipping.'

The discussion went on for another two hours, a military establishment being confronted with the reality that its weaponry had somehow slipped behind in the glamour stakes. At the far end of the table Colonel Unwin had been keeping his silence, biding his time until the right psychological moment. Now, with the meeting drawing near its natural end and no one apparently in a mood to prolong it, he decided the moment was ripe.

'There is one more systems possibility,' he said diffidently. 'Though it's a little too early from the publicity point of view.'

'Yes?' said the civil servant testily. He didn't like surprise interventions just before lunch-time.

'We do have some very high-tech stuff available in ballistic delivery-point analysis. There's Cracksman, for example.'

Another colonel snorted. 'From what I've been hearing it's not exactly combat-ready, is it?'

'They say it is now. Anyway, the manufacturers are prepared to send a full support team at their own expense. Something else, too – they have an experimental missile system that few of you will have seen yet. It's called Dodgem. Random path stuff. Very impressive. Beats enemy countermeasures. We know the Yanks have something, but this goes at least one stage further. They're prepared to take out a unit, again at their expense.'

There was a silence while they thought about it, then lunch resurfaced in all their minds.

'No skin off our nose,' said the wing commander.

'Can't see any harm in it,' said the civil servant.

94

The wing commander stayed behind for a brief word on the way out. 'You don't think the Americans are selling us a line about the Scuds? It wouldn't do to get over-confident about their ability to deal with them.'

The civil servant smiled. 'It wasn't the Americans who told us about it. A spot of good work by Six. It seems General Moiseyev himself handed over all the details to the embassy in Moscow.'

'The Red Army C-in-C?'

'The very same.'

'It's going to make their Patriot system look rather better than it really is.'

'What do you mean?'

'Well, if your anti-missile system knows exactly how an incoming threat behaves – how big it is, what speed it's going at, how hot the nose-cone gets – it gives it one hell of an unfair advantage. Cuts most of the guesswork out of the interception programming.'

The civil servant smiled. 'That, I suppose, is what you get when Russian bears start bearing gifts.'

'I only wish the French were as helpful.'

'Are you still having difficulties?'

'It probably doesn't matter, but we'd like to know if Saddam's Mirages have anything funny up their sleeves we don't yet know about. Sounds as though we'll get the lowdown on his Migs before we hear about the Mirages.'

'You must be aware of the sensitivities,' said the civil servant. 'They helped us a great deal in the Falklands. Well, indeed you were involved, weren't you?'

'Wasn't I just. Practice interceptions all day long out in the Western Approaches. Mock attacks with Super Étendards, Mirages, dummy runs with Exocet, the works.'

'Yes, but they say it's cost them dear since then. The word's out in the Third World that you can't trust the

French because they are only too ready to sell out their customers to the other side, if the other side happens to be a NATO member.'

The wing commander laughed. 'They really think you can trust anyone in this business? The Israelis have got the right idea. They modify everything they get their hands on, so even their suppliers don't know what they've got.'

As they all went for lunch, David was riding back towards Dhahran in Yanna's passenger seat, followed by an incredulous Nick Nielsen, who was wondering how his partner had been able to conjure a beautiful French girl out of the middle of an unprepossessing desert. The road, which had seemed a depressing ribbon of barren dust on the way out, now seemed exotic, almost picturesque.

'Why the helmet?' David asked.

'You don't know the rules? The rules that say no woman in Saudi Arabia may drive a car? The rules that say if we walk together I have to be twelve paces behind you? The rules that say I must not have bare arms or legs?'

'I suppose I hadn't realized they applied.'

'You ask the women with the American forces if they apply. You see these girls who are GIs. They've fought for their equality. Now the American men treat them pretty straight up. Over here these girls put on their shorts and go running to keep fit, and the Metawa police try to arrest them.'

'Have many been arrested?'

Yanna laughed. 'Many Metawa have been knocked out. There was one in the middle of Riyadh. The girl knocked him down, stood on him and put her gun to his head.'

David laughed and Yanna gave him a sharp look. 'Maybe it is not so funny, David.'

'Why do you say that?'

'It is another little bit of hypocrisy. We say we are getting ready to fight for what? Democracy? We are here in Saudi, a medieval country, fighting for the Al Sabahs of Kuwait, medieval dictators.'

'Well, we can tell it like we see it, can't we?'

'You try telling the story of the women GIs and see what happens to your copy. It has not been printed any-where.'

'Well, I'm not too surprised. At a time like this the Iraqis would seize on a thing like that. It's just what they need to divide Arab support for the coalition.'

She looked at him and shook her head. 'That is just what the censors would say.'

They rode in silence for a while, Yanna driving one-handed. After a bit he tried to take her other hand, resting on the seat beside him, in his, but she moved it away.

Chapter Nine

Thursday November 29th 1990

The sand far off in front of David erupted, leaving a snaking curtain of dust behind, as the violent roar of the explosion caught up with the flash and then dissipated into the empty desert. It was over five hundred yards away, but he still grunted as the concussion hit him, and turned away, rubbing his ears. There was an unsympathetic laugh from the corporal to his right. Nick was sitting on the ground, shaking his head. 'Getting to you, is it?' said the corporal. 'Why not snuggle down for a nice kip on the sand?' His tone changed. 'Then if yer still down there when the next one blows, it'll crush yer bollocks, never mind what it'll do to yer spine.' His lip curled. 'If you think that was fucking noisy wait until you hear the real ones with a whole fucking minefield going up as well.'

Nick climbed reluctantly back to his feet. 'Thanks for the kind thought, corp.'

'Fucking Septic,' muttered the corporal, and Nick swung round on him. 'What did you say?'

There was instant aggression bristling between them, and the corporal looked like he was enjoying it.

'Leave it out, Nick,' said David quickly. The corporal shook his head and walked off to harangue a stills photographer who'd unwisely dared to take off his helmet. He glanced back as he went, and spat in the sand.

Nick complained. 'I'm fed up with the Septic Tanks—

Yanks routine. They'll get it shoved up their assholes one day soon.'

'A few of your countrymen have already done that, I hear,' observed David.

British squaddies found it hard to keep a straight face when they heard US marines returning salutes with the latest catch-phrase, 'Sir, the desert is our killing ground, SIR', or 'The Marine Corps own the night, SIR.' The British marines retaliated with some rude variations on their jogging chants. Friction, fanned by the intense heat, had been mounting steadily. For their part the American forces could only believe the evidence of their own eyes. They were overwhelmingly the largest contingent. It was their operation and they weren't going to be very tolerant of anyone else suggesting they should be doing things any other way.

David carefully eased his weight on to his right leg as they waited for the next explosion. The sand felt like talcum powder in the fingers but had the opposite effect on the skin. It penetrated almost everywhere, and wherever it did, it mixed with sweat to turn into an abrasive paste so that necks, collars and waistbands became inflamed, chafing patches of misery. Drills with the claustrophobic NBC suits, each one a personal sauna bath, added to the torment. They would have cheerfully ducked out of those if it hadn't been for the vivid description of the effects of anthrax germ warfare and blister gases given in the regular first-aid lectures.

Nick had given those up after his very first experience. Introduced rather graphically to the principles of triage – the sorting through of the wounded to weed out those who were too badly injured to merit any attempt at saving – he had turned pale and been found some time later, sound asleep under a table with a note pinned to his shirt saying *'Mortal head wound. Don't attempt resuscitation'* in what seemed to be his own handwriting.

Now, in the scrubby, blasted back-end of nowhere, the sheep were being sorted from the goats. Battlefield stress tests were deciding which of the press would go to war and which couldn't stand the pace. The army was using Viper, a long snake of high explosive, projected across a minefield then detonated. David was waiting for the next one, trying to look unconcerned, when there was a hail from behind and he turned.

'Anthony. Good morning. How are you?'

'I'll take that as rhetorical, David. You really wouldn't want to know, I promise. I used to think rank was all about privileges. Now I know better.'

David laughed. 'Two months as a lieutenant colonel and you're jaded already?'

'Bloody post arrived this morning. The wife forwarded my Wine Society newsletter. Saudi censor blacked out every reference to the blessed grape in it. Didn't leave very much to read, as you can imagine.'

Anthony Marshall had been at school with David. They'd met on a few occasions since, mostly during the period when Marshall had been seeing a lot of Josie's sister in the days when David and Josie were together. Now Marshall had been roped into the press training programme, though he was itching to be relieved and get back to his unit for combat preparation.

David gritted his teeth as another Viper charge erupted. 'By the way, Anthony, I hate to remind you, but it's Thursday.'

'I can't argue with that.'

'Well?'

'Well what?'

'You said by Thursday you might be able to give us an idea of the chances.'

'I didn't say which Thursday.'

'Yes you did.'

Marshall sighed. 'It's pretty difficult, David. You must know that. Every bloody meeting I go to, they seem to change the rules. I've been doing as much special pleading as I can, but it's not going to be me deciding who's going to be in the pools. Anyway, I'm still not sure it's even in your interests. You could be cooped up in the back of a Warrior bucketing around the wrong bit of desert for a month and not see a damned thing *and* the pooling system means you'll have to hand over every picture you shoot to any Tom, Dick or Harry who wants it.'

'I know all that, but if the alternative is to be stuck here . . .'

'Well, don't lose hope. My colleagues all think you're a good egg. George said he'd offer you a commission with the Greys like a shot after that little number you did on them. What did you do exactly?'

'Nothing much.'

'Scooped the pool, I heard. Better score at five hundred metres than their top sniper. More than that, you talk our language.' He dropped his voice and turned away from Nick, who was a few yards behind them. 'Mind you, I'm not sure I could say the same about your producer chappie. Might help your chances a bit if you ditched him.'

David stared across at Nick moodily. His arms still ached from the previous day's live firing exercise, scrambling a thousand yards along a ditch with bullets overhead, explosions on each side and a machine-gun kicking up the sand behind to persuade them to keep going. Nick had started puffing after a hundred yards and had been purple in the face by the halfway mark. The sergeant on the machine-gun seemed to be cutting things a bit fine for safety, but Nick's survival instinct had proved unable to overcome the handicap of his beer gut.

'I'm gonna stop,' Nick had panted.

'You can't.'

'They won't shoot me.'

'Nick, believe me, there's nothing they'd like more.'

David had heaved him over the finish line like a sack of potatoes. It was one of the times he was most inclined to agree with Anthony Marshall's assessment.

'Got to get back to work, David. Keep smiling.'

'Thanks, Anthony. You too.'

The camera crew, Ian and Norman, were dealing with a camera fault as the next Viper was being prepared. They were becoming truly expert at the emergency remedies demanded by the clogging sand. It was the last scheduled shoot of the day, and David didn't begrudge them their evenings, stretched out in their rooms, watching videos, repairing the gear or drinking the non-alcoholic beer with the other crews.

Nick usually avoided David's company when they weren't working. He would disappear off to his own nether world with some of the more relaxed elements of the US army, to scorpion or sand-snake fights, or to take part in arm-wrestling matches where his flabby stomach would sucker far tougher-looking GIs into ignominious and expensive failure against his hidden expertise. These were the forums in which he traded small quantities of his moonshine, carried in a portable oxygen cylinder 'for asthma attacks', for information, equipment or anything else he could lay his hands on.

The evenings, when they weren't filled by the demands of work, were a mixture of heaven and hell for David. Here for maybe one week in every three was this wonderful, explosive woman who set him on fire at the same time as she challenged every one of his values. Yanna spent a lot of time away, riding up and down the coast searching for new images of the build-up against a depressingly uniform backcloth. He lived for her reappearances. Sometimes he didn't even have to turn to know that she had arrived in the room; the electric buzz that seemed to discharge between them was enough. But she was not one to compromise. In the way, blocking an ecstatic free fall into openly confessed passion, was a mental barrier they were unable to bridge. Their different attitudes to the war, if that was what it was to be, blocked communication on any intellectual level, leaving only the physical attraction and a deep yearning in both of them for circumstances to be different.

They were in the middle of a world obsessed by military conflict. There did not exist a neutral no-man's-land here in which to explore the other parts of their lives. There could have been, perhaps, if they had agreed to create it, to fence it off and not let forbidden subjects stray into it, but each needed to convert the other to their own point of view on this central issue where their differences ran so deep. The circumstances of this temporary life were against them. Yanna, like Nick, was a central character in the group of unbelievers; David was widely regarded among the rest of the press corps as one of the gurus of military know-how and insight. No one would leave them alone anywhere outside their bedrooms, and sometimes not even there, without approaching to lob in the latest gossip, to attempt to cross-check some rumour or to try to prise some information out of them. Only in the relative peace of their rooms could they really be together, but between them and the shared bed which their bodies yearned for stood IT, the unattained common mental ground which neither seemed able to falsify or conveniently forget.

Then, in any case, there was always the phone to ring. The pressure of the job, the phone calls from Glass Crystal or the demands of Yanna's clients to come up with something new never lifted. The trouble was, the parts of the build-up were either totally secret or completely open to all the press to see. There wasn't much opportunity for clever journalism. The pressure to fill up the pages and the news bulletins was almost unrelenting, and then, when for a few weeks it did finally relent, that seemed even worse. The British contingent suddenly had to kick their heels complaining while the media back home became completely obsessed with the overthrow of Margaret Thatcher.

Standing in the sand, David took a swig of warm, plastic-flavoured mineral water as he watched Marshall walking off. They'd done all the available Gulf stories: Bush's mawkish, stage-managed Thanksgiving visit, the constant exercising, the anthrax jabs from which David still carried the ache, and so on. David looked around and sighed. 'So what do we do now?'

'What about going back to Riyadh?' said Nick hopefully. He had a little deal going there which needed some nurturing.

'What for?' said David. 'There's nothing going on we can shoot there. Not that there's very much here either.'

'Look, I don't like to labour the point,' said Nick, 'but I think there's plenty to shoot if you just kinda look at it the right way. The SNAFU factor. Challenger engines going in and out like yo-yos, Brit soldiers trading their mothers for desert uniform, on account of there's not enough to go around. There's even GIs calling stores back home to buy satellite navigation sets on their credit cards because that's the only way to find out where you are and Uncle Sam forgot to bring enough.'

'Nick,' said David, 'all wars have foul-ups. This one's no better and no worse. If we win it, the folks back home couldn't care less. If we lose it, that's the last aspect anyone's going to be worried about.'

They were three weeks away from their first programme. So far it wasn't looking too different from the run-of-the-mill daily news coverage, and David was starting to worry about where he was going to find the extra ingredients to justify their presence.

In the evening they went back to the hotel. There was a player and a monitor set up in David's room, and they looked at the day's tapes. There was a knock at the door, and as he crossed the floor, David knew from the sudden prickling in his body that it was Yanna. He opened it and she was there, a foot away, with an ability to concentrate his entire attention into that little bit of physical space she occupied. Her face was serious, full of meaning, but her eyes did their trick on his and a shiver ran through his soul. His arms opened and his lips met her cheek, dusty with sand, as she twisted, contorted by something anguished within.

'Come in,' he said. 'What's the matter?'

She shook her head, speechless, walked past him with a mechanical stiffness and sat on the sofa. Nick looked at her and waggled his oxygen cylinder invitingly. She shook her head and looked at the screen. 'More whizz bangs? Haven't you shot enough?'

David stared at her, unable to fathom her mood. 'What else is there to shoot?'

Unknowingly, she echoed Nick's earlier words. 'Quite a lot if you know where to look, and if your eyes work.'

She'd been holding her light cotton jacket bunched up in one hand. Now her hands started to shake and she dropped it. It fell open on the floor and all across the cream front were dark splashes of dried blood.

'Yanna! What happened?'

'A tank happened. A tank happened to a little Pakistani boy on his bike.'

'What sort of tank?'

She rounded on him. 'What does it matter what sort of a tank? What do you want to know? Whether it was an M2 Mark 9 A4 whatever?' Her voice rose. 'What does it matter? What does it fucking *matter*?'

What a stupid thing I said, thought David. 'I'm sorry. I didn't mean that. I meant who did it? What nationality?'

There was a silence while she looked down at the jacket on the floor, breathing in long shaky breaths that vibrated in her throat like sobs. 'It is not important,' she said. 'No one blamed the tank driver. The Saudis need to keep the tank drivers on their side. They blamed the kid. It was easier. He was just some poor foreign worker's son on his tatty old bicycle. Just a little bit of – what is that horrid expression they say when they mean killing civilians? Collateral damage. He is just a little bit of collateral damage.'

'Did you see it happen?'

'I saw it. I was taking pictures. The kid looked at me. Perhaps that was why he fell. That is what the soldiers said. They said it was my fault.' She started to tremble again. David put his arm round her, but she convulsed angrily.

'Is he dead?'

'Oh, yes. Completely. The tank crew said there was no point in even trying. I asked them to give him morphine in case, but they showed me his . . .' She trailed off into silence.

'Yanna, it wasn't your fault.'

'That was the first thing the sergeant said to his driver. "It was not your fault." Whose fault was it, David? Was it George Bush's fault? I suppose you would say it was Saddam Hussein's fault, would you?' She fell silent. 'I am sorry,' she said. 'I took pictures. Bloody pictures.'

106

'What will you do with them?'

'I will send them to Paris,' she said in a calmer voice.

'Will they publish them?'

'Yes. All of them I hope. Then people will understand the real price. Not like this firework display you are showing them.'

Nick broke his silence. 'Our viewers couldn't take your reality, Yanna.'

'No, Nick. I know. You understand what I mean, but tell me, David, do *you* know that is why your countries are so hungry to fight their little wars? Why they are so proud of their boys, their Desert Rats and their Red Berets? So tough when it comes to putting on their white hats and loading up their six-shooters from their armchairs in front of their sanitized televisions?'

She needs to get the anger out of her system, thought David. Better like this than keeping it inside. 'You may be right,' he said. 'But that doesn't really give us the choice.'

'Don't patronize me,' she snapped back. 'You don't think I am right at all. Why do you say so? So the silly girl will keep quiet?'

'No, I . . .'

'You ought to look at what you do. It is your responsibility. What are you making, David? Cowboy films where only the bad guys die? Where you don't see what is left of a boy's head when a tank has been over it? Don't you think all those armchair warriors back in England who happily let their politicians lead them into war might pass on a different message if you showed them what it is really like?'

'Maybe,' said David, tight-lipped. 'Maybe I could single-handedly overturn the whole of British broadcasting culture. I doubt it, but maybe.'

There was complete silence in the room for some time,

then Yanna reached out and took his hand and her voice sounded dull with fatigue. 'No, it is not your personal fault, my David. You are only one little bit of it after all. Let's talk of something else now.'

He stared at her. 'I don't know if we should. Wouldn't that be hiding?'

'Yes,' she said firmly. 'Let's hide. I want to hide now. I have earned the right today.' She put on a bright, artificial voice. 'Anyway, I have other things to tell you. I have seen my French friends again. They are very bitter.'

David was silent. Nick played the game with her. 'How come?'

'They say Schwarzkopf is impossible. If he does not like what they say to him, he is just unbelievably rude to them. They say the Americans are planning the fight so they keep all the glory to themselves and the others will be out in the wilderness.'

She looked at David, but his mind was still on the previous conversation. 'Look, Yanna . . .' he began, but she thought of something else to forestall him.

'Oh,' she said, 'I brought you up a letter from the desk. From your brother maybe.'

Nick got up. 'I gotta go,' he said. 'Gotta see a man about something. Do this later, OK?' and he went out.

David watched him go with mixed feelings, unsure whether he could handle Yanna in this unpredictable, emotional state. 'No,' he said, looking at the writing, 'it's from Josie.' He opened it and held it out sideways so Yanna could read it. Her mood had passed away. She clasped her fingers together and leaned her arms on his shoulder so that the smell of her hair was in his nose. The letter was tender and concerned. Josie said she was amazed and very pleased to hear from David's letter that he had met Yanna in Saudi. She said how beautiful Yanna was and how well she thought Yanna and David went together. Yanna laughed at that bit.

'I am not so sure she really means what she says.'

'Why do you say that?'

'Well, it is clear, isn't it? She is still a lot in love with you.'

David looked at her in astonishment. 'Of course not. She married Duncan.'

'Only because you more or less made her.'

'No, I didn't.'

Yanna looked amused. 'I talked a lot to her that week-end.'

'She didn't say that, I'm sure.'

'No, of course. She didn't need to. It was clear to me.'

'You're teasing me.'

'No, I am not.'

'Anyway, what else does she say?'

What she said was couched in light-hearted terms apparently intended to make David think that all was well. Receiving letters in a war zone was like being in hospital. People wrote as if you had quite enough on your plate and only the blandest reassurances would do. It had an opposite effect on David. Josie said they were apparently going to be OK for money. Duncan had something up his sleeve, a big payment from one of his company clients or something like that.

'You think it is Bamco?' asked Yanna.

'I don't think he's got any other clients,' said David, 'whatever he tells Josie.'

'What do you think it means?'

David looked at the letter and shook his head. 'I hope he's not trying to lean on them.'

'You mean the test I saw?'

'Something like that.'

'They were faking it up, I am sure, after it went wrong. Duncan was helping them. They tried to push me away.' She thought for a while. 'He would be very foolish to – what did you say? – to lean on them. There is one there who is that type you sometimes see. Not like a soldier, something a whole lot worse.'

'A keeny-meany?' asked David.

'Yes, maybe,' said Yanna. 'What is that exactly? A keeny-meany?'

'Well, the way I see it, you can split up men who fight by choice into groups. There's the ordinary bloke, the grunt as Nick would say. He thinks of his gun just as the tool of his trade, no more and no less. He's fit and he's pretty foul-mouthed, but there's usually a bit of humour when you look in his eyes.'

Yanna nodded and smiled. 'I know what you mean.'

'Then there's the officer class. They may be the type who join up for the social life and some of them never quite grow up, or they may be the few who go beyond that. There's one or two like that out here. They're the ones with real charisma, the kind men will follow any-where. They don't always come over like Action Man though. It's almost like they live on a different plane, mili-tary scientists perhaps. They could almost be academics, historians or philosophers maybe.'

'And the keeny-meanies?'

'Ah. They're the ones to watch out for. They're way off to one side in a class of their own. They're the ones who are in it for the buzz, who like the idea of legal murder. In the ordinary armed services, officers may not even want them in their squads. These guys are just too much into weaponry. Most officers see them as a bit unhealthy, too untrustworthy. Some get pushed out. Then they turn into mercenaries or if there isn't a good war to sign up for they may take to robbing banks. Some stay in and manage to get into the special forces or the SAS, though even in units like that they're often viewed with a touch of suspicion, as if they've got their own hidden agenda of violence. Something sexual maybe.'

Yanna agreed, soberly. 'This man they have at Bamco – Busby – I think that fits him well. Your brother should be very careful what he says to them.' She walked to the window and looked out at the runway lights boxed in by the heavy blackness of the Saudi night. A jet took off and roared into that blackness. 'I didn't tell you because it sounded silly. You know I kept a roll of film of the Bamco tests? I don't know why. I took it back to Quiberon with me when I went home. I hid it there. Only my mother would know where to find it.'

'Why?'

She shivered. 'I just had a feeling.'

'Quiberon,' said David. 'Tell me more about Quiberon.'

She turned and smiled curiously. 'Why?'

'Because it is so completely, definitely not this place. In fact it's the very opposite, isn't it? Surrounded by water, not sand. The perfect antidote to all this.' He got up and joined her at the window. 'Away from the noise of planes and the single-minded purpose of all these people.'

'I will take you there. I will show you my friend, Er Vam Vraz.'

'What sort of friend is that?'

'You would like her,' Yanna smiled. 'She is a lady who has six breasts.'

'Six? Two is quite enough for me.'

It was as if a key had turned and unlocked their feelings. The keen Atlantic air from far-off Quiberon seemed to blow away the desert and its stifling complications. They looked straight at each other, then she came to him. Her body,

111

delicate and feline, moulded to him. He raised his hands to cup her upturned face and their lips met in sweet softness. She pulled away for a moment, breathing hard, looking at him, then came back to him, abruptly, violently, digging her fingernails into his shoulders.

That was when the door flew open. David's first thought was of the Saudi police and the consequences of offending against Islamic law. He turned awkwardly to see it was the very opposite. It was Nick.

He burst in, then stopped suddenly, belatedly registering that he was interrupting something, but he was too far in and his fury was too great to backtrack. He thrust some pieces of paper under David's nose, shaking with anger.

'There you are. What do you say to *that?*'

'Nick. Go away.'

'No, I goddam well won't. Read that and tell me I'm wrong about the bloody pool system.'

'I don't give a stuff about the bloody pool system.'

Yanna got off the bed and went into the bathroom. In self-defence David took the document from Nick to protect himself from having it thrust down his throat. It was a photocopy, ten pages long, entitled *Amex Foxtrot*. David leafed quickly through it. It was the complete, secret US plan for dealing with the media in the Gulf. Nick had highlighted one key sentence in orange.

'Read it,' said Nick. 'Where I've marked it.'

Yanna came back. David looked at her helplessly. She smiled sadly at him. 'Go ahead.'

To get rid of Nick, David read it out loud. 'News media representatives will be escorted at all times – repeat, at all times.' It went on in the same vein, making it quite clear that there would be no opportunity for freedom of expression if the US armed forces could possibly prevent it.

'How much did this cost you? A pint of moonshine?'

112

David said, but Nick was not in a mood to be sidetracked.

'Snap out of it,' he said. 'This is genuine. It was written by Captain Wildermuth, Schwarzkopf's chief press man. No one else outside the top brass has this. This is the way they're planning to treat us.'

He looked so affronted, David couldn't help laughing again. It didn't help. 'Look, Nick, this is a *war* for Christ's sake, or at least it will probably turn out that way. A few things get sacrificed in a war. Total freedom of action is one.'

To his surprise he found Yanna and Nick joining sides vehemently against him, and that was the end of that.

Chapter Ten

There was a strong smell of burnt propellant, hot earth and singed plastic. The drizzle was coming in again, blotting out the headland and the grey Atlantic beyond, and fizzing on the hot wreckage. A very nervous Bamco technician called Marcus O'Neill wished it would blot out Spencer Purkiss as well, but his bulk was too close at hand and too solid for that. Purkiss and Busby were both staring into a large hole in the ground, speckled with torn pieces of carbon fibre and wiring. The Scottish rain reached them then, matting O'Neill's unruly hair down on to his scalp and blurring his view of the world as it dripped down his glasses. It made him feel at even more of a disadvantage.

Purkiss straightened up and looked across the range to the launcher. 'It was nearer the fucking target when it took off,' he observed caustically.

O'Neill quailed. 'It's still early days, Mr Purkiss. The trick we've got to crack is making sure the flight path isn't so random that it takes the missile out of the critical window for the downward vector trigger to . . .'

Purkiss cut him short. 'Look, son. As far as I can see, two things happen. One, you switch on the Dodgem gizmo and it farts all over the sky and comes down anywhere it fucking pleases, or two, you switch it off and it goes up and comes down wallop on the target just like everybody else's fucking missiles but twice as fucking expensive.'

'Well, not really. It just needs a bit more development time. It's worked perfectly three times.'

'Basic mathematics, son. Nine launches. Nine minus three is six. That's six times it hasn't worked. Don't make me weep. So far the only thing that's saved our asses is the fact that the Allied army is still farting around the desert learning what sand looks like. That isn't going to last for ever. This rig has to be on a Hercules heading for Saudi before the end of next week, or they're going to change their mind about letting it go at all, and do you know what that means?' He addressed the unfortunate technician, who just gaped at him. 'It means without having "combat proven" stamped on its record book, Dodgem is as good as dead, and in that case, Bamco's electronics and missile division is as good as dead, and that means you,' and he stabbed the man in the chest with his finger, 'are as good as dead.'

He turned away and Busby muttered darkly at him. 'Little fucker's got an earring. What do you expect?'

'I don't care if he's got one through his nose, so long as he sorts this lot out,' Purkiss retorted loudly and strode back towards the Land Rover, Busby alongside him with the man hurrying after. In the vehicle he turned to O'Neill. 'As of tomorrow, you work under a new Head of Project. I'm sending Martin Donaldson up from head office to sort this out.' Busby turned and gave him a quick, sour look. Purkiss was oblivious. They left O'Neill at the airstrip to prepare for another day of adjustments and firing and took the chopper on the long noisy haul back down to Glasgow and the private jet that was waiting for them. Busby stood it until they were just airborne, when he could contain himself no longer and gave voice to what was on his mind.

'Big job to give the kid, Spence. What the fuck does Donaldson know about missile systems? Why don't I do it?'

Purkiss smiled at him seraphically. 'Sure you're not just jealous cos he's smarter than you, Geoff?'

Busby exploded. 'Smarter? Smart tongue maybe, but I haven't seen him kick ass yet.'

'I've seen him kick your arse. I think he's probably up there with the best of them. Anyway, I've got something else for you to do.' He looked out of the window for a while, leaving Busby brooding, then turned back to him again. 'We'll talk about it later. Just for a kick-off, give yourself a laugh. Read what our dear little film-maker's gone and written to me.'

Chapter Eleven

Friday January 25th 1991

'All right, what about this then. A black screen. You don't know what it is, then it widens out and there's this winking light, all fuzzy and out of focus. You hear a whine. The camera's tracking round, then suddenly you've got this face and just as you realize it's a Tornado cockpit – wham, the motor fires up. That's when you hear Macfadyen's voice.'

'It's crap.'

David sighed. Nick was in an uncompromising mood. In the end Anthony Marshall hadn't been able to get them chosen for the pool. As a consolation prize, just before getting his keenly awaited release back to his unit waiting out there in the desert, he had arranged for them to be allowed in, after strictly agreed terms of confidentiality, to Chief of Staff Ian Macfadyen's send-off peroration to the RAF crews. Day One of the air war had started with Macfadyen, a man fond of references to Biggles, switching instead to Shakespeare – 'Gentlemen in England, now abed, shall think themselves accursed they were not here' – and their camera had recorded it all, the rousing message from Riyadh, piped to the Dhahran flight line, and the apprehensive Tornado crews moving off towards their aircraft. No one else had it. No one else had even known the air war was starting until the take-off of the noisy armada blasted them from their beds and the messages started to come in from Baghdad – the voice of CNN's Bernard Shaw, over a map of Iraq, describing the flashes in the sky, and the more laid-back descriptions of the BBC's two Simpsons, John and Bob.

'Since you ask me, David, I think it's goddam obscene.'

They were crammed in a tiny, sweaty interview-room waiting for an RAF pilot to arrive.

'Why?'

'Henry the Fifth. King Hal's address to the troops before the Battle of Agincourt.'

'I know. So?'

'Jesus, Shakespeare's your goddam heritage, not mine. He was outnumbered six to one by the French. Here's this guy, steals his words to send off massive aerial overkill against a starving bunch of conscripts, forced to fight by a madman. This isn't Agincourt, it's shooting fish in a barrel.'

David was poised to reply when the door opened and the RAF minders appeared with the pilot they were due to interview. Ian and Norman picked themselves up out of the chairs where they'd been slouched, listening without much interest to David and Nick squabbling. They were only too used to it. Ian switched on the 2Ks, the big lights they'd left off until now to avoid excessive heat build-up. The pilot had come straight from the flight line, his face stretched tight by the mission from which he'd only just returned. David felt embarrassed by Nick's comments and hoped they hadn't been overheard.

He looked at Nick, who'd shambled back to his corner and picked up his clipboard to take notes on the interview. Under the Budweiser baseball cap – its logo clumsily taped over to make some sort of perverse Nick Nielsen protest to the Saudis – Nick's face had turned pink under the tan. He was wearing the latest in a succession of T-shirts with

118

tasteless Gulf slogans which he was collecting. The pilot slumped down heavily in the chair they'd arranged, moving it out of position, but they'd set it up with sticky-tape markers on the floor and it was soon set right.

They'd worked hard to get permission for this interview, something more extensive than the usual quick question-and-answer conducted out on the apron to a set formula. This was meant to be a detailed background investigation of how it really felt, for showing later on, though they knew it would still have to go through the strictest scrutiny of the military censors. The pilot was from 31 Squadron and was showing the strain of the low-level missions he'd been flying. Massive overkill indeed, thought David. Take a look at this guy. He hasn't been on any cakewalk. He glanced across at Nick, but Nick was refusing to meet his gaze.

'This is Flight Lieutenant Rutherford,' said the minder, a squadron leader. 'I would remind you, Mr Challis, though I'm sure it's unnecessary, of your agreement that none of this footage will be used without notification to us and without obtaining our express approval. On that basis you may proceed.'

Ian switched on, checked the focus and, when the camera was up to speed, gave David the nod. The first five minutes of the interview were little more than a longer rerun of the stuff the news crews were shooting every day, laconic replies with just a trace of the 'Phew, it's tough out there' showing through. Then David came to the run of Tornado losses.

'Would you say it's getting more dangerous each time you go back?'

The pilot drew his lips back in a grimace which showed the gap between the simple question and the complex, lethal reality. 'Not really. The Triple-A patterns they've been putting up have been pretty deadly from Day One.'

'Triple-A? That's the anti-aircraft fire?'

'That's right. It was like they knew just how we had to deliver the weapon.'

David's antennae had started twitching. 'You mean from the very first attack the Iraqi defences have been ready for you?'

The pilot narrowed his eyes and glanced round at the minder for a moment. 'More than ready. There's a delivery pattern for the main weapon we're using, the JP233. You have to fly low and straight in the right direction. They had a barrage all worked out to deal with it, right from the start.'

David was aware of some agitation off to one side, where the minder was sitting out of his line of sight. Guessing he didn't have much uninterrupted time left, he pressed on. 'Would you say, then, that the JP233 is compromised?'

'We need a smart version, something we can drop from well out of the way. Let the electronics take the risk. These bastards know just where to expect us, how low, how fast, what bearing. Someone's told them. We're losing too many planes –'

'All right. That will do. Hold it there, please,' said the squadron leader, standing up and walking between the camera and the flight lieutenant. 'I'm sorry. You'll have to stop. This is not the sort of subject we can have discussed here.'

Ian switched off. David sighed. 'Why not? We've agreed not to use it unless you say so. It's not for use now. It could all be over by the time we want to show it.'

'I'm afraid that doesn't help. It's not on. Wait here, please.' He took the pilot from the room, shock added to the exhaustion on the man's face. Poor bastard, David thought.

The minder came back in and held out his hand. 'I'll have the tape, please.'

Nick sprang up from his seat. 'Hold on there. We agreed. We'll let you see anything we want to use but that's our tape and we'll hold on to it.'

'I'm afraid not,' said the squadron leader. 'Not in these circumstances. Please be co-operative. It would be for the best if you would give it to me now.'

'Aw, come on,' said Nick, but David turned to Norman and nodded, and the sound recordist slipped the tape out of the machine and passed it over.

'You'll understand he's been under great strain,' the squadron leader said. 'For your information and *not* for use, none of the Tornado losses have been due to enemy artillery fire.'

'But what he said about their artillery patterns? Is that right?' asked Nick.

'I'm not in a position to answer that.'

'What's going to happen to the tape?'

'We'll keep it safe. We may let you have it back when the war's over. You can take it up with Riyadh if you want to.' He turned to go.

'That's outrageous,' Nick said. 'Blatant goddam censorship as soon as there's any sniff of trouble.'

The man stopped in the doorway and slowly turned back. His face was impassive. 'You should mind the lessons of history, Mr Nielsen,' he said. 'Are you familiar with the story of the counter-attack on the Allied beachhead at Anzio?'

'No, I am not,' said Nick aggressively.

'Italy, January 1944. It looked like the Allies were going to be swept back into the sea. Churchill ordered the correspondents' radio transmitter to be closed down. He said they were spreading alarmist reports of another Dunkirk in the making. Later, he had to justify his action in the House of Commons. I have always taken his words as my text for moments such as this. I know what he said by heart. He said, "Such words as desperate ought not to be used about the position in a battle of this kind when they are false. Still less should they be used if they were true." '

He left them thinking hard.

David and Nick rattled back to the hotel in the old Toyota, sharing for once the same black cloud.

'It's about time you gave up playing Mr Co-operative, I'd say,' remarked Nick, giving an unwarranted finger to some military policemen driving the other way, who were fortunately unable to see in through the Land Cruiser's dust-caked windows.

'What the hell could I have done? They'd have taken the tape anyway.'

'Maybe. Maybe not. How would you explain it to Yanna?'

'What's that got to do with it? I don't have to explain it to Yanna. Anyway, I haven't seen her for nearly a month.'

Nick laughed. 'Counting the days, huh?'

David's anger switched immediately to his producer. 'Put a sock in it. You know bloody well how things were with us when she left.'

'Me and half the hotel. She didn't exactly keep her voice down. Never heard anyone so worked up. She must care a lot about you.'

David braked the Land Cruiser to a halt. An army truck swerved round them from behind, horn blaring furiously. 'I don't want to hear this, Nick. It may be your idea of a joke. It's not mine. She was pulled out by her people in Paris. She didn't have a choice. You known bloody well we had a row. We just see the job differently, that's all. If it gives you any satisfaction, I wish to hell she hadn't gone, but I guess she was glad to see the back of me so don't fucking rub it in, right?'

122

Nick hadn't seen David lose control before. 'Jeez. Sorry, guy. Didn't mean to hit the firing pin.' He fell silent, wondering whether to keep the news to himself, to let David find out his own way, but he couldn't. 'Thing is, I didn't tell you before because I kinda thought it might distract you from the interview . . .'

'What?'

'She's back.'

David stared at him. 'Who's back?'

'Yanna's back. She phoned this morning, trying to get you. Told me to tell you she'd be here this evening, coming down from Riyadh. She's got a bit of cash together and she's going unilateral, the way we ought to go.'

Since the short lists of those chosen for the pools had been released and the people concerned had headed out into the desert to join their units, those left behind had divided into two camps. Some became couch potatoes, happy to sit around the hotel and the briefing-rooms, filing what they could from what they were told. Others decided to ignore the military's instructions and headed out on their own, running the gauntlet of the Allied forces, and occasionally of the Iraqis too. They were known as the unilaterals.

Emotions were running high. The unilaterals saw themselves as independent journalists doing what they were paid to do, at considerable risk. Some of those in the pools saw them as dangerous deviants, upsetting a relatively comfortable and totally controlled system by introducing the disconcerting possibility of a scoop. Occasionally a pool reporter went so far as to call on the military to detain any unilaterals found on their patch and ship them back to the rear.

David was still trying to take in what Nick was saying to him. 'Yanna's coming? Today?'

'I think you're getting there.'

'She wanted you to tell me?'

'Seems like she musta been thinking about you. She was kinda keen to get hold of you. That makes you the luckiest guy in the Gulf in my book. Just my luck I'm not her type.'

David didn't answer. Nick glanced at him. He was staring out of the window and there was a smile on his face.

'David?'

'Er, yes?'

'You want to start the truck?'

'Sorry, what?'

'You want me to drive?'

David snapped back to the present. 'Oh, right. I'm with you. Let's go.'

'David. One more thing . . .'

'Sure, what?'

'Let's go unilateral too, for Christ's sake. We ain't gonna do any good back here when the ground war starts.'

'Might not do any good out there either,' said David quietly, but Nick noted that he hadn't dismissed it out of hand.

David drove back to the hotel faster than usual. They dumped the Toyota in the car park and went in. Up the stairs there was a knot of people standing talking in the information bureau. That was not unusual, but the expressions on their faces were. Even from yards away they all looked grim. David and Nick slowed down, wondering why.

Nick spotted an American friend. 'What's happening, Gordo?'

'Bob Simon and his crew.'

David's pulse rate jumped. Simon was a popular man, an experienced CBS correspondent. 'What about them?'

'They've gone missing. Their vehicle's been found in the

desert, right on the border. No sign of them. Looks like the Iraqis got them.'

'Oh, Jesus.'

A man in crisp uniform strolled through the crowd. Captain Cato. He heard Gordo's words and stopped by Nick. 'Well, Nielsen,' he said, 'that's what happens to unilaterals.'

'Mr Nielsen to you,' said Nick, but Cato looked him up and down and laughed.

'Nielsen's enough for you. I hear you've got a few little scams going down. If I should happen to find any US Army property in your vicinity, you'll be out of this theatre of operations before you can –'

'– break wind. I know. Freshen it up a bit, Cato. I've got a thesaurus you can borrow if you like.' Cato looked puzzled. Nick walked off.

David went to his room and showered, thinking about Bob Simon but even more about Yanna. He felt like a boy getting ready for his first date. Yanna was coming back. Yanna. He gave himself a lecture. Don't blow it. Don't say anything that might upset her. Don't answer the phone when she's here. Don't get into any conversations about war. He sat on the bed and read a book. He was hungry, but he didn't want to go away from the one certain place where she could find him. The phone rang and he jumped, but it was only Nick from his room next door.

'The gear's come. Wanna take a look?'

'That's quick.' They'd only asked London to send out a new edit machine four days earlier.

'Yeah. Open the door, I'll wheel it in.'

David thought quickly. He didn't want to be unpacking boxes with Nick when Yanna arrived, but he could hardly say that. Just get it over quickly and out of the way. 'OK,' he said.

He opened the door and helped Nick haul in a giant-size aluminium travel pack on little wheels. It stood three feet high. They got it into the room and Nick said, 'Open it up, I've just gotta take a leak.'

Nick closed the door as he went out, and David still didn't rumble anything until he flipped the catches on the lid and it burst open, pushed from inside. He gasped and jumped back, then saw it was Yanna who had sprung up, thrusting her hands in the air with a broad smile and a loud 'TA RAAA.'

'Hello, Challis, you old misery,' she said. 'I have missed you so much.'

He helped her out and into his arms. 'I'm glad you're back,' he said. 'I've thought of so many things to say while you've been gone.'

'Tell me some,' she said.

'In good time,' he said, and pushed the box back out into the corridor.

'That was Nick's idea,' she said. 'I saw him downstairs. He borrowed it.'

'Why did you come back?' he asked.

She sat down on the bed and he sat beside her. He took her hand and she smiled at him. 'Because it was possible. I could not stay here before. It was all so one-sided. I have tried to go to Baghdad, but that was not possible. I have been to Jordan to see what it is like there. Now the real war will soon start, I must be there. The best place to start from is here. I could not stand it before, just seeing all the planes take off and nothing more. Soon we will be seeing both sides, I think.'

'And me? Did I come into this?'

'Oh, Challis. You seem to come into my whole life. I cannot help it. I didn't want you to. I was so angry at you. How can you be the other half of me and not see things as

I see them? I still don't understand why I cannot get you to see things as I do.' She stopped and frowned. 'I must find the right words to explain. In my photos I feel the same as all the victims whose bodies I show. That is my emotion. I want everyone to see them. For you it is so different. You take pictures and when they are too strong then those are the ones you leave out, as if you cannot afford to let those emotions come through. That is still too big a gap between us for me to cross, but I need you and I have missed you so much that I must try again.'

The phone rang and his hand moved towards it then stopped. She watched him. 'I don't want to answer it,' he said. 'Whatever it is, it will get in the way.'

Very slowly, very, very slowly, her head moved towards his, eyes questioning him all the way. They kissed and slowly, kissing all the time, they turned and lay down. David's hands gently pulled her shirt loose from her waistband and lifted it up over her breasts. His fingers reached her hard nipples and she opened her mouth over his. A siren began to howl outside the window. Her eyes sprang open. 'What's that?'

'Air-raid warning,' he said thickly. 'Forget it. Happens all the time now.'

There were running steps in the corridor. 'Could be gas. Get that goddam suit on,' shouted an excited American voice.

'Should we get our suits?' asked Yanna nervously.

'It's all right,' said David, 'forget it,' and he pulled her back towards him again. She was stiff to start with, but he persisted and she gave way.

'Will the Scuds come?' she asked in a small voice. 'I have not been near one yet.'

'We've had fifteen in the last eight days,' he said. 'Don't worry. They're pretty harmless.'

She laughed nervously. 'Well, it is new for me.' The corridor outside was silent. 'Have they all gone to the shelter?'

'Most of them. Relax.'

She kissed him again and he peeled the shirt off her shoulders. She reached for his belt and began to undo it, and then the room lit up with a bright yellow glare, immediately followed by a series of ear-splitting, thunderous explosions which seemed to be right outside their window.

Yanna was up in a flash, grabbing for her shirt and staring out of the window to where two trails of light were climbing into the sky.

'It's the Patriots,' said David, joining her resignedly. There was a bright flash, which again lit up the room, and a rumble of thunder from the sky. 'They've hit a Scud.'

There was a hammering on the door. Nick, Ian and Norman were standing there with the gear. 'Where the fuck have you been?' demanded Nick. 'I was trying to ring you. Let's move it.'

'Hi, Yanna,' said Ian.

Shit, thought David.

They went across town to where the Scud debris had come down across a road junction. Ian and Norman were shooting, hunched together. The news crews around them were using the latest equipment, radio mikes to let the cameraman and the recordist move independently. Glass Crystal's gear was a year behind. Ian and Norman were still linked by a clumsy umbilical cable. Yanna was off to one side taking stills and David was looking at her, cursing the Scud, the feel of her skin still fresh in his mind, when he saw an army truck coming too fast round the bend from the far side of the barricade. The back of the truck started to slide on a drift of sand. Nick shouted at the camera crew. Ian looked round and jumped, but Norman,

128

the sound recordist, insulated from the world by his head-phones, didn't react quite fast enough and was caught out by the cord. The back of the truck caught him a glancing blow, sending him spinning though the air. David got to him first, moving as fast as he could and dreading what he would find. Norman was lying unconscious with one leg doubled back under him at an angle which told the whole story. The medics who'd come for the Scud descended on him, their sole casualty.

It was late by the time they finished, and David packed the others off, staying on at the hospital to make many phone calls back to the UK, passing on the news of Norman's broken arm and leg and trying to make arrangements. He got back to the hotel at three in the morning and unlocked the door of his room, wondering if Yanna would be there.

Chapter Twelve

Thursday February 7th 1991

Hilary Stoughton was not yet certain where her job started and where it finished. She'd only had it for a couple of months and it had a wide brief. She was team leader to the Prime Minister's personal advisers, occupying a small office at the back of Number Ten looking out into the Downing Street garden. It had a very dark portrait on the wall of a man who might have been Lord Salisbury's private secretary, as well as two filing cabinets, a desk and an armchair.

It was just before ten in the morning, and she'd already been in the office for four hours. The war called for long working hours and today was Cabinet day so she liked to be in even earlier than usual. She was part academic, part journalist, which allowed her to skim documents quickly, then dive unerringly to the sections containing their deeper meaning for a more careful perusal. Where her background gave her little help was in the area of natural authority. She was a nice, clever person, unused to winning power struggles with Whitehall mandarins, and the man in her armchair was much more experienced in the game than she was.

'He's not at all happy, and quite frankly I don't blame him,' she said. 'It doesn't fit with his view of the world. All right, it was simple enough for Maggie. She'd have been in there, egging the Americans on and loving every second, but he's not like that.'

The man was Alex Harvey, who normally occupied a senior job in the Ministry of Defence but who was now serving as M.o.D. liaison with Downing Street.

'He's got to stay the course, Hilary. He can't leave Peter de la Billière to fight it out for himself.'

There had been a ferocious row between the British and American High Commands. Only after weeks of enormous pressure had General Schwarzkopf agreed to let Britain's Desert Rats join the US Army's 7th Corps for the land attack, instead of being stuck on the flank, providing cover for the inadequate tanks of the US Marines in a part of the main assault that looked sure to be far less glamorous. It had stretched the 'special relationship' to the limit.

'The trouble is, Alex, it all gets a bit tricky when he starts asking questions about motivations.'

'What's bothering him at the moment?'

'Nothing new. He'd just like to be able to keep it simple, concentrate on sorting out Saddam and not get sidetracked by the hidden agenda.'

'Hilary, would it sound ungracious if I suggested that was a little naïve?'

'I'm not sure it is naïve. Look back at the Falklands now. What happened? The Navy was about to get slashed. Instead, it covered itself in glory and fought off the cuts.'

'No bad thing, surely?'

'No bad thing? We just ended up with a stronger Navy than we needed. Yet another case of fighting the last war, not the next one.'

'So what's the problem, Hilary? You think the army's out for glory this time and that's going to stop the peace dividend being paid out?'

'No, not really. Not the army, Alex. Maybe this comes more from me than from him, but the whole thing's starting to sound terribly like a sales campaign.'

131

'Look, Hilary, there's a simple enough answer surely.'

'I know, I know. The two aims are completely compatible. We've been right through that. I have to say I don't think I'm totally convinced. It's straight from the spin doctors, that one.'

'It's a spin doctors' world these days. Things are the way you tell them, or the way you get others to tell them.'

Hilary looked out of the window at the garden. The subject made her uncomfortable. Clarity of purpose seemed to float away. She was realistic, but one part of her hated the way moral certainty had become a matter for presentation committees and PR experts. Doing what you were sure was right seemed to have given way to doing what a committee of experts thought the public would perceive as being right.

'Look, to be brutal, it's a perfectly straightforward argument,' said Alex. 'The end of the Cold War means lower defence spending for everyone involved. We're going to be buying fewer weapons from our own manufacturers. We're going to cut the size of our armed forces. That's a huge hit on the economy, on just about its most productive, high-technology sector, so we've got to export or else. It's as simple as that.'

'Yes, but Alex, we had this argument word for word the other day, and in the end he just got a bit stubborn and shirty and said that was nothing but a recipe for chaos.'

'You wait for the first by-election in a marginal seat where there are defence jobs on the line.'

'I don't think he's like that.'

'Oh, no? Remember what they thought when Bush took over? All that nonsense about how he'd be tough on arms sales after the Reagan free-for-all?'

'We'll see. Anyway, he was listening to Radio 4 FM yesterday, and he said our briefings from Riyadh were starting to sound like adverts. They never miss a chance to dish out the weapons' brand names. He said he doesn't know why we don't go the whole hog and give the makers' phone numbers on the end.'

Alex shook his head. 'Well, anyway, I've got a bit of news for him. They'll tell him tomorrow at the War Cabinet, but if you want to earn some Brownie points you can slip it to him ahead. It's about the JP233. We think we know what went wrong.'

Hilary looked at him and held up a hand. 'OK, but give it to me from the start. I want to make quite sure I get this one right.'

'JP233. Airfield denial weapon, call it what you want. Hunting's clever little gizmo for knocking out airstrips. Delivered by Tornados and thence the rub, because they've been flying into very well-designed concentrations of anti-aircraft fire.'

'I know that much. Hence the losses.'

'Well, not directly. Those are down to SAMs and other things, but there's no doubt it's made it bloody difficult and it's upping the stress level, which knocks on. Gives the air crews less time to think about all the other threats. The thing is, it's not just bad luck. You have to fly a very specific pattern to drop these things. Straight and level and bang on the right height. The RAF thought they'd be able to get away with that a few times before the Iraqis cottoned on, but it wasn't like that. They had their barrage all ready and waiting the very first time.'

'And?'

'And it now looks like somebody told them exactly what they had to do. Anyway, it seems Six have come up with a name. It's a front company in Jersey that's been doing some naughty things.'

She nodded slowly. 'So what happens next?'

'Well, apparently we have to be grateful to one of our foreign friends for the info on this. I'm not sure how far we can push them for more.'

She digested this. 'But something will be done?'

'Something. Yes, certainly.'

'There's another thing I need to be briefed on, Alex. I believe it's called FAE? There was someone on the radio saying it was more or less the worst thing –'

Alex cut her off. 'I know, I know. That bloody man on Radio 4 knows a little bit too much for comfort. I'm seeing if we can put a little indirect pressure on to remind him who's side he's on. Just tell the PM it's nothing to worry about. Fuel Air's old hat. Been around since Vietnam. It's just another bomb.'

That was exactly the sort of line she had feared he would take when she'd rehearsed this part of the conversation earlier that morning, trying to second-guess his likely responses.

'But what exactly is it? He's worried. He says no one's giving him straight answers.'

Alex shrugged. 'Well, there's the BLU-95, that's the five hundred pounder, then the 96, that's the two thousand pounder. It's the simplest thing in the world, really. You don't even need a proper bomber, you can just drop the ramp in the back of a Hercules and push them out like oil drums.'

'But what do they do exactly?'

Alex looked at her. 'They make the biggest bang you can –'

But that was as far as they got. Two hundred yards away across Whitehall a white van had just been driven into a parking space – a white van with a large square hole cut out of its roof, disguised with an old sheet. The driver jumped on the back of a waiting motor bike, and only seconds after he had roared away the mortars inside the back of the van fired. As the van burst into flames, one of the bombs, sailing over the roof-tops, plummeted into the Downing Street back garden and exploded, bulging the reinforced glass inwards and bringing the Cabinet meeting and every other conversation inside Number Ten to a sudden halt.

Geoff Busby heard it as a newsflash on Radio 4 FM. They cut one of their pundits off in mid-sentence with the news of the Downing Street attack. Busby was just going through his documents one last time before he headed south to catch the RAF VC10 from Brize Norton. He stopped what he was doing and stared at the radio as if he could will it to turn into a television. The set had barely been switched off since the air war began and now, with the ground war so close, he didn't want to miss a thing.

The intercom buzzed. 'Geoff?'

'Listening, Spence.'

'Got time to pop in before you go?'

'I'll be up in two ticks. Heard about Downing Street?'

'I'm listening to it now.'

Purkiss was alone in his office when Busby got there, looking out across the factory to a Birmingham roofscape broken up by chimneys, cranes and the ramp of a motorway. 'All ready then?'

'Yeah. I've gotta be at Brize by one o'clock.'

'Are we going to be in time?'

'Yeah, I reckon. The transport with the Dodgem gear's getting to Jubayl about now. They've got a chassis ready for it. We should be ready to go by tomorrow.'

'Will it work?'

'Dunno, but by the time we've finished, they're not going to know the difference.'

'Have you left anything outstanding?'

'Nothing that can't wait a month or two.'

'Any more comeback from Challis?'

'Nah. I bunged him a grand and a stiff warning. He's not exactly a tough guy. He knows what'll happen if he tries it on again.'

'OK then, good luck.'

Great, thought Busby as he slung his bag into the back of his Land Rover and climbed in. Great send-off. Me off to risk my bloody neck and all he says is 'good luck'. His mood soured further as Donaldson's car pulled in through the gate. He drove off towards his plane, looking the other way to avoid acknowledging his rival's cheerful wave. The letter was lying on the passenger seat. He'd made his choice from the latest batch after a few jars the night before. Just right, not too much of a looker, nice tight body. He slowed up by the postbox, then thought, sod it, it can wait till I'm back.

Chapter Thirteen

Friday February 22nd 1991

Five seconds at most saved David from a prison cell. That was all the time there was from the moment Nick's door closed behind him to the eruption into the hotel corridor of Cato's squad of military police hell-bent on catching Nick red-handed. The day which marked the end of what passed for normal life in Dhahran had begun almost quietly, if a rumbling line of army vehicles stretching to the horizon and beyond could be described as quiet.

They had been out filming the massive equipment movements. David watched Yanna running back to the hire-car for fresh batteries and wondered for the hundredth time whether he should ever have agreed to this deal. He hadn't realized what the price would be when he'd said yes, and anyway Nick and Ian had both been twisting his arm.

It was almost a month since Norman had been flown home with his leg and arm in plaster, almost a month since the other two had persuaded him that giving Yanna a crash course in sound recording was a much better bet than wasting time trying to get a visa for a replacement to come out from England. Yanna hadn't been in his room that night when he got back from the hospital and she hadn't been there on any of the successive nights, not unless they'd all been there. She'd had very firm ideas about it. It wouldn't be fair on the others, she had told him. They had to work as a team. Better to put everything else on hold, and he knew perfectly well that it suited her in many ways to play it safe.

'We have a lot to work out, you and I, David. Now I have to do the story with you, the way you see it. Better it is just professional for this short time.'

'It might not be a short time.'

'It will be. Then we will have as long as you want.'

She'd seemed almost relieved at the prospect, as if it simplified her life, as if it was a way of covering over all her raw nerve-endings and seeing the war through someone else's eyes.

'I'm not sure I can handle this,' he had said. 'I'm not sure I can stand there day in, day out, fancying my sound engineer and not doing anything about it. It's not natural.'

'You can do whatever you like,' she said, smiling. 'But only if you do exactly the same to Nick and Ian as you do to me.'

'That limits the possibilities, then,' he said, but his face was grim and she looked at him doubtfully.

'Are you always so serious, Challis? You don't laugh much.'

'It's just this place. It's hard to laugh.'

'That is what I am hoping. Afterwards, there must be room for laughter in our life.'

He nodded. 'Afterwards. Yes. In the meantime, if not touching you gets too unbearable, I'll just have to fire you.'

If Yanna's rules had seemed like a joke to start with, she had stuck all too rigidly to them. It lent a further touch of personal unreality to this unreal desert world where even the climate was turning weird on them. Rains came and violent, cold sandstorms. Nick continued to run his unique

138

black market in alcohol, information and equipment, and to propound his view of the war. There was a clear divide on that, Yanna and Nick on one side, David on the other, with Ian occasionally backing him up.

There was always something. In early January it had been Nick's conviction that the American Dazer, Stingray and Cobra laser systems were intended to blind enemy soldiers and set fire to their clothes rather than knock out sensor systems as it was claimed. By the start of the air war his obsession had switched to the claims being made by the US briefers for their smart bombs. Nick's sources told him the videos being shown were very selective. They went further: they claimed some of the targets were only hit because Allied special forces troops, operating inside Iraq in civilian clothes, were lighting up the targets with hand-held laser designators or planting homing devices for the bombs in the weak points of key buildings. Then it was Fuel Air Explosives, those shattering weapons nobody quite wanted to talk about, which Nick said were as bad as nukes and, far from being used for minefield clearance, were simply yet another way of roasting Iraqi troops to death. David and Nick had a real set-to about that.

'These are the Republican Guard you're talking about, Nick. What would you rather drop on them, food parcels?'

'Who says it's the Republican Guard? My pals say the CIA is making up its assessments as it goes along, simply to justify maximum force.'

'Your pals have drunk so much of your wood alcohol they don't know which way up they are.'

Right through that argument Yanna had kept her silence, but she wouldn't meet his eyes when he tried to make silent contact with her afterwards.

Most recently Nick's obsession had been one with which David could very nearly agree: the carnage of the bombing of the Amiriya shelter by two F-117 Stealth fighters on February 13th, bringing with it the deaths of over three hundred civilians, nearly half of them children. David thought the Americans had been suckered by a clever Iraqi propaganda trap, decoyed by deliberate radio activity into hitting something made to appear to be a military installation. Nick thought his fellow countrymen had just been plain stupid.

So it went on, this uneasy little group, groping their way towards their next deadline for another film. There was a request from London to see if they could make one more on the build-up to land warfare. David hadn't been very happy with the way the last film had turned out. He still felt they shouldn't be trying to turn over too many stones at this stage in the war, but he was forced to give ground to Nick's insistence that taking that line didn't leave them very much else to do.

Yanna came back with the fresh batteries, and David adjusted the lie of the moulded earpiece so that it fitted snugly. A spring clip held the other end of the tube to the back of his collar, and from there the wires ran down his back, out of sight, into the connections to the pocket tape-player hidden in his right hand. A gust of wind with some rain in it blew damp sand into his face. He glanced round yet again at the crossroads behind him. The line of vehicles was still moving slowly, but it was just about to come into shot.

Ian, peering through the viewfinder at him, looked up for a moment. 'OK,' he said, 'in five. And for Christ's sake get it right first time.'

David pressed the start button and heard his own voice in his ear, counting down 'Five, four, three, two, one . . .'

140

Then he heard the first words of the piece he'd just recorded on it coming into his ear, and his mouth took over, automatically duplicating those same words to the camera. 'It's not official yet, but the Allied ground forces are going to war, and the weather isn't helping . . .' Forty-five seconds later it was all over, a perfect first take, with the armoured vehicles going past, exactly on cue, in the background.

'Bloody good idea, that. Just right for a long piece when you're only going to get one chance. I'm surprised more reporters don't use them,' said Ian as David took the earpiece out and disconnected the little recorder.

They were on the outskirts of Dhahran, the exit point into the desert for the Allied supply trail. Walking back to the car, David looked again in wonder at the moving column. It seemed to have been going on for ever. You wouldn't have known there could be so many military vehicles in the world. Then he frowned. Overtaking them all down the outside came a battered white American saloon, and it was a car he recognized all too well. The Chevrolet swayed to a dusty halt by their hire-car, and out stepped Yussef, the driver Nick had been employing out of his own illicit earnings for various indeterminate errands. 'Mr David, Mr Nick says come back quick. Come back to garage. All you come. Right now.'

'What's happening?'

'Don't know. Just come.'

Nick had stayed behind to fix a few things. That had been all he would say. They piled in the hire-car and headed back towards Yanbu Street. Nick was just pulling out of the garage driving the old red Land Cruiser. He jumped out.

'You guys. You're just in time. Listen, get back to the hotel. Get your grab-bags and come back here. Try and do it so no one sees you're leaving. We've gotta go.'

'Come on, Nick, what are you talking about?' David objected.

'Just do it. Trust me. Have I ever been wrong?'

'Yes. Lots of times.'

'Talk to him, Yanna. Tell him to do it. I'll explain it all later.'

Yanna looked doubtfully at Nick and looked back at David, not knowing what to say. He gave in.

'What about your stuff, Nick?'

'That's already here, but there's a plastic bag in my room. It's on the top shelf of the cupboard. Bring that. Hurry. There really isn't much time.'

They told Nick's runner to follow, and took their hire-car back to the hotel. 'Shall we check out?' said Ian.

'No. We haven't a clue what's going on so let's keep the rooms on. Just turn in the hire-car keys at the desk. We can always get it back later if this is a storm in a tea-cup.'

Ian and Yanna ferried the camera gear and their bags down the back stairs to the Chevrolet. David's grab-bag was permanently half packed. He threw some extra clothes in and then went next door to Nick's room. It was all but empty, except for the thick layer of rubbish that always accumulated wherever Nick had been. He found the carrier bag as directed and looked inside. It seemed to be full of old underwear. With a resigned shrug he headed for the door. At the last moment he heard Nick's tap dripping and nearly went back to shut it off. It was just as well he didn't. The door closed behind him and he'd barely got into his stride down the corridor when a posse of American Military Police burst, shouting, from the stairwell. Captain Cato was the one making the noise, briefing them at the top of his voice as they rushed past David without a second glance. 'Grab the bastard first. Then look for the alcohol, and above all, find that goddam tape.'

142

David walked quickly away towards the stairs. Behind him, they burst through Nick's door.

Wondering what was happening, but seeing no signs in the otherwise normal level of activity around the hotel, David squeezed into the remaining space in the Chevrolet, between the door and a pile of equipment boxes. Ian and Yanna were in front, next to the driver. Nick's garage was locked and they waited for a long time, trying to work out what was going on.

'This had better be good,' said David. 'If this is all because Cato's rumbled one of Nick's scams, I'll have his guts.'

'Dead right,' said Ian.

'It will be good,' said Yanna. 'Didn't you hear it in Nick's voice?'

David looked doubtfully at her, but then Ian pointed down the street and said, 'Here he comes,' and a moment later, 'oh, sorry, no it's not.' The confusion was understandable. An old Land Cruiser that looked like theirs had lurched into sight, leaving a smoke trail behind it, but the colour was wrong. Instead of dull red and sandblasted bare metal, this one was bright yellow and shiny. All the same it was indeed Nick who jumped out and stood looking at it unhappily.

'Wrong colour,' he said. 'Best my man could do in a hurry. Gotta make it look rufty tufty, that's the word.'

'Rufty tufty?' said David.

'Yeah, I thought you spoke fluent Army. Rufty tufty, like it belongs with the battle wagons.'

The paint was still sticky. 'Come on,' said Nick, picking up a handful of dusty sand from the edge of the road and throwing it at the Toyota, 'get working before it dries.' They watched as most of the sand fell off. 'Shit,' said Nick and he tried again with equally little result. He rooted around in the garage and came out with a big catering bag of brown sugar.

'Whoa there, Nick. Time to let us in on the secret.'

'As soon as we've done this.'

After ten minutes' effort they all had sticky hands, but it had sort of worked. The Toyota was a mottled brown and yellow, rough all over and horrible to behold. The texture made you shy away from contact.

'Time to talk, Nick,' said David. 'What's happening? Have you been caught doing things you shouldn't?'

'It's a bit more than that.'

'How much more?'

'The land war. That's what's happening. And I know where and when.'

'When? How do you know?' asked Ian and David together.

'Oh, no,' said Yanna.

'Load up the gear. I'll tell you on the way.'

Nick paid Yussef off, and they piled Nick's stored rations and equipment in the back and wedged themselves as best they could into the remaining space. Not until they were heading out on Ras Tanura Road, Nick at the wheel and David beside him, did he open up. The other two were craning their heads from behind to listen.

'I got rid of the rest of the hooch, David.'

'Good,' said David, remembering Cato's words.

'I traded it.'

'Oh, right.'

'Dontcha wanna know what I traded it for?'

'I'm sure you'll tell me.'

'I traded it for the entire Allied forces battle plan.'

David opened his mouth, but couldn't think of anything to say. Ian and Yanna were leaning forward trying to hear. 'What did he say?' demanded Ian.

'He's got the battle plan from someone.'

'Jesus Christ!'

'No, not quite so senior,' said Nick. 'Moral: never trust a thirsty man in a dry place.'

'We're not going to get away with this,' said David gloomily.

'Sure we are. They'll never find out. My guy will never tell.'

'They already found out, Nick. Cato was breaking your door down when I left.'

Nick looked startled. 'Oh, shit.'

'He was bellowing about a tape. That was what he was after. What tape?'

Nick brightened up. 'Oh, is that all? That's OK then. You brought it with you. You know, in the bag.'

'That bag I carried straight past him? God Almighty,' said David remembering how close he had come to discovery. He pulled the plastic bag out from where he'd stuffed it under the seat. Delving distastefully into a wad of grey Y-fronts, his fingers touched something hard. It was an unmarked domestic-format VHS videotape, not one of their own broadcast-quality Beta-SPs. 'So what is it?'

'The Riyadh horror show. All the footage Schwarzkopf decided wasn't fit for our eyes. Remember all those party tricks with the smart bomb tapes, showing them going down air vents? All that surgical warfare crap? The stuff the wonderful press corps bought hook, line and sinker? This is the other side of the coin.' He put on a gruff military voice. 'And now, gentlemen and pretty little ladies of the press, lemme show you the luckiest man in Baghdad as our wonder-bomb saves lives yet again.' He snorted. 'This is the rest, put together for the macabre delectation of the intelligence corps. This is the tape with the close-up of the lorry driver's eyes staring at you a microsecond before the missile hits his cab. It's got the market on it, too – the one when the bomb missed its target by a mile and took out thirty Iraqis who were armed with deadly vegetables. All the stuff the spin doctors, with their surgical warfare crap, said never happened.'

'And Cato wants it back?'

'Cato wants it back for a very good reason, David. It's got a night-time shot on it they don't ever want anyone to see. It's pretty harmless really, just an everyday shot from the front of a bomb heading for a bunker. Only it wasn't really a bunker, it was the Amiriya shelter.'

'Nick. We have to get rid of that. We have to get rid of that *now*.'

A note came into Nick's voice that David had never heard before. 'You get rid of that, David, you get rid of me too. Understand? It's about time you realized what I've done for you. It's midday Friday. The ground attack starts in less than forty hours and we're the only hacks that know that, right? If it were just down to you, we'd be sitting on our butts round the pool without a clue what was coming.'

'Yes, Nick, I've already conceded that. You were right all along about going unilateral. I know that. It's a question of your methods.'

'Stuff my methods. You know goddam well it's always been about timing. Head for the desert too early, you just get swept up and sent home. Go too late and it's all over. Go to the wrong place and you'll be lucky if you even see a glow on the skyline. Get it right and we'll be waltzing right through the middle, nicely hidden in the fog of war.' He reached into the glove compartment and slapped a wad of documents on David's lap. 'Listen, shithead, I've got you the crown jewels and all you do is worry that I've been going around breaking the rules. You're not a goddam school prefect now.'

David took a deep breath. 'OK, Nick. I'm grateful. I won't say any more. What do we do?'

'Right then, listen. You remember that border town, Ruq'i? There's a place west of there that's goddam perfect, the Seven Corps area. The British First Armoured Division is lined up alongside the American First and Third Armoured Divisions. We'll go for the gap. Look in the envelope.'

David pulled out a document imprinted with the Riyadh Command heading. It accredited them to the First Armoured Division without saying whether it meant the British or the American one. He looked at it as they jolted along in a never-ending column of army vehicles. 'Is this the real thing?'

'It's as near to the real thing as it could be, bearing in mind there ain't no such thing as a real thing of this particular type.'

'It says we're a BDA team. What's that?'

'Battle Damage Assessment. We can't be a news pool – we've got no army minder with us. This is a cute trick. Believable. Means we're on the army payroll. Shooting video, as the army advances, of the way the weapons do the job.'

'Will it work?'

'If they don't find out.'

'What else have you got on board you might just have forgotten to tell me about?'

'A GPS satellite navigation system, a set of maps, some of those fluorescent pink vehicle-recognition panels for warning off friendly air attacks, and all the rations you can eat. The GI stuff is terrible except the chocolate drink, but you get twelve sheets of paper for the john in every pack. The Brit stuff's better. The bacon grill's too salty and the beans are too sweet, but they're OK if you mix them together. Mind you, there's only two sheets of paper to a pack. They must reckon Brits shit less than GIs.'

'Is that it?'

'Hell, no. There's three sets of uniform, desert issue, for each of us, just in case. US, French or British pattern, but I guess your conscience will stop you wearing that.'

'More my instinct for self-preservation than anything to do with my conscience.'

Yanna's voice came from over David's shoulder. 'David. It is time you learned to appreciate Nick.'

They came to a hold-up where a big truck had bogged down in the soft stuff beside the road and had slowly keeled over on to its side. That had become a familiar sight over the past few weeks, but this one had equipment spilling out everywhere and looked more spectacular than most, so they pulled off to film it. Yanna, hair hidden under a forage cap, dark glasses over her eyes, crouched by Ian as he shot first the truck, then the column of support vehicles grinding past it. David had his brain in neutral, waiting for Ian to finish, tired of wondering what they were heading into. He glanced casually along the immense line of vehicles slowly moving past them, then stiffened into alertness. Something he'd never seen before was approaching. It looked hastily put together. There were crude brackets freshly welded on to a tracked tank base. On the top, where the turret would normally have been, there was a boxy, square launcher. He moved across and tapped Ian on the shoulder, interrupting the shot.

Ian looked up, annoyed for a moment before he saw who it was. David pointed. 'Get that,' he said.

'What is it?'

'No idea. Get it in the can just in case.'

Grinding along behind the big machine was a sand-coloured Nissan Patrol looking decidedly civilian among all the boxy wide-tracked Humvees. David stared at it as Ian filmed. A man stared back at them from the passenger

148

seat, looking at the camera. The Nissan suddenly stopped a few yards up the road, bringing the entire column to a halt behind it.

The man, in desert fatigues but with no unit badges, ran back to them. 'Give me your tape,' he shouted. 'Right now. No pictures allowed.' His accent was English, harsh, North Country.

'Hold on,' said Nick, 'we're on BDA. This isn't a press pool.'

'I don't care if you're fucking Father Christmas. Give me that tape. *Now.* Don't fuck me around or I'll have you.'

Nick looked at David, but the stationary Nissan with the convoy piling up behind it was attracting a lot of attention, and there was nothing to be done if they didn't want military police down on their heads in swarms. There was an overpowering sense of threat coming from the man. Engines were revving. The traffic jam was building up fast. Someone was soon going to demand to see some ID.

'I'll get it,' David said, trying to sound American. He went to Yanna, the far side of Ian. She was bending down awkwardly, facing the other way. 'Give me the tape,' he said, and looked at her curiously. She fumbled it out of the machine and passed it to him without looking up. He handed it over and it was snatched from his hand. The man went back to his vehicle. The traffic started moving again.

He turned back to Yanna, thinking maybe she was feeling ill. She was still crouched down. 'What's the matter?'

She looked down the road at the departing vehicle. 'What is the matter is that the man who took the tape is Busby. Busby from your brother's friends Bamco. And that is the machine that does not work.'

Chapter Fourteen

Sunday February 24th 1991

David felt someone pulling him by the ankle. He stopped swearing and extricated his hand with difficulty from the tight space up beside the gearbox, ripping the skin of his wrist on a bent, oily metal edge as he did so. He wriggled out from under the Land Cruiser, sat up in the damp sand sucking the wound, and looked at Nick in the gloom with undisguised malevolence.

'What?' he barked.

'Time for your nap.'

'Don't be bloody stupid. Who's going to do this if I get to sleep?' Then he looked at the hand being proffered to him and the NAPS anti-nerve-gas pill in it and realized his mistake. 'Oh, I see.'

'Are you getting anywhere?'

'The gear selector's come loose from the linkage. I think it's a splined shaft and the clamp's slipped. Trouble is, I can just about feel it, but I can't get the spanner to stay on it enough to tighten it. I'll give it another try.' He looked at Nick's sagging shoulders. 'Why don't you climb in and try to get some sleep with the others?'

'No space. Anyway, I'm on scorpion duty. You make a pretty soft target, lying there. Reckoned I'd better keep an eye out all round you.'

Scorpions. David had forgotten scorpions. He felt a sudden surge of affection for the scruffy American. 'Thanks, Nick.'

'Anyway, don't figure I could sleep if I wanted to. You're swearing so loudly.'

After a day and a night of slow, difficult progress, they'd been pretty close to their destination when the transmission had finally packed up. The satellite navigation set stopped working at about the same time. Nick swore and tried to remember if it was guaranteed, but it came back on all by itself after an hour or two. They weren't to know that troops right across the desert around them were also looking at dead instruments. The satellites that fed the position data didn't give full coverage of the Saudi desert all the time. The company that sold the sets dealt mostly with sailors and, understandably perhaps, never expected its clients to be quite so far aground.

David looked around in the darkness. Never again would he be able to think of a desert as an empty, parched waste of sand. Freezing rain started drizzling down again, driven by a biting wind which hurled a spray of gritty mud into his face. They were on a slight ridge. The expanse below them had degenerated into a quagmire and was far from empty. Engines were revving in all directions as the massed divisions prepared for war. To the north sudden flashes on the horizon marked where the forward positions of the Iraqi army were being hammered by an incessant bombardment. There was a constant rumble from far off and occasionally a more distinct sound, a rapid double thud like huge doors slamming.

Crawling back underneath, and manœuvring his damaged wrist carefully back into the Toyota's intestines, he spent another fifteen minutes trying to wrestle the bulky adjustable wrench which was all he had by way of a tool kit on to the end of a rounded-off nut in the tiny space available. His fingers and arms were aching. In the end he tried to tighten it with his bare hands, but there was nothing he could do. He crawled out, thankful for the tank overalls Nick had provided from his stash, and took the poncho Nick was holding out to him. They looked in the windows of the Land Cruiser and decided not to wake Ian and Yanna, sprawled uncomfortably over the gear. Nick took a mess tin off a sputtering solid-fuel stove and passed it to him with a plastic spoon.

'What's this?'

'Corned beef hash. Smells like cat food until you're hungry enough.' David was.

Nick looked out across the desert. 'Oh-four-hundred. Oh-four-fucking-hundred. So bloody near and we might as well be on the other side of the moon.' The sand thumped to another big concussion. They didn't know, because Nick's troop disposition map didn't say, that the first phase of the advance wasn't concerned with their section of the line at all. Far to the east, towards the sea, the US Marines and a mixed bag of Saudis, Omanis and other Arabs were making a sucker punch towards Kuwait City to draw out the defence, while to the west Schwarzkopf's 'Hail Mary' football tactic was sending the XVIII Airborne Corps, including the French Daguet Division, racing round in a huge encirclement. For the two of them, though, standing there in the cold rain, there was the conviction that they'd come all this way only to miss the final act.

Then, into the already disconcerting sensory confusion of a freezing, wet desert stinking of diesel smoke came another unexpected element. David grabbed Nick's arm. 'Listen!'

A vehicle of some sort was grinding towards them. It

152

stopped below the ridge. They held their breaths, realizing that the Toyota was highlighted against the sky. It must be Allied forces, surely, and yet their disorientation and total ignorance of the situation around them was so complete that when a polite voice from out of the darkness said, 'Mr Challis? Mr David Challis?' in an enquiring tone, David was more amazed by the upper-crust English accent than by the fact that anyone in the middle of the desert could possibly know his name.

'Hello?' he said, thinking this is ridiculous. 'I mean, yes, I'm David Challis. Who's that?'

A young British officer stepped into view as they goggled at him. He smiled at their astonishment. 'We've been looking at you through night sights for a while. Saw you were having some trouble. I've been sent over to bring you in for a chat.'

'How did you know who I was?'

'My CO recognized you.'

They woke Ian and Yanna, who were both confused. The lieutenant had a Warrior personnel carrier and his driver hitched a chain to the front of the Toyota. In a warm fog of relief they were hauled no more than a quarter of a mile to a group of trucks and a large tent, draped with pink sheets of gas repellent. The others were given hot drinks while David was ushered into the tent, and there, sitting on a folding chair glowering at a map, was Lieutenant-Colonel Anthony Marshall.

'Anthony! My God, am I glad to see you.'

Marshall looked up at him in a preoccupied way. 'Don't be so sure of that. There's a lot of people looking for you. It's pure chance we were the ones who spotted you, and you might not have any reason to rejoice when I tell you the rest of it.'

'OK, tell me.'

'There's a message out from Dhahran. Comes from this Cato chap. It says all units are to watch out for a red Land Cruiser and detain one Rick Nielsen who is immediately to be choppered out, together with all video equipment and tapes found in his possession.' He looked at David. 'Doesn't give me much choice, I'm afraid.'

David thought quickly. 'Look outside, Anthony. Tell me if you see a red Land Cruiser.'

Marshall shone a flashlight out through the flap in the tent. 'OK,' he said, 'no red ones out there. That still leaves Nielsen.'

'Rick Nielsen?'

'That's what it says here. Isn't that what your man's called?'

'Anthony, ask me if I have anyone called Rick Nielsen with me. I promise to tell the truth.'

Marshall looked at him uneasily. 'Have you got anyone called Rick Nielsen with you?'

'No.'

Marshall seemed to come to a decision. 'Right, I haven't any more time to waste on some rear-echelon goon's idea of priorities. I'll trust you. I can hardly leave you wandering around the battlefield, though. We're attacking this evening. Those are Republican Guard divisions facing us. You'll have to be taken back by then.'

'We're in your hands.'

But they weren't entirely. Nick got busy that morning with his remaining personal supply from the little oxygen cylinder, and while a stream of officers flowed to and fro from conferences in Marshall's tent, an efficient-looking squaddie surreptitiously crawled under the Toyota with a tool roll and emerged half an hour later winking and holding up a thumb. They huddled in the freezing dawn listening to the planes screeching overhead and the never-ending roll of thunder beyond them, wondering if an opportunity would come to make a break.

Yanna was curled up against him. It was the first real physical contact they'd had for weeks apart from the occasional brush of a hand. The excuse was the need to share a big groundsheet, wrapped round both of them. Nick had been sampling and throwing away the freeze-dried American rations, and was now stirring together a new mixture of tinned compo rations over his stove. Away to one side the lightening sky suddenly filled with angled sheets of flame.

'What are those?' asked Yanna.

'MLRS,' said David. 'Multiple Launch Rocket Systems. Twelve rockets, six hundred and fifty anti-personnel bombs in each one.'

'Six hundred and fifty? What does it do?'

He was reluctant to tell her. 'You use it against troop concentrations.'

'And?'

'And it blankets a pretty large area.'

'It wipes them out?'

'Yes.'

'What can it be like to be the man who thinks up that?'

'How do you know it was a man?'

'Oh, yes, Challis. It was a man. Obscene, yes?' She looked at him in the grey desert dawn and shook her head. 'People,' she said. 'Those are people over there.'

'Those people are the Republican Guard,' said David, 'the toughest soldiers Saddam's got. Spare your sorrow. You may be glad of a few rockets before this is over.'

They fell silent. She was lost in her own thoughts. There was a swirl of violent, wind-driven sand which had them turning their heads away, then they jerked them back. Through the desert air, pushing the continual bombardment into the background, an incredible noise came soaring, different to any part of the barrage they'd heard so far. It was a shrieking, wailing howl. A mile or so away the morning sky was torn apart by a sheet of white flame with electric blue edges. Unlike the MLRS, it didn't arc up into the sky. It careered around like a giant squib, moving higher and higher in frenetic lunges. At its zenith it rushed around in a random circular motion, then steadied and streaked to the ground too far ahead of them to see much of the explosion that followed its impact.

David knew what it was from Duncan's video. Yanna knew too, from a day long ago on the ranges. Bamco's new product was going on sale.

Chapter Fifteen

Same day

'I'm sorry, David. I've stretched it as far as I can. I haven't mentioned Nielsen to them, but it's a direct order. You're being picked up and that's the end of it.' Anthony Marshall didn't like having to pass the message on, but his radio net was full of far more important matters than the disposal of one maverick TV crew. They'd been eavesdropping as much as they could throughout the morning and lunchtime, and it was clear from the pace of events on the radio that the battle was moving faster than expected. Civilians round his neck – even friendly, self-sufficient civilians – were more than Marshall needed.

'Supposing we just disappear?' David suggested. 'You could deny all knowledge.'

'How can you? That old banger of yours is bust, isn't it?'

'Oh, well . . .' Then, unusually, a lie came easily to David's lips. 'Yes, of course, I wasn't thinking.'

'Anyway, no can do. There's a Sea King already on its way. I'd do a lot of things for an old pal, but being court-martialled isn't one of them.' Marshall looked around the tent. There was a lull in the radio traffic. He jerked his head towards the flap and David followed him outside. 'Your ears only. I just want you to understand. We're due to breach the berm this evening. The Yanks make the hole, then we're the exploitation force.' Another salvo of rockets streaked overhead towards the Iraqi defences, and they broke off for a second. 'It's not going to be a cakewalk, David. There's some bad guys out there. They'll hit us with everything they've got on the way through, probably bring out the gas and the bugs too, if you ask me. I really can't have you tagging along and I certainly can't leave you here. I mean, supposing the attack fails? You'll have the Republican Guard swarming all over you.'

He was called back to the tent. The weather was as bad as ever, but between the gusts of rain and the blowing sand David could see the groups of Challenger tanks, scattered across the muddy desert, revving their engines, ready to go whenever the signal came. Around the Warrior personnel carriers soldiers were loading up most of the remaining tents.

Nick was asleep in the Toyota. Ian had shot everything in sight and was talking to a couple of squaddies. Yanna was standing by herself staring towards the distant line of the sand berm, which was mostly covered by a pall of smoke and eruptions of sand as shells and missiles continued to hammer it. She looked round as he came up to her. 'What do you think?' she said.

'I think we're on our way back whether we like it or not.' He was standing right behind her and she leaned slightly back against him. It was a rare moment of intimacy. She tilted her head back and her hair brushed against his cheek.

'What would you rather do?' she asked.

'Go with them.'

'Yes. Me, too. There should be witnesses to all this.'

'Witnesses? That sounds as though it's criminal.'

She looked towards the berm. 'I cannot think what it must be like to be over there,' she said.

'Save your sympathy,' he said. 'They have all the advantages. They're deeply entrenched. They've had months to

158

get ready. They're Saddam's bad guys and they're tough as hell. Think of this lot going in across open desert, through the minefields.'

'They are people,' she said. 'Only one of us is right about them. When we find out which one of us that is, then I hope we can be together. I want to be with you, somewhere more simple, but I think that is the fence we have to jump first.'

She turned to look at him and his eyes, as ever, were hypnotized by the curves of her cheek-bones and the fall of her hair, but before either could say anything more a corporal came out of the tent, shouting.

'Mr Challis?'

'Yes,' he said.

'CO's compliments. He says the Sea King's five minutes away and will you get your lot ready straight away, please.'

They called Ian over and woke Nick with difficulty. 'No luck then?' he asked sleepily.

'No,' said David. 'The chopper's nearly here.'

'Shit,' said Nick. 'That's it then, unless you fancy making a break for it?'

David was silent, thinking about the chances. They couldn't get far. There were units everywhere around them. He was about to say so when he saw Nick's eyes were no longer on him. Nick had stiffened and was looking over David's shoulder towards the berm. He pointed. David swung round. Three soldiers were running for a low sand ridge beyond them, carrying guns. Throwing themselves down, they got into the aiming position. A tank, a hundred yards off to their right, revved its engine and swivelled its turret. Anthony Marshall came out of the tent in a rush with two of his officers behind, all lifting binoculars to their eyes.

159

'Ian,' said Nick, 'turn over.'

Ian lifted his camera to his shoulder, nudging Yanna into action. She bent to inspect the lights on the recorder. Coming towards them across the desert from the Iraqi lines, in a shower of spray and mud, was a small, unfamiliar vehicle, travelling fast. As its shape became clear, it was revealed as a strange device, a kind of dune buggy, skeletally framed in metal tubes with a machine-gun mounted on top. It crossed the low ridge ahead of them, travelling almost in silence. The soldiers relaxed. 'SEAL vehicle, sir,' one of them called to Marshall, and he strode over to where Ian was filming. 'That's enough of that,' he said. 'US Special Forces. No filming allowed, I'm afraid.' But then his attention was distracted by urgent shouts. The buggy bounced into the middle of the camp and they realized that all was far from well. Two of the three men on board were inert, sprawled over the tubes surrounding their seats. The driver was conscious but not much more than that, driving with his one good arm and his head lolling weakly. His face was a mask of blood, and the other arm hung limply over the side.

'Medic,' shouted Marshall, 'get to it,' and everyone started running towards them.

'Ian,' said Nick softly, 'switch back on. Don't get noticed.'

Ian was an old hand. He thumbed the lens to full wide-angle, started the camera turning and, holding it apparently casually by the top handle, started to walk to one side where there was an uninterrupted view. Yanna, unused to this, didn't immediately realize what was going on, so Nick quietly picked up the recorder from the ground, slung the strap on his shoulder and strolled after Ian before the umbilical cord between them could bring him to a halt. He kept his hand on top of the machine just in case anyone should notice the red recording light was on.

The men were carefully lifted out of their seats. One was losing blood fast from a huge exit wound in his back. His face was blue-grey. Someone ripped open a morphine pouch, took out the green and yellow cylinder inside and punched it against the soldier's thigh. A field dressing was pushed into the hole in his back. Other soldiers were quietly, urgently, working on the remaining two men. Into the scene of hushed but fevered movement broke the thrashing of rotor blades and a Royal Navy Sea King clattered down to a noisy landing fifty yards away. Marshall looked at it. 'Good timing,' he said. 'Whatever the chopper wants, tell him he's on medevac now. Get these men on board right away.'

David and Nick moved slowly away from the group while their attention was distracted. Nick whispered to Ian. They walked casually back to the Toyota and stood out of sight behind it, Ian filming the loading of the helicopter from round the corner. The chopper took off and it was only then that Marshall turned, and a look of intense annoyance came over his face as he saw them still there, remembering after five hectic minutes what the original purpose of the flight had been. He waved his arm in a summoning gesture and David walked over to him, but before he got there, a shout came from the tent and Marshall ran to it. David stopped.

Thirty seconds later Marshall was outside again and the tent itself was already coming down. He was issuing orders with an extra layer of calmness imposed over the speed, his personal reaction to stress. Men were moving fast to their vehicles. David walked closer. Marshall broke off and looked at him. 'No time, David. Get out of my hair. H Hour's been brought forward. Schwarzkopf's plan's going so well he's advanced Seven Corp's attack time by six hours. Stay here, with the vehicle. Don't try and walk out.

I'll get a message on the net that they're to come back for you.'

'Good luck, Anthony' was all David had time to say, then he and the other three were left standing in a cloud of diesel smoke and stinging rain as the unit moved out. They stood there, Ian filming, as the tanks and the Warriors disappeared towards the Iraqi line. Armour was moving as far as they could see.

'OK, boss, what now?' said Ian, hefting the camera.

David looked at the Toyota. 'No point in staying here. No point in going back. If this thing really works, let's give them ten minutes' start and go after them.' He looked at Yanna, who was carefully polishing the lenses of her stills cameras. 'Anybody disagree?' There was silence. He went on. 'It's not going to be comfortable.'

She looked up. 'We have not seen this war yet. How can we not go?'

David looked at Ian. He shrugged back. Nick grinned. 'Onward, ever onward, I say,' then he looked across with interest at the Special Forces vehicle, standing abandoned. 'Being a good citizen, I'd say it's my solemn duty to look after the American taxpayers' investment represented by that SEAL buggy. I mean someone might steal it, and that would be a terrible shame.'

So it was a strange-looking convoy which snaked its way north in the paths of the speeding tanks. Nick was gloating over the extra-sophisticated satellite navigation system in the buggy. He'd unslung the machine-gun from its bracket and left it in the desert. The giant sand walls, thrown up by the Iraqis to protect their lines, came nearer, the way towards them marked by a mass of tank tracks. They were keyed up for a battle – instead they found a traffic jam. It took them half an hour to get close to the gaps in the berms. Paths that had been cleared through the minefields to the breaches, and marked with poles and bundles of chemical light-sticks, were now a chaos of roaring engines and bad-tempered men, impelled by their adrenalin and held back by the traffic. The Toyota looked wildly out of place and they got some curious looks, more in fact than Nick, who had found a slouch hat in his stash and was driving the buggy alone, looking far too eccentric to be taken as anything other than the real thing. The chaos of war, plus the bad weather and the fact that everyone was hell-bent on catching up with the fighting, wherever it might be, protected them. They had their anti-chemical jackets and trousers on for the trip through the berms, with respirators at the ready, but they weren't necessary. They drove in near-zero visibility for several minutes, following a big tracked vehicle in front, sliding in the muddy, rutted sand under their wheels.

Time stopped passing in the normal way. David felt he was starting something unending, where the normal time signposts of hunger and sleep could be postponed indefinitely. The only reality was the grumble of the exhaust, the back view of the vehicle ahead and the jolting bounce of the wheels. There seemed to be no other images available to Ian's hungry lens. The weather sealed them in. Then, out of the grey loomed up a shape, the turretless hulk of a tank.

David pulled over and Nick stopped behind them. Ian got out to film and they all looked at the wrecked machine.

'You know,' said Nick slowly, 'apart from bits of Scud, this is the first concrete sign we've seen for ourselves that there is another side in this war.'

The camera was set up and ready to start when the wind died for a moment. The sand seemed to fall out of the air and they saw clearly around them for the first time.

They were on the edge of . . . what? A scrapyard? An abattoir perhaps, where high-tech weaponry had ripped an Iraqi division to pieces. Torn, smoking metal lanced out of the ground in all directions. With careful study David could see the pattern where a gun emplacement once stood, but only by piecing together the evidence of tiny fragments of wheels, barrels and gun-carriages. The soldiers themselves seemed to have vanished, until he reinterpreted the unfamiliar shape draped over the rear of the tank's hull into the crisp, black torso of the human being it had once been and, taking an involuntary step back, stumbled over a dismembered arm. The eyes soon learnt then to search out the less familiar sight of people, not machinery, shattered into components.

The smell was acrid and sweet – cooked paint, explosive fumes, diesel and flesh. Ian didn't so much stop filming as slowly grind to a halt, as if the imagery was too much for him. He lowered the camera and shook his head. Yanna gave a great shudder and put the recorder down. No one spoke for a long time. She recovered first and, still in silence, reached for the bag with her stills camera. It had been in the back of the Land Cruiser and somewhere on the way one of the side pouches had been ripped off.

'My film has gone,' she said in a dazed voice. 'I must have film.'

David came back to life, relieved to have a mundane task to justify turning away. 'I've got some Fuji Reala. It's colour print. Would that do?'

'Anything will do. Anything that will remember this for me. Thank you.'

He found it. Each film cassette had the processing company's little personalized label stuck on it, bearing his name and account number. She almost smiled at that. 'Very English,' she said, and it helped give him his balance back. Through the viewfinder she too recovered her poise.

164

They drove slowly on, trying to stay out of the way of fast-moving army vehicles without straying off the tracks. The traffic had spread out in all directions now and they chose one at random. They'd only gone four or five hundred yards when a smoking dugout entrance disgorged a dozen soldiers into their path. Ian was driving now, and he slowed.

'Jesus, they're Iraqis.'

Their general background fear coalesced into a sharp pang of direct danger before David took in their bedraggled state and the pieces of paper they were holding up. More than half of them were stumbling, wounded. One lurched towards the Toyota, tripped and fell over the bonnet as they stopped to avoid running him down. His face was flat on the metal, only inches from David through the glass. He turned it with an effort. He had no eyelids, lips or nose left, just a sheet of flayed, charred flesh in which one red eye was weeping.

'Oh, God,' said David, 'What the hell did that?'

Then more and more men appeared out of the sand and they were all the same – thin, ragged and wounded. Soon there was too big a throng to let them move. The men were banging on the sides of the Toyota, pressing the pieces of paper against the glass. David had seen those same pieces of paper being loaded into the C130s at Dhahran when they were still in neat bundles ready to be dropped. They showed a cartoon soldier on the left with his hands up and a thought bubble coming from his head containing pictures of a wife and family. He was surrendering to another soldier on the right, who was framed by the American, British and French flags. They all had them, holding them like holy relics.

'What do I do, David?' said Ian. David couldn't see Nick through the crowd and thought he must be feeling even more vulnerable in the open buggy.

'Yanna,' he said, 'pass me a box of MREs.'

He started shovelling the American ration packets out of a gap in the window as fast as he could. The crowd came to his side. 'Throw a whole box out of the back door,' he said. Yanna did and the Iraqis all began to shuffle, limping, to the rear. He saw the buggy again. Nick was seizing the opportunity and getting clear. They followed.

'Are those . . . what did you call them? Saddam's bad guys?' asked Yanna in a deceptively neutral voice.

'I think they were just ordinary conscripts,' said David. 'Not every unit is Republican Guard.'

The next moment his head was cracking against the windscreen as Ian slammed on the brakes. Something on tracks, with a slab-sided, angled-back front end, came hurtling towards them out of the increasing gloom. A turret with a slender gun barrel swivelled towards them. There were three more behind it. 'Bradleys,' said David, 'going the wrong way.' He held his breath as they looked down the gun barrel, but Nick's scheming had extended to providing them with the fluorescent pink Allied recognition panels, which were draped over the fronts of both their vehicles now, and no one fired. The Bradleys stopped.

A sergeant climbed down from the first one, looking gingerly at the ground, and came over. 'What's it like up ahead?' he asked, looking in curiously at the three of them.

'I'm afraid I wouldn't know. We haven't been up ahead, we've been back behind. That's where we're going next,' said David, puzzled.

'Pardon me, sir, but you're heading south so you must have been.'

'No. We're heading north.'

The sergeant shook his head. 'No way. I guess you're just goddam lucky you didn't meet any unfriendlies.'

They had to agree to differ, so he gave up, got back on

166

board and led his little troop off in a track-juddering, sand-slamming charge towards Saudi Arabia. 'I hope they're careful who they shoot at,' said Ian, switching the camera off.

As evening approached they groped their way into an area of complex bunkers and triangular sand-forts, and the carnage around them took on an entirely new dimension. David started to feel the first real doubts enter his soul. All along, the briefings on the massive Iraqi strength, and the difficulties of breaching their defences, had prepared him for some vast apocalyptic trial by fire in which the Allied armies would eventually win through by superior tactics, but only after the softening-up process of the air bombardment to even up the defenders' natural advantages. What he saw here bore no relation to that. This was a ragged army put through a food mixer. The sand was equal parts metal shards and minced soldiers. Smoke was pouring from the reinforced entrances to bunkers, and the smell of the smoke left no doubt at all as to what it was that was burning down below.

Ian was working mechanically now, with a dead expression on his face, moving on wooden legs. David had long ago stopped suggesting shots to him. Between Ian's shots Yanna would put the recorder down and take out her stills camera. Her face was a mask. Nick was singing a hymn quietly to himself, the same lines over and over again, 'He has loosed the fateful lightning of his terrible swift sword, his truth is marching on.' His expression gave no clue to his feelings.

There were huge bands of Iraqis wandering through the battlefield, holding up their scraps of paper. Sometimes they were shepherded by one or two British or American soldiers. More often they were by themselves, desperate to give themselves up to anyone who looked as though they might have something to eat. David felt uneasy and was relieved when, as it was getting dark, they came across an American refuelling point, where giant rubber bladders of fuel, airlifted in by Chinooks, had guards posted around them. They filled up, no questions asked, then parked for the night beside one of the guard vehicles. They got a few hours' fitful sleep, sitting up in the Land Cruiser, sleeping-bags doing little to keep out the cold.

Monday February 25th 1991

They woke with emotional hangovers from too much horror, and continued their sleepwalk through the total annihilation of the front lines, the damage continuing. T-62 and T-72 tanks, some destroyed, some merely disabled by sapper teams after they'd surrendered, littered the ground. They came across a devastated logistics site with a few soldiers mopping up. No one had time for them.

They drove slowly on and suddenly, ahead, there were muzzle flashes, heavy artillery and tanks in action, fountains of exploding sand mushrooming in a fierce engagement, the first real fighting they had seen. A British NCO leaped out in front of them and moved quickly round to the driver's window, looking curiously at the out-of-place Toyota. Nick was in the buggy behind.

'Password, please, sir,' he said.

David stalled. 'Terribly sorry, corporal,' he drawled in his best Sandhurst accent, 'gorn clean out of my head with the excitement.'

'Well, that won't do, will it, sir?' said the man, recognizing an officer's style, 'You say nine and I say six, sir.'

'Oh, of course.'

'Password, please, sir.'

'Nine.'

'Six, sir. Very good, sir.'

'What's going on up ahead?'

'Staffords are having a spot of trouble, sir. Objective Lead, it's called. A few of the ragheads still want to fight. Lost a man to an RPG so you want to watch your step. There's an infantry battalion in there and they're making it tough.'

'First trouble you've come across?'

'Well, first organized trouble, you could say, sir. Objectives Zinc and Platinum were a pushover. Lots of targets along the way. Not many of them managed to shoot back.'

They were stalled there for the rest of the day, unable to see clearly what was going on in the messy fighting, and they passed another uncomfortable night.

Tuesday February 26th 1991

The last resistance had been overcome and they could move forward again, following the tanks which were racing towards their encounter with the Republican Guard's Tawakalna and Medinah Divisions.

'What day is it, David?' said Yanna. 'I don't know any more.'

David had to look at his watch. 'It's Tuesday, the twenty-sixth. Four o'clock. Why?'

'I feel like a carrion bird, condemned to pick at abandoned battlefields for ever.'

'Not for ever. They're going so fast it has to end soon.'

'Oh, God. Look.'

They had reached another area where the Multiple Rocket Systems had had their way. No one talked much now. They looked at the acres of shattered equipment and bodies. They had to watch their step. Some of the showers of little missiles had failed to explode, captured by the soft sand. Every few yards their plastic fin sections, cream-coloured, stuck out from the sand at forty-five degrees like the aftermath of some mad darts game. They skirted them carefully. A leg was standing upright in a boot, stuck between a tank track and the upper half of a burnt body. Ian raised his camera.

'No, Ian,' said David. 'Save your batteries. We've got more of that than we could ever use.' Yanna looked at him. Their eyes met, but she looked away. 'I know what you're thinking,' he said, 'that's reality. But you have to stop somewhere, don't you? Don't you? What's the point in just going on and on with it? One shot's going to be enough to make them throw up in Woking.'

'No, David. They will forget one shot. They will say to themselves it was just one shot. The rest was not like that. You can open your eyes now, dear. That is what they will say.'

It was a dead land they moved through for a long time, and they had to go very slowly. The tracks were not clear and, in the areas where the rocket bombardments hadn't destroyed everything, they could see anti-personnel mines lying on the surface in many places. They crept from this dead sector to one that suddenly came alive. They got out to look round and a crackle of small-arms fire snapped at their ears from behind a sand berm. They dropped flat. There was much revving of engines ahead. They crawled forward to the top of the berm and looked cautiously over it. A group of armoured vehicles was gathered round a bunker. There had just been some sort of action. Now a curious vehicle moved into sight, a tank chassis with a bulldozer blade on the front. It was freezing cold again and getting dark rapidly.

170

They watched as the bulldozer dug its blade in and shovelled sand forward, wondering what it was doing. Then they saw it was filling in the entrance to the bunker. Yanna exclaimed, 'They're burying them alive.' They stared in horror. David tried to think up another possible reason why anyone would bulldoze a bunker entrance. He couldn't. Something broke inside Yanna and she turned openly on David.

'You tell me. You think all this is so good. What are they doing? Is that what you call war? You are always ready to justify your army. Where are all these big strong enemies? I don't see them. All I see is starving Iraqis or dead Iraqis.' She pointed to the bulldozer. 'Can you stand by and watch that and say it is right?'

David looked at her and saw anguish in her eyes, but he was still too stubborn to admit such a complete change in his values. 'Don't jump to conclusions. Let's go down and find out.'

Nick intervened. 'Leave Yanna and Ian here. Let them film it. We'll go down and talk. That way, if it's what Yanna thinks, we'll have the pix without any interference.'

They slid down the far side of the berm and cautiously crossed the hundred yards to the knot of soldiers and vehicles. All activity stopped as they approached. A balding, red-faced American officer looked them up and down for any evidence of rank or unit, finding none in the strange selection of desert wear they had adopted. Nick was still wearing his Special Forces slouch hat, and the officer gave most of his attention to that.

'Who are you?' he said abruptly.

'Battle Damage Assessment video unit,' said Nick unhesitatingly. 'Got out of touch with the rest of our guys. Wondering if you could fill us in.' David knew his English accent wouldn't help and kept silent. The officer laughed a sudden, raucous laugh. 'Fill you in? Only after I've filled in these. You took a helluva risk just then.'

'What do you mean?'

The man waved back at the berm. 'You two just walked straight through a minefield. Must have been born lucky. We were waiting for the bang and the red rain.' There was another burst of small-arms fire from one side, and he stopped to listen. 'The boys are still flushing out a few survivors.'

'What's the dozer for?'

'Closing up the bunkers. What do you think?'

Nick tried to make it casual. 'Trying to suffocate them in there?'

'They ain't breathing. They had a last little breath of Fuel Air, then they all said their prayers. When those babies come down, you generally find they turn up their toes pretty quick.'

'Oh, right,' said Nick. 'So, er ... what kind of barrage was that?'

'Just regular Fuel Air drop. Them things are just great big aerosol sprays. Ain't you ever seen one?' The officer looked at Nick curiously. 'You're doing BDA and you ain't never seen the effects of those babies? Man, that's the biggest battle damage you're ever going to assess.' He looked around. 'That sucker puts down a fireball quarter of a mile wide. Flattens the men and burns 'em crisp. Beauty of it is, you cain't run and you cain't hide. Goes right down into these holes, fills up the bunker and when it sparks, whoomp, that whole baby blows.' He punctuated his description with short bursts of high-pitched laughter. He'd seen too much.

'Sounds like we'd better bring the guys down and shoot some video around here.'

172

The officer shook his head violently. 'No way. This ain't even for private consumption. They say we're doin' the dozing for health reasons. Ain't that at all. You should know that damned well. It's down to the fact that when this is over, they don't want to talk about Fuel Air. They don't even want to whisper about it. Next best thing to a nuke without the radiation, and they don't want anyone trying to take their toys away.'

They heard a distant shouting and looked round to see Ian waving his hands in a beckoning gesture on top of the sand berm. The officer nodded in his direction. 'Guess your friend wants you back. Can't go that way. Not unless you need a foot massage. Might not be so lucky this time.'

'So how do we get back there?'

'Only sure way is the way we came in. Follow our tracks back south, then turn when you're well clear. It's all Indian country, so don't blame me if you step on something.' He looked back and they saw with dismay that Ian was starting to come down the berm. David shouted 'Stop!' and held up both hands in a warding-off gesture, but Ian kept coming.

'Time for a bit of direct action,' said the officer. He took a gun from the soldier next to him, and for just a moment David thought he'd gone off his head and was going to shoot Ian, but instead he put five rounds of rapid fire into the sand a few yards short of Ian's feet. That stopped him.

The visibility had clamped down again before they got back, groping through the rain and the stinging sand, following the other edge of the berm, each waiting for the blasting obliteration of a land-mine. They saw a light being flashed on and off ahead and were relieved to find it was the buggy.

The relief didn't last long. The Toyota was missing and Ian was beside himself. 'What the hell's going on?' he shouted at them as they approached. Why did that fucking idiot shoot at me?'

'You were about to walk through a minefield,' said David. 'He had to stop you. Anyway, what's the fuss?'

Ian could hardly get the words out. 'She's gone off.'

'Yanna?'

'Who else. She just disappeared.'

David went cold all over. He looked around into a deepening night, filled only with far-off explosions and the smell of burning. Night was no time to be moving around, not without thermal-imaging night-sights to look through and Chobham armour. Out there were things waiting to eat them, both animate and inanimate – desperate enemy soldiers, jumpy friendly ones and uncaring anti-personnel mines sown like grass seed across the sand.

'How long ago?'

'Ages. Soon after you went down. That's why I was shouting, as soon as I realized.'

'Tell me exactly what happened.'

'I don't really know. I was concentrating on shooting what was happening down around you. She was kneeling down, back to one side. I heard a vehicle moving around behind us.' He stopped and thought hard. 'I glanced round, She was looking at it. The mike was lying on top of the recorder. I was a bit miffed because I thought she ought to be concentrating on the sound, but it was more or less OK where it was and I didn't want to miss anything that happened down around where you were, so I turned back. Then you two reached the soldiers and after that I was concentrating hard. The funny thing is, I thought I heard her mumbling a bit, but I didn't look round. I just thought, shit, silly girl, she's buggering up the natural sound, but you were far too far away for us to be getting any sound off you, so I wasn't too bothered. I knew we could always dub it later. Then there was a great gust of wind and bloody sand everywhere and I couldn't see or hear a thing. When that stopped I heard the Toyota start up, and the next thing I knew, she was driving off.'

'Which way?'

'Further on. The way we were going. Anyway, that was when I started shouting for you to come back and that moron started shooting at me. I was so scared I pissed myself.'

David, desperately worried, looked round again. 'I'll take the buggy,' he said. 'You guys stay here.'

'No,' said Nick. 'That's just plain crazy. You won't find her and then we'll just have two people missing. We've got to wait for daylight.'

'Listen, Nick, she's gone because of me. I'm responsible. She couldn't take all this. She thought I didn't care about it.'

'Maybe she has, maybe she hasn't, but it won't help if you go too. We need the buggy to find her and we need daylight.'

In the end, miserably, he had to accept Nick's view. Nick took no chances, wedging himself into the buggy's driving seat while the others wrapped themselves in groundsheets to spend a freezing, miserable night.

Wednesday February 27th 1991

At first light they moved off. The Land Cruiser's tyre tracks had been obliterated by rain and blowing, wet sand. David was now covering up his guilt and fear with anger at her foolishness in going off.

'She's got all the bloody gear in it, too. It's bloody stupid.'

175

'She's not like that, David. You should know. I don't believe she meant to abandon us.'

'I do. She's very emotional. She thought I needed my eyes opening.'

It was ten a.m. and the GPS device gave them a read-out which put them south-west of Medinah Ridge, where, unknown to them, the last stand of the Republican Guards' tanks was taking place. Ahead they saw yet another column of Iraqi prisoners trudging towards them.

'Jesus, David. Look at that.'

'What?'

'Behind them. It's the Toyota.'

And it was. The familiar shape of their old Land Cruiser was grinding slowly along in the wake of the column.

'What the hell's she been doing?'

'I told you she'd be all right.'

'Phew.'

They studied the Toyota closely as they approached. It looked normal. David jumped out and ran towards it, waving his arms. It stopped, the door opened and a tall, black GI got out with a gun in his arms. David slowed to a halt, bewildered, looking at him, then at the truck, expecting to see Yanna there too.

'Where's Yanna?'

'Don't know no Yanna. Who's he?'

'That's our truck. Yanna's a she. We're looking for her. Where have you come from?'

The GI didn't answer. He turned back to the Toyota, picked up a radio set and called in. 'Captain, I got three guys here. They sound like Brits. They're in a SEAL buggy, an' they're asking questions 'bout a girl.' He looked at them. 'You guys stay right here. Someone's coming. I got prisoners to attend to.'

He went to get back in the truck. 'Hey, stop. What's going on? That's ours,' said David.

The GI looked at the buggy. 'Well, that one surely ain't. But I don't mind taking it off your hands.'

They stood by the Toyota and watched the buggy disappear.

'They must have picked her up last night,' said Ian.

'I suppose so,' said David.

It was a very long five minutes, but then a Humvee raced up and a gaunt officer got out. 'You with the girl?' he asked.

'Yes,' said David, relieved. 'Where is she?'

The man looked him up and down. 'She's in a bodybag,' he said. 'Now start at the beginning. Who the fuck are you?'

Chapter Sixteen

Monday July 8th 1991

David sat on his rock, feeling the grit under his boots, not even moving his head to watch when an RAF Tornado streaked low across the sky to his right. He had walked a long way that day, skirting the areas to the north where the army's signs warned you to keep an eye out for live shells. There'd been firing in the distance as he had eaten lunch in the scattered ruins of an old encampment, inhabited now only by a few sheep. As the evening came, he'd climbed up this granite outcrop and sat perfectly still for an hour or more, gazing down across the gentle hills of the South Hams towards the sea, where the length of the River Teign glistened silver in the last of the sun, from Newton Abbot all the way to Teignmouth. Beyond it the coastline stretched from the far side of Exmouth all the way round to the last rearing-up of Devon at Jennycliff on the eastern edge of Plymouth Sound. He looked around. Below him the quarries and the old granite tramway bore witness to the times when this edge of the moor had been a centre of industrial endeavour. Behind, Dartmoor rolled away for mile upon mile, north and west.

In the past three weeks he seemed to have crossed every inch of it, walking and walking through rain and sun to get away from the devils at his back. Twenty-five miles in a day sometimes, and it hadn't done a great deal of good. He knew he couldn't go on doing it, trying to drive away thought and the need for human contact by putting himself beyond reach and pushing himself to his limits. It was getting near time when he would have to abandon the anonymity of the pleasant, undemanding hotel in Ashburton and go back to face a future with all the people he had alienated since he came back to England.

It was the summer holidays, and during the daytime the moorland roads and car parks were choked with cars, but the tourists didn't venture far into the real moorland, content on the whole to totter up the grassy tracks to the nearest tor then totter back down to feed the pot-bellied ponies. David had made a point of being up early each day, leaving his car before the car parks filled up and walking deep into the heart of the moor, with just the occasional hail from other like-minded walkers to contend with. Now it was evening and the crowds had left, and he felt it was safe to go back down to the road again.

He patted the rough granite beneath him. Haytor, at least, was just the same as ever, one old friend who wouldn't die on him. He had come here many times in childhood with Duncan and his parents in the periods when his father was back in Plymouth from some long trip away. Up here the deep anger that still consumed him could be put away for a while, put into context by this massive, dependable, unchanging landscape. For a short time it was replaced by a patient sadness which he found more easy to tolerate.

Getting up to leave was a major decision. Advancing evening and mild hunger hardly seemed good enough reasons, but what else was there? He climbed down the iron staples set in the steep face of the rock and headed down the grassy slope to the car park. The ice-cream van was still there, and four or five cars. Someone was flying a stunt kite, which was weaving and zooming all over the

179

sky, but at least the coaches had all gone. Still a long way off, he searched out the familiar shape of the old Jensen to reassure himself it was safe and saw with great irritation that there was someone sitting on the bonnet.

He broke into a gentle downhill jog, watching his footing among the little outcrops of granite, and staring, when he could look up on the smoother sections, at the stranger by the car. It was not until he was crossing the road that the man turned and he found himself looking with immense surprise at Nick Nielsen, a waving, rising, relieved-looking Nick Nielsen. This was not what he wanted at all. This was a far too sudden return to a world for which he had no great appetite. He stopped, facing Nick.

'Good God. What are you doing here?'

Nick had the air of someone who knew his presence would not be entirely welcomed. 'I got dragged back, David. Glass called me up. Sent me to find you.'

'How did you do it? I didn't leave a number.'

'You don't have to tell me. I've paid the price. You just mentioned to Sally in the office that you were thinking about going to Dartmoor.'

'It's a big place.'

'Listen, sunshine, I can tell you exactly how big. I've called every goddam hotel and guest-house for fifty miles. I was just praying you hadn't decided to sleep in a tent. I'd nearly given up.'

'So you found the hotel. How do you come to be up here?'

'I was going to wait for you down there, but you know the Danish couple that's staying there? The woman came in and she said she'd seen your car here.'

David still couldn't make sense of it. 'So why are you here?'

'One-word answer? Glass. Our dear friend Bertram has a

hole in his schedule in sixteen days' time. He's changed his mind. He now thinks there's enough material for one more Gulf programme. He wants you to do it.'

'Nick, I don't work for him any more. I haven't renewed my contract.'

'David, don't think I don't know. The after-shock's still rating five on the Richter scale. The office has thin walls, He said to point out to you that it doesn't technically end until the end of this month.' Nick imitated Glass's affected voice. 'As forcibly as you can, Nick, as forcibly as I would if I were there.' He reverted to his own voice. 'If he were here, he wouldn't dare say a word. Listen, David, he's shit scared of you. He needs the programme and he's about as desperate as you've ever seen. He sent me to talk to you.'

'Why scared?'

'Well, I guess your little encounter in the desert might have had something to do with it. That's passed into legend pretty damned fast.'

David thought back to the scene. Yanna had been dead for five days and he'd been working like an automaton, crawling into his little bivouac tent at night only to lie awake through the intermittent rain, staring at the fabric just above his head. Nick made sure he ate and drank. In the desert outside Kuwait City, Britain's Defence Secretary suddenly appeared, whirled out by air to congratulate the troops. With him came a small group of Fleet Street and TV editors. David was slumped on the sand, leaning against one front wheel of the old Land Cruiser, watching Nick and Ian shooting pictures of Tom King, when a shadow fell across him and, bizarrely, Bertram Glass's unmistakable drawl said, 'Hello, David, old boy. Well met. Hoped I'd bump into you somewhere round here.'

He remembered getting to his feet and taking in the almost impeccable safari suit and military jacket. He could hardly believe what he was seeing. Glass was only a few hours' easy travel away from his central London office and restaurant habitat. David was months away from it and those months seemed more like years. He remembered looking down at his own filthy clothes and looking back up to find his boss staring in a slightly puzzled way around the horizon. 'Where are you staying?' Glass asked. 'Decent hotel, I hope?'

For a man not normally given to obscenity David's reaction had been savoured by all those who'd heard it. Now, suddenly, he felt unexpectedly glad to see Nick.

'Come on,' he said, 'let's go and have a drink.'

David led the way down off the moor, taking his favourite back-road from Halshanger Cross past the cliff-like walls of Belford Mill in its sheltered valley. A heron flapped into the air from the splashing stream of the Ashburn. He slowed to pass two children riding their ponies back from the moor, and as he came into the little town of Ashburton, he realized that for once he didn't mind his evening return to the world.

Nick sat in the hotel lounge, waiting for David to change, feeling a little apprehensive. While he waited, he relived the scenes in the Glass Crystal cutting-room as they had tried to put together the first of the post-Gulf films. At that stage he had hardly been able to talk to David any more. Since Yanna's death David had been in the blackest of black moods. He didn't even want to see the footage of the carnage on the Iraqi front lines. He wasn't interested in the morality or otherwise of the use of Fuel Air weapons or the Multiple Launch Rocket System, and he wouldn't listen to any of Nick's suggestions that this should be even a peripheral part of the film.

182

Nick had tried to talk quietly to Bertram Glass to see if he could change David's mind, but Glass now looked on David as a dangerous wild animal that might maul him at any moment, and in any case he thought of Nick as somewhat less than sound on the principles and purposes of the war. David had specifically forbidden Nick from explaining to Glass anything about his relationship with Yanna; Glass's version of sympathy was the very last thing he wanted.

In the postwar, gung-ho relief at the low level of Allied casualties, it was as if the one-hundred-hour land campaign had barely happened. The armed forces pool arrangements for TV had the effect of delaying the footage from the front until the pictures of liberated Kuwait had already been shown all over the world, consigning the images of the land war to the waste bin of old news, way behind events. Nick's belief that the land campaign was nothing but a massive overkill sounded wilfully eccentric to Bertram Glass, as it would have done to almost the entire TV-watching population of the Western world.

Nick remembered his final attempt. 'David, why don't you at least look at this? All I've done is cut a few pictures together of the Iraqi front-line positions. Nothing in close-up, but it makes the point.'

'Leave it, Nick,' David said, with a low and lethal quality in his voice, 'just bloody well stop going on about it,' and he left the room.

Fran, the picture editor, and Nick looked at each other. Nick shrugged. 'I'm only trying to save him from himself. OK, he's got a good reason to hate the Republican Guard, but this is right over the top. Nobody, but nobody else has told this part of the story. If we don't, no one will.'

Fran pulled a face. She was a natural conciliator, always ready to agree with whichever side in television's frequent cat fights happened to be in the cutting-room with her at the time. This time, though, the greater god of romance was also involved. 'I'd feel like that if I were him,' she said. 'I mean, he was in love with this girl Yanna, wasn't he? And it was dreadful what they did.'

Nick looked at her. More dreadful than you can know, he thought, his mind going back to the terrible encounter in the tent in the desert when he and David had been brought to her and the zip had been undone. 'Yes, it was,' was all he'd said.

The first film had been done in a rush. They'd brought back a stack of tapes, which had still been in the Land Cruiser, undisturbed, when they were reunited with it. Captain Cato had been too tied up in Kuwait City to harass them further, exercising the last of his authority before the inevitable return to civilian life as a mere reservist, selling soft-drink machines in Alabama. They'd been questioned at second hand about the smart bomb video, but by then David had already seen to that in his own way. Nick could remember that vividly too. He'd woken up early, the day after they'd seen Yanna's sad, shattered body. There was a noise outside the tent he couldn't place, a tearing, cracking sound. He crawled outside into a cold dawn and found David standing by the back of the Toyota, ripping tape out of the cassette, pulling and stretching it until it was piled on the ground round his feet in a heap of shining brown destruction.

'Jesus, David. What are you doing?'

David was breathing hard with a disconcertingly blank look in his eyes. He tossed the emptied, broken cassette at Nick. 'Yours, I think.'

Nick picked it up and realized what it was. 'Chrissakes. What did you do that for?'

'They don't deserve our pity. They *don't deserve our pity. They don't fucking deserve* . . .' Then his voice broke.

184

The film they made had not been about the ground war. It had not been about the dawning realization that the CIA estimates of Iraqi battle strength were way over the top. It had not been about the hundred-hour slaughter. When David had shouted himself to a halt, Bertram Glass found Nick by himself and administered the *coup de grâce*.

'Nick, dear boy. Look at it this way. Even accepting all that you say, would you really have been happier if there had been twenty thousand Allied deaths instead of two hundred? Eh?'

That was when he had stopped arguing full-frontally and had begun guerrilla tactics to try to slip in the odd hint of what they had seen. To no avail. Instead the film had been about the untold military cleverness of the strategy, the electronic war, the fooling of the Iraqis by Schwarzkopf's 'Hail Mary' hook to the west, and the electronic faking that left them thinking the encircling divisions had never left their original location. To that extent it had been a good, professional job, ahead of the competition.

What had worried Nick most had been the vehemence of the subtext. David was utterly convinced that the Iraqi Republican Guard had surrendered all their rights to be treated as humans, and was determined to make that point in every syllable and every stress of the film's commentary track. Nick even tried to argue that David couldn't know for sure it was the Republican Guard who had killed Yanna. David lost all grip on reason then. 'Look at what they did to her,' he'd shouted. 'They did the same in Kuwait City. The petrol and everything. Who else would it have been? Do you think those pathetic specimens we saw wandering round like lost souls would have been capable of thinking up something like that?'

*

Nick's train of thought was interrupted as David came down the hotel stairs into the lounge. He could see for certain now that part of his anxiety was unnecessary. This was a different, calmer David. They crossed the road to the old Golden Lion, still showing the grandeur of its days as a coaching inn, though it now marched to the beat of a more raucous drummer.

'So what does Glass want us to do?' asked David when he'd got the drinks, and Nick noted the implied surrender with relief.

'The high-tech stuff. Not just the smart bombs but the way they reacted to the problems on the ground. Things like bringing in the Buccaneers with the Pave Spike laser equipment while they were still fitting the Tornados out with laser gear.'

'I don't remember shooting much footage of the Buccaneers for a start. Have we got enough?'

'Well, no, I guess not. That's why we've got to shift ass. We have to be somewhere called Yeovilton tomorrow morning to shoot one of them being put through its paces.'

'Yeovilton? That's a Fleet Air Arm station. Those Buccaneers used to be Fleet Air Arm, but they're attached to the RAF these days.'

'Yeah, well, I guess you'd know better than me. Anyway, that's where they're going to be. Ten o'clock tomorrow morning. Are you on?'

David thought about it. A contract was a contract. A man's word was still his bond whatever circumstances might have done to him in the meantime.

'Yes, I suppose so,' he said.

'Right, let's get on with it then,' said Nick.

Nick watched surreptitiously as David sipped his Scotch. The strain showed clearly in David's face. For all the exercise and fresh air, there were oily grey shadows under his

186

eyes, which hadn't been there before, and something less definable. It was as if all the muscles had slackened just a bit and the sharp edge of that chiselled profile had blurred.

'Have another one,' he said, getting up.

An hour later they'd had several more. 'You're trying to get me drunk,' said David with just a little difficulty as Nick put a fresh tumbler of Glenlivet in front of him.

'Wouldn't hurt,' said Nick.

'I don't get drunk,' said David. 'Got drunk once when I was seventeen. Bloody room started going round. I threw up in the wastepaper basket in the end. Decided I never wanted to do that again.' He beamed slightly owlishly at Nick. 'So don't get any ideas. Won't get drunk. You just forget about any of that therapy nonsense. I don't want to talk about it, OK?' But then he grinned and missed the glass at his first try when he reached for it.

'Therapy?' said Nick. 'Who's talking about therapy? I'm talking about alcohol. That's an end in itself. Anyway,' he said, putting his own glass down, 'I forget to tell you. Your sister-in-law's been phoning you.'

'Josie?'

'Yeah. She sounds real nice. She's worried about you. Couldn't get you at your house, so she tried the office. I promised I'd make you phone her if I found you.'

'I'll phone her. Sweet girl.'

'That's what I thought, real concerned. There's loads of other messages, but I guess they can wait. Glass says to tell you that you might be up for an award.' Nick paused as David belched loudly and giggled. 'And that soldier friend of yours called up.'

That got through to him. 'Who? Anthony Marshall?'

'Yeah, that one. He was on a satellite phone from somewhere. I couldn't make much sense of him. He's still out there. I think he was saying he'd call again.'

Chapter Seventeen

Tuesday July 9th 1991

'We're trying to find out, Mr Challis. It shouldn't take too long.'

David paced round the operations room at Royal Naval Air Station, Yeovilton, trying not to show his irritation at the delay. The elderly Buccaneer jet that was needed to fill one of the holes in the programme was going to be late. As yet, no one quite seemed to know why. The Buccaneer was to play a central role in the next film. It had been an unlikely star of the RAF's air war. A handful of them, only half a squadron to start with, had been dusted off and rushed out to the Gulf at short notice when the RAF had to abandon low-level attacks in the face of early Tornado losses and turn to laser guidance from a safer height. Only the Buccaneers already had the laser target-acquisition equipment in place, so they were pressed into service, the bulbous aerodynamics of a much earlier era contrasting sharply with the high-tech razor edges of the Tornados that accompanied them into battle.

A phone shrilled and the lieutenant picked it up. 'Right you are,' he said. 'Most grateful, I'll pass the message on.' David looked at him and he grimaced. 'Spot of trouble, it seems. Got off all right from Scotland then had some sort of fuel system failure so it had to return to base. They're working on it now. Won't be here before this afternoon, though, I'm afraid.'

'I see. They will definitely fix it, will they?'

The lieutenant put on a mildly superior air. "Fraid you'd have to ask the RAF that one, sir. Anyway, they'll have to. It's coming down for a ship attack exercise, joint services job, so they'll have to put up another one if need be. I'm sure if it was down to us it wouldn't have gone wrong in the first place.'

'Of course. They used to be yours after all, didn't they?'

'That's right, sir. Bit before my time. Can't say I'm quite clear on how they wound up with the RAF at all.'

'Well, I can tell you the answer to that one,' David said. 'Once the Navy gave up the big carriers and switched to Harrier jump jets, you didn't have anywhere to land them any more. They were still needed, though – maritime interception and so on – so you gave them to the RAF. Great plane, in its day, Blackburn's best.'

The lieutenant raised his eyebrows. 'You know your onions, sir. Speciality of yours?'

'My name is David. Forget the "sir". I'm interested, certainly. Bound to be, really. My father was Fleet Air Arm, war service and afterwards.'

'Was he now? Which squadron?'

'899.'

'Well, well. You're in the right place then. Pity they're not here at the moment, or we could have taken you over to see them. They'd have been tickled pink, very hot on the history. What did your old man fly?'

'Seafires mostly, until the end of the war. Everything that was going afterwards, right up to Sea Vixens.'

'Retired now, I suppose?'

'No. I'm afraid he died a long time ago. Silly really, after all that. A car accident.'

'I'm sorry.'

The door opened and David looked round. Ian, just

arrived from London, was ushered in with his camera. After him came a face David hadn't seen since Dhahran and the aftermath of the Scud attack: it was Norman, back in action with his leg mended.

'Norman. Good to see you again. Are you all right now?'

'Thanks, David. Good to see you, too. Yes, mostly. Aches a bit when it rains.' There was something a little wary in Norman's manner. The man had clearly heard all the stories of what he'd missed, and David realized that the impact of his rampage in the desert would take a long time to die down. Norman's presence gave him a strange inner twinge. It brought back so many scenes.

'Isn't Nick here?' asked Ian.

'No, he's gone back to London to get on with things. I'm afraid we've got a bit of time to kill. The plane won't be here until this afternoon.'

'We could have stopped for breakfast after all.'

The lieutenant stepped forward. 'There's the café over by the museum.'

Ian brightened. 'Sounds good. What sort of museum would that be?'

'The official Fleet Air Arm museum, sir. Very good indeed. First-rate collection,' said the lieutenant. 'Plenty to see if you've got a bit of time to kill.'

'What about that then, David?'

'I've been round it lots of times. I'll have another wander round, I suppose. Better than sitting here.'

They were having breakfast in the café when the phone behind the counter rang. The woman who picked it up waved it at David. 'Are you Mr Challis? It's the Ops. Room for you.'

The lieutenant's voice said, 'ETA's 12.45 now, Mr Challis. I'm sorry you'll have such a long wait.'

'Not to worry. At least we'll be able to shoot it coming in.'

190

'Fine. One other thing. I called the museum. I remembered they've got some stuff there I thought you might care to see. We had an old boy in from 899 last year and he spent ages going through their wartime line book. I thought that might be right up your street, unless you've already seen it, of course?'

'No, I don't know anything about it. What's a line book?'

'Oh, you know, as in "shooting a line"? Sort of an unofficial squadron history, written by the pilots themselves. A kind of scrapbook, I suppose you might say.'

'I'd love to see it.'

'Just say who you are at the door. They'll be expecting you.'

When they'd finished breakfast and left the Swordfish restaurant, they didn't go straight into the museum. Immediately outside the steps up to the entrance was a Buccaneer on display. It made the perfect shot for the programme, with the museum behind it, to emphasize just how old the plane was. David left Ian and Norman doing it and walked in through the doors.

A school party was filing past the ticket office and he had to wait. Finally the way was clear. 'Hello. My name's David Challis. I think they rang you.'

'Yes, certainly, Mr Challis. I'll just call the library for you.' In a minute or two a girl appeared and escorted him down the steps into a display of First World War aircraft. She ushered him through a gap in the barriers into the middle of the display, past a Spad biplane that was tipped up on its nose in a mock battlefield. They went through a doorway concealed in the backdrop, where taped sounds of shellfire were playing. It led to a collection of quiet offices, lined by shelves stacked with files and books. Off the main archive area was a small room marked RESEARCH STUDY.

It was all ready for him. A thick black tome was waiting on the table, a leather-bound scrapbook, bulging in the middle, and with the familiar 899 crest – a mailed fist accompanied by the Squadron motto 'Strike and Defend' – on the cover. The crest was as familiar to David as his own face in the mirror. He had looked at it, framed, ever since he was a baby, first on his parents' walls, then on his own. Unexpectedly it made his eyes prick with tears, with a sudden sharp memory of his parents' death brought to the surface of a mind sensitized by the loss of Yanna.

He opened the book as if it were a Shakespeare first folio. It started with an inscription in stylized block letters: *All characters and events portrayed in this book are entirely ridiculous and any likeness to actual persons is intentional.* After that the tone, to start with, was a little formal. It described the Squadron's formation at Hatson, in the Orkney Islands, in 1942, around a nucleus of experienced pilots from other squadrons, filled out with rookies fresh from the training schemes in Canada and America. His own father's name leapt at him out of the page, nothing more than one in a list, sending a tingle down his spine. But then in that same list, hitting him from his blind side because the intervening months had driven away old Mr Middleton's words, there was another name, unexpectedly crashing at him from the page, so that his eye, slipping past, lurched back to it. Sub-Lieutenant Jackie Mainwaring. Middleton's voice came sharply back to him. 'He didn't make it. That's all.'

Doubly absorbed, he read on. Dummy deck-landings around Scapa Flow as they had worked up to readiness. Then the first Squadron tragedy, reported in detail, as a young pilot prosaically lost control in clear weather. *At this time, Sub-Lieutenant Douglas Barber lost his life in an unfortunate accident when his machine crashed into Kirkwall harbour.* Then as they started doing the real thing – landing their Seafires on an aircraft-carrier deck – the wrinkled fuselages, torn-out arrester hooks and shattered propellers induced a joky tone. The CO was a very old man: he celebrated his twenty-seventh birthday. Serious mishaps were still few and far between, and they could afford the luxury, away from the action, of describing them in full. *Rooky attempted a half-roll on take-off, no one being more surprised than himself, and then had a ticklish quarter of an hour before landing-on downwind. This all due to a very ropy aircraft that workshops had foisted on to the squadron, which had something wrong with its rigging and preferred to fly in a continual roll to the left.*

Time passed without David being aware of it, as he read on. The Squadron was getting used to danger in stages. *On the 28th the ship left harbour and the section from Machrihanish was flown on. Stan Jones, who was the last one on, went over the port side, tearing his hook out, severely denting and bending the second radio mast as he went. He was under for some time and when he finally surfaced, no one could see him to start with.*

Action was coming nearer. *A Buster scramble to twenty thousand reached in fourteen and three-quarter minutes.* Then a shorter entry on May 29th. *Unfortunately, Pat Fitzgerald spun in from about one thousand feet while in the circuit and nothing more was seen of him.* Shorter still at the end of June. *Bob Lawson's engine cut out on approach and he was lost in the drink.* The spectre of death was now sitting firmly at the mess table, and from then on only life's more trivial matters got a full description.

Now they were on their way to war in the Mediterranean, and a long doggerel poem, listing all the squadron members, appeared. David noted down two sections, one about his own father, the other about Jackie Mainwaring. His surname was rhymed with *hammering . . . at the keys of his typewriter, in the days when lights were brighter.* It said that in Civvy Street he had been a journalist and playwright. It concluded, *He never goes up in the air, without his faithful teddy bear,* and there was a cartoon of a man standing by a Seafire, clutching a teddy, which was wearing a leather flying helmet.

He turned the page and there it was, that same familiar photo of the pilots lined up, swinging their legs over the side of the flight-deck, his father looking piratical in his dark glasses. This one was signed by all of them, and there was Mainwaring, a fair-haired slim echo of the 1930s public school system. A few pages later, the ultimate in understatement. The only mention of the torpedoing and near sinking of the carrier they were on, HMS *Indomitable*, was a picture of a torpedo and a clipped newspaper headline, which just said *Miracle in the Night.*

Force H turned back to limp to Malta, where they were constantly attacked by the Germans and then told they were transferring to a much smaller escort carrier, HMS *Hunter*, with a new model of Seafire. That was not, of course, how they put it themselves: *Our old cabs had been thoroughly teased by the visitors and we were re-equipped as a result with LIICs.*

Then the squadron took part in the Salerno invasion, which David knew from his own separate studies had been crucial and where aircraft losses had been extremely heavy. There was just the briefest of mentions, a pasted-in signal: *N.C.W.T.F. has asked me to express to your ship's company and flying crews his sincere thanks and appreciation of a job well done. He reports air situation critical and he asks for early morning cover tomorrow, which I have agreed to provide. Programme starting 0615. Maximum numbers for first two periods.* The squadron flew ashore. The book went on to mention two of their aircraft which were destroyed by enemy shell-fire. *During a rather heavy bombing attack, it was rather amusing to see pilots sheltering under a petrol tanker feverishly passing a bottle of Scotch to and fro.*

After that they returned to the UK to regroup. Two pilots left: *Charlie has slight twitch and went for a rest. Gerry has returned to the RAF for a wing leader's course.* In November 1943 there was a photo which had him looking closely, a group of pilots enjoying themselves on an airfield, posed with the Squadron spaniel. Behind them was a magnificent vintage sports car, head on to the camera, and David looked hard at it. It was a four-and-a-half-litre Bentley, that was clear, and that would have been quite special enough, but this was something even more. The distinctive ribbed casing of an Amherst Villiers supercharger projected from the half-round cut-out in the bottom of the radiator. It was a blower Bentley from 1929 or 1930, one of the supercharged cars, and from what David could see it looked like one of the Dorothy Paget team cars developed by Henry Birkin. Below the picture someone had written *Sally the spaniel and the boys, with Jackie's hundred-pound bus, the other love of his life.* A hundred pounds, thought David. Good Lord. More like a million now.

There was bad news again over the page. Away from the war they felt freer to write about it. *We regret to announce the death of Gordon Elwell while flying a Seafire LIIC to Abbotsinch with Peter and Jimmy. He spun in on a turn in bad weather over the Isle of Bute just when turning back to Ayr. In him we lost a good pilot, a promising Stores Basher and above all a very fine chap.*

That wasn't all. The circumstances of Jackie Mainwaring's end were filled in just one page further on. Middleton's words – 'He didn't make it, that's all' – echoed again in David's ears as he read it: *We regret the loss of Jackie Mainwaring, one of the Squadron's founding pilots. Jackie disappeared without trace somewhere near Newcastle while ferrying a new cab back to the Squadron. Visibility was poor and it is believed he went down in the sea. Jackie had flown almost ceaselessly since the first days of the war, initially in Rocs and Skuas, then in Fulmars and since the formation of the squadron in Seafires. Words cannot express what we feel. He had to bear more than his share of the load.*

David looked through the rest of the book, reading the references to his father's exploits, but his mind kept drifting back to the young pilot and the old man, keeping his memory alive in his remote Northumbrian farmhouse. Then the door opened and the archivist came in. 'Sorry to disturb you, Mr Challis, but the tower's on the phone. They say your plane will be here in fifteen minutes.'

Chapter Eighteen

Thursday July 11th 1991

'Take that tin can away and park it somewhere I can't see it,' Purkiss said. It came as a complete and unpleasant surprise. Donaldson had driven into the Bamco executive car park in the usual way and there was a flashy 5 series BMW, brand new in bright red, sitting in his designated space. He'd stopped, annoyed, then that annoyance turned to concern when Spencer Purkiss appeared like a jack-in-the-box and addressed him like the lowest of the shop-floor low. Was his brief ascendancy at Bamco over? Had Geoff Busby fought back? Careful not to let his feelings show while he flicked through the possibilities, he drove the Vauxhall round the corner, locked it and walked deliberately back to the front door.

Purkiss was still there, waiting for him. 'Couldn't stand the look of your heap out here,' he said. 'Lowers the tone.'

'Whose is that?' said Donaldson, looking at the BMW, keeping his voice even and trying to read something from Purkiss's voice.

'That? That belongs to the new head of special projects. Just appointed this morning. Today's his first day on the job.'

The sinking feeling got worse. 'I didn't know there was one. What's his name?'

'Martin Donaldson,' said Purkiss, laughing aloud at the look on Donaldson's face. He pulled a bunch of ignition keys out of his pocket and dangled them in front of him. 'Happy Christmas,' he said, 'courtesy of the Bamco management. What do you think?'

Donaldson looked at the BMW, dizzy with relief but keeping it to himself. 'It's a beauty, Spencer.'

'Least I could do after all your hard work. Can't say how much I've appreciated it.'

I'm there, thought Donaldson. I'm an insider. When Purkiss goes soft on you, you've been elected to the chosen few.

Purkiss pointed at Busby's Land Rover. 'Look at that bloody thing, will you? I've been on at Geoff to go for something a bit more suitable, but I just can't get him to change his mind.'

'Each to his own, Spencer,' said Donaldson, thinking what could be more suitable for that bullet-headed dreadnought of a man.

They went their separate ways to their offices, Donaldson with a new spring in his step, looking forward to a busy morning. The final technical specifications for the Cracksman 2 upgrade were due and he couldn't wait to get to grips with those. Geoff Busby had just come back from the Middle East and by now Donaldson's in-house information system should be giving him full details of all the bits of Busby's trip that Busby himself might just decide not to mention. Donaldson was under no illusions. Busby bitterly resented his ascendancy in the organization and would do anything to thwart him. Purkiss's left-hand and right-hand men were at each other's throats.

He'd only been in his office for five minutes, going through the booking dockets for Busby's travel and accommodation, when the intercom went. 'Mr Donaldson? Mr Purkiss says would you join him in his office as soon as possible, please?'

He put down what he was doing, then on second thoughts crossed to his own private filing cabinet and locked the papers in the drawer. He crossed the lobby, walked into the other office and raised an eyebrow at Purkiss, who was staring at a letter.

'What's up?'

'Read this.'

The letter was headed 'Duncan Challis Productions, Chalice Hall'. It started, 'Dear Spencer, I have just been looking through all my video material on Dodgem. What a splendid job we made of that. I do hope you agree? I do feel, however, that in the end what we produced went far beyond the normal requirements of our agreement. I was disappointed with my contacts with Geoff Busby on that score . . .' He went on reading to the very end, taking on board the elegantly phrased threat and raising his eyebrows.

'Do we have to take this seriously?'

Purkiss didn't answer because at that moment Geoff Busby walked in.

'Morning, Spence,' he said, and nodded curtly at Donaldson.

'Give Geoff the letter, Martin,' said Purkiss. 'It's his pigeon.'

'What's that then?' said Busby.

'Our video friend,' said Purkiss. 'I thought you'd sorted out that little misunderstanding.'

Busby took the letter. 'Yeah. Challis you mean? Yeah, I had a word. Told him there wouldn't be any more cash.'

'When was that?'

'When you told me. Months ago.'

'Well, he's having another go. Have a look at that.'

Busby did. Donaldson watched him, seeing his lips move. Purkiss shook his head. 'What do you make of it, Martin?'

'Blackmail's what I make of it. He must have been doing a bit more homework.'

'So in answer to your question, Martin, yes, we have to take it seriously.'

Busby came to the end of the letter and looked up with an angry expression on his face. Purkiss looked at him.

'So, Geoff. Ball's back in your court. Perhaps you're losing your touch?'

'He's just a snotty little shit. I'll soon sort this.'

'That's what I want to talk about.' Then Purkiss checked himself and looked at Donaldson. 'No need to bother you with this, Martin. We can handle it.' And Donaldson left the room, thinking maybe I'm only in the inner circle until the gloves come off. There are still some things they keep to themselves. Then he was struck by a fresh thought. Purkiss had only wanted him there to wind Busby up a bit more with the exposure of his failure. Interesting, he thought.

Chapter Nineteen

Friday July 12th 1991

David had never expected to walk into the Glass Crystal offices again, so it felt extremely odd despite being totally familiar. He was greeted with cautious enthusiasm, as if he were a favourite family dog that had suddenly and unpredictably started biting people. There were a few minutes before the meeting, so he went into the office he used to share, where his table looked unused, and rang Josie. He felt guilty about his long silence, but she was too sensitive to remonstrate. 'Hello, love,' he said, 'Sorry I've been out of touch. Nick said you were trying to get hold of me.'

Her voice was clear. 'I was just worried, that's all. Did you have a good time in Devon?'

'Oh, yes,' he said in a tone that meant no.

'Why don't you come up here for a bit?'

'Well, maybe in a while.' He realized that wasn't a very adequate response. 'Sorry, that doesn't sound very grateful. It's just . . .' Just what? 'Just that I don't think sympathy would be very good for me at the moment. I'm probably better on my own.'

She came straight back at him with a no-nonsense note in her voice. 'I wasn't going to offer sympathy. Company, maybe. Anyway, I need to talk to you.'

'Dunk?'

'Yes.'

'What's happened?'

'Well, I don't want to trouble you and that wasn't the only reason I was calling.'

'I know. Go on, Josie.'

Her voice suddenly sounded close to tears. 'I expect you can guess. It's the same old thing. He's been hitting the bottle again. I had a big row with him on Sunday. I told him we were going to be in real trouble if he kept this up. He's already had a warning from the programme. We're hardly keeping our heads above water as it is. He got all cocky, told me he was fixing that. He said he wasn't going to let Bamco off the hook.'

'Where is he now?'

'London. It's his show tonight.'

'Of course it is. Look, don't you worry. I'll talk to him.'

'I'm sorry to burden you with this.'

'It's not a burden. How about you? I don't suppose you've got anyone to talk to up there?'

Her voice sounded cheerful again. She was always resilient. That was one of the things that had originally attracted him to her. 'Well, I have in fact. George comes round most days. We have coffee and we talk about things.'

'George?'

'Yes, you know. George Middleton. You met him.'

'I didn't know you were friends?'

'I probably didn't get a chance to mention it, what with everything that's been going on. He's so sweet. I don't think he's had anyone to talk to for years and, since you told him about your father and the Squadron, he's been a bit like an uncle really.'

'I'm glad. Tell him I was in the Fleet Air Museum this week. I looked up some old 899 history.'

'Will you come up soon? I'd love to see you.'

'Well, I might. I'll see.'

Josie put the phone down, wondering if she'd been right

to inflict this on David but still believing her instinct that his readiness to take on other people's problems might be just the trigger he needed now. David put the phone down, distracted from his own situation for the first time since he got back. He thought of phoning Duncan, but realized he would be in the middle of the preparation for the show, so he decided not to disturb his brother until afterwards.

He looked at his watch and went along the corridor to Bertram Glass's office for the script meeting. Glass was still nervous of David and gave him an over-effusive greeting while managing to avoid looking directly at him. Nick and the others filed into the office. There were nods all round. Glass cleared his throat.

'Now, first things first. What we need is a title.'

David, to whom that seemed the lowest priority, saw Nick's eyebrows rise.

'Wants something serious. Shakespeare, maybe,' Glass went on. 'What was it that Air Force chappie Macsomething said when he sent the first air strikes off? You used it, David, didn't you?'

An earnest young researcher jumped in. 'You mean the quote about gentlemen in England now abed holding themselves accursed they were not there?'

'That's the feller. Richard the Third.'

'Henry the Fifth,' said Nick, and David laughed. Everyone else looked surprised.

'No, Bertram,' said David, 'Don't ask why. Just no. Anyway, why don't we talk the script through first, then you'll have a better idea what to call it.'

Glass looked at him, trying to fathom his mood with as much chance of success as a palm reader staring at a gloved hand.

'Great programme last time, David. We want to keep the temperature up. One of your best scripts ever.'

'Yes, Bertram. Thank you.'

It meandered on for an hour and a half. The only person who came out of it knowing more than when he went in was Glass, and that wasn't saying a lot. David went into a smaller conclave with those that mattered: the editor, Nick and two researchers. They had already roughed out the structure of the script. Now, an afternoon's concentrated work put it well on the way to completion.

As the rush-hour traffic began to fill the streets, David went back to his flat. He knew he had to have another shot at writing a letter to Yanna's mother. He had written to her from the Gulf, a stiff, inadequate letter because it was either that or an uncontrolled outpouring. Somewhere deep in his mind were echoes of a commanding officer doing his duty after a casualty in his unit. He had received a short note back from Quiberon. She had asked him to write again, or to come and visit her when a little more time had passed. Now, pen in hand, he found it was hard to express himself precisely enough in French, and he was nowhere near finished when he realized it was time for Duncan's show to start.

By the time he'd found the remote control down the side of the sofa and switched on, it was halfway through the opening titles. David had never liked them, a flashy mixture of obvious business images and some pretentiously portentous music. As the title sequence ended, they cut to a wide shot of the studio set with Duncan behind his desk, and that was when David had his first inkling of disaster. Duncan seemed to be bending over, fiddling with his earpiece, unaware that he was already in vision. David could imagine the urgent words being barked into his ear, and he seemed to collect himself suddenly. Then he opened his mouth for the lead-in to the show and David knew with sickening certainty that he was drunk. It wasn't that obvious. You would have to know him pretty well, but his timing was out, his stresses were more random than usual and there was just the trace of a slur to his voice.

His letter forgotten, David sat with his attention fixed on the screen. Duncan staggered his way through the menu for the show and navigated with some difficulty through the introduction for the first film. That came on and there was five minutes' remission, but David knew perfectly well there was nothing anyone could do for Duncan in five minutes, though he could imagine the scenes in the gallery as the seconds ticked by. When the film ended and they came back to Duncan, he seemed to be just finishing some sort of argument with someone out of shot. He was red in the face. Next up was a live studio interview with a captain of industry, who looked distinctly ill at ease, clearly having been privy to some goings-on in the studio that the audience couldn't see.

'Mr Beasly . . .' Duncan looked down at his sheet of paper. 'Er . . . Breasly.' David groaned to himself. Everyone knew James Beasly.

Duncan deliberately and obviously read the first question from his notes. 'Would you say the ress . . . the, er, the recession has affected the engineering sector more . . .' He didn't say more than that, and Beasly waited for a puzzled second before giving some sort of answer. Duncan hunted for another question and eventually found it. He even managed to deliver it without a mistake. 'Is your decision to move out of power station equipment a result of that?' Beasly answered, looking a little happier, with Duncan nodding over-emphatically. Then he started on the next question. 'Is your, er, decision to move out of power station equip . . .' The producer must have shouted into his earpiece at the same moment that David put his hands to his head. Whatever it was, it didn't help much. Duncan searched around for another question and was rescued, appallingly, by James Beasly taking the initiative.

'Well, let me tell you, Mr Challis, while you collect your thoughts, on the export side we have . . .' and off he went. Duncan managed a further question, then with a huge effort, seeming to get drunker by the second, wobbled through the introduction to another film. David waited with bated breath for the end of it to see if he'd managed to pull himself together, but the studio never reappeared. Instead they cut to a slightly flustered continuity announcer who said there had been technical trouble in the studio. Then they put on a cartoon.

David was horrified. He searched for the number and called the studio. No one was available to talk to him. He left a message that he was coming to collect Duncan and went straight outside to the car. He was there in twenty minutes, and they were expecting him when he got to the desk. He was shown into an open-plan office. Duncan was slumped in a chair in the editor's glass cubicle at the far end. Two people were standing looking at him. The girl who had taken David in went and tapped on the glass. The programme editor, Tim Bygrave, came out. He was in a poisonous mood.

'There he is. Have you brought a car? You might need some help. He can't stand up.'

David sighed and Bygrave, who was clenching and unclenching his hands, went on. 'Look, if you've got any influence over your bloody brother, this is the time to use it. I've had enough of it. Do you know what he's known as now? Drunken Duncan. Not just here. Right through the business. These things spread, you know. Take him home. I'll have to think what we're going to do.'

They helped David load Duncan into the car, and he thought about where he should take him. His own flat only had one bedroom so he drove him to Lancaster Gate, to the flat Duncan sublet for his weekly visits to London. Maurice Henbest, who owned and lived in the rest of the flat, wasn't home. David didn't like him at all and was relieved by his absence, though he could have done with some help getting a comatose Duncan inside. He had to put his brother over his shoulder in a fireman's lift in the end, aware of passers-by stopping to watch. He lowered Duncan into a chair and the phone started ringing.

He picked it up. 'Hello?'

'Hello. Who's that? Is that Maurice?'

'Josie. It's David. I've just brought Dunk back.'

'I was watching the show. It was ghastly. Is he all right?'

David glanced across at Duncan. He hadn't moved. 'He's right out of it, love. He needs to sleep it off. I'll put him to bed and come back to see him in the morning.'

'Did you see Bygrave? What did he say?'

'He's not very pleased.'

'Oh, God. David, what do we do? He's never been as bad as this before.'

'I'll call you tomorrow after I've talked to him.'

'David?'

'Yes, love.'

'I'm so glad you were there.'

David tucked Duncan into bed. He was surprised to find his brother was now not only immobile but almost rigid. It was with some difficulty that he straightened him out enough to get him on the mattress. He looked at him thoughtfully, wondering whether to call a doctor. It seemed a panic measure, but he'd never seen anyone in quite that state before. He sat down in a chair, trying to decide what to do, but the rattle of a key in the lock announced the return home of Duncan's landlord.

David only knew Maurice Henbest from occasional encounters at the flat, but what he'd seen didn't make him anxious to extend that acquaintance. Henbest was supercilious and wholly dedicated to the pursuit of money. He worked in an expensive West End antique shop, and all his stories were of the various ways in which he'd ripped off his customers to his own benefit. He was tall, beaky, stooping and altogether reminiscent of a Walt Disney vulture.

'Well, good evening, David,' he said with an irritating stress on David's name. 'To what do we owe the pleasure?'

'I brought Duncan back. He wasn't too well.'

Henbest looked at him questioningly. 'On the bottle, I presume?'

'Well, maybe.'

'Silly Duncan.'

David hated bringing Henbest in on it, but he was worried. 'I'm thinking about calling a doctor. He's sort of stiff. I've never seen anyone quite like that before.'

They went to look. Henbest felt one of his arms. It was still locked across his chest. 'Don't worry. Standard operating procedure for your kid brother. He's been like this before. He'll be fine when he's slept it off.'

There was something in his voice David couldn't quite place. He nodded slowly. 'OK. I'll be back in the morning.'

Saturday July 13th 1991

He had slept badly, worrying, and was back there by half past eight. Henbest had gone to work and Duncan was sitting in the kitchen, white-faced, drinking coffee.

'Morning, Dunk. How are you?'

'Ha bloody ha. I bet you had a good laugh last night.'

David sat down. 'I wasn't laughing. How did it happen?'

'I don't know. I must have been ill. I didn't drink much. I can handle it, you know that, David.' He said it imploringly. David just looked at him. 'I can. Don't give me that silent censorious bullshit. I wasn't just pissed. I never fall down on the job.'

David couldn't duck it. 'Listen, Dunk, that might have been true once, but it isn't now. It's getting to you.' Duncan shook his head. 'No, you mustn't deny it. You're heading for full-scale alcoholism.' His brother's head lifted. 'You may already be one. It's time to get some help.'

Duncan went on shaking his head, but the phone rang. He made no move to pick it up so David did it for him.

'Duncan? It's Tim Bygrave.' The voice was curt.

'Hello, Tim. It's not Duncan, it's his brother.'

'Oh, David. Is he there?'

Duncan was waving his hands and shaking his head. 'No. Well. I should say he's still asleep, Tim. I think he was pretty ill yesterday. It wasn't just drink.'

Bygrave snorted so loudly that Duncan could hear it clearly from the other side of the room, and lowered his head into his hands. Bygrave went on. 'OK. You're family so I'll tell you. He's on two weeks' sick leave while we think about what to do. I'm not risking that happening again *ever*. Tell him I suggest very strongly that he gets some sort of treatment if he wants to stand any chance of keeping his contract.'

Sunday July 14th 1991

Geoff Busby finished his Heineken, staring round the side of the can at Martin Donaldson sitting alongside Purkiss on the sofa. It used to be the two of them. Now it was three and that was one too many for Busby. Donaldson was a bit too slidy for him, too smart, always two jumps ahead. Still, this was a victory party, so maybe they should call a truce for the afternoon.

Purkiss tossed him another can. 'Want to see it again, Geoff?'

'Yeah, why not?'

It was a huge screen, taking up a major slice of one wall in the den of Purkiss's big, big house near Solihull. Busby knew Purkiss usually watched war videos on it. He looked at the row on the shelf: *Platoon, Hamburger Hill, Full Metal Jacket, Top Gun*. There was one at the end Busby had never heard of: *All Quiet on the Western Front*. Didn't sound very interesting.

They watched it all through again, Purkiss chuckling when Duncan Challis seemed to lose his questions. When it was over, Busby hit the off switch. 'So much for him. Nobody'll believe anything *he* says from now on, eh?'

Purkiss looked at him and shook his head. 'Maybe, Geoff, maybe not. I dunno though. He's been stirring it some more. Just had a bell from our man at the M.o.D.' He stopped, deliberately goading Busby. Donaldson smirked and Busby knew, with a sudden leap in his aggression level, that the other man had already been let in on the secret.

'So? What's he say?'

'Challis sent them a letter saying he had information for them about us. They're inclined to think it goes with the pink elephants, but can we take the risk?' He looked long and hard at Busby. Then he handed round another beer and turned his gaze to Donaldson. 'So come on then, Martin, what's next on the agenda?'

Donaldson clasped his fingers behind his head and leaned back in his chair. 'We're squeaky clean on the M.o.D. assessment. We fired a total of . . .'

210

It was like a red rag to a bull. Busby rocked forward in his chair. 'Just hold on there, Martin. What's this WE crap. You might have thought it up, but you were back here in nice cosy Brum while I was doing the naughty bits. Mind if I tell it?'

Donaldson smiled at him infuriatingly. 'Be my guest.'

The others had heard it all before, but they let Busby have his day. The news that the people who did the Ministry of Defence evaluations had bought the whole stunt was, after all, quite a special moment.

'Worked like a charm,' said Busby. 'We only had twelve and we fired eleven of 'em. The other bugger stuck in the tube. Nearly had us, that one. After each firing, it was all about timing. We had the radio net on and we were picking targets just before arty or the multiple rockets took 'em out anyway.'

'Couldn't have been easy, Geoff.'

'Too right, Spence, but the old pals act helped a bit. I made sure we were near an arty battery where I knew the gunnery control bloke. It went a bit funny two or three times and I got 'em to bend their field of fire a bit for us. We were going for troop and vehicle concentrations. Some places the targets were so big, fucking Dodgem could probably have hit them without help.'

'Well, don't be like that, Geoffrey.' Purkiss wagged an admonishing finger. 'It's going to be a fucking good system one day.'

'One day, sure. Anyway, then we used the shotgun trick . . .'

'My trick,' put in Donaldson smoothly.

'Well . . . yeah. Anyway, we had the pellets with the isotopes loaded into shotgun cartridges. All the M.o.D. knew was we were putting radioactive pellets in the Dodgem warheads so they could do the assessment

afterwards just by running clickers over the targets.
Anyway, the thing was, we had to get in there right after
the bombardment. That was the dodgy bit. I had to go
looking for dead targets and bits of wreckage in the right
place and blast them with the pellets. Fucking hairy it was.
I thought I was surrounded at one point. Had twenty
Iraqis all round me but all they wanted to do was surrender.'

'No one saw you doing it?'

'Nah.'

Chapter Twenty

Monday July 22nd 1991

They took the tape to Television Centre for a viewing on Monday afternoon. David didn't want to go at all. Wise in the ways of BBC committees, he knew no good would come of it and there was a better way to handle it. Nick didn't want to go either, but Bertram Glass was halfway through some high-level contract renegotiation with the mandarins of Wood Lane and was playing all kinds of devious, buttering-up games in which the straightforward demands of making a good programme came way down the priority list. It wasn't a final cut. The edges were still rough. The start was right, but there was a sequence in the middle which didn't work as well as it should and needed an extra shot or two to be slotted in.

They'd been working on it, flat out, for the whole week. Some films come together almost by themselves, others have to be wrestled into submission. Two factors combined to make this one more difficult than most. Nick persisted in staging a last-ditch attempt to dilute David's message, to run at least some of the suppressed images of the devastation of the Iraqi front line. The thaw in their relationship looked temporary, however, as David responded by disagreeing even more violently than before. Seeing the pictures again brought back in spades his hatred of what the Iraqis did to Yanna. That led to difficulty number two. It was hard to accommodate that degree of raw passion in a film which was meant to be about the mechanics of war. At first the searing words of David's voice track jarred oddly with the impersonal, megabuck technological images of the film.

That gradually drove the film in an odd direction. It became a hymn to surgical war, a glorification of smart weaponry. It was, finally, vintage Challis, a punchy script which was, after many rewritings, beautifully matched to the pictures. It started with a shot so well known that it could have been boring – the view from the nose of a smart bomb being guided slap into the middle of a Baghdad bridge. But fading in and out of that shot, over and over again, was another image – World War II aerial footage of a thousand-bomber raid on Germany, the sky black with a rainstorm of bombs falling haphazardly on a city.

Over that came David's voice, with that special, hard, important edge in it which he could produce when the subject required it: 'Desert Storm. The first moral war. Might and right, hand in hand, empowered by modern electronics. Now the overthrow of dictators need no longer bring devastation to their cowed subjects.' After that, up came *Double Exposure*'s theme music over pictures of a broken bridge, with normal life going on around it, mixing to black and white footage of the abandoned rubble of Berlin in 1945.

Nick had fought it all the way. He had reminded David of the tape he had destroyed, of the other images of the supposedly surgical war. He had tried to show him the pictures they had shot of the land campaign. He got no-where. David became more taciturn as he went on and Glass seemed entirely happy at the way the film was going. For a brief moment Nick thought he had made some progress, when David accepted they couldn't do the film without some reference to the Amiriya shelter catastrophe,

214

but when Nick saw that part of the script, David had written it as if it were simply the necessary exception which proved an altogether admirable rule.

The pressures of programme-making held sway in the end. Sitting in a darkened cutting-room either side of the picture editor, endlessly laying and relaying shots to make sequences work smoothly, trimming words from sentences to make them fit, picking just the right bit of an interview to stand by itself and make its point, the complexity of the process and the shortage of time combined to push things David's way. When it came down to it, the film had to be made and it was quite clear that if it wasn't made David's way, it wasn't going to be made at all. Nick hoped that the other half of the show, a film made in New York, might serve to balance it, but knowing his fellow-countrymen's attitude to the Gulf conflict he doubted that very much.

They agreed on the ending, however. It was a two-minute tribute to Yanna which David had made part of the film, the pictures of her which Ian had shot in quiet moments and the voice-over which David knew syllable by syllable: 'We cannot end this film without paying tribute to Yanna Le Bihan, who came into the desert as part of our crew, and left her life behind there, one of so many victims of the cruelty of Saddam Hussein's Republican Guard. Yanna was the only journalist on the Allied side to die during the war. We do not know exactly how or why she died, but we do know that the brutal manner of her death bore the hallmarks of the Republican Guards' disciplinary squads, who were charged with preventing mass desertions among the conscripted troops. We also know that, at the time of her death, she was acting out of concern for the fate of those same conscripted troops. Yanna was just one victim of Saddam Hussein's regime, but to those of us who had the privilege and the joy of her company, she

215

stands for all the others whose deaths have gone un-marked.'

David and Nick found themselves fighting on a united front, though, when Glass suddenly announced that he had agreed to show it to the BBC two days before trans-mission.

'Why, Bertram? They okayed the idea. They've seen the script. They don't normally want a preview until the day. For God's sake, we're still working on it.'

Glass got pompous. 'Reasons, David. Reasons of my own. It would be, let us say, politic, to show it to them now.'

'Tell them to stuff it,' said Nick. 'We're working our asses off to get it done. We don't need any extra hassle.'

'I'm afraid Nick's right, Bertram. You know very well it's asking for trouble. They're bound to want changes. They always do. The only way they can feel like pro-gramme makers is by screwing us around. Why not tell them we'll show it to them Wednesday morning, when the final cut's finished.'

'No,' said Glass petulantly. 'They're paying the bills. They want to see it. We're going in half an hour.' He went out of the cutting-room, then stuck his head back round the door in time to intercept an upturned finger Nick had been thrusting towards his retreating back. He looked startled, and Nick swung his arm up, trying to make it look as if he'd simply been combing his hair with his fingers. 'Oh, er, Nick,' he said, 'try to borrow a jacket from somewhere, would you?'

In the taxi David knew they were heading for an un-pleasant experience. Glass had no further interest in support-ing him now that his contract was over; he had every in-terest in rolling over backwards to the people who paid for the programme. 'Listen, Bertram, they're doing this be-cause they're worried about political sensitivity. They know

216

there's an election coming, maybe even this autumn. They're not exactly the bravest people in the world at the moment. We mustn't let them bully us.'

From the taxi's jump seat, crammed into a researcher's tweed jacket which was at least a size too small, a borrowed tie contrasting uneasily with his lumberjack shirt, Nick guffawed. 'If that's what it is, no problem. The Conservatives will be begging to borrow it for a Party Political Broadcast.'

The head of the department had been called away suddenly to an urgent meeting, they were told. No one seemed to be expecting them. In the end they showed the film in a spare cutting-room to one of the head's deputies, who seemed to be in his late twenties at most. He spoke with the slow and artificial cadences of one who felt he had great wisdom to impart. At the end he pursed his lips and steepled his fingertips. They waited, unwillingly but by necessity, for his verdict.

'Ye-es,' he said. 'I confess to feeling just a shade unhappy about the run of the argument in the middle.' They looked at him. 'It's just I think we've done Amiriya to death,' he went on, and Nick winced. 'I don't think you have to make a meal of that all over again.'

David looked at Nick a little smugly, but that didn't last long. 'One other thing,' the man said, 'and here I think I must put my foot down. This strange thing on the end. The bit about the girl. A trifle out of place, just a touch mawkish, don't you think?'

'Yes, maybe you have a point,' Glass started, but David interrupted him with steel in his voice.

'No, you don't,' he said. 'It's a perfectly proper tribute to include. Whatever else changes, that stays.'

The deputy department head was taken aback, but authority was new to him and his spine was made of marshmallow.

'Well, I suppose you could say it gives a little *frisson* to the ending. It just feels rather, shall we say, personal.'

'*Frisson?*' David started. Glass cut him off.

'Suppose we just did it as a caption in the end credits?'

'Yes, fine,' said the man.

'Certainly not,' said David. 'Change anything else you like, but unless that stays in, you'll have to find someone else's voice because I'm not putting the final track on it.'

In the taxi on the way back Glass was full of weary recriminations. 'You don't understand what's at stake, David. You can't go rampaging around like that. They're the ones who call the shots.'

David shrugged, lost in fresh misery, staring out of the window. Nick pulled off his tie and inspected the split that had opened up in the seam of the borrowed jacket when he had flexed his shoulders. He grinned. 'Call the shots? That guy's barely out of nappies. He wouldn't know a shot if it landed in his Sugar Puffs.'

Wednesday July 24th 1991

Transmission day came without further incident. The final polish was put on the film. Some extra sound effects were added for sections where the real acts of war seemed just a shade too distant. Everyone except Nick professed themselves satisfied. David was emotionally and physically exhausted. He shunned Bertram Glass's company until the evening, when everyone concerned attended an obligatory gathering in Glass's plush office to watch the film go out. By that time, as tiredness sapped the anger which had guided David, little doubts began to surface. He watched the film objectively for the first time and wondered whether it might not, after all, be flawed. However, Ian's camera work had been truly superb, and the combination of David's scripting skills and the persuasive steamroller of his voice mixed to form a blindingly powerful end-product. In the crowd of backslappers afterwards he wasn't about to admit to any second thoughts, and anyway only Nick would have had a clue what he was talking about.

As soon as the film ended, the office phone started ringing with well-wishers. There was even a call from a senior minister's PA passing on the minister's appreciation. That added to David's secret qualms, but he didn't let them show. Bertram Glass's secretary, a good-looking Sloane, volunteered to cook dinner for him, but he disentangled himself and headed back to his flat as fast as he could. There had been no call from Duncan or Josie and that left him feeling let down. He moped around for a while, then, feeling childishly sorry for himself, decided to call them.

The phone rang several times. Eventually a strange man's voice answered, a voice he couldn't quite place. For a moment he thought he had the wrong number. 'Hello? I'm sorry, I was trying to reach Duncan,' he said.

There was a slight pause, then the man said, 'Who is it speaking, please?'

'This is David Challis,' he answered, slightly annoyed. 'Who's that?'

The voice took on a different, less cautious tone. 'Hello. This is George Middleton,' and he remembered the old man. 'I'll just get Mrs Challis for you.'

Then Josie's voice came on the phone, low and full of tears. 'David? I'm sorry. Oh, God. He's dead. Duncan's dead.'

Chapter Twenty-one

Thursday July 25th 1991

David was fighting leaden eyelids when he reached the open moorland beyond Kirkwhelpington. The white line of the A696 suddenly divided in front of him as his eyes crossed, and he snapped fully awake as the car swerved. He shook his head and decided to stop again, pulling into the side of the road and getting out to pace up and down, drawing the cold morning air into his lungs to try to fight off the fatigue. Nearly there, he thought. Just as well. He was having to stop every fifteen minutes now and he couldn't have stood much more.

Walking back to the car, looking east, he saw the first line of pink dawn in the sky towards the coast. It struck him with violent poignancy that this was the first day in thirty-four years that Duncan would not see. The misery, kept at bay by the purposeful act of driving, hit him then. He got back in the Jensen and sat still, collecting himself for a couple of minutes until he felt lethargy stealing up on him. Then, with the window right down to give him a cold draught, he started it up and got back on to the road.

He'd gone another five miles, driving faster now on the sweeping open roads, using the adrenalin to help fight the tiredness, when he had to brake hard into a tricky left-hander. He was concentrating on the road, correcting an incipient slide with a twitch of the big steering-wheel, when he saw the tyre marks on the outside of the bend, the glass and the broken stonework, and he knew this had to be the place.

He pulled off the road after the bend and looked at the map. He was just short of a hamlet called Raylees. The sky was lightening rapidly. He walked back. It was a deceptively sharp bend and the outside had a stone wall protecting a steep drop into a copse of trees. There was a hole in the walling and a swathe of damage down through the smaller trees on the edge, ending at the shattered stump of a larger one. The trunk had been dragged away, presumably to let the rescuers get at the crushed car. He could see signs of the efforts they must have made, the efforts that had done no good. He squatted on the ground. There were bits of trim and glass all around and a section of plastic grill carrying a broken Volvo badge.

That kept him awake for the last handful of miles. He drove quietly up the driveway to the house, intending to sneak in without waking anyone, but the door opened before he'd even stopped the car and Josie appeared wearing track suit trousers and a loose sweater, the baggy coverings of grief when all you want is warm clothing and it doesn't matter any more what it looks like. They didn't say anything, just held each other on the step for a minute or two until she shivered and they went inside.

There was a log fire burning in the sitting-room and Josie put a finger to her lips and pointed silently. George Middleton was sitting in an armchair, with a rug over his lap, fast asleep. They went into the kitchen and she put the kettle on.

'He's been so sweet,' she said. 'I couldn't sleep so he decided to stay up and keep me company. He's such a wise man. He was telling me all about the history around here. It was terribly exciting, everyone taking shelter in their

221

peel towers and bastle-houses, and raiders all over the place, then suddenly he stopped in mid-sentence and just went fast asleep.'

'I wish you'd slept too,' he said.

'I couldn't. I just couldn't think of you trying to stay awake all the way up in that old monster of yours.' She paused. 'It's silly, I thought something would happen to you too if I nodded off. I felt like I had to stay on guard. Not that there was much danger of going to sleep.'

'You'll have to sleep sometime.'

'I know. The doctor's given me some pills. I'll sleep when you do, but I've got to tell you about it first.'

'No, you haven't. Not now. I've already seen where it happened. Sleep first.'

She didn't argue. She went upstairs in front of him, looking so like a lost child that he wished he had a teddy bear to give her to keep the nightmares away. He watched her swallow the pill and sat in the room with her until she was asleep, then he went and crawled into the guest bed and finally let his own eyes close.

In what seemed like no time at all he was being shaken awake. He opened his eyes, disoriented and muzzy-headed, to find George Middleton standing there with a cup of tea. 'I'm sorry to wake you, Mr Challis, but I'm afraid the police are here and I thought it better to let Mrs Challis sleep on.'

'Yes. Yes, of course. What time is it?'

'Quarter past ten. In the morning, that is,' added the old man, seeing the look of uncertainty on David's face. He went to the door. 'Shall I tell them you'll be down in a few minutes?'

'I'll put some clothes on and come right down.'

It was a businesslike inspector with a WPC. They were standing in the kitchen when David walked in.

222

'I'm sorry to disturb you, Mr Challis. I understand you've been driving all night. I'm very sorry about your brother. I didn't have the pleasure of meeting him, but it must have come as a great shock.'

'Yes. Thank you.'

The inspector looked at the pad he was holding. 'The accident happened down the A696 on a bend just beyond the second Elsdon turning. I don't know whether you're familiar with the area?'

'Yes. I saw the spot this morning, on my way here.'

'The car's been taken away for examination, sir, but there's no sign of any mechanical defect. I'm afraid it took the brunt of the impact on its roof. It must have tipped as it went over the edge. Those cars are pretty tough, but I don't think anything would have helped really. It seems your brother was travelling at pretty high speed. He'd passed a lorry driver a few miles before who said he seemed to be having a bit of a burn-up with another car, weaving around a bit, he said.'

'I see.'

'He wouldn't have suffered, sir. It would seem the direct cause of death was a broken neck and a crushed windpipe.' The inspector said it gently and impersonally, but it hurt David to hear it. The inspector paused for a second, looking at him, then went on. 'His blood alcohol ratio was just a little over the legal limit, I'm afraid, sir. Do you mind if I ask you if your brother drank regularly?'

'Yes, I'm afraid he did, inspector. But he was very used to it. He's been like that for a long time. It might have been illegal, but he was still capable of driving fairly safely when anyone else I know would have been under the table.'

'Well, that's as may be, sir, but it looks as though that played the major part on this occasion, I'm afraid.'

They made arrangements for formal identification, and

left. David went back into the kitchen and found George Middleton there. He'd clearly been waiting tactfully somewhere else in the house. 'I'll be on my way for now,' he said, 'If there's anything I can do, just call. My number's on the board over there.'

'I'm very grateful to you,' said David.

'I'm so sorry for Mrs Challis, and for you of course. I do mean it. If there's anything at all.'

He went quietly off in his old Riley, its paintwork worn thin by too much polishing. It was comforting to know that at least someone out there, in the world beyond the end of the drive, knew and cared. David went back inside, feeling very tired again. He went back to bed, set his alarm for 2.00 p.m. and was soon asleep. His mental clock woke him just before the alarm did, and he showered to clear his head. He went downstairs and, while he was making a sandwich, Josie came in, looking still three-parts asleep.

'David? Have you been up long?'

He gave her a hug and told her about the police and what the inspector had said.

'But Duncan had sworn off alcohol, or at least he said he had.' Her voice sounded indignant.

'When was that?'

'Well, only at the weekend, but I think he meant it. We went round together and got rid of every bottle in the place. He was quite shaken up by what happened on the show.'

They sat down at the table. It seemed better to focus on something definite, so he gently said, 'Why don't you tell me what happened yesterday?'

She thought. 'Well, he spent quite a long time on the phone in the morning. He seemed pretty pleased with himself. I asked him what he was doing, but he was a bit mysterious about it.' She sighed and took a sip of coffee,

224

then frowned and went on. 'Someone called him after lunch on the line in his office. He seemed to be expecting it. I went to answer it, but he stopped me. He said it was the one he was expecting. Then I saw him out of the window, loading a box into the back of the Volvo. He came in and told me he had to go to a meeting for a couple of hours.'

'He didn't say where?'

'I didn't ask. I was on the phone to the plumber. I just waved at him.' She closed her eyes. 'I didn't even see him drive off.'

David reached across the table and squeezed her hand. 'Then what?'

'Well, he just ... he just didn't come back. I didn't worry too much until your programme was about to start, then I thought it was a bit funny. I knew he meant to see it. Then the police arrived and told me. George was right after them. He'd been on the road and he'd seen the car ...' She stopped.

The mechanics of death took over for a while then. There were phone calls to friends and their small handful of relations, undertakers to find, arrangements to make. It was dreadful but numbing at the same time. Informing people was the worst. It was hard to keep control, as if telling it made it new all over again and, anyway, no one at the other end knew what to say once the first shocked reaction was past. By the time that was done, it was early evening and David was groggy with fatigue. He could see Josie was starting to crumble.

'What we need is a drink,' she said, and laughed with a touch of hysteria. 'Pity I've thrown them all away.' Then she held up one finger. 'Ah! Not all. If you feel like going through the bin, there's the end of a bottle of Scotch somewhere. I found it in the bloody car yesterday before he went. He said he'd brought it up from the flat and forgotten it.'

David went out to the stable yard at the back, where the bins were kept. He didn't have to look far. Jammed down among the potato peelings and coffee grounds, there was a nearly empty bottle of Glenmorangie, Duncan's favourite Scotch, with a couple of inches still in the bottom. He took it inside, staring at it, rinsed the muck off under the cold tap and split its meagre contents between a couple of glasses, hoping there would be enough to have the desired effect.

'Here you are,' he said, holding one out to Josie.

'It feels, I don't know, sort of disloyal,' she said, looking at it doubtfully, 'after getting him to stop.' But she drank it. They flopped into neighbouring armchairs. David sipped his, feeling the warmth in his throat. Neither of them said anything for a while, then Josie broke the silence.

'The thing is, really, I lost him a long time ago.'

David was startled. 'What do you mean?'

'Well. The drink thing. He was quite like a stranger in the end. Not the Duncan I married. That's why it feels so ... odd. I keep thinking of the way he used to be.' She looked at him very seriously. 'Isn't it strange, I'm grieving for someone I used to have and then didn't have any more, and you're grieving for someone who ... someone who you didn't quite have and wish you had done.'

He looked at her and unexpectedly she started laughing. She's drunk, he thought. Then, to his surprise, he started laughing too, and that was the last completely coherent thought he had that evening. Later he could remember various parts of it – Josie trying earnestly to explain to him that she'd cared for Duncan and him equally but differently; him, just as earnestly, telling her he had only given her up because he felt his little brother needed her more.

Then a silence in which he'd tried unsuccessfully to stand up, broken by Josie suggesting in serious, slurred words that she would try crying for Yanna and he could concentrate on Duncan, which led into more strange laughter followed by unstoppable tears.

He opened his eyes, with a painful effort, to a grey morning. He was in an unfamiliar bed. He lifted his head and saw he was in Duncan and Josie's room and the bedroom light was still on. He was under the duvet, but he felt constricted and stiff. Josie was lying next to him, tucked into his shoulder with her arm round him. He had all his clothes still on, down to his shoes. He groaned and looked at her. It made things just a little simpler to find that she had all her clothes on too, though she'd kicked off her shoes, one of which was wedged painfully under his leg.

She opened her eyes, frowned in surprise, tried to sit up and fell back clutching her head. 'God. What happened?' she said.

'I don't know. We must have had a few too many.'

They got out of bed, constrained and a little embarrassed. In the kitchen Josie put the coffee on. They were both moving slowly and carefully. She was thinking.

'We didn't, you know. We didn't have a few too many. We only had one glass each. That's all there was.'

'You're right. What the hell happened then? Maybe it was because we were both so tired.'

She shook her head slightly. 'When I'm tired it always seems to stop it working, not the other way round.'

David got the bottle from the side-table where he'd left it. He opened it. It was completely empty. He sniffed it, but it smelt perfectly normal.

'Did you say it was in Duncan's car?'

'Yes. He drove back from London with it. When I first found it, I thought he might have been swilling it on the way back, but I think he was so shocked by the show he hadn't touched a drop.'

'Nevertheless,' said David, thinking. 'it could easily be the same Scotch he drank before the show. There's no way that's normal malt whisky.'

'You think he's got hold of something extra strong and put it in that bottle so it looks better?'

'No,' said David, 'that's not what I think at all. I've tried most of the world's fire-waters, from Nick Nielsen's moonshine to Stroh rum and Norwegian home brew. None of those tastes remotely like Glenmorangie. I think maybe it was doctored.'

For a moment, as he said it, it sounded absurdly fanciful, but then an overwhelming sense of the truth of it came over him. They stared at each other as the chilling realization started to dawn that Duncan's problems, and his death, might have had a less straightforward explanation.

'Listen, Josie,' he went on after a second, 'just tell me all over again what happened before Dunk went off in the car.'

She went over the phone calls once more and the box he'd loaded into the Volvo.

'Come with me,' he said, and led her into Duncan's offices. His business line was separate from the phone line in the house.

'I wonder who he was phoning?' said Josie.

'Let's find out,' said David, looking at the phone. 'It stores the last number you call.' He picked up the receiver and pressed the redial button. It rang twice, then a female secretary's breezy voice said, 'Bamco. Mr Busby's office.'

Chapter Twenty-two

Friday July 26th 1991

Inspector Percival buzzed through for coffee and looked at his visitors with a slightly jaundiced eye. They'd gone to all the trouble to track him down to Ponteland, which showed their determination. When he was off his usual patch, the desk at Hexham wouldn't normally have handed out his whereabouts. Mind you, that was no surprise considering who the brother was. He recognized him from the box, and that was what reporters like him were supposed to be good at. It didn't make much sense, though.

'Mr Challis, I have to say I've always found there's a lot more to be gained by going for the simplest explanations in life. I know it's not a very pleasant thought for you to dwell on, but death by drunken driving is a distressingly familiar occurrence to us.'

David took the bottle from a bag and put it on the table in front of him. 'I know, but the fact is we had one small drink each last night from this bottle and it had a quite extraordinary effect.'

'Can you be absolutely sure it was only one drink? It would have been very understandable under the circumstances . . .'

'We're quite sure,' said Josie firmly. 'That's all there was left in it and there was nothing else in the house.'

The Inspector took the bottle and tilted it, holding it up to the light. 'There's not going to be much to go on, I'm afraid.'

'If I might make a suggestion,' said David politely.

'Of course.'

'We're entirely certain that my brother's last call was to this Mr Busby at Bamco. Wouldn't it at least be worth finding out what that was about?'

'Did he have any business normally with Bamco?'

'He made videos for them sometimes.'

'Would that not be a sufficient explanation then?'

'Inspector, I'm fairly sure he had a major disagreement with them. I think he was taking lots of their videotapes back to them. He'd done a deal of some sort. All the tapes that were usually in his studio aren't there any more.'

'Had you seen them recently?'

'Well, not for a while, but he loaded a box into his car just before he left.'

The inspector turned back to Josie. 'Mrs Challis, you didn't see what was in the box?'

'No, but it could have been the tapes.'

'Would you have any idea why someone at Bamco, which is after all a pretty big, well-established company, might have wished Mr Challis harm?'

David took a breath. This was the difficult one. He'd been wondering how to answer it in a way that wouldn't have the inspector leaping straight to the conclusion that he was off his trolley. 'I think there was some friction between my brother and some of the people at Bamco. I think he had video footage which cast doubt on the effectiveness of one of their weapons systems.'

The inspector had a look in his eye which indicated that he had indeed leapt to the conclusion David feared.

'I think I should tell you,' he said, 'that we have already made some checks. Mr Challis had been stopped for speeding earlier yesterday evening on his way back through Newcastle. He wasn't breathalysed, but he would have

230

been if the officers hadn't been called away to something more urgent. He was returning in the Otterburn direction. Do you have any idea why he might have been in Newcastle?'

'That fits. Bamco have a big factory there,' said Josie. 'He often went there for meetings. Their head office is in Birmingham, but they're always using the firing ranges up here, so a lot of the work he did was at this end with the Munitions Division.'

The inspector sniffed. 'I'm well aware of Bamco's factory. There's a great many other people in Newcastle as well. In point of fact, the Bamco factory is at Dunston. Your husband was stopped heading west between Gosforth and Kenton Bar. It's a different direction.'

It ground to a halt then, and Josie looked so miserable that his heart softened a bit. He was a kind man, but he was also down-to-earth, and tales of the arms trade were a lot harder to swallow than a simple case of another boozer turning the wheel too late. 'I will telephone Bamco,' he said. 'I'll do that soonest. I'll be in touch.'

'And the bottle?' asked David.

'We'll have to see about the bottle, Mr Challis,' said the inspector, and after they left he sat there looking at it doubtfully for quite some time before he reached for the phone. There was nothing discernible left in it. He shook his head gloomily as he waited for someone to answer.

David and Josie did a sad tour, which involved a great deal of driving between offices in different towns and villages. The undertakers, the Registrar of Births, Marriages and Deaths, and the mortuary. When they drew up outside, David turned to Josie. 'I won't be long,' he said. 'You stay here.'

231

'No, we'll both go,' she said.

'There's no point, love.'

'Yes, there is. I'm not leaving you to do it on your own.'

When they came out, David had his arm round her shoulder and they were both very quiet. They sat in the car for some time without David making any move to start the engine. 'It wasn't really Duncan, was it?' said Josie. 'He'd gone.'

They must have cleaned him up a bit, thought David. He didn't look too bad. He thought back to the sights he'd seen in the desert, but one dead, distorted brother was far, far worse than a thousand charred, shattered enemy soldiers. There was only one image in his memory that compared in any way, the nightmare image of Yanna when they unzipped her bag, and he'd been ruthlessly suppressing that one ever since. Now he couldn't keep it at bay, it mixed with Duncan, the white face and the burnt one. The burnt one.

'David,' said Josie, alarmed. 'Oh, David,' and he felt the tears pour down his cheeks. It brought out new strength in her. She seemed to sense what was going on in his head. She didn't ask him anything, she just held him tightly, murmuring, 'Poor David. It's all too much. Poor David.'

He was angry with himself and got back under control quite soon. 'I'm sorry,' he said.

'No, I'm sorry. You've had twice as much to bear.'

'Let's go.'

Their next port of call was the tiny town of Bellingham, and they got there with a quarter of an hour to spare before their appointment, so they found a snack bar down a little side alley and went in for a cup of coffee. They were sitting at the table when Josie looked beyond David and he heard an avuncular voice greet her.

'Mrs Challis. I was coming to see you later on. How are you?'

'David, this is Dr Lyle, our GP. Doctor, this is Duncan's brother.'

'Yes, indeed. I know your face well.' Lyle was an old-style tweedy country doctor somewhere in his sixties.

'Will you have a coffee?' said David.

'No, but I'll join you for a moment if I may. How well did you sleep last night?'

'I took your pill in the end.'

'Take another one tonight.'

David had a thought. 'Are those pills safe with alcohol?'

The doctor paused. 'I wouldn't recommend mixing them, but they're not barbiturates. They wouldn't do any major harm.'

'Doctor, could Duncan have been taking any medication which could have increased the effect of alcohol?'

'Not that I know of, I'm afraid. Of course there are quite a lot of things, the powerful analgesics, like Distalgesic. Then there's the dihydrocodeine group, like Paramol, and of course there's Ativan and Valium.'

'What do they do?'

'Well, they're the very devil if you mix them with alcohol. It can be like drinking ten times as much.'

'I see.'

The doctor peered at him. 'But these are prescription drugs. Your brother wasn't taking any of those. Not through me anyway. I'd remember. Why do you ask?'

'Just an idea. Never mind.'

There was to be one more surprise that day and it wasn't a pleasant one. Their last appointment was with Duncan's bank manager to sort out immediate financial affairs. Josie hadn't been able to give David very much advance information.

233

'Well, he's always made sure there's money in a joint account for household things.'

'What about the rest?'

'David, you know your brother. He was a law unto himself. He was always doing conjuring tricks, juggling debts between accounts. He said that was the way to keep the creditors at bay. I have no idea how much there is, except that there isn't much.'

There was less than that. The bank manager was polite, concerned, and very worried about who was going to pay off Duncan's overdraft.

'But surely his life insurance is going to cover any immediate problem?' asked David. One thing he did know was that when Duncan had bought the house, against David's advice, he had at least twisted his little brother's arm into getting expensive and wide-ranging life cover.

The bank manager writhed like a worm on a hook. 'I'm very sorry, Mr and Mrs . . .' – realizing it sounded wrong, he tried again – 'er, Mr Challis and Mrs Challis, but there was a problem there. You see, Mr Challis came to see me three months ago about his overdraft. He'd kept saying that he was expecting a lot of money in, but then he told me it hadn't materialized yet. We had to find some way of cutting down the outgoings, so in the end I'm afraid we had to agree that he couldn't keep up the insurance premium payments. He was having enough trouble meeting the mortgage.'

They stared at him as it sank in. 'You mean you advised him to let his life insurance lapse?' said David in a tone of unmistakable menace.

'Well, no. It wouldn't be fair to say I advised him. It was his own decision,' said the bank manager, flustered. 'I could only go so far in drawing the alternatives to his attention. I did say he should try to find a different solution.'

David suddenly felt sick. He wasn't sure, looking at her, whether Josie had yet realized the full implication of this.

'So exactly what is the situation at present?' he asked.

'Your brother's main account was overdrawn by £34,832 at the close of business today. He has a monthly standing order for his mortgage of just over £2,000. Other standing orders total a little bit more than £700 a month. I should tell you we have a second mortgage to secure the overdraft, but I'm afraid that probably doesn't leave much, if anything, in the way of unencumbered assets. The household account is overdrawn by £400, which, I'm afraid, is in breach of the agreed limit.'

'Do you know of any other assets?' David asked.

'I'm afraid not. I was rather hoping you did. There does seem to be a pressing shortage of immediate funds.' The bank manager looked at them and added, 'I expect you'll want to take stock. Perhaps we should arrange another meeting?'

David saw the anguish in Josie's eyes and pulled out a cheque-book. He made out a cheque for £5,000 and handed it to the bank manager. 'Pay this into the joint account, please. That should take care of the immediate situation.' Inside, despite it all, he found himself relishing the theatre of the moment, the temporary securing of the moral advantage over a bank manager who only believed in liquid funds. Josie gave him a look of gratitude, but it was no kind of permanent answer and he left the bank feeling intensely depressed.

They got back late and tired and sat in the kitchen, their spirits in their boots, having a cup of tea.

'I wasn't sure about the house to start with,' said Josie. 'I thought it was just one of Duncan's grandiose ideas, but I love it now. I'm going to lose it, aren't I?'

David searched for something helpful to say, but he

couldn't see an answer and it was quite clear that even selling it was going to be difficult in the current market. Then the phone rang.

It was a far-away, distorted voice and he had trouble making it out. Eventually it cleared a little.

'Is that Duncan? It's Anthony Marshall, Duncan, I'm trying to find David. It's urgent.'

'This *is* David, Anthony. Where on earth are you?'

'I'm dealing with the Kurds. I'm up in the bloody mountains on a satellite phone. It might go down any second. Bloody glad I found you. How are Josie and Duncan?'

David considered. It was too big a question to answer under the circumstances. 'What's the problem, Anthony?'

There was a long crackle and a whistle, and he thought he'd lost the call, but it came back after a few seconds, louder than before. 'I'm still clearing up a few things about the remaining prisoners. I've had a message up here. Seems the Saudis found an Iraqi among their lot with a cassette of film in his pocket. There's a stick-on label from the film processing company on the outside. It's got your name on it.'

'How?' said David, remembering in the same breath the films he'd given Yanna.

'That's what I wanted to talk about. He's told a story that ties him into your girl's death. I've got to look into it. I've had a hell of a job finding you.'

'I'm sorry. Something unexpected came up here.'

'I've got a translated statement. Well, it's a transcript of the interrogation, really. I want to send it to you. We've got the gear this end, portable fax I can hook up. Question is, have you got a fax anywhere nearby at your end?'

'Yes. There's one here.' He covered the mouthpiece. 'What's the fax number, Josie?'

He passed it on, said goodbye and they quickly went to

check that the machine was switched on. Within three minutes the lights came on and the paper began to roll. It started with a handwritten note from Anthony Marshall telling David it was to be regarded as confidential and saying he was inclined to believe the story. He said the circumstances made it necessary for them to have the film developed at that end, but he would make sure it was sent to David as soon as possible. What followed was badly typed, badly copied and had suffered in the transmission.

There was a preamble:

Subject is a 24-year-old Iraqi named Naji Awatif. His pay book shows him to be a member of 26th Division. He is a conscript and entries show he has been subject to punishment for attempted desertion. He was part of a unit (no officers) that surrendered to VII Corps after spending two days fleeing from the Allied advance.

It was three pages long, close-typed. David skimmed through, then stopped.

Interrogator: When did you leave your position?

Awatif: Some of the officers left four days before the attack. Many of them died when the fire-bombs were dropped. They had a bunker. We did not, but the fire filled up the bunker. My friends were killed too. I was burnt, see here on my arms. We would not fire our guns because, when we did, the planes came to attack us. Then the rest of the officers left. We had no food but, thanks to the grace of Allah, we had water from the rain. We saw helicopters dropping soldiers near the sandbanks and we knew the tanks would come, so we left in the last vehicle.

Interrogator: Where did you go?

Awatif: I do not know. Just onward to get away until we had no more fuel. Then we walked, but Ali was shot by an officer who stopped us. Then we knew he was Republican Guard.

237

We stopped still and hid in a bunker, but then the planes came so we came out in case they dropped more fire-bombs. The Republican Guard tanks left and we waited for the American soldiers. We had picked up the pieces of paper which told us how to surrender ourselves and we talked about how we should hold our hands up, and whether we would be shot.

Interrogator: Where did you get the film?

Awatif: I did not steal it. I did not.

Interrogator: I just want to know where you got it.

Awatif: The sand was blowing and I could not see. I heard engines and I thought it was Americans. I stayed still and a truck came. I saw two men get out, but they did not see me. They fired a gun, then they kept quiet, then I heard shouting and running. Someone ran past me, but the sand started blowing again. There was another bang and the two men ran near me too. I kept very still. Then there was some flame and then they went away in their truck. I waited until the sand stopped blowing and then I found the body of the woman lying in the sand. The fire was still burning a little. I went quickly away and I saw something green. I picked it out of the sand. This was the film.

Interrogator: How far from her was it?

Awatif: Perhaps ten steps. She might have dropped it or thrown it.

Interrogator: Were these men Republican Guard?

Awatif: No, NO, I tell you. They were not Iraqis at all.

Interrogator: What then?

Awatif: Maybe American, I do not know. I could not see much, but not Iraqis.

Interrogator: Can you be sure?

Awatif: They drove away towards the Americans. Even the Republican Guard would not have done that.

Chapter Twenty-three

Same day

Bad news travels fast in television. On Wednesday night David had left London without telling anyone what had happened or where he was going, but the phone calls he had made to Duncan's friends on Thursday multiplied in the fast-breeder reactor of the media world. The news was passed around with two parts genuine shock mixed, it must be said, with one part titillation. There were many conversations of the 'Have you heard?' type. It reached the Glass Crystal offices late on Thursday afternoon when a producer who had once worked on Duncan's show was rung by his lover, who still did.

He put the phone down, the script in front of him forgotten, thinking rather of who else he could tell. Nick Nielsen came immediately to mind. He got up from his desk and went in search of him. The offices weren't very extensive, but Nick didn't seem to be anywhere. Instead he bumped into Bertram Glass.

'Oh, Bertram, do you know where Nick is by any chance?'

The question wasn't a happy one. Glass had been trying to find Nick and David for a couple of hours. It was typical, he thought, for bloody reporters to think the job was done as soon as their film was screened. That was when the hard work started. There was a whole sheaf of invoices to check, expenses to clear, sheets to be filled in. Glass glared at him. 'No, and I would very much like to. If you happen to find out where he is, would you be so kind as to remind him from me that we are still paying him a salary and in exchange I do expect to see him here during the day.'

'Oh, right. Um, I suppose you've heard about David Challis's brother?'

'The drunk one? No, what's he done now?'

'He's dead. Car accident.'

That stopped him. 'Good God. I suppose he finally had a few too many. Where was this?'

'Somewhere up north.'

'So presumably that's where David has disappeared to.'

'I suppose so.'

'Anyway, if you see Nielsen, tell him I want to see him at once.'

Nick had awarded himself a day off. He had no intention of staying at Glass Crystal any longer. He didn't rate any of the others as highly as he rated David, for all his faults, and he was busy trying to set up an escape route. The work on the film had meant some enforced healthy living, so in the evening he went off to catch up on the dissipation stakes. He was so successful in this that it wasn't until nearly eleven o'clock on Friday morning that he wandered rather uncertainly into the office and was immediately caught by the receptionist.

'Mr Glass wants to see you straight away, Nick.'

'Ah.'

He knocked at Glass's office door and went in.

Glass put down a copy of *Horse and Hound* and quickly picked up a file.

'Where were you yesterday?' he said aggressively.

'I took a day off. Why?'

'You have to ask first, you know. I was looking for you all day.'

'Come on. We worked right through last weekend to get your film out for you. Anyway, what's the panic?'

'You don't seem to realize. Your job doesn't just end there. There's a lot to clear up. I need someone to sign the crew's time sheets. There's all the other bills.'

Nick sighed. 'David and I can knock that off in no time.'

'David? Of course David can't. Not in the circumstances.'

Nick was alarmed. His first thought was that sorrow over Yanna, stirred up by the film, must have got to him. 'What circumstances?'

'Well, his brother, of course. Didn't you know?'

It was a sad and angry Nick Nielsen who made his way down to the basement a few minutes later. His heart went out to David and his fist was longing to go out to Glass. Of all the things he could be doing that morning, Glass's instructions seemed about the lowest priority. There were sixty-eight as yet unsorted tape cassettes in the stuff they had brought back from the Gulf. Glass wanted them viewed and checked. As part of his latest economy drive he wanted the best shots edited on to a few big compilation tapes so that the used cassettes could be wiped and put back to work. Nick doubted the wisdom of reusing tapes which had been through the sandy destruction-test of the Gulf War, but he knew this was more Glass's idea of a punishment than anything else, so he might as well get on with it. He sat down in a vacant editing-room, thinking about David and Duncan, and settled in for a long, boring job.

Later that afternoon, Geoff Busby was hammering north on the motorway. He took a perverse pleasure in the looks he got as the Land Rover raced past other, sleeker vehicles.

241

The ride was hard and the wind roar was deafening, but the power of the stretched Range Rover engine under the bonnet made it tolerable. You could almost see the fuel gauge moving like the minute hand on a clock when you had your foot flat down, but Bamco paid the bills for that and he didn't want a chauffeured company car on this trip, not with so many loose ends to tie up. He didn't feel so much like a bloody civilian, travelling like this. Mind you, he thought, I'm going up and down this bloody road like a yo-yo these days, should be on a 'Frequent Driver' bonus scheme. Southbound yesterday, northbound today. He flashed his lights angrily at a Metro that started to stray into the fast lane in front of him, then the phone squawked and he answered it, casually driving one-handed.

'Mr Busby? Can you hear me all right?'

He suppressed a flash of irritation. His Newcastle secretary wasn't a patch on the one he had in Birmingham. She was nothing to look at and modern technology seemed to be a complete mystery to her. She always started off like that when she called him on the car phone, as if the things couldn't really be expected to work at all and every syllable that got through was some sort of bonus.

'Yeah, course I can hear.'

'You've had an Inspector Percival on, from Hexham Police Station. It's about poor Mr Challis. You know about that, don't you? It's been in the papers.'

The Land Rover jinked slightly, but Busby kept his voice level. 'Yes, I know about it. What did he want?'

'Just a routine inquiry, he said. Do you want his number?'

There she goes again, he thought, thinks I can sit here writing down bloody phone numbers. 'Tell him I'll call him later. Don't let on where I am, Meg, I haven't got time to get dragged into all that. Oh, and call Mr Hanmer for

242

me. Ask him to meet me in the office in an hour and a half.'

In less than an hour he was pulling into his reserved space in the car park. He appreciated the implied indispensability which went with the parking space and the second office set-up, sitting here idle for so much of the time. The gilt was slightly tarnished when he saw the board with Donaldson's name on it in the next space and thought back to the times when there were just two.

Meg was a bored, sallow girl who sometimes helped out in filing when her boss was at the other end. Busby registered Donaldson's new girl as he went past the office. A bit of a looker, he thought sourly. Sleazy. Bet he gets his leg over that.

'Get me a coffee, Meg,' he shouted. 'Did you get hold of Sledge?'

'Mr Hanmer will be here in half an hour, Mr Busby.'

Why does she have to sound like she's whining all the time, he thought, and he picked up the phone to call the inspector's number.

'Hexham Police? Could I speak to Inspector Percival, please? It's Geoff Busby here, from Bamco.'

It was a soft Northumbrian burr which came on the line, but Busby knew the locals well enough not to let that put him off his guard.

'Mr Busby. Thank you for calling. I expect you've heard about the accident to Mr Challis?'

'Yes, I have. A great shock. How can I help you?'

'I understand he did some work for you?'

It struck Busby to wonder why he personally should be the recipient of this call. An outsider would normally have had to penetrate several other layers of the Bamco system and would by rights have wound up with Spencer Purkiss, not him. It racked up his caution another notch.

243

'He did some video work for Bamco from time to time. Not for me personally.'

'I see. Did you have any contact with him recently? Meetings or phone calls?'

'Nothing very special that I can remember. Why do you ask?'

'It's just that your direct line was the last number he called on his phone.'

Bugger, thought Busby. 'I don't know, I'll have to check. He may have talked to my secretary.' He tried a different tack. 'He could be quite difficult, you know, inspector. Bit of a boozer, I'm afraid. He used to hassle us over bills and that.'

The inspector sounded conciliatory. 'Yes, I do understand, Mr Busby. That's the picture I'm getting. It's just that there's a suggestion he may have organized a meeting with someone from your office on Wednesday, possibly returning some video material to you, and it would help us to build up a picture of what happened to him that day.'

'Well, I can check. I doubt it, though. I'm pretty certain we already hold all the video material. He was getting a bit unreliable, you see. It can be a terrible thing, alcohol.'

'Could you give me any idea of what sort of material that would be, Mr Busby?'

Better stamp on this one, thought Busby. He put a hard edge of battlefield command into his voice. 'Inspector Percival, you must understand we're talking about classified material here. I'm afraid I can't discuss that sort of thing on the telephone. In any case I would normally expect to be talking to your Special Branch man about anything in that area and even then only if I was satisfied he needed to know, and it doesn't sound to me as if it's very relevant. Just a drunk driving job, wasn't it?'

As he said it, he wondered if he'd made a mistake. It

244

could just serve to whet the man's appetite, but to his relief the inspector backed off. 'I understand. No need to pursue that one, sir.'

Busby put on a tone of innocent inquiry. 'What makes you ask?'

'Nothing to trouble you, Mr Busby. It's just Mr Challis, that's Mr David Challis, the brother, came to see me with a whole lot of worries about the business. Seems to have a bit of a bee in his bonnet. Sort of thing you get with the bereaved, I'm afraid. They sometimes start thrashing around with all kinds of ideas when they can't accept what's happened.'

'David Challis,' said Busby. 'I didn't know there was a brother. That must be a support for the poor wife, then.'

'Oh, yes, indeed. I dare say you'd recognize him if you saw him. Quite well known. He's the one on TV. The one that was out in the Gulf. His programme was on the night his brother had his accident.'

Damn, thought Busby. 'Oh, right,' he said casually. Better sound concerned. 'By the way,' he said, 'do you know how Mrs Challis is taking it?'

'She was holding up when they came to see me. And of course the brother's staying up here for a bit to see her through.'

Busby drummed his fingers on the desk when he hung up. There was a whole new element here that he didn't like. Less that two days after the event and already there was someone throwing bouncers. A bloody reporter at that. Time to find out how many loose ends Sledge had left around. Then the intercom buzzed at him. His secretary's voice from the outer office said, 'Mr Hanmer is at front reception, Mr Busby.'

'Ask him to hold on there. I'm coming down. If Mr Purkiss or anyone else calls, tell them I've gone out and I'll be back in half an hour.'

They walked down to the banks of the Tyne and stood on the edge of the crumbling concrete. Busby looked at Sledge's balding head with something approaching affection. The long-term equilibrium of Bamco's management team might be tilting, but Sledge's loyalty was still his to command. The same platoon in Aden. Then they'd both been picked for Hereford and done some very murky things together in the old Sports and Social. Sledge had left the SAS before Busby. Gone private. Done a bit in Africa here and there. These days he was on Bamco's payroll in an on-and-off sort of way. He'd got bigger as he got older, but somehow it didn't look like fat on Sledge, more like body armour. A Londoner in Geordie-land, but nobody messed with him, leastways not after they'd taken a good look at him. Officially he did some of the Bamco munitions assessment for them, running riot on the ranges in commando warfare simulations. If the things still fired after Sledge had put them through the old rock and roll, then they'd stand up to anything, Unofficially, he was Busby's private army.

'Give it to me from the top, then.'

'Went a treat, Skip,' said Sledge. 'Met up like you said. Fixed it for a meet over Longbenton way, so there wasn't anything on our patch. 'E was like a kid at Christmas. Couldn't fuckin' wait to hand over the tapes. I give 'im the cheque an' 'e starts grinning for all 'e was worth. Then I brought out the old 'ip flask an' 'e went all dribbly. I give 'im bottoms up, an' I've got me tongue over the 'ole, but 'e thinks I'm drinking. Then I passes it to 'im an' 'e glugs the fuckin' lot. I got a bit worried then, cos it wouldn't take nearly that much to do the trick, an' I though 'e might just flake out then and there, but 'e gets in 'is car an' off 'e goes. Must be 'ardened to it.'

Busby nodded, thinking of that venial little sod Henbest and the bottles he'd been doctoring down at the London flat. Never as strong as this time though.

'And?'

'Well, the thing is, 'e'd only gone just up the road, an' I was hanging back a bit cos 'e was going like a bat out of 'ell an' the Old Bill pulls 'im over for speeding.'

'Yeah?'

'Yeah. I thought fuck it, that's the end of that one. Then I 'as a bit of a brainwave, so I nips into a phone box and dials the old three nines. Tells 'em there's a woman being killed two streets away. Took a bit of a chance, cos there could 'ave been another unit around, but it worked a treat. Only took thirty seconds for them to come on the blower, and the cops took off like there was no tomorrer. Chummy gets back in the motor an' off we go again. I tell yer, 'e's used to knockin' it back, though. Wasn't driving 'alf badly, considering.'

'He was used to it all right.'

'We got clear out in the sticks, an' he's dodging around a bit, but it looks like 'e might get all the way 'ome. There's this bend I knew about, a bit before you get to Otterburn, an' there weren't no more cars around, so I comes up behind 'im as 'e's slowing down and gives 'im a wallop up the arse. I've got bull bars on the front of the Trooper, so I knew I could do it. Bang. Bob's yer uncle. The wall tipped 'im over, right down the bank. Musta bin doin' seventy. Roof first, straight into a tree.'

'Did you stop?'

'Yeah, course. I 'ad to 'elp him along a little bit, but 'e was on the way to croaking. Just 'ad to make sure. I got the cheque off 'im an' I was going to torch it, but I 'eard this truck coming way off so I got out of it.'

'You did well, Sledge.'

'Yeah. Neat.'

'It's not quite over, though.'

'Oh?'

'I had a call from the law. He had a brother and the brother's sniffing around a bit.'

'Want me to snuff 'im?'

'I think two might look a little bit obvious. No, I want to know what he's thinking. He's staying at the house. I think we should be listening in.'

Sledge frowned. 'Full set-up?'

'Only if you can find a safe way into the house, or maybe hook up to a phone junction that's well out of the way. Bloody house is right out in the middle of nowhere, that's the trouble. Otherwise it's the laser job on to the front window-panes, but only if you're absolutely sure you can get close enough without showing up.'

'Good as done.'

Chapter Twenty-four

Saturday July 27th 1991

David woke soon after seven from a tortured night full of confused dreams into the stark realization that this was to be the day of Duncan's funeral. He looked in on Josie. She was sleeping soundly, the duvet slipping diagonally off the bed to leave a leg and an arm showing. Tenderly, like a father, he tucked it back over her, because the wind blowing in through the open window still had a northern chill to it, and stood looking at her for a while. The pills will give her another hour or two, he thought, and feeling the need to blow the cobwebs out of his system he went to find his track suit and headed downstairs for a run. Outside, the grass was wet with dew. The cold air woke him thoroughly and the scent of the moorland pleased some deep level inside him. He started towards the stream valley without thinking, but then remembered the last time he'd been that way, when he'd met Yanna, so much alive, and he veered away sharply as if from a direct physical threat. He ran down the drive instead, up the road and on to the slope in front of the house.

As he got into a rhythm, his mind went crashing back to the fax from the Gulf. What did it tell him? It wasn't enough to go on. Some terrified Iraqi, scared stiff of being implicated, coming up with an unlikely tale to get the investigators off his back. Of course he wouldn't have blamed other Iraqis. He had concocted the story to get himself out of trouble.

249

It didn't read like that, though. He had to admit there was a ring of truth in it that distance and translation couldn't quite filter out. Whatever logic he could conjure up, it still worried him. It worried him a lot. He'd always been one for hunches and gut feelings. He'd made his career out of them to an extent he would be reluctant to admit to anyone else, often letting them guide him, without quite knowing how, in deciding where to be, who to phone. Now those same gut feelings were telling him something in his analysis had been very wrong. He wished he could talk about it with someone else, and Nick came immediately to mind. Why Nick, he asked himself? I've been pretty tough on him, he might not want to listen, but he knew that wasn't so. I'll phone him later on, he thought, when the funeral's out of the way, he won't be up yet anyway. Then he stopped thinking and ran hard, trying to leave the doubts behind, but however hard he pushed himself, the doubts seemed effortlessly to match his stride.

He was wrong about Nick, at least in the sense of his getting-up time. That morning Nick was doing something totally unprecedented for him. He was up early of his own free will and he was going into the office on a Saturday. No one else would be there, and that was the point. On his first trawl through the tapes Nick had found a treasure trove of good, completely untransmitted material – all the footage of the front lines that David hadn't wanted to use, hadn't even wanted to see. It was too good to waste. Nick had no illusions about it. If he just put it on the master tapes it would sit gathering dust in Glass Crystal's archive until one day they too were wiped. He couldn't let that happen. He had no clear idea what use he could put it all to, but he was determined to keep a copy of it for himself so that somewhere, someday, it might see the light of day, flying someone else's flag.

That could only be done when there was no one around, so he let himself into the offices with his key, hoping nobody else would show up for any reasons of their own, and sat down to work.

David had run himself into the ground. He had completed half of the circumference of a wide circle and he stopped, gasping, staring down the slope at the distant house below. He wasn't ready to head back yet. Instead he walked slowly onwards, fighting to get his breath back. There was a grassy-bottomed cutting in front of him and fat rabbits raced away in all directions as he came into view. It looked man-made, some sort of ancient quarry or mine workings perhaps. He slid down the bank into it and walked along the bottom. It was peaceful, cut off from the wind. There was a slope at the end and a little hillock with a hardy, wind-blown tree angling up sideways out of a pile of old masonry.

To occupy his mind he walked round it, looking closely. It was the stump of an old round tower, with an opening in the base leading into a small vaulted chamber. He sat on the bank staring at it, wondering about its origins. It could be something industrial, like a limekiln, but he guessed not. In that fought-over landscape it must have had a defensive role during the bloody time of the Border reivers. He looked across the bowl of landscape it would once have dominated, and that was a mistake.

His eye was caught by the stream bed down there, beyond the house, and he could see the slope of hill down which Yanna had come running that morning last year. He realized he was wearing the same track suit as then, breathing the same air. The trees down in front of the house had been in the same state of leaf. The same small flowers had been poking through the heather. He thought about dates and realized with a shock it was just one week short of a whole year ago. One more week to the first anniversary of their meeting, and Yanna was five months in her grave and Duncan just about to go into his. What a waste.

He sat very still then, so still that the rabbits came back to the smooth green grass in the little cutting below him, and if they heard him crying, they didn't seem disturbed by the noise. Why had he been so stubborn, he thought? Why had she gone off in such anger that she hadn't even told him she was going? The fax made it worse. He had used the certainty of his hatred for what the Iraqis did as a crutch. If it wasn't the Iraqis at all, then where was that crutch now?

The dew on the grass had coated the sides of his running shoes. Now it was soaking through the seam, making a cold damp line along the side of his feet, which seemed to match the twisted ache behind his wet eyes. He was staring up at the crumbling archway of the tower. Into his mind, unbidden, came a half-remembered short story, about an old, eccentric, reclusive man, custodian of some great building, a cathedral maybe? Yes, it was a cathedral. This old man knew its structure like his own body, had lived with it since the day it was finished, when he was barely more than a boy. One day, far into his advancing madness and isolation, he had fallen victim to the conviction that somewhere in this huge edifice was one vital keystone, a block, which if it were ever loosened would bring the entire structure crumbling down. He searched until one day, at the top of a remote stone stair, he discovered a small locked door of thick oak. He found in a forgotten corner of the vaults the key that opened it, and revealed a precarious narrow gallery, far up above the nave, ending at a small archway topped by its keystone. It came to him that this was the all-important stone, and he became obsessed by the idea that he must guard it night and day from those who might also find his building's weak point and decide to destroy it. Then one day he saw the mortar round the stone had begun to crumble. After that, day by day, week by week, however much he tried to cram the fragments back into place, the rot spread through it, until one dreadful day the stone slipped askew, hung there and fell. The building was unmoved; it was the mind of the custodian which had collapsed into wreckage. David, brooding, felt the edifice of anger which constituted his defence against Yanna's death to be in danger of the same collapse.

The rabbits below him suddenly bolted for cover again. He stirred, wondering if he'd unwittingly made a noise, and looked around. There was a sound of muffled footsteps in the heather, and round the side of the tower walked George Middleton. He stopped, surprised, and David wiped the back of his hand across his eyes.

'Mr Challis?' His voice was concerned as he took in the look of David's face.

'Hello. Sorry, I was miles away.'

Middleton took a step nearer. 'How is she?' he asked.

'She's taking it very well.'

'She's a brave girl, Mr Challis.'

'Please, make it David. I'm so grateful for the support you've given her. Even before this happened, I mean. It's obviously meant a lot to her, getting to know you.'

'It has meant a lot to me too,' the old man replied quietly. He looked closely at David. 'Is she by herself?'

'She was still sleeping soundly when I left. I don't think she'll wake for a while yet. Pills, you know.'

'Would you care to come back to my house for a cup of tea, then? It's not very far if we go across the beck.' He smiled. 'I'm afraid we should have to walk. I don't think I would be able to keep up otherwise.'

'Yes. I'd like to. Thank you.'

'I often come this way,' said Middleton. 'It speaks, don't you think? This tower, I mean?'

'I was wondering what it was.'

'I'm sure it's from the time of the troubles. I often wonder what it would have been like to stand here and see Douglas's horsemen winding their way down from the north. Bloody fighters they were. I think it has seen a great deal of death in its time.'

He started off down the slope and David followed. By the road he stopped, turned, and said surprisingly, 'If I might say so, David, you mustn't let one grief get in the way of another.'

'What do you mean?'

'Mrs Challis told me about your own misfortune with the young lady. And of course I knew a little from the papers. It's doubly hard for you.' David was unable to answer and the old man went on. 'I've lived for many years alone. I had Mrs Mainwaring to look after, but she was a proud lady and she didn't want me over at the house much. Circumstances, such as they are, dictated that I should be by myself and I have regretted it on many occasions, but I know something of loss and I know it must be faced fully at the time it happens. Blame may be used as a sticking-plaster, but it doesn't heal.' He paused. 'Forgive me. Does this sound like a lecture?'

David could only shake his head and listen as he went on. 'I know one thing of war, one thing only that is certain. It is this. When you return from a war, it is impossible to relate your experiences in a way that can convey their

254

true meaning to those who were not there. Anyone who says war is a simple matter is lying.' He swung round and looked back in the direction of the stump of the old tower. 'Even in the time of the Percys, the boy peering fearfully from that tower at the enemies who were coming to kill him would have been kept there by all the propaganda of fear and hatred his elders had heaped upon him – the fear of letting his tribe down and the hatred of an enemy that he must not be allowed to perceive as like himself.'

'It's worse today, surely. It's more sophisticated,' said David with difficulty, wondering at this deep, thoughtful, expressive old man.

'No. It's just closer. That's all.'

David listened to him most of the way back to the farm-house, a philosophical monologue on the nature of hatred between races. When finally they were sitting at the table in the neat, simple kitchen, David tried to express what he was feeling. 'The thing is, I knew while I was out there that it wasn't that simple. Because of Yanna, I feel I've wound up lying to myself. There you are, with Saddam Hussein turned into the embodiment of all evil, like Hitler, and it's easier if you forget about all the little men under him who have no choice.'

Middleton just looked at him, waiting, and he went on. 'I had this producer in the Gulf, a mad American, but he was the one who saw it. He told me all kinds of things, like how the Apache helicopter pilots were fed on Kuwait atrocity stories every day so they'd feel angry enough to keep on attacking defenceless targets. He kept saying it was just like Vietnam, where the GIs couldn't tell the difference between North Vietnamese gooks and South Vietnamese gooks so they simply blasted them all. I didn't listen to him.'

Middleton gave a slight, sad smile, and David suddenly

255

remembered the Spitfire model and Jackie Mainwaring. 'I
was at the Fleet Air Arm Museum the other day. I looked
up the 899 Squadron line book.' Middleton's head lifted.
'I found pictures of my father and of Jackie Mainwaring. I
read about his death.'

'I didn't know they had it,' said the old man quietly.
'What does it say?'

'Just that he disappeared without trace, ferrying a new
plane. They thought he'd gone down in the sea. It said
he'd flown non-stop since the start of the war and he was
a very good guy.'

Middleton seemed greatly affected by this and David,
taking a leaf from his book, felt it would be kinder if he
carried on talking about safer generalities. 'I read a lot
more. It all seemed so much more straightforward then.
Simple weapons, simple issues.'

The old man shook his head vehemently. 'Oh, no. No.
Simpler maybe, but not simple.' He got to his feet. 'Jackie
Mainwaring didn't die from anything simple, I promise
you.' He went out of the room and came back with a
wooden box. He took out of it a book and a folder of
papers. 'David, these are my most treasured possessions.
No one else has read them. They came to me from Jackie
Mainwaring. I think you might like to read them, just so
you know that war is never a simple matter. I know I can
trust you with them.'

'Thank you,' said David, wondering what they could be
and feeling honoured. 'I'll look after them.'

Middleton smiled a far-off smile as he looked down at
the papers. 'I won't be at the funeral. Will you tell your
sister-in-law that? I thought I would come over to the
house and be there while you're all at the church. That
way I can make sure everything's ready when you come
back.'

256

'That's very kind. I think Josie will be very pleased.'

David walked back, carrying the papers in a plastic bag, resisting the urge to peep inside them until there was time to do it properly.

It was only 8.30 when he got back to the house, and Josie was still asleep. He went into the kitchen and sat down at the table. He didn't look out of the window, and even if he had done he would have needed to squint sideways to make out the small van, just visible through the hedge, that was now parked further down on the side of the road. He settled down and took out the diary with anticipation, but the phone rang. He picked it up, irritated.

'David?'

'Yes?'

'It's Nick.'

'Good heavens. I was thinking about ringing you, Nick. How are you?'

Nick was clearly unsure of the reception he would get, but David was suddenly extraordinarily glad to hear his voice.

'How are you is more to the point?'

'I'll be better when today is out of the way. It's Duncan's funeral at three o'clock.'

'Oh. Look, David, it's probably a very bad time to phone you, but I've come across something that's got me pretty bothered. Would you rather I kept it until later?'

'Something about Yanna?' asked David sharply.

'Yes,' said Nick in surprise. 'How did you know?'

'I've got something too. Tell me yours first.'

'I've been going through all the tapes. You know we never even viewed the stuff we shot when they were bull-dozing the bunker?'

'Yes, I know. My fault. You were right. We ought to have done.'

'That's not what I mean. I was playing it back with the sound up, and suddenly there was Yanna's voice on track one. I remember now, Ian said she'd been mumbling something. We never thought to look.' He paused for a second. 'We should have. She was leaving you a message.'

David stopped breathing for a moment and his heart thumped. 'What sort of message?'

'I've got it here. I copied it down. It's personal in places, but I thought you ought to know as soon as possible.'

'Read it to me.'

'Are you sure?'

'Nick, just bloody . . . I'm sorry. Yes, I'm sure.'

'OK,' Nick sighed. 'It sort of starts off with her saying "Ian, Ian", trying to get his attention, but he's obviously filming and he doesn't even seem to hear her. You know how bloody deaf we all were after all that artillery stuff. Then she says hurriedly, "Shit. They're going. OK, message to David. Can't wait. Busby has just driven past behind us. The Bamco man. Like he is looking for something. I am going to see what they are doing. Wait for me here, I won't be long." Then there's a slight pause. "Just writing a note to say play the tape. David, I love you. It's silly, but just in case, go and see my mother. Tell her to take you to . . ."' Nick trailed off. 'There's some funny words. It sounds like air fan france or something.'

'Er Vam Vraz,' said David, his voice strangled.

'What's that?'

'I don't quite know. I think it's where she hid some photos.'

'That's where it ends,' Nick said. He waited. 'David, are you there?'

David felt like a man drowning. 'Ian never saw a note. There wasn't a note.'

'There was a wind. It must have blown away.'

258

She loved me. She didn't leave in anger. Awatif was right, David thought. She wasn't killed by the Republican Guard at all. Nick said something. 'Sorry. What?'

'I said what's your news?'

'Same thing in a different way. An Iraqi soldier, under interrogation, said he more or less saw what happened. It wasn't the Iraqis.'

'We need to talk.'

He blessed Nick for not saying, I told you so. 'Yes. Nick, look, I'm sorry. I've been looking at everything the wrong way round.'

'Yeah, don't worry.'

'There's already more. I need to think. This is to do with Duncan being killed as well.'

'Being killed?'

'That's what I said. Look, the funeral's at three. I'll phone you later.'

He hung up and the window-panes ceased their tiny, unnoticeable vibration. The laser device focused on them from the van was a very sophisticated piece of equipment, usually only found in the hands of intelligence services. It had its limitations. It was only useful when there was a line of sight to the windows of the room in which the person was talking. Double glazing and thick curtains hampered its effectiveness, but neither was a problem this time. When David hung up the phone, it stopped emitting the signal to the computerized amplifier which turned it back into recognizable speech and recorded it on a cassette. Sledge Hanmer, out in the lane, realizing all too well the importance of what he had just heard, started the van and drove off rapidly in search of Geoff Busby.

Chapter Twenty-five

Same day

George Middleton turned up an hour before they were due
to leave. He parked his car unobtrusively round the back
of the house and quietly took over the preparations from a
protesting Josie, sending her off to change.

'Will tea and biscuits be enough?' said Josie, worried.
'They will have come an awfully long way.'

'I'm sure it will be fine,' said Middleton. 'I brought some
cakes with me. I don't think in these circumstances people
will be expecting too much.'

'They'll probably want a drink,' said David, who had
been to Otterburn to restock. Josie looked at the bottles of
Scotch, gin and brandy in the cupboard and made a face.

'I don't much like seeing them there,' she said. 'It's only
a week since I cleared the last lot out.'

Middleton came to the door to wave them off, but the
door was out of the line of sight from where Sledge Hanmer
had arrived a little late at the top of the far hill, so Hanmer's
binoculars caught the Jensen pulling out of the gate without seeing the man left behind.

In the car Josie was nervous. 'I hope there aren't too
many people,' she said.

'There won't be. Your mother and your sister, assuming
they get there in time. No one from our side. Apart from
Uncle Ted in Alberta, there isn't anyone. That's all the
family. I don't know about friends.'

'I don't even want to see Mum. She'll be on at me about my clothes not being smart enough, and Lottie always looks as though she's robbed a clothes shop.'

He smiled and squeezed her hand. 'Five hours in the car from Suffolk will have rumpled her a bit. Anyway, I'll protect you.'

'I wish Dad was still alive,' said Josie.

They saw Josie's mother and sister, waiting anxiously at the church gate, before they even stopped the car. They were talking to two old university friends of Duncan's. Josie's sister waved when she recognized the Jensen, and David parked a little way down the road. 'Deep breath,' he said. 'Time to face the enemy.' Josie gave a little smile.

Then it was hugs, kisses, the smell of freshly applied face-powder, and expressions of restrained bravery. They walked up the path to the door of the church and David was surprised at the long line of wreaths and all the bunches of flowers propped up alongside the path. Josie read out the labels as they went. There was a big one from Duncan's show as well as several individual ones from members of its staff. There was, surprisingly, one from Bertram Glass and a bunch of flowers from Nick, which touched David. Then Josie bent down and flicked over the label of an ornate shiny creation of ivy and lilies. *From all at Bamco, it said, in fond memory of a valued colleague.*

David picked it up and everyone behind him stopped. He looked around. Out on the pavement was a rubbish bin. In front of the astonished mourners he walked back down the path, stuffed the wreath with difficulty into the bin and retraced his steps. The small group parted in front of him as if he had suddenly developed rabies. Josie looked at him calmly. 'Is that because of what Nick told you this morning?'

'Yes.'

'I wish you'd tell me what it was.'

'Later. One thing at a time.'

It was a shock to walk in and be confronted with the reality of the coffin, drawing everyone's attention into the middle of the aisle. He found it confusing. It was and it wasn't Duncan all at the same time. On one level it was just a heavy polished box. On another it contained that terrible object, the body that no longer looked exactly like its former inhabitant. If this is a ceremony of parting, thought David, it just doesn't work. We shouldn't be saying goodbye to a lump of wood, we should be able to see him.

During the short service he tried to put it all together in his mind. The organ struck up the opening chords of the hymn. It was 'The Battle Hymn of the Republic', the only one they could think of that could possibly be called a favourite of Duncan's. As the few, thin voices started to sing, 'Mine eyes have seen the glory . . .', David's mind swung sharply back to the last time he had heard it, hummed over and over again by Nick as they had walked through a desert littered with torn, dismembered bodies. He looked at the coffin. So much fuss for you, dear brother, he said to himself, so much individual pain. Out there you would have been just one more ravaged patch of sand.

As they sang, George Middleton, fastidiously polishing tea-cups with a clean drying-up cloth, was half listening to the radio. His watch had been playing up and he wanted to be completely ready for when the family returned, so he had tuned the set in the kitchen to the nearest pop station. He hated the music, but at least they gave lots of time checks. It was an FM station and he'd had to put the radio's telescopic aerial up. Every time he walked past it at a certain angle, his presence affected the signal and it slid off

262

into an irritating sideshow of distorted hissing. When he was out of the room, it was fine. He was wondering whether David had yet started to read the Jackie Mainwaring documents and trying to guess what he would make of them when the announcer said, 'And with the time just coming up to . . .' Because he was in the next room, he stopped and listened carefully, but the distortion suddenly set in again and he couldn't make it out.

How can that be, he thought? I'm in here. It should be fine. Blast it. Then he heard another noise and realized someone must be out there. That's why the radio's gone all funny, he realized, but they shouldn't be back for a good hour yet. He put down the cloth, set the cup carefully on top of a saucer, wiped his hands on his trousers. Maybe a delayed guest who'd come straight to the house because it was too late to head for the funeral? He went quietly towards the kitchen, with a welcoming smile, and found himself face to face with a large, bald man who had walked in as if he owned the place. Realizing straight away that this was unlikely to be a guest, he started to open his mouth and saw a fist arcing towards him.

Nick Nielsen was doing over ninety miles an hour in a purloined Granada Scorpio belonging to Bertram Glass, heading flat out down the Otterburn road, navigating dangerously by the Ordnance Survey map spread out on his lap. The snap decision to take the tape in person to David was an emotional and quixotic response to the need and the fear he had suddenly heard in David's voice. Weeks of being ignored and sat-on hadn't changed the fact that he liked the guy, and he was nearly as angry as David at Yanna's death, though less likely to apportion blame. Glass had left his car at the office while he flew to Paris for a few

263

days. It still had his golf clubs on the back seat. Nick was almost sure it wouldn't be missed.

He was very bothered. He was all too willing to read between the lines of what David had told him on the phone and, coming from a more violent culture, he was afraid David and Josie might not be sufficiently on their guard.

Even had he known the funeral was in full swing, he wouldn't have been tempted to go to it, dressed as he was in his usual disarray and unwilling for once to embarrass David by it. He overshot the turning, went straight past the Percy Arms, unable to believe Otterburn could be such a small place, and did a violent U-turn in the road, which took three months' life off Bertram Glass's tyres and made the small funeral gathering inside the church just up the road turn their heads in surprise. Nick zigzagged out on to the moorland, still driving much too fast, and in consequence overshot for the second time, going straight past Chalice Hall's gateposts. This time it was a little more excusable as he had difficulty believing that so large a house could possibly be the right destination.

It was as he was looking for a place to turn in the narrow road beyond that he saw the van parked in an entrance to a field and the trail of footmarks in the damp grass leading towards the house. Alarm bells rang in his head. It was the kind of scenario he had been imagining all the way up. He stopped the car, got out and looked at the van. There was nothing inside it to point either way, but he could now clearly see that the footsteps led across the grass to a low place in the garden wall. That was enough.

Alert now, he retraced his route, turned quietly into the drive and stopped at the foot of it. He got out of the car, looking carefully around, then a thought struck him and he went back and opened a rear door. He took a club out of Bertram Glass's golf-bag and hefted it in his hand, then walked slowly up the drive to the front door, not taking his eyes off the house. The door was ajar. He pushed it gently open and waited for his eyes to get accustomed to the lower light level inside. An old man was lying on the floor, bleeding heavily from the mouth and nose. He knelt down and checked to see if the man was breathing, but then the light changed and he ducked out of the way as something from the side crashed towards his head, striking him a glancing blow. He caught a glimpse over his shoulder of a big man turning for another go at him and, using both hands, he brought the golf club round in an awkward backward swing that just caught his attacker on the side of the head. It seemed to have little effect. The man was built like a tank. He lurched towards Nick and pulled his feet from under him as Nick swiped again with the club, feeling it hit home as his own head hit the ground.

Five cars made up the little convoy back to the house from the church. David was driving Josie and her mother. Josie, sitting in the cramped back, was thoughtful but silent, silent at least until her mother, in the front, started sobbing into a handkerchief. Josie leant forward towards the front seat.

'Mum, enough now. Come on.'

'I don't know how you can be so brave, Josephine.'

'Well . . . I can. That's all that matters. So you must be too. For me.'

'But what are you going to do?'

'Well, I don't know yet, but something will come up.'

'But he was so young.'

'Oh . . . *Jesus*.'

The exclamation wasn't prompted by her mother, however, but by the fact that she had just been propelled head
first into the narrow gap between the front seats. Turning
off the main road into the lane, David had found himself
head-on with a speeding ambulance, blue light flashing.
He backed up and the ambulance squeezed past almost
without stopping and sped off down the road in the direction of Hexham.

'What on earth is that doing?' gasped Josie as she pulled
herself back upright.

'Haven't a clue. Maybe some walker got hurt or something?'

It was a measure of David's inner belief, despite all the
recent events, in the orderly ordinariness of his own life
that it wasn't until they turned into the drive and saw the
police cars drawn up outside the house that he suspected
for a moment that the ambulance might have any connection with them.

Inspector Percival arrived hard on their heels, summoned
by the sergeant on the spot. He was a little more open to
suggestion this time, but only a little.

'Mr Middleton's colour and breathing sounded pretty
bad, I'm afraid, Mr Challis. Apparently the ambulance crew
thought there was a good chance he had a fractured skull.
They'll take the best possible care of him at Hexham, I'm
sure.'

David, sitting at the table, nodded.

'Your friend here, Mr Nielsen, turned up at the right
time.'

'Yes, he did, didn't he?' said David, turning to look at
Nick, who was lying on the sofa with Josie holding a cold,
wet cloth to the swelling on the back of his head. Nick

managed a smile. The bruising on his shoulder wasn't serious and despite the bang on his head there was no sign of concussion.

'What do you make of it, inspector?'

'Happens all the time, I'm afraid, sir. A bit unusual out here, perhaps. You get people who watch out for the funeral notices in the papers, you see, looking for addresses that sound on the rich side. They look for the time of the funeral, then they know they're going to get a clear run for an hour or two.'

'We didn't put a notice in the paper.'

'Well, yes, but there's a story in the local paper about your brother's death, and that did give details, I'm afraid. House like this attracts them like bees to honey, I'm sorry to say. They wouldn't have known someone like Mr Middleton would be here. It's just as well your friend came along when he did and frightened them off.'

'Inspector, I hesitate to bring this up, but we've come up with some more information that may well point to this Bamco outfit. I'd like to come and talk to you again when I've had time to consider it.'

The inspector looked doubtful. 'Well, I'm always available, Mr Challis, but I'm sure this was a plain and simple burglary. Now, I'm sorry we're disturbing you on a day like this. If you want to get back to your guests, I'll just finish up with the scenes-of-crime officer and we'll leave you in peace.'

He went out. Nick got carefully up off the sofa.

'Take it easy, mate,' said David gratefully. 'I'm glad you came. You did bloody well.'

'I didn't do all that well,' said Nick. 'Same old problem I always have with golf. Picked the wrong club. If I'd used a wood instead of a 3 iron, we'd still have the bastard.'

Josie had already checked over the house quickly. There

was nothing apparently missing. They didn't know they'd got it the wrong way round. They should have been looking for extra things, things that were there but shouldn't have been – the four little radio bugs with their one-week batteries, sitting hidden in the two phones, on top of the Welsh dresser in the kitchen and in a gap on top of a beam in the drawing-room ceiling.

Chapter Twenty-six

Same day

'No, I'm not family. He doesn't have any family, I told you. I'm a close friend.' Josie listened, 'I see. I do understand. Yes. I'll phone again tomorrow.' She hung up the phone and turned to David and Nick, looking distraught. 'You would have thought they'd realize some people don't have families. They just didn't want to tell me much.'

'What did they say?'

'We can't go and see him. He's deeply unconscious. They're considering some sort of exploratory operation.'

'Is he in any danger?'

'Well, of course he is,' she snapped, then stopped herself. 'I'm sorry, David. I just can't stand it. Not George, on top of everything. It's my fault he was here.'

The kitchen door opened and Josie's mother came in. 'Is there any news, Josephine?'

'Not really.'

'Well, I do think you should come in and see your guests then. Everybody's just sort of standing around, waiting. I'm sure Mr, er . . . I'm sure he'll be all right.'

'I'll come,' said David. 'You stay here if you'd rather.'

'No, it's OK,' said Josie. They left Nick, who was studying the transcript of the Awatif interrogation, and went through the hall into the sitting-room, where the vicar and the doctor stood with Duncan's friends and Josie's sister.

Josie's mother looked back darkly after they closed the door on Nick, and turned to David. 'He's a bit peculiar if you ask me. Are you sure he wasn't something to do with it?'

'Oh, Mum,' said Josie, exasperated. 'I'm quite sure.'

'He's an old friend of mine,' said David, finding an unexpected sense of truth in what was meant to be reassuring exaggeration.

Half an hour of stilted conversation over the teacups just about killed it. The vicar and the doctor broke ranks first. Duncan's friends, clearly feeling there should be something more on offer after driving such a long way, went off next, leaving only Josie's mother and Lottie.

'Mum and I have been discussing it,' said Lottie, 'and we've decided there's nothing so absolutely urgent for the next few days that someone else can't take the strain back home. We think your need is greater than theirs, so we'll stay for a bit to help out.'

Josie's face indicated a sudden sharp increase in strain. They'd been careful to keep everyone else out of the conversations with Inspector Percival. Her mother and sister had no idea that Duncan's death might have been more than a simple accident, or that the day's events were anything other than a burglary that went wrong. They needed clear air to try to sort it all out.

'I wouldn't dream of it, Mum. You're far too busy.'

'You shouldn't be up here all by yourself.'

'I won't be. David will be here.'

Lottie joined in. 'If your family can't help you at a time like this, when can they?'

'No, I really mean it,' said Josie. 'I'd love to come down and stay with you soon, but I must clear some things up first. Anyway,' she said, 'you've got so much on your plate with the school governors and the Conservative Association.'

270

'Well, that's true, of course,' said Lottie, 'but that's not what matters,' though there was an unmistakable note of relief in her voice.

David started asking detailed questions about their route back and whether they minded driving in the dark. He suggested one or two places where they could break the journey if they got too tired, and within ten minutes they'd been shoehorned into their car and seen off. It was a huge relief when at last the three could talk freely. They poured fresh cups of tea and settled round the kitchen table.

'I'm sorry,' said David. 'Apart from tending to the wounded hero's head, you two haven't really met properly.'

'That was a pretty good introduction,' said Nick.

'I've heard so much about you, I feel I've known you for a long time,' said Josie.

Nick looked at David. 'Oh, dear,' he said uncertainly, then he looked back at Josie. 'Do you want to get straight down to it, or would you rather wait for tomorrow? I guess it might feel a little weird to be talking about Yanna on a day like this.'

Josie looked tired but defiant. 'With me in my widow's weeds?' She stopped and thought for a moment. 'No. It's funny, isn't it? I don't want to think that Duncan died just because he was pissed. Revenge is a powerful drug. Let's get on with it.'

'OK. First things first. You'd better hear Yanna's tape.'

They went into Duncan's studio and put it in the machine. Before he switched it on, Nick cast a worried glance at David. 'You sure you're ready for this, boss?'

David wasn't sure, but he nodded. He'd tried to keep in his mind the soft, low, accented sound of her, but the subtleties of sound are elusive and it rocked him to hear the real thing. Poor, dead Yanna spoke directly to him from a four-inch speaker in a black cabinet. As he heard her first words, 'Shit, they're going. OK, message to David,' he froze into immobility and his eyes blurred. All his muscles knotted at 'Wait for me here, I won't be long.' He couldn't have moved if he had tried, and his whole being was focused on the speaker as he fought to keep control. 'David, I love you' undid him. A great sob was wrenched from him before he clamped his mouth shut to hold his feelings back. The tape ended and no one moved. There was a long silence before he blinked a few times and opened his eyes again. Nick was staring steadfastly at the wall, swallowing. Josie's eyes were red and, as he moved, she reached over and stroked his head in a desperate way.

'God,' he said. 'That's a bit . . .'

'Yeah,' said Nick. 'I'll get the Scotch.'

Half an hour later they'd covered every angle they could think of. They'd looked at the route on the map Nick had brought up with him, from where they'd last seen Yanna to where her body had been found. David had described what he'd seen of the video Duncan had been shooting and they'd gone over the encounter with Busby in the desert traffic jam. Josie had recounted what little she knew of Duncan's dealings with Bamco.

Nick summed up. 'If Duncan had been drinking doctored Scotch before his show, that could mean someone gave him more of the same stuff in Newcastle before he drove back. If we're going to tie that into Bamco, we need to know a whole lot more about that appointment.'

'Yanna was quite positive that Bamco had been trying to fake up the Dodgem tests and she was always saying Duncan shouldn't have anything to do with them,' said David, whose voice still sounded strange and hoarse to himself. 'She kept back the photos she took of the first test because of it. Josie, you wrote to me that you were worried about something Duncan was planning to do. Come to that, he told me himself that he had something up his sleeve.'

Nick turned to the computer sitting on Duncan's desk. 'Have you checked his mail?'

'In there? No. Try it.'

Nick switched on the monitor and groped around the back of the machine for the on/off switch. It booted itself up to show a rather good version of Challis Video's logo. Nick hit the space-bar and the logo disappeared to be replaced by a prompt. He got into the root directory and found the right file names, and they all leaned over it in anticipation, but then the screen came up with the two words: ENTER PASSWORD.

'Do either of you know it?' Nick asked.

'No.'

Nick tried the obvious ones, like Duncan's date of birth, his name, Josie's name and everything else he could think of. They got nowhere. Nick sighed. 'I've got a password search programme, but it's back in London.'

'What on earth have you got that for?' asked David in surprise.

Nick looked at him innocently. 'Part of every well-equipped journalist's kit for dealing with the 1990s. Courtesy of my mate, Ove the techno-whizz.'

David had heard of Nick's friend Ove, a brainy Scandinavian with a mania for electronic security in all its forms, and especially its more illegal countermeasures.

'Ah,' said Nick with a sudden funny look,' 'that reminds me, Ove's first axiom.' He tapped away again. 'Bingo!' The screen scrolled into a long list of letter headings.

'What?' said Josie, startled. 'How did you do that?'

'Like I say, Ove's first axiom. I should have thought of that before. He told me that when some people are facing their private thoughts and sharing their secrets with their computer, they use moral icons for their passwords, names of things they look up to.'

'So what was it?' David asked.

'You're the key, pal. The password's David.'

That twisted something inside him, and David quickly bent to an examination of the sub-directory called LETTERS. The file headed BAMCO had letters numbered from .001 to .089. Many of them were invoices, or administrative notes about times of shoots. Then, on July 9th, just two and a half weeks earlier, this:

Dear Spencer,

I have just been looking through all my video material on Dodgem. What a splendid job we made of that. I do hope you agree? I do feel, however, that in the end what we produced went far beyond the normal requirements of our agreement. I was disappointed with my contacts with Geoff Busby on that score.

With all that in mind, it occurs to me that you may want similar end-products in the future, and it is therefore important to be clear at this stage what constitutes proper remuneration for this kind of special production. I'm sure you would agree it would be difficult to go out into the open market at this stage to find another supplier prepared to fit in with your wishes so closely. It seems to me that a one-off extra payment of £40,000 would be suitable in this case, and that should you agree to that, it would then be better if the video material at present in my keeping were returned to you. As it is classified material, if you should decide that is not the correct way of handling things, then I suggest the nation's interest would be best served if I were to pass on the video material to the Ministry of Defence for safe keeping.

Yours faithfully,
Duncan Challis

'Well, well,' said Nick. 'That's it, isn't it.'

'What do you make of it?' asked David.

'It's the businessman's version of a blackmail note. Duncan chose his words carefully, didn't he? So he could look whiter than white in court if Bamco were stupid enough to take him there, but basically, when you add it up, it's a sting.'

'You're right,' said David. 'The trouble is, he chose the words so carefully you wouldn't see it that way if you were a policeman, would you? Not unless you started from our point of view.'

They tossed it around for a little while more and checked back through every other Bamco entry in the file, but Nick's head was hurting and Josie looked exhausted, so they decided to call it a day and drifted off to bed. Only when silence fell after the last 'Good night' was there a tiny little click as the high-powered relay from the microphones switched into its 'wait' mode. Only a badger heard the click as it strode past the plastic box covering the relay in the little patch of woodland a short way down the road.

David couldn't sleep. It was one o'clock in the morning, and it was all going round and round in his head. Nick was snoring in the other spare room. He pushed Josie's door open quietly and looked in at her. Her breathing was deep and even, and she looked very young in the moonlight. He remembered how sweet it had been ten years earlier when they first went to bed together. He indulged his memories for a minute or two, then suddenly feeling embarrassed by them he went out and closed the door. Downstairs, he went looking for something to read and only then did he remember the book and the documents which George Middleton had given him less than twenty-four hours ago.

275

He made himself some cocoa, switched on a sidelight, settled into an armchair and opened the book. It was a thick ledger, with plain, unruled pages, stiffened by age. He was soon deeply immersed.

The book was an occasional diary; it was not a banal daily record of events. It contained a series of what were almost essays, detailed glimpses of wartime life, written with enormous skill by someone used to the careful assembly of words. It clearly carried on from another volume. It started at the end of April 1940, with the Norwegian campaign. David skimmed through it, then his eye was caught by one sentence and he started to read with care.

I woke this morning to the sombre realization that this is a war we may very well manage to lose. Judging by Mother's latest missive from the moors, Britain's mood has not yet turned the same way. The overconfidence seems absurd, unless she is too remote from the rest of the country to judge. It may be just the effect of having Father on hand. She says he's out in the garden with his shotgun every day, hoping a Jerry might come over. She says he's terribly proud of me and tells everyone all the time what he imagines I'm doing. His last letter to me was another long account of his part in the Battle of Jutland, almost word for word the same as the one before it. It doesn't help. We are up against a ferociously efficient enemy, and what are we? A callow band of unseasoned youths, doing our best with popguns. No one in their right mind would suggest that the Blackburn Skua is a suitable riposte to the latest products of Messrs Heinkel, Messerschmitt, Junkers and Dornier. Every time I look at my Skua I am irresistibly reminded of a greenhouse perched on top of a London Underground train. It is a lumbering, slow camel of a thing with no redeeming features, the product of years of neglect when the RAF has made decisions for the Navy and our wonderful First Lords of the Admiralty had not the slightest clue about the real needs of naval aviation. On a good day it is one hundred and fifty miles an hour slower than the machines of Fliegerkorps 10, which we are flying against. We are outnumbered by five to one, and the empty spaces in the mess are growing to the point where the jokes are wearing thin. We have to hide a hundred miles offshore and trek slowly in to do our pathetically limited damage. The Skua is a bad dive-bomber and an even worse fighter. Walter looked it up in his encyclopaedia yesterday. It says a skua is a bird that folds its wings and drops into the sea. Precisely.

It would be shooting a line to say this in the mess, so I shall confide here what yesterday's dogfight really felt like. I was so scared I started singing to let myself know I was still alive. A bottle of bubbly would have had about the same effect, I should think. I was up against a Heinkel 111. That of course is a bomber, and fighter boys like us are supposed to be able to knock spots off bombers. Unfortunately, bomber or not, the Heinkel is faster than the Skua. We were trapped in a fjord. It was like being inside a giant box. The cloud ceiling was halfway up and the sides were sheer. I had to keep turning, he was doing the same. Fighting only came into it in the odd second when we weren't both trying to stay clear of the rock walls. Walter was in the back seat, shouting for all he was worth. I don't think he knew he was doing it. I popped off the odd shot every now and then, more to cheer myself up than anything else because he was never really in my sights. I was flying the arse off the poor old crate, then whomp, the Heinkel pilot touched a wing-tip and that was that. I have to confess to you, dear diary, that the old trousers will never be quite the same again.

David read on. As the army was forced back to the evacuation point at Narvik, the aircraft-carrier *Glorious* was sunk by the German battleships *Scharnhorst* and *Gneisenau*. Jackie had been transferred to another squadron to balance up losses and, in an attempt at revenge, his new squadron was detailed to attack the *Scharnhorst* in Trondheimsfjord. It was a hopelessly badly conceived attack. The Skuas were totally unsuitable. Only eight of the sixteen returned. Jackie's writing showed unmistakable anger at the stupidity of those who planned it:

I extend an open invitation to any one of our commanders who might be dreaming up another stunt like that. Come along with me for a ringside seat. Walter won't mind, I promise. Walter won't be minding anything ever again and the fitters will have plugged up the holes by then.

After that it had been Dunkirk, still in the dreadful Skua, attacking German tanks and attempting to engage far superior ME 109s over the beaches. The anger flared up again from time to time in the writing. Then a little peace. Jackie wanted to join the group of Fleet Air Arm pilots who had been seconded to the RAF to help fight the Battle of Britain. He suspected he had opened his mouth a bit too far. Instead, he was put on the Skua's replacement, the Fairey Fulmar, a much more kindly but still desperately slow aircraft. In 1941 and early 1942, between operations – the dangerous convoy trips to the Mediterranean and beleaguered Malta – he escaped from the increasing vacuum in his stomach by returning to his pre-war activity. He was writing a play about what war is really like, more of a series of monologues really, letters home from a number of young men – a pilot, a stoker, a gunner and the carrier's captain – interlaced with their personal diaries of what they felt inside. It was perhaps a form of therapy.

Jackie, it was clear, felt let down, forced to fight with one hand tied behind his back by an Admiralty which had arrogantly specified its aircraft without even considering asking its pilots what they needed. As 1942 began Jackie analysed himself for signs of 'twitch':

I dread it more than death. At least with death, people will always think the best of you and forget that you were only a passenger in your own war story. We talk about almost everything except what we feel like before each take-off. Am I the only one? I know we all feel the flutter, you can see that in the way everyone behaves differently as the moment approaches. Jonno whistles incessantly. Dougie sits there with his eyes shut. We all visit the heads a lot and we hear Peter Warwick being sick, though no one mentions it. I should say we heard, not we hear, because Peter, who has done quite well as my wing man, after a dicky start, was sent to a shore hospital. Reggie found him in his bunk in the morning. He was just staring open-eyed at the deckhead, hands clenched at his sides. No one could get a word out of him. Poor Peter, I can't think what his father will say.

Then, later in 1942, Jackie joined the newly formed 899 Squadron and David stopped skipping sections and started to read every word. At last, Seafires. Modern, high-performance, single-seater fighters, capable of taking on the best the enemy had to offer. The elation had a savagery about it.

First flight in a proper plane. I took off from Hatston and after the usual shenanigans with the temperature gauge and the undercart, I pointed the nose at a cloud and pushed the throttle through the gate. WELL. We scampered up the sky like Pegasus on heat. That Merlin engine is a real beaut.

It didn't last. He harked back time and time again to what

was becoming a favourite subject. Many of those with whom he had started the war were now dead. The RAF had realized long ago that pilots were under a specially intense strain. They got rotated through limited tours of duty with proper rest periods. The Navy didn't see it that way. Fly until you die seemed to be the idea. Sitting on the pitching deck, at readiness, expected to be in the air eighteen seconds after the order. Coming back afterwards, if you're lucky, on the dregs of the fuel in your tank, to look for a tiny grey dot in a heaving sea and then to persuade your aircraft to meet precisely that rearing, slick metal deck and to stay on it.

The new recruits, who hadn't sweated through the last three years, were more able to take to the challenge of yet another unsuitable plane, because, beneath the veneer of myth, that's what the Seafire was. This made David sit up. He'd only heard the Seafire spoken of in the same glowing terms as its more common, land-based parent. The Spitfire might have captured the imagination of the English-speaking world, but its naval equivalent was a killer.

Jackie Mainwaring had encapsulated all he felt in an impassioned essay:

Landing a Duff Cab

I'm coming back in after a long patrol. No more than ten gallons left. A bit of the usual ill-disciplined ack-ack fire from one of the escorts. I do wish they'd learn that Jerries don't have elliptical wings. *Indomitable*'s in sight now, steaming nicely into wind. A good bus will land between seventy-four and eighty miles an hour. A bit too slow and it will stall, a bit too fast and it will rip out its arrester hook on the deck wires which are meant to catch it. Death therefore lies at both extremes of that narrow window of life. That is the starting point for my task. However, there are other factors. This isn't a good plane. It might have been once,

280

when it rolled out of the Castle Bromwich factory, but now countless hapless erks, thrown off-balance while they have tried to put it right on a rolling deck, have slid and thumped their way around it, bending its cover panels out of shape so they only fit where they touch. That and the coating of salt that has got in everywhere have combined to push the stall-speed higher. My little window of life, the allowable range of speed to let me be sure of walking away from this landing, is just three miles per hour.

That being so, you could think, dear reader, if there ever is a dear reader, that the air speed indicator, my most crucial means of staying alive and returning His Majesty's property in good working order, would be somewhere where I could easily see it, would you not? It will come as no surprise to find that it isn't. It is instead on the left-hand side of the cockpit, which is a ridiculous ninety degrees to the pilot's line of sight while he is landing-on.

Now join me again as I approach *Indomitable*'s deck in the descending turn made necessary by the fact that the plane has such a long, high nose that approaching in a straight line would blot out my view of the ship altogether. Only by curving in, looking over the side, can I have any idea of where I am going. In a calm sea this would be just a shade on the difficult side; however, the sea is not calm. The round down at the start of the deck is rising and falling perhaps forty feet in the waves. On land it is no problem to put a Spitfire down. The pukka RAF way is to come in on a two-degree glide path and flare at the last moment, stuffing the tail down in a three-point landing to kill the speed. It is of no importance that the plane floats along for a few seconds, suddenly not losing any more height in squashy ground-effect. You have time while it is doing that to twirl the ends of your moustache neatly into place with one hand and rehearse your account of the day for the popsies in the pub later on.

It matters in a Seafire, though. That is just one more way of

281

dying if you let the plane float over all the arrester wires, either head-on into the crash barrier if you're lucky or straight over the bow and down, down, down, plummeting behind the weight of that great big Merlin engine as the hull of the carrier rolls over you at thirty knots. So on a Seafire you simply dump it down, tail first to get that hook engaged. To hell with the life of the fuselage. The harder the better, but the bastard's still got a few tricks up its sleeve. That undercarriage isn't meant for violent treatment. It's designed for a sink rate of eight feet a second on land. At sea it's normally twelve, but if the deck's lurching up to meet you on a big wave that can easily be twenty-four. The pivots on the undercarriage legs don't like that. The gouges in the deck show just how often they shear. Then it's in the laps of the gods – a crash and maybe a fire if both legs go, or a wild sleigh-ride over the side if it's only one.

If you're really lucky it's just the lightweight rear fuselage you buckle, and that's what happens this time, in full view of all the off-duty types lined up in the Goofers' Gallery by the bridge. So now all I have to do is face the wrath of Commander (Flying) for my ham-fistedness and the fact that yet another of the taxpayers' contributions to the war effort will have to be pushed over the side as scrap. One sore elbow and a cut on the forehead is, I suppose, a small price to pay.

Being the light-hearted souls we are, of course, we have made a game of it. We have an aristocratic league of barrier prangs. One makes you a Baronet, two make you an Earl, three gets you a Dukedom. Bill Challis, that most impeccable of flyers, achieved his Baronetcy today, after a big engine blow-up. We couldn't let him off. He wanted to know if it was hereditary. There's optimism for you.

The mention of his father brought it very close to David. Distance was suddenly no barrier to the feelings contained in the essay. It spoke directly to David across the years, and he felt his palms sweat in sympathetic fear.

282

Jackie was by now approaching the end of his very long tether. He tried to use the skills at his disposal to do something about it. His references to the attitudes of his own and other pilots' fathers gave the probable clue as to why he so much feared the stigma of 'twitch', but he was clearly showing all the warning signs, at least in his private thoughts. In the end he wrote an article about the problems of Fleet Air Arm pilot fatigue. He had sent it to a magazine or newspaper, it wasn't clear where exactly, but it was quite clear that the censor had come down on it like a ton of bricks and that Jackie had received some very rough handling by the Admiralty as a result.

That was interrupted by the torpedoing of HMS *Indomitable*, an enforced sojourn under enemy attack in Malta, then transfer to the little, slow 'escort' carriers. That had at least resulted in new, updated aircraft, as David remembered from the Yeovilton line book. Then came Operation Avalanche – the invasion of Italy at Salerno – and the part the squadron had played. This, David quickly realized, was the final 'Balaclava' for Jackie. He was merciless. There was no attempt now to keep smiling.

This is what I believe the Americans would term a snafu. There is no wind here. Our little carrier *Hunter*, with its short deck, can only manage eighteen knots flat out. That's not fast enough to produce the draught over the deck needed to land the planes back on safely. Not only that, but whoever planned this operation didn't see any need to give the carriers sufficient sea room to get up to maximum speed for the landings. We have lost cab after cab in unnecessary but inevitable landing-on accidents. We are told the invasion is in danger of failing. We are the only air cover, and there is a Panzer tank division preventing capture of the airfield ashore, which was meant to become our forward base. It's now the third day and Dicky, Gerry, Bill and I are the only ones still flying. In the whole fleet there are just twenty-seven Seafires left in working order out of the hundred and ten we started with. We are flying non-stop and we don't even get close enough to the Jerries to shoot at them. We seem to be turning back their raids, but we're just not fast enough. Now we're told we're flying ashore at last. There's a strip ready at Paestum. Paddy tells us he reckons it's under fire from artillery and from the Panzers still. Brilliant. Bloody brilliant.

The rest of his account was dry, laconic. It concentrated on his dislike of Italian tomatoes, the only food available in the dusty surroundings of Paestum. He'd come by a German helmet in circumstances he did not divulge, and seemed oddly obsessed by it, putting it on his head and trying to think like the previous wearer.

Once it was all over and they were on their way back to the UK to regroup, he seemed to allow the cracks in his mind to widen again. In November 1943 they were taking it relatively easy. Jackie had at last had some proper leave. The Lords of the Admiralty were starting to see the light, but there was personal news for him.

On my second to last day at the Hall, Father died. Mother came in the night, with great dignity, and asked me to come. He had got up to look out of the window, as he always did if he heard an aircraft, and he was slumped down on the floor, blue in the face. We laid him on the bed and tried to reach the doctor, but the telephone lines seemed not to be working, so I went on one of the horses. He came, but, as we thought, there was nothing to be done.

David read on. He had rejoined the squadron in Scotland, but barely mentioned flying after that. He talked more of his car, the old Bentley David had seen in the line book photo.

Had a letter from W. O. Bentley himself to my great surprise. Didn't think he would write back. He confirmed it was a Birkin team car from the photo, but he couldn't tell me which one. Said he'd never been in favour of supercharging the old four-and-a-half litre and he'd left Birkin to get on with it. Wished me luck. Nice to think the old girl probably did Le Mans in her time.

Then the book simply ended. It was three in the morning.

Chapter Twenty-seven

Sunday July 28th 1991

David woke at nine with his mind already going full tilt. He knew what George Middleton was trying to tell him. War never is simple. The old men decide and the young men suffer from their mistakes. It might have been ignorance rather than commercial pressure that made them pick the wrong technology last time round, but the final result was the same for the people on the sharp end.

He dressed and went down to the kitchen. Josie was just hanging up the phone. She gave him a sleepy hug, looking rumpled and vulnerable. 'No news. He hasn't regained consciousness. It was a different sister, a bit more forthcoming this time. They're thinking about doing a scan.'

At the table, Nick, wearing only a baseball cap and a pair of shorts, was having a beer and a breakfast which consisted of cold baked beans mixed with mayonnaise on a huge slab of bread. He waved a hand in greeting with his mouth full.

'It was his idea,' said Josie defensively. 'He made it himself.'

'What a horrible sight,' said David.

He poured a cup of coffee and sat down. Nick swallowed enough of his mouthful to speak round the edges. 'Council of War?'

'I suppose so. We can't just sit here.'

'Supposing we try again with Inspector Percival?' said Josie.

David shook his head. 'I don't think so. There's nothing solid.' He realized he had already made up his mind. 'I think I'd better go to France. The only thing I can think of which might add up to a row of beans as far as the police are concerned is the photos Yanna took. If her mother really has got them, that's the best hope.'

'Have you met her mother?'

'No.'

'Are you going to phone her?'

'No. I think I'd rather just turn up.'

He didn't look very happy, so Josie pushed him a bit. 'Don't you want to?'

'I'll have to tell her all about it.'

'Isn't that a good thing?'

'I don't know. Yanna told me she never leaves her little village. She sounds pretty rural. I don't suppose it will be easy.' He stared at the fireplace. 'Anyway, I suppose at the end of it all I still feel pretty guilty.'

'You shouldn't,' said Josie, 'not now we know what really happened.'

'She wouldn't have been there if I hadn't . . .'

'Bullshit,' said Nick. 'Knowing Yanna she would have been somewhere else just as bad.'

'Anyway, I'm worried about leaving you here by yourself.'

'She won't be by herself,' said Nick. 'I'm staying until you get back.'

'What about work?'

'The hell with work, I've had enough of Glass.'

'One tiny point. You've still got Glass's car outside.'

'Oh, yeah, so I have. Now isn't that something.'

'I'm still not happy. I don't think one of you is enough.'

'OK,' said Nick, considering. 'I reckon I can fix that. There's a few guys owe me a favour.'

'What sort of guys?'

'The sort of guys that make gorillas cross to the other side of the street and pretend to be window-shopping. Pals of mine from the arm-wrestling game.'

'Will they come?'

'Sure they will. They owe me money.'

David looked at his diary. 'I'll go down tomorrow. There's this bloody silly event at the War Museum on Tuesday. I said I'd be there. I'll go on to France after that.'

Nick was as good as his word. It took him an hour on the phone, but by the time Monday morning came around and David was ready to leave, Nick's friends were already on their way. Josie hugged him in the kitchen. 'Be very careful, David,' she said. 'We've only got each other now.'

'I will,' he said, 'but if it really is Bamco, they won't know I'm going and they won't know what I'm after. I'm far more worried they'll try something here.'

Tuesday July 30th 1991

He knew it was a mistake from the moment a gust of wind slammed the taxi door against his leg. He paid the cab driver, glad to have got one who didn't recognize him, and looked across the expanse of bleak south London pavement at the barrels of the huge naval guns stamping their military message across the approach to the Imperial War Museum. He'd been here many times in the thirty years since his father had first brought him as a five-year-old. There was little inside the museum that held any technical mystery for him. He could recite type numbers, calibres and battle history with the best of them. Now, though, for the first time ever, he glanced at the guns with something almost approaching distaste as he walked past them to the

288

door. It crossed his mind briefly that someone might have followed him, but he dismissed that as melodramatic. That was a mistake. He had been watched all the way in.

A Japanese couple were staring sadly at a notice telling the public that the museum was closed for the inauguration of a special exhibition. A banner proclaimed the name of that exhibition: *The BBC and the Gulf.* Inside the crowded foyer hands were waved at David, by those who were more interested in watching the arrivals than in listening closely to their opposite numbers in small talk. Many of them were media desk-warriors, those who'd stayed behind, living the war vicariously through the satellite links, some supportive, some quick in their criticism to let others know they could have done it better. Here and there were the real faces he recognized and valued – reporters, cameramen, picture editors, technicians. They were outnumbered. He acknowledged a few greetings, swerving away from contact like a plane evading ground fire, and thought, wrongly, that he would find safety in the exhibits.

The far right-hand corner of the floor had been taken over, rearranged for the exhibition. Next to Montgomery's tank from El Alamein stood the first of a series of glass boxes. Beside it was a display placard, black on khaki. *Allied military forces were in place, ready and prepared for war, when the UN deadline passed on January 16th, 1991. They were not alone. For the BBC's own army of journalists and technicians this was a foreign assignment which required all the experience, expertise, resources, technology and sheer staying-power at its disposal.* He winced and read on. *Pressures to be first with the news had to be met within the context of accuracy and sensitivity, and there were strict guidelines on reporting, with the safety and security of the troops of paramount importance.*

289

He lingered, brooding over the wording. 'The context of accuracy.' A week ago he would probably have agreed with that. Now he was not so sure. Then his eye fell on the contents of the display cases. There was reporter Joe Paley's yellow A4 pad carrying his handwritten impressions of the Allied ground attack. Next to it was the compulsory protective suit for the nuclear, biological and chemical threats which had never materialized. His skin prickled in the remembered discomfort of claustrophobic, sweaty heat as he looked at it.

The second cabinet had Kate Adie's canvas bag, with her good-luck charm of three knitted bells, red, white and blue. Alongside it was a black book with John Simpson's writing in red pall-point: . . . *this is a very strange war* . . . Amen to that, he thought.

By the wall was the sandpit used again and again as the studio set for the *Newsnight* programme, a tatty little miniature desert reducing war to the status of a harmless children's game. Behind it, wall displays gave long lists of the deployment and technical resources of the BBC's mini-army. David's feelings of unease suddenly crystallized. It all seemed so gung-ho and out of step with any ideal of dispassionate reporting. The exhibition made the BBC seem no more than a wholehearted player in the military game, the Queen's Own Broadcasting Brigade. Then a dissident note caught his ear from a TV monitor mounted high on the back wall, playing a looped tape. He glanced up and was drawn into the familiar images. The lunar terrain of the Saudi–Kuwait border. The scrim nets camouflaging HQ vehicles, gun emplacements. The Desert Rats and the languid professionalism of their officers, anxious to display the merits of their Challenger tanks against the American M-1A1 Abrams. It looked familiar, but it didn't feel familiar. The smell was missing. The smell of diesel smoke in a damp, cold, muddy desert. The smell of the aftermath, the grotesque barbecue of the final assault.

He watched it, brooding, then the tape turned full circle and there was that dissident note again, a brief reminder of the way it had really been – a short clip from Jeremy Bowen's searing report of the civilian slaughter of the Amiriya shelter. Just a hint in the heavily edited shots – blackened bodies being removed through a tunnel of wailing mourners – of the real smell of modern war.

He turned away from the screen and that was when he saw one last display case, standing apart from the rest, in the corner of the room. The exhibition seemed so far removed from his personal experience of the war that he walked over to it without the slightest inkling of what it might contain, and only then saw Yanna's black-edged photo.

He slowly turned his eyes to it and saw her looking out at him, her mass of pale curls drawn back and tied behind her head, crinkled eyes tightened, smiling into the Dhahran sun in front of the Airport Hotel, and a savage ache constricted his throat and his eyes.

He just stood there, lost and staring at Yanna's face, the sadness and horror of the past week suddenly eclipsed by this overwhelming sorrow from five months earlier. In the end it was a voice next to him that dragged him back from his double mourning. It was a languid, affected voice, the last he wanted to hear – Bertram Glass, still technically his employer, but only for another twenty-four hours, until the end of the month brought the end of his contract, and freedom.

'Hello, David, old boy. I was looking for you.' He glanced at the display. 'Gives us a mention, anyway,' he said. 'Seemed a good thing to do with the stuff they forwarded to us. Just as well you never gave her a contract, though. I really don't know if we would have been covered against a claim.'

Glass didn't notice David's fists clench. He had a memory which emptied itself of all personal details that didn't directly concern him. If he had ever been told about the relationship that had flowered for so short a time between David and Yanna, it had long since gone into his private garbage can, pushed out by more pressing details of programme proposals, contracts and deadlines. David controlled himself, and Glass blundered on.

'Had my bloody car stolen over the weekend.'

'Sorry to hear that, Bertram,' said David, trying to keep any expression off his face.

'Taken from the bloody office.'

David let it pass and Glass rather gruffly had to go on. 'Have you had any more thoughts on what I said?'

'No, Bertram.'

'You don't have to make up your mind yet, you know. You could have a new contract from the autumn if you want a bit of a break.'

'No, Bertram. I'm not interested.'

Glass looked at him and started blinking as he always did before he mentioned money. David felt weary, but it wasn't easy to stop the man. 'We could go up a bit. As long as you didn't tell anyone. I could probably add on another ten K.'

'It's not a question of money.'

'Well, you've got to live on something. What are you going to do?'

'Bertram, thanks for your concern. I have plenty of savings. The answer's no.'

Glass looked sulky. 'I don't think you played it very straight, David. You know perfectly well I planned to take up the option on the second year.'

292

David had suddenly had enough of fending the man off politely. 'Look, Bertram,' he said, 'it was all in black and white. Either one of us could invoke the option clause as long as it was done by the end of June. I didn't want to. You forgot. End of story.'

He looked back at the display and Glass misunderstood. 'Not still feeling guilty about that, are you? You weren't to know she'd go rushing off. It wasn't your fault.'

'Forget it,' said David with considerably more force. 'You haven't a clue what I'm talking about. Just drop it, OK?'

Glass paused, nonplussed by the vehemence in his voice. 'Well . . . anyway, you're OK for tonight, aren't you? I'm sorry to drop you in it. No choice. I've got the speech here for you.'

David looked at him and at the document he was holding out. 'You mean you want me to just stand up there and read your words?'

'Well, yes. Didn't I make that clear?'

David took the papers without enthusiasm, shook his head looking at them, and then walked away without another word. Glass looked after him in puzzled frustration, then gave up and went back to talk to the type of people he understood.

David wandered on, away from the crowd. People he knew only slightly kept coming up to him with words of praise or with banal questions. He didn't want to talk. He didn't want to be a Gulf War media hero. He took the stairs to the lower halls, away from the knots of guests wandering through the exhibits, but there were people down there too. This was a voyeur's evening, TV management and paper pushers vastly outnumbering the people on the sharp end. He looked for an escape from the canapés, wine glasses and recycled, second-hand stories of other people's doings.

He saw a sign he'd never noticed before, pointing the

way to a new exhibit. On the spur of the moment he followed it away from all the people to a door made from a sheet of bent, stained corrugated iron. It opened when he pushed it and closed behind him, leaving him in unexpected darkness, which brought with it a sudden, vivid and immediate illusion of being in the open air. He was in a trench with a parapet of sandbags close by and the dome of the night above him. There was a faint whiff of explosive and the steady rumble and flicker of an artillery barrage out ahead of him on the horizon. For a moment he was transported back to the desert war in the long, freezing night before the advance. Then he looked at the dummies of the soldiers poised by the ladders to go over the top, and took in the extraordinary atmosphere of the museum's recreation of a First World War trench somewhere on the Western Front.

Recorded sounds of quiet conversations followed him as he walked slowly through the twists and turns of the trench. It was good. It had the feeling all right, but it was sanitized. This was a sombre place full of the lurking danger of the giant animal of war, just out there, but it had little of the muddy squalor of the Somme, of the Ypres Salient and Vimy Ridge. And now he knew something else. It mercifully lacked the unforgettable smell of explosive slaughter. He stopped and, in a dim light from a dugout, took Glass's speech from the pocket where he'd stuffed it and looked at the opening words.

Never before it began, *has a war been brought before us all so instantaneously. The Allied media were entrusted with a serious task – to tell that part of the tale which should be told, and to do their part in protecting our fighting forces. For once, there was no grey area between right and wrong.*

He snorted in disgust and looked around. In the dugout a dummy officer was conducting a taped conversation into a field telephone. In front of him on a rickety table was a box full of messages, orders and plans of attack. He stuffed the speech into it, saluted the dummy sardonically and left.

Later that evening, just by Piccadilly Circus, the Café Royal was full to the brim for the annual awards ceremony of the British Electronic Media Association. The dinner itself was passing in the usual way, spiced with a mixture of gossip, tall tales and one-upmanship. The telecrats and the deals men outnumbered the screen faces and, at each table, conversation was interspersed with much neck-craning around the room to see who else was there.

At Table H, right in the middle, the wife of the sales manager of Wessex TV looked at her celebrity neighbour and sighed to herself. What a face, she thought, the television doesn't do him credit. Any thinner and those sinews and shadows would look emaciated. As it is he's just plain uncompromising. He looks caged in here, she mused, as though he should be striding a poop deck in some Errol Flynn swashbuckler. It was an outdoor face, and she could imagine the dark hair blowing free in a mountain wind. She looked at her husband and sighed again, thinking, not for the first time, that what was left of his hair looked as if it had been dropped on him from a great height. She'd been hoping for a fun evening. She didn't often get to share the perks of her husband's life and tonight had sounded like a bit of a treat. Looked like it too when she found herself seated next to David Challis. As it was turning out, though, conversation was, frankly, a bit of a strain, and because she didn't pay very close attention to the newspapers, she didn't know why care seemed to sit so deeply upon him, why he seemed to be so lost in his thoughts. She looked at that strong profile and tried again.

'Mr Challis? What are you working on at the moment?'

Even that question seemed to cause him difficulty. He put down his coffee-cup, turned to her and said, 'Well, nothing specific really. I'm on my way to France for some personal –' but at that moment a gong sounded loudly and he turned gratefully towards the high table, where the Master of Ceremonies was calling for their attention.

It was time for the awards and, had he been a bit less preoccupied, David would have worked out that Bertram Glass must have known they were getting one to have bothered to prepare a speech. As it was, it only dawned on him towards the end of the huge build-up from the Master of Ceremonies that his own Gulf War documentary, *In the Path of the Storm*, had won the top billing. The man was laying it on thick. 'Brilliant, uncompromising, tough . . . leaving no one in any doubt how richly Saddam's forces deserved their fate . . . sensitively chosen imagery conveying the full horror of that tragic but necessary conflict.' In his present state of mind nothing could have been worse. He just wanted them to stop. Then the chairman of the association got to the point. 'Ladies and gentlemen, a leading commander in the Gulf said there was among the press corps one man he wished he'd had helping him fight the war, and not just filming it. We're very glad he chose the camera and not the gun. I give you that man . . . David Challis,' and the applause propelled him, unwillingly, to the rostrum.

As he looked down on a sea of people, the doubts he'd faced all evening disappeared. Her voice came to him from a great distance, and his mouth opened. He looked at the audience, all smiling from their tables, a few faces he knew well sprinkled through the massed ranks. Used to talking to ten million people at a time, hidden away beyond the camera lens, it was disconcerting to address, instead, three

296

hundred people in plain view, three hundred breathing, moving, reacting people. Still, his mind was made up. They were expecting a gracious speech of acceptance and they weren't going to get it.

'Few of you have seen a man get shot,' he began. Then into the startled silence that followed he went on. 'It's not like the movies any more. People don't clutch their chests, stagger a few paces and slump slowly to the ground. Modern ammunition has seen to that. Modern ammunition fired from weapons designed for annihilation, not for chivalry. Let me tell you about it. Two things happen. If you're lucky and you just get nicked, the force spins you violently round or even hurls you through the air.' He looked at all their open mouths. 'But if you get hit full on, the energy destroys your central nervous system. You fall like an armful of wet rags, just like that, before the eye can take it in. The camera can't cope with it. People disappear from your field of vision so fast it's like trick photography. You can't film death any more, only its aftermath.'

He let a count of three pass. 'This association has just been kind enough to give me an award. I feel ashamed to accept it. I have only learnt in the last few days that I have been wrong about many things that happened out there. Yanna Le Bihan taught me that. Most of you will remember that she, alone of the press corps, did not return from the Gulf. I say what I am about to say in memory of her. I have been praised here tonight for the sensitivity of the pictures we shot and edited together. She would have said that those pictures were squeamish, that they avoided the hard, brutal obscenity of death. She would have gone further. She would have said that by making war acceptable, we play along with those who see it as a satisfactory policy option.'

There was a murmur. He ignored it. 'We are used to the

style of the cinema, the long shot. The low angle on the feet, legs and covered-up torsos of corpses. The despatchers of bullets flailing away shooting from the hip, claiming more footage than the explicit disintegration of those who receive the bullets. Every time we have used those cinematic conventions in our news coverage, we have played our part in a conspiracy which makes war acceptable by suggesting it is little more than just another movie. Don't get me wrong. My camera crew, like all the others, shot the right pictures, tapes and tapes full of them, but in the edit suite we consigned them to oblivion, labelled them too strong to be shown, put them back on the shelf and so, perhaps, we played our part in the build-up to the next time bullets are used to solve a quarrel.'

The muttering grew. One man got up and ostentatiously walked out.

David looked around the room, 'The French, to take one example, don't do that. They show pictures on their news that would have the switchboards to Television Centre and to ITN jammed for hours. Many people here would say that shows they are more bloodthirsty, more callous than we are. That's what I used to say too. Now I think perhaps they're just more honest than we are, more able to be –' he searched for the right word '– mature about their attitudes. Maybe that's why it was the French who tried to find a diplomatic solution in the Gulf right up to the last possible moment.

'Our major failure, and the thing which brings me closest to despair, was that in the heady rush of the hundred-hour victory we leap-frogged right over the truest images of the land campaign. We went from tanks charging towards the Iraqi lines straight to liberated Kuwait. Logistics stopped the news teams bringing into all your living-rooms the unacceptable images of the damage done to the Iraqi army by some of the weapons of our own armed forces, by the Multiple Launch Rocket System and in particular by the Fuel Air Explosives.'

He stopped there and looked round. Several more people got up. Individual voices could be heard talking loudly in the hall. Three of the committee were conferring at the back. 'Disgraceful,' called out a voice. There was a little burst of applause and a few shushing noises. Might as well be hung for a sheep as for a lamb, he thought.

'Let me tell you a little about Fuel Air. It is a weapon of near-nuclear horror. It makes a huge fireball which fries people indiscriminately over a huge area. If its effects had been shown they would have aroused a storm of public protest. If you read all the gaudy colour picture-books of the war, you will hardly see it mentioned. Even if you study the more thoughtful books which are starting to appear, it barely slips in. No credit has been claimed for it by the military, because they want to be able to use it again and they know it would never stand up to public scrutiny. When questioned, they say they used napalm, as if that was perfectly all right. In comparison I suppose it would have been.'

Something else made him pause, the feeling that he wasn't being quite honest with himself. His central doubts resurfaced and he worked hard to turn them into words. It was plain to his audience that they were watching something unusual, an unprepared speech, straight from the heart. In some that was enough to make them listen despite the unpalatable nature of the message. Many were not so generous.

'I find myself torn,' he said. 'I was a strong supporter of the war. I still see no alternative response to that kind of aggression.' Some of the dissident voices in the hall fell silent. 'But from what I know now, I wish the war had been fought in a different way. People talk of the hidden agendas of the Gulf War. They discuss endlessly whether it was oil or whether it was Saddam's nuclear build-up that really lay behind the politicians' decisions. The other hidden agenda came not directly from the politicians but from those who supplied the hardware. They were the ones who saw the Gulf War as the biggest marketing opportunity they were ever likely to get, an opportunity to show what their products could do against living tissue and to stamp "Combat Proven" across all their glossy catalogues.' The voices started up again.

'I speak in shame. I had the pictures that could have brought it home, pictures of a tattered conscript army, shredded and burnt where they stood by weapons you have never guessed at. I had the time to use those pictures, but I chose not to do so because I made my film in anger. That is something I now intend to put right. Thank you for your award, but I only wish that I had made a different film.' He bowed his head and turned away from the microphone. A tiny ripple of applause was extinguished by several angry voices. Most of the audience were simply sitting in dumbfounded silence.

He got down and thought of marching straight out of the hall, but that seemed too melodramatic, so instead he made his way back to Table H, looking straight in front of him, and sat down again beside the sales manager's wife, who smiled at him uncertainly. A large, florid-faced man in a dinner-jacket got up from the next table and tapped him on the shoulder.

'Balls, that's all balls,' he said, nearly shouting. 'What did you expect the military to do? Go into battle with one hand tied behind their backs just to give the Iraqis a fair chance? Well?'

But David, overwhelmed by the power of his conversion

300

and the release of so much of his pent-up contradiction, could only shake his head at a question he knew he couldn't answer. The sales manager's wife summoned up all her courage. 'Leave him alone,' she said. 'He's had a very hard time.'

Chapter Twenty-eight

'He was definitely still in London last night?'

'Yeah, I told yer. Sim sat outside the museum, then this joint in Regent Street. Follered 'im all the way 'ome. Could 'ave done 'im, no problem.'

'Don't even think about it,' barked Busby. 'Not on our own doorstep. Even that plonker from Hexham might get excited if you did that.'

He pressed the button on the cassette player again. 'If it really is Bamco, they won't know I'm going and they won't know what I'm after. I'm far more worried they'll try something here,' said David's voice, and Busby turned it off.

Sledge chuckled and Busby turned on him. 'What's so fucking funny?' Sledge fell silent. Busby thought fast. Mostly he was thinking about Purkiss and Donaldson. This was not what he needed right now. He knew all too well that Purkiss valued him for his skill at keeping things under control. This was not under control at all, not at all. It felt like a wheel was about to come off. Most of all it was this sodding brother. But for him, things would be fine.

He added up the pros and cons. They'd got the videos back. The police still thought Duncan had boozed himself into a tree. If he had followed up his threat and sent any letter to the M.o.D., it hadn't done any apparent damage. Since he'd snuffed it they were bound to decide it was just

302

drunken ramblings. On the other hand there were the bloody French girl's photos. They were an unknown factor. He thought back. They had to be from the first Dodgem test. He knew they shouldn't have let an outsider in. Purkiss fancied her, that was the trouble. She was only meant to be there for the silly shots of him in the body armour. It had been Purkiss's idea to stick her in the chopper to come on the test, thought he might get off with her or something, but she'd left with Challis in the end. Course that must have been how the brother came into it. The pictures sounded like they could be the real problem. France had certain advantages. It wasn't England for a start, and he remembered Sledge had some mates in France.

'OK, Sledge. You fucked up at the house. Time to put things right. Here's what we do.'

All David had was an address. He'd rung round while he was in London. There was no easy way to get to where he was going except to drive there. He booked the car on to Brittany Ferries out of Plymouth on the midday Wednesday sailing, sorted out some fresh clothes and set off, thinking about the exhibition and about the dramatic effect of his speech. I bet they wish they hadn't given me the award, he thought, and I bet everyone who knows about Duncan just thinks I've gone off my trolley because of that.

It was a three-and-a-half-hour drive thanks to some road works around Bristol. He only stopped for fuel, so Busby and Sledge Hanmer, flying in a private charter to Morlaix, were in France, picking up the cars Sledge had fixed, long before David was finally turning into Plymouth's Millbay Docks.

*

David stood on the starboard deck of the ferry *Bretagne*. He'd eaten on board and watched a film to while away the long crossing. Now he was staring at the rocky North Brittany coastline looming up and wondering what he would say to Yanna's mother. The letters they'd exchanged after the French military gave her the bad news from the Gulf had given him no clue about her. What do you say to the grieving mother you've never met of the woman you loved? Especially when you can't shake the feeling that but for you she'd still be alive.

The docking was delayed. It was getting dark and raining as he drove out of the echoing hold, where colliding ramps of metal made vast, shaky, booming noises, down the ramp and through a cursory immigration check. David was worrying about the fact that he suddenly felt free from danger. He felt certain that the focus of their opponents' attention was still on Otterburn and that in some way he was letting the side down here, hundreds of miles away, insulated from all that by the width of the English Channel. In this his hunches were letting him down. If he'd looked very carefully into the gloomy drizzle, he might have seen a man in dock workers' overalls compare the Jensen's registration with something written on a piece of paper and walk rapidly off to dial the mobile-phone number he had been given, thereby earning by far the easiest thousand francs of his dissolute life.

Sledge's ex-Legion mate from Brest reckoned there were only two likely routes the man could take. It took a bit of working out because the name of the place on the tape hadn't been very clear, but when they played it to Jean-Philippe, he got it straight away.

'Quiberon,' he said. 'Southward. On the coast. The obvious way would be down to Landivisiau to join the N165 at Le Faou, then it is a fast drive, a good road all the way past

Quimper and Lorient. If your friend wants to stay off the big roads or he wants to waste time, there is the other way, more to the east. It is very twisty, through Pleyber-Christ and Carhaix-Plouguer. We could wait for him right outside the ferry port, before the roads separate, to see which he chooses.'

'No,' said Busby, 'if he's going to twig us, that's where he'll be most watchful. We ought to be down the road a bit so we get him when he's relaxed.' They looked at the map. 'Just as well we've got two cars. We'll watch the first route. We'll park up somewhere around this place here, Ste Catherine. You take the twisty one. That way we're more likely to see him and then you can catch us up cos you know the roads better, right?'

Jean-Philippe nodded. Sledge was looking at the phone in his lap with a puzzled frown.

''Old on, Johnny,' he said, 'Just tell me 'ow this bugger works again before you piss off. Right from the top.'

They'd been waiting in the village, peering at the cars passing, for some time when the phone went off, its harsh tone making them jump. Sledge prodded it doubtfully and the ringing went on, so Busby snatched it out of his hands and pressed the button.

'I am behind him,' said Jean-Philippe. 'He has chosen the slow way. It is an easy car to spot.'

'Bugger it,' said Busby. He went to start up, then considered the chances of Sledge successfully managing the map-reading and changed his mind. 'Jump out,' he said. 'You're driving.'

In the Jensen, oblivious to the cars behind him, David had chosen the indirect route for a very good reason. He had no intention of arriving unannounced on Madame Le Bihan late at night. He was feeling sudden enormous anxiety at the meeting ahead, trying his best to deal with the resurfacing of all kinds of painful memories, and was only too pleased for an excuse to delay it until the morning. He stopped at several likely places. They were all full. The rain came and went and he was very tired. In Pontivy he nearly rammed a Citroën 2CV, unable to see the markings of a road junction properly with the street lights reflecting on the slick, wet tarmac. He decided that was definitely a signal to stop, so he tried a few hotels before finding a room at the Hôtel de l'Europe by the big market square. He had no appetite for food and went straight to bed.

Thursday August 1st 1991

Waking, disoriented in his small attic bedroom with its sloping ceiling, he lay there rubbing his eyes, reassembling the fleeing shreds of his dream. He had been with Yanna in the little house she had described to him, the divided cottage overlooking the sea, she in one side, her mother in the other. He had been dressed in uniform and she had been slowly undressing him, teasing him and telling him how much better he would feel without it. The transition from the soft dream of Yanna alive and a warm future in front of him to the brutal reality of Yanna dead and nothing ahead but sorrow curled him into foetal misery.

He breakfasted in that self-conscious silence which comes from being alone in a hotel dining-room where everyone else is in groups. It made him feel he was eating terribly fast so he deliberately paused a long time between mouthfuls, but that made him even more self-conscious, so in the end he finished as quickly as he could and left. The bill was larger than he expected and he went out into a fine, blustery morning. Jean-Philippe, watching from the far side of the car park, glanced across the road to Busby's car and nodded his head, but David didn't make straight for his car. He was still in no hurry to confront the day so he walked round the little town for a while, knowing that all he was doing was putting off the last leg. He looked at the French women in the *boulangerie*, imagining each of them as Yanna's mother, trying to anticipate the kind of conversation he would have and failing. He wondered if she would even be there, but he knew she would.

Yanna had told him her mother had had a very eventful life in the past. 'My mother and my father they always had adventures, busy times,' she had said. 'It seemed normal when I was young. Always the exciting life. Now he is dead a long time and she has taken root. Like a tree. She says she will never travel again. She laughs at me. She says for me it is all zoom, zoom, but one day I will be like her.' Well, that's true, he thought bitterly. Yanna's taken root. Her travelling's done. There was a sudden grey gust of wind.

Even when he was back in the car, it was an effort to start up. Eventually he took the little road through St Nicodème down to Auray, where an arm of the nearly land-locked Gulf of Morbihan reached into the town bringing the fresh scent of the sea on the air. Yachts were moored down the centre of the river, their rigging rattling with impatience in the gusting wind. Seagulls cried. At Plouharnel the signs to the Carnac standing stones nearly diverted him from his track, but by now he was getting irritated at his own time-wasting and he forged on.

A mile or two later he was into the final section of his journey, as the land narrowed around him and he was suddenly skirted by sea on both sides on the thin strip of the Presqu'île de Quiberon. Left to itself it would only have been a matter of time before it became a complete island, but man's determination to assert his chosen state of affairs over nature had put a stop to that process. The first half of its ten-mile length was barely more than a road, with some trees struggling in the sand-dunes and a beach on each side. He drove slowly. The traffic behind him seemed in no great hurry. To his right the wind was hammering great Atlantic breakers on to the rocks that dotted the sea. He tried unsuccessfully to remember his history, details of the Battle of Quiberon Bay. It must have been a hell of a place for combat between ungainly square-riggers. The technology of modern sailing was all around, a dozen wind-surfers tearing at enormous speed across the waves, leaping from wave tops. The tide was out and on the sand itself there were more sails, three-wheeled sand-yachts bowling stiffly in curving darts up to the seething edge of the water, then turning awkwardly to shoot back to the shingle again.

At the Fort de Penthièvre the land widened enough to give it some feeling of permanence, and for the last four miles there were little villages, windswept clusters of houses and even side-roads. After passing the village of St Pierre he saw Quiberon itself ahead. He remembered Yanna's description and bore left towards the south-east corner of the long promontory, looking for the road that ran around its very tip. There was a little fishing port called Haliguen, with its original stone walls engulfed by a marina development, leaving its small lighthouse, if not exactly land-locked, then certainly no longer representing the outer frontier of safety. He parked on the Quai des Sinagots to seek directions.

A pretty, dark-haired Breton girl was passing and was all too keen to stop when he spoke to her. Her intonation was very like Yanna's. She pointed out the road winding round the far side of the little harbour. She knew Yanna's mother well, it seemed. 'Mais Madame Le Bihan, elle n'est *pas chez elle.*' That seemed almost a reprieve to David, but it soon turned out she wasn't far away from home. The girl said he would find her where she usually spent her time, around the Fort Neuf, just a short way down the road, not at the Maison Blanche du Conguel, where she lived. The girl smiled after him in appreciation as he drove off, toying with the idea of dropping in, just by chance, on Madame Le Bihan later on.

The Fort was by a bend in the road, an ancient stone redoubt, solidly built and with its double gates open. There was a historical marker board declaring that this was the place where the emigrants of the Quiberon expedition surrendered to General Hoche in 1795. That meant nothing to David. He went inside through the gates in the perimeter wall. It encircled a series of well-kept stone buildings with smart, red-painted doors. It was clearly some sort of sailing centre. There were boat trailers, masts and sailboards, and a caravan. No one was there. He climbed up on a grassy mound on the seaward side and found himself looking out across a wild seascape. Down to the right, just a little further along the road, was a car park, a beach and a slipway. Two boys in wet suits were getting their windsurfers ready on the slip in the rising, tearing wind. There were more sails out to sea. Then, with a sinking heart, he saw a woman of perhaps sixty, swathed in a bulky grey woollen coat, who was sitting on the low wall by the slip, gazing glumly out to sea.

He stood there for a while looking at her, then pulled himself together and walked back the way he'd come, out to the road and round to the car park. He approached her slowly, and her gaze never wavered from the sea in front. 'Madame Le Bihan?' he asked, and she turned slowly to look at him. She was older than he thought, with a coarsely wrinkled face. He noticed a very cleft chin with two or three bristly white hairs. She looked at him uncomprehendingly and he repeated her name, then she shook her head silently and pointed out to sea.

For a moment David thought she was saying she wanted to be left alone with the elements, then he followed the line of her pointing hand and saw a figure, far out, in among the reefs, on a rocketing windsurfer with a bright red sail. He looked again at the woman. '*Madame le Bihan*,' she said emphatically, in a gravelly voice. '*Voyez.*'

He stood watching, all his preconceptions blown away in the now nearly gale-force wind. The other windsurfers on the slipway were giving up, packing their gear away again, grumbling about the conditions. Those who were still out in the bay were heading in. The woman with the red sail, furthest out of all, didn't seem troubled. He stood there watching her for the best part of another half-hour, long after she was the only one remaining out there, as she tore back and forth, weaving in and out of the rocks, before at last she too turned for home. She came back in like a speedboat, flying from the wave tops. As she executed a stylish duck gybe and stepped into the water, he walked down the slipway. She pulled the board on to the beach next to the slip, turned and took off her helmet, shaking out her hair. David was frozen to the spot. Standing before him was an older version of Yanna. The blonde hair was cut shorter, the face was more seasoned, but the figure inside the tight black wet suit was the same and so was everything about the smooth grace of her movements and the way she held herself, as if stretching up to receive the blessing of the sky. He felt a sudden pain as he watched.

She bent to deal with the board, and David stood there like a statue as she derigged the mast, the boom and the sail. She seemed so busy that he thought he was unobserved, but she suddenly turned to him, arms akimbo, and challenged him. '*Monsieur, pourquoi vous me fixez comme ça?*'

He was flustered and quickly answered that he was just waiting for a good moment to introduce himself. Hearing the slight English accent, she gave him a searching look, then her defensive expression disappeared and she smiled a broad, beautiful smile, so completely Yanna that it was as if she had been brought back to him from the dead.

'No need,' she said in English. 'I know who you are. You are David Challis. Am I right?'

'How did you know?'

'My daughter told me enough about you.' She saw the look in his eyes and, reaching out to shake his hand, turned it instead into a warm clasp of steady pressure. 'I am Gwenaelle. We have both lost something precious. Now we will be friends. Come back to the house and we will talk.'

'Let me help you with that stuff.'

'That would be kind. I leave it here, inside the fort.'

They put it away and he opened the car door for her. 'I will make your seat wet,' she objected. 'I usually walk. It is not too far.'

'It's all right. Leather soon recovers,' he said. Indeed, the house was only a few hundred yards further on. It was a long, low cottage of white-painted stone, standing on a gentle grass mound which descended on terraces of rock into the sea. The bay in front of it was dotted with rocks and reefs. It was just as Yanna had described it, a place of great natural grandeur, or it would have been if someone hadn't built some immensely long, curved holiday apartments along the road immediately behind it.

She poured him a glass of rough, red wine, took one herself and went to shower. He sat in the room, looking out across the sea, wondering how he would start to tell her and trying to work it all out. Yanna had been twenty-six. He was thirty-six. Yanna's mother must be maybe

311

forty-five, but she certainly didn't look it. She came back wearing jeans and a floppy sweater with a white towel round her head.

'That feels better,' she said. 'How is your wine?'

'Very good. I'm sorry just to turn up like this. I should have written, but there were some pressing reasons.'

'I am very pleased to see you here.'

She was so like Yanna in every way that sitting there with her was part delight and part agony.

'I've had a fax from the Gulf,' he said. 'It has made me feel rather doubtful about some of the conclusions I had come to.'

'You mean the answers of the young soldier, Awatif?' she said, watching him.

'Yes,' he said, surprised. 'Have you seen them too?'

'Yes. What do you make of it?'

'There's this company called Bamco,' he began, and ten minutes later he had told her all he knew of Yanna's last hours, including to his great surprise his own misunderstandings and recriminations. He told her about the tape Nick had found with Yanna's message, trying his utmost to keep his voice from cracking. 'I'm still waiting for the film,' he said. 'I hope that might show a bit more when Lieutenant-Colonel Marshall sends it.'

'Have these people from Bamco made any threat or done anything against you in England?' she asked, and he realized he had left out any mention of Duncan's death and what had subsequently happened. It was as if focusing again on Yanna had locked away the rest of his mourning in a separate compartment. Her eyes widened as he told her all about Duncan. Again he found himself saying much more than he expected to. It wasn't at all like talking to a country-dwelling Breton mother. It was more like a conversation with a very intelligent policeman. Gwenaelle put in the occasional pertinent question, but otherwise she just listened and occasionally nodded. She never seemed to doubt what he said for a moment.

'Is your sister-in-law safe at the house?'

'I have this very tough producer, Nick. Yanna knew him. He's there.'

'Ah, yes. The amazing Nick. Yanna wrote to me of Nick, but is that enough?'

'He was bringing some friends to help.'

'Phone them,' she said, 'phone them now. Just to check.'

He dialled the number. It was picked up on the second ring. Josie's voice answered. 'David. I'm so glad. We were going up the wall wondering how to get hold of you. You didn't leave us a number.'

'What's happened?' he asked in sudden fear.

'Well, a few things. Nick will tell you in a moment.'

'Are you OK?'

'Yes, I'm being very well looked after. There's Donnie. He's out by the front drive. He's one of Nick's goons. The Millwall arm-wrestling champion. Then there's Gunk. He doesn't talk much. Nick's put him on night duty so he's upstairs asleep at the moment. Cross between an oak tree and a Rottweiler. Then there's Ove.'

'That makes me happier. What about George Middleton?'

There was a hesitation, and her voice changed, and then before she had said more than a word he knew why she had sounded so brittle and bright. 'Not very good news, David. He was conscious for just a little while. I went to see him, but he couldn't really talk, and then he got much worse again. They think it's a blood clot. They don't think he's going to survive, I'm afraid.'

He waited for her to go on, but all he heard was a small stifled sound. It was as if her bravery was finally exhausted.

313

'Poor love,' he said. 'I'll be back as soon as I can. I'm in . . .'

'*No*,' she said sharply. 'Don't say. Here's Nick.'

Wondering at this, David heard Nick's voice on the line. 'Dave. Don't tell me where you are, just in case.'

Jesus, David thought. 'In case of what?'

'In case there are any more little electronic nasties in this house like the ones my pal Ove found this morning with his sweeping machine.'

'Start at the beginning, Nick.'

'Have I told you about Ove? He runs his own electronic outfit. Snooping and sweeping and all that. It's a long story and I'll give you most of it later, but he's going to be very useful. Anyway, first off, he starts doing party tricks with bits of gear and showing us this new bug sweeper. He hides a bug and sniffs it out. Trouble is, after he takes the bug away the machine goes right on bleeping. We ribbed him a bit about what a crap machine it was. He thought it was up the creek too when the lights kept flashing, but then he decided to try believing it instead, and it found four more.'

'The house was *bugged*?'

'On the button. You catch on quick.'

'Maybe they'd been there a long time.'

'Ove says no. They had one-week cells in, maybe still half charged.'

'So that means . . .'

'So that means I'm very glad we've got Nick Nielsen's private army on hand, and if anyone shows their face we'll have him. It also kinda makes me think the guy I found in the house was putting them in place. But there's one more thing which bothers me quite a lot. I don't think we're the ones who should be worrying, because it also means our friends probably know just where you are, pal, and just what you're doing, so you take care. A lot of care.'

314

Chapter Twenty-nine

Same day

David hung up the phone and became aware that Gwen-aelle had been watching him closely.

'Is everything all right there?'

'Not really. They're all safe. The hospital says the old man, George Middleton, is unlikely to pull through. Josie will miss him a lot.'

'You too, I think?'

He looked at her and nodded. 'Yes, I will. He's a very wise man. He's lived this quiet, isolated life. All he did for years was to provide company to an old lady, but he sees things terribly clearly. He did more to make me think about war and its values than anyone else, except Yanna.' He stopped short there. 'There's something else, though. They've found microphones in the house. Nick thinks the Bamco people must know I'm here. They would have heard us talking about the trip. He thinks there may be much more danger at this end than back there.'

Surprisingly, she smiled. 'Good,' was all she said.

'Well,' he said, nonplussed, 'I think I'd better be off quickly in case he's right. I rather think I may have brought trouble with me.'

'You think someone followed you?'

David tried to cast his mind back. 'The truth is, I simply wasn't even thinking about it. There were certainly cars

315

behind me most of the time, but then there would be, wouldn't there?'

'Let me make a telephone call.'

She came over to him, lifted the receiver and dialled a number. She asked for someone by name. When he came on the line, she gave a short series of terse instructions. 'I want to know about any strange males in town, probably foreigners.' She listened. 'I know it is the holiday season. I mean males without accompanying families, especially those in my immediate area or seeking directions. Get on to it, please, Grégoire, and stay in touch. I may need to get back to you quickly.'

He looked on in astonishment as she put the phone down. 'Who was that?'

'The police.'

'How can you do that?' he said. 'It sounded as if you were giving them orders and they seemed to be taking them.'

Gwenaelle looked at him, half smiling, half thoughtful, and pursed her lips. 'David, I presume that Yanna took her responsibilities seriously and didn't ever tell you her parents' life story?'

'She never had much time,' he said flatly, and she gave a thoughtful nod.

She turned and looked out of the window at the sea. 'Yanna's father and I, we worked together for very many years in a government department, attached to the DGSE. You know what that is?'

'The French Secret Service?' said David incredulously.

'Yes. That was where we met. He was killed in Africa. He was, well, let us say he was doing something he probably should not have been doing in the old French colonies where our government has found it so hard to give up its influence. Yanna was only thirteen, but I kept on with it.

It was difficult, but she gave me good cover and the service helped a lot. Anyway, these days I am still on the books in a limited way. I have some special skills which I am called on to use, for advisory purposes and training, that sort of thing. The result is I still have my links when I need them, and the head of the police here is an old friend.'

David could only stare at her, and she swung round to him. 'So you see, David who my daughter loved, you and I both want to meet the men who killed her. I want to meet them very badly indeed.'

David nodded, belatedly recognizing that he was in the presence of someone much more used to this kind of problem than he would ever be.

'OK. What do you suggest we do? I mean, for all we know, they may not even be here.'

'We have to hope they are. We must find out. We will put out something to act as bait. The jam that will bring out the wasps. I think they will come buzzing.'

'If they listened to us back there when we were discussing the photos Yanna took, then yes, I expect they will.'

'The photos. Yes. That will do it and then we will be ready for them.'

Jean-Philippe had done well. He had a mate he sometimes did business with, who worked in a scrapyard on the Vannes side of Auray, and the mate produced a little Citroën truck – local plates and anonymous enough to pass anywhere. Sledge Hanmer and Geoff Busby weren't too comfortable sliding around in the back when Jean-Philippe forgot himself on corners, but it allowed them to stay out of sight, so even though the gendarmes were soon on to the two strange cars that had been seen earlier cruising round Quiberon, they took no notice of the van. The cars had been tucked away safely, in a warehouse the scrap man had access to.

'So that is the house. What now? Do you want to drive past it again?'

Jean-Philippe had the worst breath Busby had ever smelt and he was glad to be some distance away in the back. 'No,' he said. 'Use your eyes. That's them further along, walking, see? Leastways that's Challis, so the other one's got to be the mother. Why don't you pop out, Jean-Philippe, and trot along after them. They don't look like they're just out for a stroll.' And, he thought, that will give us a break from the halitosis at the same time.

'They will see me. There are not too many other people here. I am not dressed like a tourist.'

It was true that blue overalls weren't the most likely thing to be wearing on the beach. Busby craned over the back of the seat, looking out through the windscreen. 'Pretend you're fishing.'

'I do not have a rod.'

'What's that sign about? The big one right over there?'

'It is about the rules for the searching for the er . . . the *huitres* and the *belons*. What is the word?'

'*Huitres*? Oh, right, shellfish. Oysters and that. Right then, there you are.'

Gwenaelle hadn't explained. She had just taken a torch and led the way out of the house, with a mysterious look on her face, and eyes that searched ceaselessly without being given away by too many movements of her head. It was only half a mile along the beach to a flat area of rock pools stretching far out to the falling tide. In the dunes above the high-water mark a single stone stood pencil-thin, pointing to the sky, and by it, in the entrance to a mound of sandy earth, a stone lintel was set above the gateposts to a dark doorway. There was faint carving in relief on the stone. The megalithic men who built this dolmen five thousand years before had covered the vertical surfaces of the subterranean corridor with richly worked symbols, and time had failed so far to obliterate all of them.

She went in first, David following, stooping to walk with difficulty along the low, narrow passageway lined with slabs of stone. They turned a bend and it got darker as the light from the doorway dwindled, then she stopped and he bumped gently into her. 'David,' she whispered, 'I would like to introduce you to Er Vam Vraz.' She clicked the torch on and a crudely carved face leapt at them. They were in a wider chamber off the curving passageway. 'It is what Yanna and I called her when we first saw her here. In the Breton language it means Big Mother,' explained Gwenaelle. She shone the torch up and down the small stone. The figure carved on it covered it completely, and David could see the row of simply represented breasts. 'Later, Yanna used to call her Er Vaouez Chansus, the Lucky Lady. From when we very first lived here, she would come to this place and talk to the lady, all by herself.'

They fell silent and David tried to get a feeling of Yanna's presence. It eluded him and left him with a sense of failure. Then Gwenaelle, listening to his silence, put an arm round him, and he smelt her scent in the warm darkness and realized that here, in this woman, was the most tangible form of Yanna's presence he could ever hope for now. They crouched like that in the silence for some time, thinking their own thoughts, then Gwenaelle stirred.

'Now we will see if my guess is right. Shine the torch for me.'

She went to the carved stone, took a knife from her pocket and, using it as a lever, began very carefully to pry it from its place among the surrounding stones. 'Do not worry,' she said, 'I am not a vandal. They took the real one to the Carnac museum years ago now because all the tourists wanted to touch it here. This is a copy. When they put it in, Yanna and I found we could move it, so we started using it for treasure hunts and as a secret place to put surprises for each other.'

She placed the stone carefully on the floor, and David shone the torch beam into the recess behind it.

'Yes!' she said. 'There it is.'

In the space behind the stone was a plastic bag. They opened it. Inside was a flat brown envelope, full of colour photographs. In the torchlight it was hard to make them out. 'We will take them outside,' she said.

'Is that wise? They may be watching.'

A hard edge came into her voice then. 'Of course it is wise. That is the only reason for doing it.'

Outside, in the sunlight, she made no attempt to conceal the pictures, quite the reverse. She held them up, looking at them, showing them to David as they walked, even gesticulating using them. They went and sat on a rock with a good view all round, both to see and to be seen, and that was where they first looked at them carefully.

It was clear enough when you saw it all in sequence. Two launches on motor drive, with Yanna's Nikon eating a whole roll, thirty-six frames, for each one. Ten or eleven seconds probably covered each launch. She had kept it on wide angle so the surrounding sky gave a good frame of reference to the missile's path. The first film had that familiar jinking trail as the missile soared crazily into the air and circled. Six frames had been enough to cover the second half of its flight, still jinking, to explode in quite the wrong place, as the startled men in the foreground, crouching and turning to look behind them, showed all too clearly.

320

The databack had printed the time and the exposure number on each one. There was no doubt. The second missile had hit the target bang on the nose. No one could have disputed that. The only little problem was that the smooth curve down to earth was matched by the smooth upward curve of the launch. Whatever made Dodgem dodge had been given the heave-ho for that one. Then David remembered the jump-cut in Duncan's video. These were the same two dud launches, cut together by his brother to look like one successful one, and he understood for certain exactly what had made his brother think he could put the squeeze on Bamco.

'Don't look up,' whispered Gwenaelle. 'Show me that photo again. Look excited about it.'

'Why are we whispering?'

'Fat man in blue trousers. He's on the rocks down to our right. He's the one.'

David waited a while, then looked casually all round. 'It's not Busby. I don't recognize him. How do you know?'

'He's pretending to gather shellfish, but it is the off-season. He picked up some over there.'

'Perhaps he just doesn't know?'

'No, he's looking towards us and he's just walked right through the best patch of oysters this side of La Baule. He didn't even bend down.'

'OK. What now?'

'Wait for him to go past and we'll walk slowly back. Try to keep him in front of us and see where he goes.'

Ten minutes later Jean-Philippe was back in the van and driving off.

'Wait a minute, where are you going?'

'Be quiet, Busby. They were just behind me. I cannot

321

stay without risking that they may notice.' He drove for a couple of minutes, then parked round the corner. 'They have something. They went to a pile of rocks on the beach, one of those old grave things. When they came out, they were waving these photos around as if they could not believe it. They sat down and looked right through them. Maybe forty or fifty of them.'

'Right,' said Busby, relieved to have something solid to justify the trouble. 'Better get our thinking caps on, Sledge. Tonight's the night.'

Gwenaelle came back downstairs. David was looking carefully out of the window round the edge of the curtain.

'They have gone,' she said, 'but not far. I can see the top of the van from the window in the attic. They are deciding what to do next.'

He looked at her a little doubtfully. 'Gwenaelle, I'm sure you know what you're doing, but these people play it very rough. How do you want to handle it?'

'In my own time and my own place. Not now. First we consider their options, then we cross out some of them. Why don't you pour us another glass of wine.' She picked up the phone again.

By six o'clock in the evening Busby had finished off the planning to his own satisfaction. Straight in at a quiet moment. Sledge would snuff them both, then he and Jean-Philippe could fake up something with the dinghy and the canoe they could see in the lean-to by the cottage – take them out to sea in the dark and tip it up. They moved the van back a hundred yards or so, to where they had a view obliquely down to the cottage and the flats behind it. They

322

let an hour and a half pass, until all the holiday-makers had gone home and those who were going out to eat had drifted off again. Then Busby gave the word and they got out, with the promise of violence adding a spice to the air.

It was as if a button had been pressed. As the van doors slammed behind them, a rising howl of rubber stopped them in their tracks. A Peugeot 504 appeared, swaying and snaking at high speed round the bend, and screeched to a halt in front of the holiday apartments. Two men in business suits jumped out of it, one holding a suitcase, and ran into the building. Busby held up a hand and they shrank back behind the van because once again rubber was howling, but this time there were the sounds of sirens in addition. They got quickly back in the van, watching through the windscreen as two police cars came in the same way and a third shot past the van from the other direction and blocked the road.

'Fuckin' 'ell, let's get out of it,' said Sledge.

'No, wait. This isn't about us,' said Busby. 'Sit tight.'

So they waited and watched nervously, Jean-Philippe's fingers toying with the key in the ignition. The police stormed into the building. Ten minutes later they came out, frog-marching one of the two business-suited men. There was no sign of the other man or the suitcase. A police car took him away, but the others didn't leave.

'One of them's hidden, I reckon. What do you think it is?'

'Dunno,' said Sledge. 'Drugs maybe?'

'Could be,' said Jean-Philippe. 'What now?'

'Well, we can't do anything while they're around. Let's give it an hour, go for a drive.'

An hour later the only thing that had changed was that some very obvious plain-clothes men in two dark saloon cars were staking out the house with a police van to back them up a hundred yards away, tucked, not very cleverly, half out of sight.

'Bugger this,' said Busby. 'We'll come back tomorrow.'

'They might be still 'ere,' said Sledge.

'There's more than one way to skin a cat,' said Busby. 'Jean-Philippe, we need a bit more help. I wonder if your friend might know someone.'

The phone rang and Gwenaelle answered. She made noises of agreement a few times and hung up, looking pleased.

'Good,' she said. 'I think we are clear until daylight. The police will stay out there all night.'

'And tomorrow?'

'Tomorrow is another day. There are many things I want to talk about before then. Now I will cook you something.'

While she prepared the food, David wandered round the kitchen filling her glass and enjoying her company.

'At the slipway,' he said, 'you knew who I was straight away. What had Yanna said to you?'

Gwenaelle looked at him steadily before answering, as if weighing up whether he could take it. 'She told me you looked like an Arctic explorer. The sort of man who always looks as if his eyes are searching for the North Pole.'

David let out his breath. 'Not quite as certain as saying I was six foot two with black hair.'

Gwenaelle carried the plates through to the table and they sat down. 'Do you want to know what else she said?'

David hesitated, weighing the pain and the pleasure, but knew he couldn't say no. 'Tell me.'

'She said you were a rock she felt she wanted to wreck herself on. She told me that when you came back from the Gulf she wanted to make love to you for ever and she told me she wanted to marry you.' Gwenaelle measured the pain in his face and went on. 'She knew she and I had the same opinions about men, so it is no surprise that I recognized you.'

David looked at her across the table, through the candle flame between them, and felt, suddenly and confusingly, a little return of that electric buzz he had once known with Yanna. Disconcerted, he made a bid for neutral ground. 'Did she write to you often?'

'Very often, but not for the final two weeks.'

'Is there anything else I can tell you?'

'Thank you. I know that is not easy, but I have read all your statements and everything else I could get. I pulled some strings, you see. You have helped to fill in the blank sections.' He nodded, but she hadn't finished. 'There is one thing I do want to know.'

'Of course. What is it?'

'Yanna told me what it was like between you. She said it was better to wait until the war was out of the way before going further. She said too many bad emotions were in the way of your love. But that was before you went into the desert. Did you make love then?'

David hesitated. This wasn't a conversation he had ever expected to have, but it seemed surprisingly natural. 'No. It was just . . . Well, it just wasn't possible.'

'Would you have married her?'

'I . . . I never had time to think of that, we were always rushing around. But yes, I couldn't have imagined leaving her.'

'Why?'

'She was so beautiful. As beautiful as you are. But it was more . . . I think she was the only woman I've met who had the need to move as fast as I do.'

Gwenaelle drew in her breath. 'And you think that would have been good for you?'

He just shook his head slowly and she left the topic alone. Supper went on, a slow, intense meal. There was a complicated bond between them and David recognized it had a strong sexual element.

After the meal Gwenaelle got up. 'Now,' she said, 'you have only seen half the house. You know the other half was Yanna's. Would you like to see it?'

'I don't know.'

'I think you should.'

There were photos on the walls of the studio, which looked out over the sea. Photos on one wall of death, photos on the opposite wall of life. The Saharan wars in terrible close-up facing a picture essay on birth. The bedroom smelt of Yanna. The walls were hung with bleached-out calico dyed in patchy, irregular light blue. David breathed it in. There was a photo on the table – mother and daughter smiling together, alike as two peas in a pod, two master-works from the hand of the same great painter at different stages in his life.

After two or three minutes a mist came over David's eyes and he turned away. Gwenaelle closed the connecting door. She put both her arms around him and hugged him. He buried his face in her hair and it was the same as Yanna's hair. He stayed absolutely still and she just went on hugging him, then after a long time his sadness turned to something else. Her face lifted to his and their mouths met and it was the same as Yanna's mouth. They kissed with increasing fervour until she broke away, breathing deeply. She took his hand and led him to a bedroom with a large brass double bed in it. 'This is my room,' she said.

'Where shall I sleep?' he asked.

'Here,' she said. 'This is not a normal night. There are many reasons why we should not be apart.'

Chapter Thirty

Friday August 2nd 1991

It was hard to close the zip. The neoprene suit fitted like a glove. David's shoulders were, if anything, too wide for it, but that was a small price to pay for protection from the savage wind gusting around them and whipping the spray across the beach. He pulled on the boots she had found for him in the shed and looked around for the gloves.

The telephone had finally interrupted the tail-end of their lovemaking that morning. They had woken twice during the night to take up where they had left off, as though they had to fit all the sexual variations possible into that brief space of darkness. David had never known its like before. Gwenaelle stripped him of his reserve with a passion and energy that had him crying out and raking her back with his fingers as her legs twined round him. That reserve might have resurfaced when he woke in the daylight reality of a strange bed, but the manner of his waking never gave him a chance. She was already astride and around him, arching down to brush her lips across his as he opened his eyes from an erotic dream which was no dream after all. Now David couldn't begin to come to terms with it and could no longer see the need to rationalize it. As he looked across at Gwenaelle preparing to sail, a sexual ache came back to remind him of the wet suit's tight fit, but it seemed as though that Gwenaelle had slipped away to be replaced by a colder, sterner, older person.

Whatever she heard on the phone had made her smile with satisfaction and look out of the window at the sea.

'They have been asking the right questions,' was all she would say, 'and they have been given the right answers. Now we will fight on my terms.' She had turned to him. 'Time to get ready now. Tell me, do you know how to sail a windsurfer?'

'Yes,' he had said, 'up to a point,' and looked doubtfully out of the window. 'I can handle one OK normally, but this wind's pushing it a bit.'

'I will instruct you.'

So they went to the Fort.

'What was the phone call?'

'All in good time.' She touched his cheek. 'I do not want to insult your masculine pride, but I must handle this in my way. You do not have the experience which I have.'

'Well,' he said, 'OK, but . . .'

'I will tell you when I need you to help. It will not work any other way.'

She selected a Mistral Screamer for him. 'You are happy handling a sinker? You can do wet starts?' she asked.

'Just about,' he said, remembering the agony of learning to use a board that was too small to support your weight unless it was already moving. It might have been more sensible to say no, but his pride was a little dented by this strong, sexy woman, and he looked at the rough seas defiantly.

She took her own custom-built board and a four-and-a-half-metre wave sail. The board had a stiff ten-inch skeg, like a glass dagger sticking down from the bottom. She was in shiny black neoprene too, with a helmet and a face guard.

They took the equipment down to the water. There were some fair-sized rollers coming in. It was more like a winter's

328

day than the beginning of August, with Atlantic rain gusting across and poor visibility. No one else was windsurfing. Gwenaelle seemed to be in no hurry. She was looking around to the east, searching for something. Then she snapped into action. 'OK,' she said, 'let us begin. Come, I will teach you how to do good carved gybes in bad weather.'

He followed her in, flinching as the cold water worked its way into his wet suit, praying it would warm up quickly and feeling not entirely up to the job of turning this inert and stubborn mass of nylon and glassfibre into a coordinated tool of wind, speed and sea.

Sledge could remember many experiences he had enjoyed more. He was well used to mad rides in high-speed inflatables. If this was a proper Gemini or something, it wouldn't be so bad. He'd be checking his weapon, hunched down against the rubber sides, waiting for the beach at the end and the buzz of a firefight. This boat wasn't his kind of thing at all. They'd collected it from a yard in the long channel out from the centre of Vannes towards the Gulf, the only one Jean-Philippe's mate could get without too many questions being asked. It was a hard, brutal sort of boat, solid and bruising as the Mercury outboards punched it through the waves. It had a very fair turn of speed, but when it bounced, it slammed down with a harshness that made his spine ache. The waves weren't too bad until they got out of the Gulf, through the narrows into the proper oggin.

He looked at Jean-Philippe holding the wheel. Last time they'd been in a boat together with shooters had been . . . where was it? Somewhere in Africa with a bloody silly name. Hot as hell and they never got paid the full whack because the bloke that put the deal together got the chop from a bloody ricochet.

'What do we do if you're wrong an' she ain't fuckin' windsurfing?' he asked.

Jean-Philippe glanced at him, twitching the wheel to meet a big roller head on. 'We go in from the sea like Busby says. On a day such as this one nobody will see us. Busby will pick us up. But I am not wrong. That's what they say there. She is out every day. Even winter.'

He was right. It was ten spine-crunching, wet, cold miles across Quiberon Bay to the point. Halfway there they took one green right over the bow, filling up the rear compartment so they were forced to slow, and Sledge, soaked and freezing, had to bail to get it dry again.

'Busby's done OK,' he shouted, 'keeping the shore job for 'imself. Behaves a bit like a bloody officer these days, though if 'e's paying the bills that's what you 'ave to expect.'

Jean-Philippe grinned. 'Maybe he is a bit softer than he looks, your Busby.'

Sledge snorted. 'Soft? Soft as fucking granite. So soft they threw 'im out of the old SAS for being too 'ard. That's 'ow soft 'e is.'

'What did he do?'

'Thought 'e caught two of 'is blokes shagging each other. 'E all but killed one of the buggers. Broke the other one's arm. Turned out 'e 'ad it all wrong. One of 'em 'ad pulled a muscle in 'is groin. The other poor sod was only trying to massage it.'

Jean Philippe lifted an arm as they came round the lighthouse, and pointed. There were two sails in the water inshore, coming out. He throttled right back and Sledge picked up the glasses. He focused them, then chortled. 'Both of them. Bloody both of them.' He grinned at Jean-

Philippe. 'Must be my birthday, you fat old git. Filthy day. Bang bang, bob's your uncle. No one'll ever know what 'appened. Let's go get 'em.'

Bobbing, battered in the waves, David was losing heart. The drill had been hard enough on a Greek island in warm, clear water. There was no easy way to learn except the grinding business of trying it again and again, and in the intervening year he'd lost some of the knack. He trod water for a second and went over it once more in his mind. Get the rig upwind of you, lying flat in the sea. Hand under the boom, swim towards the wind and heave it out of the water. When the wind gets under the sail and it starts flying, grab it, get your back foot on the board and let it pull you out of the water. All very well, but all the essence of it was in that last bit and with waves and a wind like this, he was getting bloody tired with five failures to every successful wet start. Where was Gwenaelle when he needed her? She'd shot off again, hadn't she, going like a cannon shell towards the lighthouse, tearing past the speedboat which had just appeared around it and slam gybing to rocket back down towards him. He looked at her miserably as she approached, powering down and dropping easily into the water next to him.

'Rest for a few minutes,' she said, 'just paddle gently. Don't try to do anything. I will be back.'

'Where are you going?'

'Keep still and watch.'

'But . . .' She was already back up on the board. 'Shit. Gwenaelle, what the hell are –' But she'd gone. It was a shame that this game she was playing didn't seem to include him. He was trying to keep an eye on the shore, assuming that she was hoping to lure them into the house

331

while they were out at sea. Then he looked at the speed boat, now motoring gently towards them, and suddenly, far too late, he understood. She'd known they'd got a boat. She'd bloody known. Then he began desperately to try to get back up on the board. He was too hurried and he fell back in the water, with the rig on the wrong side of it. He tried to swim round, shoving the sail in front of him, but a wave caught him and pushed him back. The boat was now a hundred yards away or less. He could see two men in it, one standing in the open back section, one at the helm. The one in the back was a big, beefy, bald man who appeared to be soaking wet. He remembered Nick's description of the man he'd surprised in the house, and then saw that the man was holding in his arms a short-barrelled gun with a big magazine.

He wanted to hide behind something, but there was nothing except the board and that represented no kind of safety. Gwenaelle could not have seen the gun, surely, because he knew perfectly well she had no weapon of any kind, and yet she was up on her board, tearing down on the boat as hard as she could. He watched her skid round its stern, duck gybing, and slam back up the other side. The man in the stern had the gun raised, but in the rolling sea seemed unable to get a good aim. The speedboat accelerated sharply, planing. Gwenaelle was going as fast as he had ever seen a windsurfer travel, broad reaching at right angles to the wind, the fastest way to sail. They were tearing across his line of vision out to sea, the speedboat catching her under full power. Then the boat was abeam of her and the man in the back was raising the gun.

To David it looked all over. They were now only feet apart and the worst shot in the world could not have missed with the entire magazine, but only then did Gwenaelle show her true colours. She raked the sail in harder,

332

with its bottom kissing the board, and accelerated, turning slightly towards the boat. David could see her looking around at the waves, working the sail with all the power in her body for every last little bit of speed. There was a big sea rolling between her and the boat, and it threw the man with the gun off balance again as it rolled under the hull towards her. Then she was climbing the ramp of the wave, feet in the straps on the back of the board, and suddenly her knees were bending, lifting it into the wind, and the board with its razor-like skeg was hurtling into the air, sweeping broadside up over the boat with her weight and all the force of the wind behind it. The cry and the thud carried clearly to David as the bald man in the stern was hurled spinning into the sea, and Gwenaelle swung the front of the board round in a perfect landing on the other side.

Then she sailed away back towards him, looking around her, and David wondered what she was doing. The other man was still there at the helm. He opened the throttles and the boat took off after her, coming diagonally towards David. Bugger this, he said to himself, she needs me, and he spurred into action, going through the wet start drill again. His mind was on the boat, which may have helped. He almost didn't make it, but driven by desperate urgency, he forced his protesting legs to straighten on to the board as it gathered speed, and suddenly he was up and in control, accelerating fast. Gwenaelle seemed to be shouting at him, but he couldn't hear what she was saying. He gybed round and tore back towards the speedboat, the cold forgotten now, feeling the spray in his face and intent only on closing the distance. He had no clear plan in his mind except to distract the man, who was fast overtaking a faltering Gwenaelle. The boat was twenty yards away, then ten, and he simply headed straight for the man at the wheel, who was raising a pistol towards him. A bullet went through his sail, a foot from his head. Then he was on the boat, trying to hurl himself into it and just missing, as the board crashed into the side of it. The next thing he knew, he was under the water, taking a blow on the head from the board on the way down, and seeing the buzzing propellers of the speedboat slash past, inches from his eyes.

He surfaced to see the disappearing tail of the boat and, beyond it, Gwenaelle, clearly in trouble. She was looking wildly around, zigzagging and slowing. The man spun the wheel of the boat and turned after her. She looked over her shoulder at him, leading him out to sea, staying a hundred yards in front, but she wasn't sailing so fast now and David wondered if she'd hurt herself in the jump. She turned once, twice, staring towards him, towards the shore, then disaster. She gybed clumsily and fell in.

There was a roar as the man opened the throttles fully and the speedboat lifted and tore towards her. She was a sitting duck and there was nothing David could do to help her except shout in impotent rage from the water. The boat was hurtling along flat out now, pointing exactly at the helpless woman trying to get back on the board. Fifty yards, forty, thirty . . . then abruptly there came a splintering crash. The speedboat stopped in its tracks, veered to one side and, as the man, arms flailing, went flying over the spray screen into the water, it turned on its side and sank. She moved fast then, diving under the sail towards where he had disappeared. After thirty or forty seconds she came back up. He didn't. Then, nonchalantly, she pulled the sail out of the water and cruised back towards David.

Chapter Thirty-one

Same day

'It nearly did not work out. The tide was falling. I had to choose the right rocks. Another minute or two and he would have seen the waves breaking on them. It had to be just so.'

'Well, you fooled me. I thought you'd had it,' said David. He put his glass of cognac down and stared grimly out to where a police launch was still circling, pitching in the blustery swell, looking unsuccessfully for the other body.

'I was worried about you. I did not mean you to join in. He could have killed you. I was too far away to rescue you.'

'So I shouldn't have tried to help? As far as I could see he was about to run you down.'

Gwenaelle hid a little smile successfully. 'Well, it worked out well. What you did helped. He got further behind me, so he had to be going faster when he hit the rocks.' He still looked angry, so she went round behind him and put her hands on his shoulders. 'It was very brave of you.'

The phone rang once more and she went next door to take it. He hunched up and looked out of the window again. He felt cold through and through, not so much from the long swim as from the personal nature of the one-to-one violence he had found himself part of. He wanted to know what Gwenaelle had done under the water at the end, but he didn't dare ask for fear of what he would hear. It was quite plain that her career had taught her to regard this kind of thing as relatively normal.

She came back and stood in the doorway. 'I am not happy,' she said. 'The police say they have one body. He even had his papers in his pocket still. He was just the hired help, a French thug from Brest who is no loss to the world. They do not have the other, the one with the bald head, but he certainly did not swim away.'

'So why aren't you happy?'

'Because in my experience dead men do not find it easy to drive. The boat came from a yard near Vannes but the truck they had been driving is no longer there. The police have found it at a warehouse. The car belonging to the man from Brest is there too, and there are tyre marks which may mean another car has been there and gone.'

'It could be this man Busby, but I don't know. It could be anyone, couldn't it?'

'The police are putting out instructions to watch the roads, but that does not give them very much to look out for.'

David could suddenly imagine Busby heading back to England, working out the next round, continuing the game. 'I suppose I should do something with the photographs. They're the only hard evidence.'

Gwenaelle shrugged. 'Evidence of what? They show two test failures. That is what Bamco would say. Put together with your brother's video, they might show something, but you do not have the video and even if you did, well, it's just a little marketing trick, no?'

'I can't just sit around waiting for them to have another go, can I?'

'No. You need more information. In any case, if you go to the authorities in Britain, it will be taken right out of your hands. You will never find out what happened.'

'You say that because it's an arms company that's involved?'

'Of course. I have some sources I can use maybe to help a bit. They have no allegiance to the British arms business. You might say the opposite in fact. I will send you any results I get.' She crossed to a desk and wrote down a number. 'This is a local fax number I use. Contact me through that. Use fax whenever you can. Do not use the same route for communications twice. If you have to use an ordinary telephone, do not say anything on it that is at all important. That is even more true of mobile telephones.'

He looked at his watch. It was still only midday. 'I feel we still have a lot to talk about.'

'There will be other times perhaps for that. I am not trying to get rid of you, David, but there is work to do and you should be back in England. That is where your Busby will be heading. Work is the only way to safety. We must find out enough to get others to take all this seriously. There are big things at stake, things like money and export sales. Do not underestimate the task.'

David looked at her, perplexed. This was a different Gwenaelle. Her mastery of the situation had widened their age gap. Though the memory of the previous night was still immediate and strong, he was sharply aware of the distance between them now. She detected in his eyes something of his thinking as he prepared to leave. At the door she took both his hands in hers and looked at him very directly. 'I want to give you the best present I can,' she said. 'Last night was one part of it.' She paused and looked at him. 'What was it like?'

He looked at her and could only speak the truth. 'It was like I had imagined it would be with Yanna.'

'It was meant to be. It was to stop you mourning something you never had. I wanted to show you that sex in the future can be good again and you should not look back. Now the other part of my present. It is this. It is to tell you that you are free. I knew my daughter very well. You and she arc very like each other. You would both leave others standing as you flew through life. Like Icarus, you move in ways which are bad for you. You make up your mind, and poof, you're gone before others have even started to think about what to do. You both have things that drive you. It would have been hard for two people like that to stay harnessed to each other. I think you were meant to zoom past each other in the skies like two comets.'

He shook his head, unwilling to accept it. She went on. 'Have you not seen it this morning? I have taken control. I moved faster than you and you were not at all sure you liked it.' That floored him and he suddenly laughed aloud and caught her in a great hug. They kissed tenderly one last time, and she propelled him towards the car.

He thought about her words all the way up past Lorient, this time watching his rear-view mirror carefully for any signs of untoward interest. By the time he got to Quimper a new peace had come to his spirit, and when he reached Roscoff and the ferry later that afternoon, he was quietly singing to himself.

Geoff Busby had been badly rattled by what he thought he'd seen. Visibility had been too bad to be certain, but the boat had sunk, that was for sure, and by the time the arrival of the police had forced him to move further off, there had been no sign of Sledge or the Frog. He thought, on balance, that they'd both had it, and he couldn't think how a cakewalk like that could have gone so wrong. There hadn't been much time to play with. Wondering if the van was compromised, he got shot of it first off, getting back in the hire-car, deciding that was the lesser risk. It was hired in a different name and he had no reason to suppose anyone would have its number.

He tried to add up the score. On the minus side, Challis had the photos. Right now, that was Purkiss's problem, not his. Sledge had got the chop. He could still hardly believe that. Up against two cream puffs. It made him bloody angry. There was definitely a score to be settled there. On the plus side, his nose was clean. In fact, now he thought about it, he hadn't even done anything wrong in France. He looked at a map and headed down the twisty roads, realizing none of that mattered as much as the fact that he'd screwed it up. This trip hadn't been very clever and Purkiss wouldn't like it one bit if he ever found out. Purkiss never liked him freelancing, and there would be a lot of explaining to do. Donaldson seemed to have ways of finding out and he had no illusions as to what would happen if that little bastard got on to it. Martin bloody Donaldson would be sitting on Purkiss's right hand and Busby would be out in the kitchen washing the dishes.

The only thing he really had to worry about was the other Challis brother's death. He reckoned he was in the clear about that, but that might not last long with this one still alive and sniffing. He hit the steering-wheel with both fists. It would have been so fucking perfect. Tragic accident on a windsurfer. No one would have batted an eyelid. Do something back home and even the sleepy country coppers round Otterburn might think lightning shouldn't be striking twice. Bugger it, he thought. If Sledge did get out of it, he'd have his guts.

Little did he know, but Sledge was getting out of it, making a steady one-and-a-half knots with the tide, heading gently out to sea just below the surface, but only the fish would be having his guts.

*

'Spencer, I really need an uninterrupted hour or so to talk about how we're going to pitch the sales of Cracksman 2. I was hoping to get Geoff in on it. Do you know when he's due back?'

Martin Donaldson had been wondering where Busby had got to for a day or two now. It was time for the next phase of his game and he needed some more ammunition to use against the man. Purkiss, though, had been used to giving his other lieutenant a bit of rope over the years and waved away Donaldson's inquiries, but Donaldson was working to his own private agenda, with his mind very much on his own position, and such information was useful. Putting to work the little intelligence system he'd already built up within Bamco, he'd soon found out about Inspector Percival's call and about Busby's surreptitious bookings to France, and he'd thought for a long time trying to add it up. Now they were sitting in Purkiss's office, waiting for the car to take them both to the airport. Cracksman 2 marketing cut no ice with Purkiss. He was in an expansive mood and he wanted to philosophize.

'Bit of relaxation over the weekend, young Martin. I'll show you some more of the island. There's some bloody good restaurants on Jersey, then just a touch of work to do on Monday with the lawyers.'

'I'm not relaxing until we've got everyone signed up.'

Purkiss looked at him fondly and laughed. 'Calm down, Martin. We're there. You've hooked them, I can feel it in my bones. The army are salivating over it. They want Dodgem and they want it now, and when they sign up, then we're in the big league.'

'That's all very well, but will they let us sell it to anyone else?'

Purkiss laughed. 'One thing at a time. What the eye doesn't see, eh? Don't move too quick. I want to enjoy the glory first. Might even get a gong. My old man would have liked that. Makes the point, you see. There's nothing evil about weapons, they're just lumps of metal. It's the people who use them who can be good or bad, not the people who make them. Better we should be doing it in good old Blighty, 'cos if we didn't there's a million other buggers out there who'd have our market in no time flat.'

A similar point was being made a hundred miles away in Downing Street. Now that Major's team had settled into Number Ten, Hilary Stoughton was happier with the extent of the authority of her job, though with never-ending speculation about the timing of the election there were simply too many things to think about for her to indulge in the visionary forward planning she had dreamed of when she took it on.

Alex Harvey had been promoted within the Ministry of Defence, partly, he was aware, because of the role he had played with Number Ten during the Gulf War. He was still summoned over to Hilary's office whenever she wanted to know something. Now he was waiting and watching while she finished the phone call which had interrupted them, wondering why she seemed so angry this morning. He'd had to give up playing the experienced Whitehall mandarin indulging the naïve outsider. She was far too smart for that, but as she put the phone down, rather hard by her standards, he reckoned he knew her well enough now to venture something personal.

'Something biting you, Hilary?'

'Why do you ask?'

'I can tell when I've only got half your attention. I don't think I'd like to be whatever's getting the other half.'

She stopped scribbling in her memo book and grimaced.

341

'Sorry, Alex. It's just so bloody frustrating. All this election stuff.'

'What's frustrating about it? That's the name of the game. It was ever thus.'

She shot him a penetrating glance and he wished he'd left out the implication that he was wiser in the ways of Downing Street than she. 'With all due respect for your years of experience, Alex, I beg to differ. We seem to have given up on running the country. Life's one long election campaign now. There doesn't seem to be any time left over for thinking about the things that really matter.'

There was a short silence in which both were aware that she had gone further than she ought, or indeed than she ever had before. She looked at him, thinking in for a penny, in for a pound, and carried on.

'You know what gets to me most? It's the loss of moral certainty. We don't seem to have the confidence to do what we think is right. Everything has to be filtered through the presentation specialists.'

He raised an eyebrow. 'What have the spin doctors said to offend you?'

'It's not what they say. It's not that at all. It's just we never decide what's right or not right ourselves any more. Instead we ask a bunch of glorified soap salesmen whether the public will perceive it as right or not. What happened to certainty? What happened to doing things because they are right?'

'They got squeezed out of the nine o'clock news by cleverly written thirty-second sound bites.'

'Oh, God. Anyway, I didn't get you here to talk about that. Luckily there are still some areas left where we don't have to worry what the public might think, because the public aren't going to find out.'

He snorted and she stopped. 'You mean to say,' he said,

342

'that the only areas left where you can make up your own mind on what's right are the secret ones?'

'Ironic, eh? Anyway, much to the irritation of some of my colleagues I've managed to get my defence sales policy paper back on the agenda here.'

'Are you sure that's necessary, Hilary? We've got a draft ready that might well have done.'

She stared at him. 'Yes, I'm sure you have, and yes, I'm sure my version is necessary.'

Alex remembered the briefing he'd had before he came over to Downing Street. 'The game's changed a bit, you know. We're projecting a drop in worldwide military demand for hardware of getting on for 30 per cent. That's mostly the Soviet situation and partly recession, but it means we're all competing for a shrinking export market.'

'All the more reason to do some serious thinking, Alex.'

He got up and looked out of the window. 'It's no time to start being too purist, Hilary. It's dog eat dog and the dogs have got American accents. It all worked out bloody well for them, you know. Clever briefing. It's turned the whole market on its head. No one's interested in buying anything that hasn't got the "smart weapon" and "combat proven" tags tacked on to it. We haven't got that much to offer. It's going to be hard enough to sell anything without getting all funny about the principles involved.' He turned and gave her a hard look. 'I'll give you the list of the main products we stand any hope of marketing. Outside the aircraft, and you know where we stand on the Saudi deal, it's not very long. You might care to reflect on the fact that if we start getting too fussy about what we're selling, then all we'll be doing is handing the market on a plate to the Americans.'

There was a short silence. She was taken aback by his vehemence. 'So you'd rather Number Ten stayed out of it?'

He just looked at her. 'The industry has to shrink. World-wide. It's not easy. Look at the Czechs, if you want a good example of what happens to idealists. Vaclav Havel's factories are still churning out tanks because no one wants the tractors he'd rather build. Every time he tries to switch the production lines, the workers take to the streets. They're good at building tanks. Tanks pay their wages and tractors don't. They'd rather build tanks than be on short time. Look at the USA. The local politicos of St Louis and every other defence town are total experts at tweaking the White House to go on ordering jet planes, and with Pat Buchanan on the rampage they'll screw Bush in the primaries if he doesn't go along. Recession knocks ideals on the head. It's a dirty world. I'd rather see our companies scale back down to cope than see them get shot in the head and hand over the market without a fight.'

She felt the argument slipping away from her. 'What about this French hoo-ha?'

'My God, you have been keeping your ear to the ground.' He looked at her thoughtfully. 'What did you hear exactly?'

'Just that the French are very unhappy about something naughty one of our companies is said to have done. Seems they think it's been carrying private enterprise a bit too far. Lost us some of our own aircraft in the process.'

'That's a big exaggeration. It's nothing.'

The nonchalant reply smacked of arrogance. She felt her blood pressure start to rise and her voice, when she spoke again, had risen in pitch too, with an edge that he picked up on immediately.

'It's not nothing at all, Alex. If it was, I wouldn't have raised it. It sounds to me like the very same thing you failed to tell me all about once before. However, the French took the precaution of informing M.I.6 as well as the M.o.D.

344

directly, and it was mentioned at the PM's briefing, so take the plum out of your mouth and tell me.'

'I'm sorry. I didn't mean to give you the brush-off. It's just that we suspect a bit of pique. One of the few French systems that got used didn't work too well, so they're crying foul. It just happens that they're pointing the finger at a company that's got one of our very best new products coming along. In fact it's something so smart even the Americans might buy it. That's why we're not too impressed.'

'I'll want to know more. The PM's latched on to it. They're suggesting some of our Tornado losses really might have been down to this. Is that true?'

'I don't think so. Look, Hilary, leave it with me. To tell you the truth, we've been thinking about this outfit Bamco for quite a long time. Good company, but some odd characters at the top. We wouldn't want it to go under, but it might be in everyone's interests if someone else was running it.'

'Shareholders?'

'It's a private company. We can't put pressure on that way.'

Hilary considered. 'Are they vulnerable? Lots of borrowings, that sort of thing?'

'Well, there's a big army contract coming up and they've spent a lot of money on the product trying to get it, so there's a good chance.'

'Why don't you talk to Sir Jack?'

Sir Jack Hitchens was an ex-minister who'd served his time at the M.o.D. before privatizing himself into the more remunerative world of merchant banking. Now, as the head of Hazzard Mackeson, he had maintained close links with his former political associates and was a useful player when the Government wanted to make its unseen hand felt somewhere in the corporate world.

345

Alex nodded, relieved Hilary had calmed down, and decided it was time to change the subject. He looked back through the window. 'Nice to see the grass has recovered.'

Something nagged in her memory. She chased it. It was to do with the IRA mortars, another conversation they'd been having at the time. 'Alex. There was something I was asking you that time when the bombs went off. Something we never finished. What was it?'

He looked at her levelly. 'Sorry, Hilary. I haven't a clue.'

Chapter Thirty-two

Saturday August 3rd 1991

The men with the guns were waiting for David. Lulled by the return to the wide open spaces of Northumberland, he wasn't expecting them. He had kept checking the mirror all the way, but there had been nothing in view behind for the last ten miles. He was in a kind of mental limbo until he came to Duncan's bend and looked down at the gash in the trees as he passed. That served as a switch to return him to the situation he was about to find at the house. He wondered about George Middleton, hoping against the odds there might be better news. There were many things he still wanted to talk about with the old man.

He'd used every moment of the drive north, going over and over every detail, every bit of evidence. He'd grudged the need to stop for the night at a Plymouth hotel, and he'd been up early on Saturday morning to continue his journey as quickly as he could. He took the left-hand route up the M5 and M6, and by the time he stopped for a quick cup of coffee and a sandwich at Forton services by the Forest of Bowland, he concluded that Gwenaelle was right. Information on Bamco came first. Without that they held no substantial cards in their hand. The problem was how to get it. He turned off past Kendal on the Kirkby Stephen road, then joined the old Roman road at Brough to hammer across Bowes Moor and down to Barnard Castle. As Newcastle and the River Tyne came into sight around lunchtime, he saw the turning down to the Bamco factory and decided desperate measures were called for.

He was still mulling it over as the Jensen's tyres crunched over the gravel outside the house, not allowing for the fact that others might have come to the same conclusion, which is why it came as a complete shock when his door was yanked open from outside and he turned to find himself looking down the black holes of a shotgun, held by a very unfriendly man he had never seen before. One detached part of his mind registered that the exposed metal face of each muzzle was still shiny and a little rough, showing how recently the barrels must have been sawn off, while the rest of him was turning to helpless jelly. His eyes flicked left, hoping for a way out, but round the corner of the house came a huge man holding another shotgun, this time with its barrels still in place. The gun looked tiny in his hands.

'Outa there,' said the first man, '*now*,' and he could think of no other solution than to obey. Careless, he said to himself, despairing. How bloody careless. Then the front door opened and Josie appeared. It took him a second to register that she looked surprisingly calm, even smiling a little.

'Put him down, Donnie,' she said. 'That's David.'

Inside the house, sitting in the kitchen over a cup of coffee, David's adrenalin drained away straight into weariness. Nick came in and gave him a bear-hug. He was followed by a very small man with a pointed face and a receding chin, unhappily augmented by a ragged moustache.

'Dave, meet Ove,' said Nick.

'Oh, yes. The bug man,' said David, and shook hands. Ove's eyes darted around and never quite met his. As that

348

would have involved looking up quite a long way, David assumed this was a habit forced on him by his physique.

'Let's hear about it,' said Nick, and David took a deep breath, wondering where to start.

'Well,' he said, 'Gwenaelle turned out to be a bit of a surprise.'

'Gwenaelle?' queried Josie.

'Yanna's mother. Madame Le Bihan,' said David. 'She wasn't at all what I expected.' He wondered, why Josie was looking at him like that. He tried to tell the tale as simply as possible, aware that events that would have seemed utterly fantastic a week before were now accepted without demur.

'So you don't know for sure if someone else was there too?' asked Nick.

'Gwenaelle said the police were pretty certain of it.'

'Either way, they'll know soon enough it didn't work. I guess if they were ready to pull a stunt like that once, they won't mind doing it again?'

'I think that's right. How long can we rely on your private army, Nick?'

He looked unhappy. 'Not too long. The guys are getting a bit bored. No one's come by. That's probably why they went a bit over the top with you.'

Until then David hadn't asked because he knew they wouldn't have hesitated to pass on any good news, but now it couldn't wait any longer. He turned to Josie. 'What about George Middleton? Is there any progress?'

There was a silence all round, then she said quietly, 'I was waiting to give you a bit of a breather.' Her face said it all. 'I'm afraid he died last night. The hospital said he didn't recover consciousness again.'

'Oh.' David closed his eyes.

Josie took a deep breath and went on talking gently to fill the silence. 'I'm sure he wasn't in any pain. I've been on the phone this morning trying to sort a few things out. I've arranged for the funeral and I've asked around to see if anyone knows of any relatives, but he kept himself to himself and I didn't get anywhere. I've talked to our solicitor about it, and he says we should probably advertise. He also says we have to go and look through the house for a will or any other documents, but that can wait a day or two.'

'Well done,' said David, and then she surprised him.

'Personally,' she said, 'I want revenge. I want these bastards dealt with.'

'I think maybe one of them has been. I didn't tell you. Nick? The man in the boat, the first one Gwenaelle knocked off, I think he may have been the one you interrupted here.'

'Kinda square body? Heavy eyebrows? Flat nose?'

David thought back to the crowded events in the water. 'I'd say so.'

'Could be, then. There's your revenge.'

Josie objected. 'But what about the others? The people behind it?'

Before anyone could answer, the phone rang. She picked it up. 'Hello. Yes? He's here. Just hold on a minute.' She turned to David. 'Your French friend.'

'Gwenaelle?'

'That's the one.'

She gave him the receiver and walked off to look out of the window. Nick raised his eyebrows.

'Gwenaelle? I just got back.'

Her voice sounded excited. 'I have a message for you. I am putting it on your fax now. We talk again later.'

He put the phone down. 'She's sending a fax. Seems to think that's safer than talking on the phone these days.'

Ove, who had been sitting silently working away on a

pocket computer throughout the conversation, suddenly came to life with a squeak. 'This is not sensible. We don't know if your fax is clean.'

David swung round. 'You mean you can bug faxes?'

'Of course. Nothing easier. I am afraid your French lady must be a year or two out of date on her procedures.'

They all went through to Duncan's office as the fax machine came to life, but they soon saw that Gwenaelle wasn't taking any risks. The fax was cursory to an extreme. It was handwritten. 'My friends do not like your friends. Find a safe fax and send the number for more.'

David was thinking. 'Ove, give me a little run-down, would you? How do you bug a fax?'

Ove had calmed down. He smiled. For some reason Nick was smiling too. 'You put an induction loop round the cable. That harvests all the impulses in the line. Then you just hook up a machine to your loop and read whatever you want.'

'But you have to get into the building to fix up the loop?'

'No. That would make life very hard for people like me. Fortunately, telecom companies are not so careful about their installations. They have to have switching points which their engineers can reach, and junctions where the cables join the main trunking. All you have to do is find a switching point along the cable like that.'

'What are the chances of finding a switching point some-where outside, let's say, the munitions subsidiary of a weapons manufacturer somewhere near Newcastle,' said David.

'Talking theoretically?' asked Nick with a grin that had nearly reached bursting point. He looked at Ove. 'May I?' he asked.

'Be my guest.'

'Well, talking theoretically of course, and I only say this because Ove swept the house again from top to bottom this morning for any snooping devices, there might just be a chamber, accessed from a cover in the roadside by a stretch of waste ground, just about here.' He opened the pad of paper he had been holding and put it on the table. Inside was a roughly drawn sketch-map.

'You've already been to check it out?'

'Great minds think alike. It's a hundred yards from Bamco's eastern fence. There's no problem getting into the chamber. Then you just go down a little ladder and it's all hanging there, ripe for the picking.'

'What exactly?'

'All the phone lines and two fax lines from Bamco.'

'You're sure?'

'Does the Pope shit in the woods?'

'Well, probably not, actually,' said David.

It was just after dark when they arrived at the factory, and it was raining again. That, they decided, was a good thing because it kept casual strollers off the streets, not that there was anything much in that corner of Tyneside to induce anyone to stroll. They parked half on the pavement so the car blocked off the manhole from view. David looked across at the lights burning in the Bamco complex. It looked a little close for comfort, but, in the dark, logic told him they had to be all right. Ove climbed down into the little chamber and turned on a powerful lantern. He gave a thumbs up to Nick, who lowered the equipment bag down to him.

'Ten minutes,' he said, and Nick settled the manhole cover back into place so the light wouldn't show.

'Just as well he's so little,' said David as they got back in the car.

David flicked the wipers on to look towards the factory

again. Nothing was stirring. 'By the way,' he said 'what happened to Bertram Glass's car?'

Nick shifted uneasily in his seat. 'Believe me, you'd rather not know. Care to forget you asked the question?'

'What question?'

'Right. Anyway, let's take a look at that fax again.'

The fax bureau in Hexham had closed five minutes before they had got there, and in the end it was a hotel which had come to their rescue after they had turned on the charm to the receptionist. David had expected a long wait for a reply once he'd sent the message to the safe fax number she'd given him, but someone at the other end, perhaps Gwenaelle herself, had been standing by. Not more than a minute later the machine had buzzed into life with the reply.

Now, in the car, David brought it out again and angled it sideways to catch the light of the street lamp. It didn't mince words:

My friends believe the Bamco company has been central to the reduction in effectiveness of at least three joint European weapons projects. They believe it has sold countermeasures to prohibited countries. They are asking for severe measures to be taken against it. They have some evidence that this has been effected by Purkiss and Busby, through an intermediary in St Helier, Jersey. They draw our attention to a company based there called BFSS. They have also been looking for information on Martin Donaldson, now thought to be Purkiss's main aide. They further inform me that French Special Forces have passed on information derived from SAS contacts that some of the actions of the SAS behind the lines in the Gulf established that UK-supplied countermeasures to Allied weapons systems were in place. Special Forces then had to be tasked to neutralize some of these. The UK Government has so far not been overtly receptive to high-level French approaches on the subject. This is perhaps seen in London as a

353

spoiling tactic by French interests anxious to extend their own markets. Our mutual purposes may be best achieved by publicity to force your Government to act in some way now that the groundwork has been laid.

Nick whistled. 'Heavy duty. Don't you think we're a bit out of our league?'

'Completely, but I don't feel like giving up just because of that.' He glanced at Nick. 'Look, I feel I ought to say this. It's my problem, not yours. These people killed Yanna, my girl, Duncan, my brother, and old Middleton. It's my battle.'

Nick shook his head. 'Yanna makes it mine too, David. Anyway it sounds too good to miss, and we can always make a film out of it afterwards.' He shrugged. 'In any case,' he said, 'there's a few people after me round town for some money they think I owe them. I'm better off up here for a while, if that's OK with you.'

David smiled at him. 'Those must be pretty serious debts if you're really better off doing this. Anyway, it's a deal. It's good to have you around, Nick.' He looked at his watch. 'Shall we let Ove out?'

Nick held up a hand. 'One more thing.'

'Yes?'

'Josie. She's a great lady. She told me you two used to be very close before Duncan.'

'That's true.'

'Is that just past history as far as you're concerned?'

'Well, yes, I suppose so.' David was surprised by the question. 'Why do you . . .'

'No matter. Not now. Anyway, I couldn't help noticing, David. She got something in the post this morning that really upset her. She went white. Took the letter away upstairs. I asked her if she was OK and she said sure, but she wasn't. I tried, but she wouldn't talk about it.'

354

'Any ideas what it was?'

'I took the envelope out of the garbage. Bit sneaky, but I wanted to see if there was anything I could do to help.'

'Yes. I understand.'

'It said Trebitsch Finance on it. That's all. I just thought you ought to know.'

'I appreciate that.'

'Mean anything to you?'

'No.'

'She's had a helluva lot to handle, that kid. I know you have too, but she needs a break. She's a lovely kid.'

'Nick! Are you lining yourself up?'

Can't see what's in front of his nose, thought Nick, shaking his head, and looked at his watch. 'Time to let Ove out of the hole.'

Ove was pleased with himself. The conversation degenerated rapidly into technicalities which neither David nor Nick could follow.

'Tell us again in English,' said Nick.

'It's not so difficult, is it? I have one machine for two lines, you see. It is switched to take messages off both. If messages come in at the same time, I have set one to be the priority line. I have loaded up with paper and set it running.'

'So what do we do next?'

'Like fishing,' said Ove. 'We come back later, perhaps on Monday when it is dark, and we see what we have caught.'

'Suppose they have someone like you on the staff?'

'Won't matter. They cannot detect this. Only if someone looks into this hole will they see it, and that is not likely unless the telephone engineers come here to do something. Then they will find the machine and we can do nothing about that, but it is only a very small chance.'

Chapter Thirty-three

Monday August 5th 1991

It was a clear morning after days of rain, and the tall trees around the house were greeting the fresh wind with a rustling that made David want to get outside and fill his lungs. They'd spent the rest of the weekend killing time inside the house. Now he suggested to Josie that they should take a walk. They crossed the road and climbed the rise, the springy moorland oozing some of its stored-up rainfall at the pressure of their boots. On the far slope they had to push through knee-deep heather until they were both panting with the exertion. Turning, they could look down on the great bowl of moorland, rock and stream below them, with the house standing, largely hidden by its trees, and beyond it the woodland marking where the farmhouse and the barns stood.

'Life carries on, doesn't it?' said Josie. 'That's the point of living in a place like this. That's what the rocks and the hills tell you. Whatever the little Busbys of the world can do to poison things, this will still be here.'

'You feel that too?' said David. Then he decided it was time to tackle the subject that was on his mind. 'You had some other bad news on Saturday? A letter?' She looked startled. 'Nick told me,' he said.

'It wasn't anything.'

'Trebitsch Finance doesn't sound like nothing.'

She turned to him. 'Nick's got no right . . .'

'Nick thinks the world of you. He wasn't really snooping. He knew you were upset and he just wanted to see if he could help. It was written on the envelope.'

She set her mouth defiantly. 'David, you're not automatically responsible for solving all my problems. I have to learn to stand on my own two feet.'

'Tell me.'

'It was just some bloody letter about some more money Duncan had borrowed.'

'What did they say about it?'

'It said . . .' She cast back for the words. 'We are sorry not to be able to grant your request for an extension of the loan repayment period and we must insist on . . . Oh, I can't remember the exact words, but it meant pay up now or else.'

David did a swift calculation to see how much was left in his account. 'Don't worry. I'll fix it. How much is it?'

She didn't answer and he turned to look at her. Tears were running silently down her face. 'You won't, I'm afraid.'

'Why not?'

'Because it's eighty-five thousand pounds, that's why.'

'No! How can that be? Did you know anything about it?'

'Of course not.'

'What could Duncan have done with it?'

'I haven't a clue. I keep thinking . . . Oh, I don't know.'

'What?'

'Well, I suppose it's silly.' She turned a tear-stained face to him. 'I keep wondering if he had a mistress or something, tucked away in London, while I was out of the way up here.'

'I'm sure he didn't.'

'Are you?'

No, I'm not sure, thought David. 'Yes,' he said, 'quite sure.'

'So what did he do with the money?'

'I don't know. We'd better start trying to find out.'

She looked towards the distant trees. 'The real trouble,' she said, 'is it makes me think horrible thoughts about having to sell George's house and I don't want to, not so soon after he . . .' She stopped. 'It's still his house. I don't want to think of it like that. Anyway,' she said, 'even if I did sell it, which will be pretty hard right now, I doubt I'd get enough.'

He put his arms round her and soothed her, staring out across the valley. 'Don't worry, love. We'll sort it out.'

'No, we won't,' she said in a sad voice. 'You know we won't. It just gets worse and worse.'

'We'll do a proper search through Duncan's papers. Maybe the money's on deposit somewhere. Perhaps he was going to use it for something.'

'You don't borrow money at 26 per cent to put it on deposit at 10 per cent, do you?'

'Is that what it's costing? 26 per cent?'

She nodded.

'Ouch,' he said.

'Anyway, now it's my turn. I've been thinking about all this. I think it's time to go back to the police. I feel, well . . . it's almost like it's a distraction for you, all this cloak and dagger stuff. You need it to stop you thinking about Yanna. It's almost as if you're enjoying it. But I think we should put it in someone else's hands now.'

'Josie, we've tried. You were there. They didn't want to know about Duncan. They're taking Middleton seriously, but only because they think it was some burglar. What can we do?'

She faced him. 'There's two more things. There's the bugs in the house. We can show them those. Then there's what happened in France.'

'There's no evidence from France. Just one body. He was a nobody. We have to have something more. Just one solid thing to show them.'

She looked at him, despairing. 'David, you're all I've got left.'

'Thanks for the glowing . . .' he started to say, but to his utter amazement she punched him hard enough in the stomach to knock the wind completely out of him.

'What was that for?' he gasped, and she looked at him wildly.

'For doing what you always do. For coming up with some smart remark when I'm saying something that matters to me.'

'Wow,' he said, holding his hands up as he took in just how furious she looked. 'Sorry. My tongue sometimes moves faster than my brain. What's going on here?'

'You've always done that, haven't you? Said something quick and trivial when I'm trying to get through to you. Why do you do it? Can't you stand anything that feels like it might be a real emotion?'

'Hey. It was just words, that's all. It just slipped out. Surely we've known each other for long enough to . . .'

'I loved you for years, you bastard. I married your brother because he was a bit like you, but he didn't do that. So don't start doing it to me again.'

'I'm sorry,' he said, amazed, and he meant it. 'Surely that wasn't the only reason you married Duncan? I mean . . .'

She caught her breath. 'I married Duncan because you kept pushing me away and whizzing off at a hundred miles an hour. Duncan married me because he idolized you and he transferred that to me as your girlfriend. We were good friends, Duncan and I, at least we were for a bit. Until the drink started getting in the way. It was horrible after that.

359

You must have seen. It was like living with a shell and seeing the person you knew sort of drip away out of it and be replaced bit by bit by a stranger.'

He reached out and took her hand. She screwed up her face for a moment and went on. 'You're the only bit of my life that is still intact. I need you to stay that way. You mean a lot to me. Don't trivialize it. I'm not making any demands. I just want you to stay alive, that's all.'

David looked at Josie as if he had never seen her before. She had stuck out her lower lip and looked all of sixteen, but the steel beneath showed through.

'OK. I promise.' He took a deep breath. 'One step at a time, though. Let's just see tonight whether Ove's magic trick has come up with anything. After that we won't do anything we don't agree on. I'll be careful, really.'

And they walked back down the hill hand in hand in silence.

That night, and with that conversation in mind, David elected to stay behind while Nick and Ove went to retrieve the fax equipment. There seemed a lot of past ground to sort out between him and Josie. They settled down on the sofa with a glass of wine to watch a film, but then Gunk appeared.

'Oh, good, I like this one,' he said, and sat massively in the armchair next to them, inhibiting conversation. Before the film ended, Nick and Ove were back, Gunk rising quickly to his feet with the shotgun to peer out of the window before David had even registered the sound of the car outside.

They came into the room like it was Christmas, grinning from ear to ear and clutching reams of paper, which trailed across the floor behind them. There was yards and yards of it, and everyone gathered round the table as Nick spread it out. Starting to read it was a thrilling moment, illicit excitement backed up by moral justification.

'OK,' said Nick. 'What have we got?'

'You mean you really resisted the temptation to look at it all the way back?'

'Yeah. I reckoned you'd want to be in on the act. So, let's see. What's this one? "Week ending August 2. Production schedule target attainment results." Boring. Travel bookings, same again. Air freight waybill notification, material delivery schedule. Jesus, this is dull stuff.'

'Nick, any company's faxes would be 99 per cent crap. We're looking for the special 1 per cent. Don't give up just yet.'

Ove had lost interest now his bit was done, and wandered off to make some coffee. Ten minutes later David felt much the same way as Nick. There were turnover breakdowns, statistical reports to head office, hotel bookings for reps, raw material orders, hire-car arrangements, but nothing to make the pulse speed up. Every now and then there would be something that made no sense, a few lines of garbled nonsense, just rows of jumbled figures and numbers.

'What is all this?' asked David, pointing at one.

'Garbage,' said Nick. 'Some kind of interference, maybe. Ignore it.'

'Nice try, but we haven't got much.'

'Not so fast. What we have got is a worm's-eye view of their office set-up.'

'What do you mean?'

'Look at the people who are sending these, or who they're being sent to. We've got the names of all the top guys' secretaries, plus their room numbers and most of their phone extensions. We know what sort of messages they send each other. We know how Birmingham head office addresses Newcastle and the other way round.'

'How does that help?'

'God knows, but it's better than not knowing it.'

Ove came back in then. 'So, how does it go?' he asked brightly.

Nick sighed. 'Not too good. There's no smoking guns here. Maybe we'd better go and try again.'

'Sure,' said Ove. 'We can give it another go.' He picked up the long train of paper and peered at it curiously. 'Next time, we just stick it on line one, yes? There's no point recording all this scrambled stuff on line two.'

'No, I suppose not,' said David, then Ove's words sank in and he sat up. 'Scrambled? Do you mean garbled or do you mean literally scrambled?'

Ove looked amused. 'Scrambled, like with a scrambler – for security.'

'That's what all those pages of rubbish are?'

'For sure. What did you think they were?'

'So line two is all scrambled material?'

'Looks like it. See, here. The first characters of each of those messages. They're the same. That's the scrambler trigger code.'

'Now you're talking,' said Nick. 'So how do you un-scramble it?'

'You don't,' said Ove calmly. 'Not unless you have access to a huge mainframe and lots of money for computer time, and even then maybe not. It's almost totally impossible to unscramble.'

'Well, at least that means it matters,' said David. 'This has to be the private line for the important stuff.'

Nick looked at Ove. 'So there's nothing we can do?'

Ove looked back at him and his mouth twitched a bit. 'Not unless we are feeling very brave.'

362

At lunch-time the next day they were all three wondering if they really were feeling brave enough. The previous day's faxes removed some of the immediate danger. They knew from the travel bookings that Purkiss and Donaldson were out of harm's way in Jersey, Busby appeared to be in Birmingham for a meeting and the local MD from Newcastle was down there too, which was one more plus point.

An hour earlier they'd put Ove down the hole again, with the car parked to block off the line of sight from the factory. Nick had been tempted to steal one of those screens that the BT line engineers use to put round the hole, but David had stopped him. They didn't need any extra risks. It all felt a bit too chancy in broad daylight, and they kept a wary eye on the factory all the time Ove was down there, but nothing stirred.

'OK,' he said when they got him back up again, 'it is all ready. I think we can transmit on that line now. Do you have the piece of paper?'

They had stayed up late the previous night preparing it. The heading had a careful mixture of ident codes to make it hard for anyone in Newcastle to work out exactly which office within the Birmingham complex it emanated from. Initials and phone numbers were similarly designed to be a bit ambiguous in case anyone decided to check. By sending it from the machine that was now tapped into the line, it would appear to have come direct from head office. They had decided the odds were on their side. Coming, as it appeared to, straight from the horse's mouth, why should anyone go to the bother of checking?

It was a simple message. It told the MD's secretary to arrange for access to the encrypted fax machine for two specialists from a security company. It gave names and arrival times for two men, Gunnar Ekblom and Vernon Whalen. The visiting-card machine at Newcastle airport was a godsend, producing convincing-looking business cards on the spot, with as fancy a logo as they could concoct.

Nick looked at his watch. 'Ove, just for me, be a pal and go over it one more time, would you?'

'OK. It's not difficult. Encryption, scrambling, whatever you call it, only happens after the fax has read the message in clear, right? The machine has to read the piece of paper just like normal. It turns it into electric pulses *then* they pass through the scrambler and get changed before they go down the line to the other machine. Messages coming back go the same way. They come in scrambled, pass through the device, then go the short distance in clear to the printer, which gives you the message.'

'So the only point anyone else can get at the message, when it's not scrambled, is between the scrambler and the bit that prints and reads messages?'

'Just so. Inside the machine. That is where we have to put the device.'

'OK, I understood that. What you haven't said is how we then get the message outside to us.'

Ove held up a little box. 'A clever little gadget. It's just another bug, but it has a tiny transmitter. It sends us the fax by radio. We put the receiver on the other machine and bingo.'

'Yeah,' said Nick, 'but if they sweep for bugs, they'll find it, won't they? It'll be zapping out all kinds of broadcast shit.'

'There are two reasons that does not bother us,' said Ove. 'First, why should they do any sweeping when they know their team of specialists sent by Birmingham head office have just swept it? Second – this is the clever bit – it sits there sleeping until we alert it with a radio signal. It has to, because the battery only has a short life with the sort of transmission power we need.'

'How long?' asked David.

'Four, five hours maybe.'

'That's not much.'

'No. It means we have to be clever, but it also means no one can detect it until we switch it on.'

They'd got a hire-car specially for the job. They drove up to the entrance gate and stopped at the barrier. It was the moment of truth. They had no way of telling what had happened since their fax arrived. Nick, at the wheel, was more than half expecting bells to go off, and had his escape route all planned out in his head. Boot it in reverse, wheel hard over and get out of it. That plan was foiled by a van that drew up behind them. He handed their cards through the window as naturally as he could, watching the guard inside his room carefully. The man betrayed very little interest. He checked a list, nodded slightly and picked up a telephone. It was the make or break moment. Was this the whistle being blown or were they in? He talked briefly on the phone, put it down and nodded at them. They were in. He directed them across the parking area to reception and wished them a friendly good afternoon.

They wandered round reception looking at the photos on the wall and the models on display in the cases, until a young, good-looking blonde girl came down the stairs and said, 'Mr Whalen? Mr, er Ekblom?'

'That's us,' said Nick.

'I'm Mr Donaldson's secretary. Mrs Humberstone asked me to come down and look after you.'

'How delightful,' said Nick, and smiled at her. She gave him a slightly arch look.

'It is the first time you've been?' she said.

'It is, but I very much hope to have the pleasure of coming again.' She giggled.

She led the way up the stairs, chatting away and playing up to Nick's flirting.

In the foyer to the executive office suite upstairs stood a woman of an altogether different disposition. She had short iron-grey hair that clung tightly to the contours of her head. The lines of her face were the fold-marks for the frown that looked permanently settled on it, and she was not happy.

'It's not the usual procedure at all,' were her first words.

'Mrs Humberstone, I presume,' said Nick with a big smile that cut no ice.

'Why have I only just been told you were coming?'

'I'm afraid that's not a question for me to answer. Didn't Birmingham tell you?'

'Yes, but at very short notice.'

'I'm sorry, I'm just following instructions.'

'But who gave you those instructions? We had the office swept last week.'

'I'm, sorry, Mrs Humberstone. I'm just the poor guy that gets given the job sheet, but I understood this was a special visit. Kind of a one-off. You want me to go away again?'

He watched Mrs Humberstone wrestle with the problem, knowing that if she decided to make check-calls, they'd be in a lot of trouble. She picked up the fax from her desk and read it through again, then sighed. 'No, you'd better do what you've come for.' Then she turned to the blonde girl and said in a voice that she barely bothered to moderate, 'And you'd better stay with them.'

The girl took them through to a small annexe with

366

machines in it. He knew the matter would continue to nag at the older woman and there was little chance of the bug remaining undetected for long once Bamco's management was back from all its journeying.

Then they swung into their routine. He used Ove's bug sweeper all round the office, playing with its dials and keeping one eye on Ove's progress with the fax machine. As soon as he saw the cover was off and Ove was reaching into his equipment bag, he put down the sweeper and turned to the girl. 'Are you the big boss's secretary then?' he asked.

She giggled again. 'No, that's Mrs Humberstone out there. I'm Mr Donaldson's secretary, or at least I'm one of them. His main one's down in head office.'

'Two offices? Twice the security problem. Does he keep duplicate papers both ends?'

'I suppose he does. I'm always filing copies here for him.'

Nick tut-tutted importantly. He tilted his head towards the outer office.

'She must be a bit of a cow to work with.'

The girl spluttered, nodding. 'Shhh.' She grinned. 'You said it.'

'How many people use this office?'

'Just Mr Purkiss, Mr Donaldson, Mr Busby and us.'

'What's Mr Donaldson like to work for then?'

She looked round to make quite sure Mrs Humberstone was out of earshot. Luckily, Ove's body was blocking her view of what he was doing inside the fax machine.

'A bit, well, spooky like. Cocky. Knows he can handle himself, and he's not what you'd call modest. Mind you, he's very nice to me.' She smiled winsomely. 'Always calls me Blondie.'

'What's your real name?' asked Nick, although he knew the answer.

'Moira. What's yours?'

'Mine?' Nick was momentarily struck dumb, because he couldn't remember. Then he reached into his pocket, whipped out a business card with a gallant flourish and pressed it into her hand.

'Vernon,' she said, reading it. 'That's a nice name.'

'Call me Vern.'

'Where are you based?'

'London.'

'Are you staying up here then?'

Nick could see that Ove had the cover back on the machine now and was giving him the nod. 'Maybe. Unless they send us somewhere else. I could call you if we're staying. We could go and eat somewhere. How about that?'

'That would be nice,' she said.

'Anyway, we're finished for now. It's all clean. We'll be on our way,' he said.

'I'll see you out.'

They drove out past the barrier with a feeling of huge relief and headed for the spot, half a mile away, where David was waiting out of sight in a disused freight yard.

'How did it go?'

'Like a dream, but we shouldn't hang about. There's an old hag there who wasn't too happy about us. She's bound to check it with someone as soon as she can. I'd say we don't have a very long shelf-life.'

'OK,' said David. 'We've got all the gear. Now we just need a way of getting the information out of them. We'll only get one shot at it. We know Purkiss and Donaldson are in Jersey and we know which hotel they're in. Gwenaelle's given us the name of this company. Shall we go for it?'

'Why not?' said Nick. 'I hope to hell she's right.'

'I'd bet money on it. Anyway, I've drafted a message from what we know and I've typed it all out on the portable. Take a look and tell me what you think.'

The fax was brought straight up from downstairs by Maurice the messenger and handed to Moira in the buff folder which was always used for confidential executive-level communications. She opened it and wondered for a moment why it had come in on the open line before she remembered Mr Donaldson was in Jersey and presumed he would have no way of scrambling it from there. Mr Busby took his portable unit with him when he went away, but not Mr Donaldson. She read it:

Blondie. Please immediately fax main documents of my BFSS files on scrambled line to BHO to await my arrival there. M Donaldson.

She raised her eyebrows at the 'please'. He's not usually so polite, she thought. Nice to see he's changing his tune. Then she thought more about the request, and frowned. He must know she didn't normally have access to his private filing cabinet. Could he have forgotten that was where all the BFSS stuff was kept? She didn't handle any of that. It worried her because she did know, just from tidying up his desk, where he kept his spare key, and that was a security lapse. Could this be a trick to get her in trouble? She wouldn't put it past him. She could fax or phone to ask, maybe that would be best. She reached for the phone, then hesitated. He hated it when she checked back with him. He always said it showed she didn't have enough common sense. What a dilemma. Should she break the rules and unlock the cabinet, or what?

There was a noise in the other office. 'Mrs Humberstone?' she called.

The usual crabby, irritated voice came back. 'Yes, Moira.'

'I've got a funny request from Mr Donaldson.'

There was an exaggerated sigh from the other room. 'There are no funny requests, Moira. Not from our employers. There are simply requests. Is it something you can do?'

'Well, yes, but . . .'

'Then for heaven's sake, girl, do it.'

So she did.

The note had taken a lot of effort. Every word had been scrutinized for flaws. In the end they'd decided the simpler the better. 'Blondie' was a bit dangerous, but in the light of Nick's information they decided it was a good touch. BHO for Birmingham head office had come from the previous day's faxes. They'd spent several minutes trying to decide between 'scrambled' and 'encrypted', and the sign-off had been equally difficult. David had argued for Martin Donaldson, typed in full. Nick felt either Donaldson or Mr Donaldson was more likely. Ove cut them short by suggesting M Donaldson, which could be simply taken as the result of some rushed typing.

When they were happy, David retyped it and Ove went back down his hole again to transmit it on the machine. After that it was all rush. He had to disconnect the machine, bring it back up to the car and couple it to the radio receiver. They drove a bit further away so they were still in line of sight but not quite so obvious. Ove started the little generator they had rented from a hire shop on the way, and switched on the fax. Nothing happened.

'Goddam,' he said. 'No output.'

'From the fax?'

'No, the goddam generator. The engine goes, but there is no power.'

'Bloody hire shop. Let's get back there,' said Nick.

'No time,' said David. 'If they reply to that fax it's going to be straight away. We'll miss it. Is there anything you can do, Ove?'

Two minutes later he almost wished he hadn't asked. It would only take a passing policeman to have them all inside. The bent inspection panel lying on the pavement was one thing, the mess of wiring pulled out of the bottom of the street lamp was quite another, so obvious that anyone coming by would see it. However, so far no one had passed and the fax's lights were glowing nicely. They sat there watching it, hypnotized by its inaction.

The machine was beside Ove on the back seat. A short antenna was clipped to the top of one of the rear windows. David was staring at the machine, thinking it would never work, there were simply too many things which could go wrong along the way. Suddenly, a thought struck him.

'Ove,' he said, 'if she does send this fax, are they going to get it in Birmingham too?'

'Yes, of course,' said Ove. 'We are just listening in on the line, not cutting it.'

'Oh, shit,' said David. 'Then when it all prints out there, they're going to know straight away, aren't they?'

'Makes no odds,' said Nick. 'Soon as Donaldson gets back little Blondie is sure to say did you get my fax OK? We're no worse off.'

But David hadn't thought that one through, and as the green 'receive' light came on before their disbelieving eyes and, against all the odds, paper started slowly edging its way out of the machine, he was left with the uncomfortable feeling that they had just stirred up a nest of vipers.

Chapter Thirty-four

Wednesday August 7th 1991

Martin Donaldson arrived back at the office with hardly a care in the world. Not normally given to counting his chickens before they were hatched, he was, nevertheless, in his own peculiar way, on cloud nine. Looking back on the last few days in Jersey, he could see it as just about the final stage in his long strategy. Purkiss had at last let him almost all the way in on the final secrets. There was just one thing Donaldson reckoned was still being kept from him. He was pretty sure Purkiss was keeping the richest titbit to himself. Still, Geoff Busby was no longer a threat. More than that, it looked as though he was out in the wilderness. Purkiss was thoroughly hacked off that Busby had again taken off somewhere by himself.

They had been sitting at dinner the previous night on the small terrace of a very exclusive restaurant high on the hillside above St Helier. There was a Formula One racing driver at the next table – it was that kind of place. The prices were astronomical. Until then it had been the sort of restaurant Purkiss had taken him to only when they were entertaining somebody else.

'Young Martin,' Purkiss said distractedly over coffee and cognac, looking down on the lights of St Helier twinkling below. 'You and me, we've got a bit of a job to do. I smell a spot of bother coming up and I need you to help sort it.'

'What sort of bother, Spencer?'

'I'm not quite sure. It might be called envy. It might be called greed. But whichever way it's got a very unpleasant smell.'

He just raised an eyebrow and waited, and in his own time Purkiss went on. 'Last month I thought we were just about out of the woods. We've got the right gear to sell now. The army deal on Dodgem is the golden key that unlocks the door. The trouble is, there's a few wanting to muscle in on our act.'

'What's going on?'

Purkiss paused while the waiter appeared with a box of cigars. He took one and sniffed it.

'Cut it for you, sir?'

'Fine.'

The boy left and he leaned forward conspiratorially. 'It's been building up in the last few days. What I want to say is you've done well on the weapons. Now I want you to front up on the corporate bit. That's our next war. There's something I don't like going on. I don't like it one bit. We need another slice of cash for the end of the Dodgem development programme, just to crack those last few problems, then we should be home and dry, but just at the critical moment the bloody bank's started being awkward, dragging its feet.'

'Any ideas why?'

'I sniff sharks, Martin. The scent of blood in the water. Someone knows we're going to be worth a bit soon, and they wouldn't mind swallowing us whole.'

'And you're saying they've got our bank on their side?'

'Don't be naïve. It's a merchant bank. It's out for what it can get. You need to get across this when we get back. We got WEPEX coming up. You know about WEPEX?'

'I know it's the biggest of the European arms fairs.'

'Yeah, well, this time it's where we cash in our Gulf chips. You know we've got a big push on to sell Cracksman 1 there. There's three, possibly four buyers lined up. The first three are all OK. They're friendlies. I don't have to tell you who the fourth one is, but you might say they're a bit beyond the pale. All the same, usual route – Belgium, let's say – and an end-user certificate from some banana republic that's on the OK list, and bingo.'

'I thought the M.o.D. hadn't given the go-ahead to release Cracksman 1 yet?'

'I'm seeing them tomorrow. I'll persuade them, no problem. I'll tell them they can have Cracksman 2 at cost if they let us sell Cracksman 1 to underwrite it. That's the sort of message they understand these days. It's big money, Martin. Very big. I don't want any fuckers in pinstripes spreading rumours to queer our pitch.'

Now, Jersey behind him, Donaldson parked the car in his space, got out sniffing a sulphurous tinge in the Birmingham air, and went inside. Upstairs, in his office, he nodded, still smiling, at his secretary Jean, and sat down.

'Moira sent you down these from Newcastle,' she said, putting a buff folder on the desk in front of him. The buffs always came first, so he opened it and pulled out a thick wad of papers, clearly a long fax, neatly divided up into its individual sheets and clipped together. The first sheet was a covering note. It read 'Dear Mr Donaldson. I've done as you asked. I knew where your spare keys were. I hope that's what you meant. Here is the material. I wasn't sure exactly what you wanted so I've sent most of it. Hope you had a good time in Jersey. Moira.'

Puzzled, he turned to the next sheet and stiffened in utter astonishment. Then he flicked rapidly through the

374

rest. It made no sense. He looked at the covering note again and it didn't help. There was every important list from the file. The file that was meant to be safely locked away in his office. The whole bloody story. He riffled through it again. No one looking at him would have noticed, but his mind was racing. He looked at the ident. It had come through on the scrambler. He relaxed just a little. That appeared to knock a few worrying options on the head.

He picked up the phone and pressed a button. 'Blondie?'

'Yes, Mr Donaldson. How are you? Did you have a good trip?'

'Yes, thanks. These papers you faxed down to me?'

'Oh, dear. Didn't I do it right? I did wonder when I got the fax . . .'

'No, no. It's nothing to do with that. I just want to take a look at the fax itself. The one asking for the papers to be sent.'

There was a short silence on the end of the phone, then she came on again, sounding puzzled. 'You mean the one you sent me?'

'That's the one.'

'Well, all right then. Do you want in encrypted?'

'No, there's no need for that. No need at all.'

When it came, he was astonished at the top line. Jersey. The hotel. Purkiss and he had been the only ones there. Purkiss? Checking up? Seeing what files he was keeping? That made no sense. He would simply have asked Mrs Humberstone to find out and send the material straight to him. What about Busby? He knew the man was desperately worried by his own ascendancy. What good would it do him? Maybe he was hoping to show Purkiss that Donaldson wasn't fireproof, that he could make security mistakes as well. He lifted the phone again to check Busby's movements, but they didn't add up to anything. Then he looked up the number of the Jersey hotel.

'Reception?'

'Good morning. This is Martin Donaldson from Bamco. I was staying with you for the weekend.'

'Yes, Mr Donaldson, what can I do for you?'

'I'm just trying to trace a message which went astray. I might have forgotten to get it faxed.' He glanced again at the codes on top of the fax in front of him. 'Could you just tell me whether either Mr Purkiss or I faxed anything to Newcastle at about 1.22 p.m. yesterday?'

'I'll call up the fax log right away, sir. Won't be a moment.' It was just under a minute. 'Mr Donaldson? No, sir. Nothing around 1.22. In fact there wasn't anything to Newcastle all day. I'm sorry.'

'That's quite all right.'

He sat back and whistled quietly to himself, then took out a Swiss Army knife, pulled out the screwdriver blade and took the cover off the scrambled fax machine. He had a good look around inside it. Nothing. Then he rang Moira again.

'Blondie? Was Mr Busby in the office yesterday?'

'No,' she said. 'I haven't seen him for days.'

'Was anyone else there yesterday?'

'No,' she said again. 'It was dead quiet. Just me and Mrs Humberstone all day. Oh, and the men who came to do the sweeping.'

'What men would those be?'

'The ones you sent up. At least I thought it was you, Mr Donaldson. Perhaps it was Mr Purkiss. You know, to check for bugs.'

'What, Karoll Associates?'

'No, not them. They're the usual ones, aren't they? That's what Mrs Humberstone said. This was some special arrangement. I thought you'd know about it.'

'Do you know who they were?'

'Yes, hang on a moment, I've got one of their cards. Here we are. It says Vernon Whalen. MX4 Security.'

'What's the phone number?'

There was a short silence. 'Well, that's strange,' she said. 'There isn't one. Funny, that. What use is a business card without a phone number on it?'

'Did they check the fax machine?'

'Oh, yes. They were very efficient. They had it all apart.'

When Martin Donaldson put the phone down, he put his feet on the desk and stared into space for a long time, weighing the possibilities of Busby being at the heart of this. It didn't add up. It was unnecessarily complicated. Another thought struck him then, and he swung his feet back to the floor. Then a funny thing happened. He started to laugh.

A little later on there was a summons to lunch. He went round to Purkiss's office. The man looked decidedly bothered. 'What's the matter, Spencer?' he asked.

'Dunno quite. All that stuff I was telling you about? It's coming up on our blind side a good bit faster than I thought. Save it for now. We'll talk about it while we eat. Geoff Busby's coming too.' He noticed Donaldson's subtly dismissive reaction. 'It's all hands on deck time, Martin.'

There was a private room at the back of the Royal Oak that they often used. Busby met them there. He's a bit twitchy, thought Donaldson, trying to put it all together. What's got into him? He's like a cat on hot bricks.

'Martin. Long time no see.'

'Hello, Geoff. Been busy, have you?'

Purkiss was steaming. When the waitress left them alone, closing the door behind her, he started straight in.

'That stuff I was telling you about, Martin? The trouble with the bank? Something's going on I don't like, lads. Something very sniffy indeed. I've had a call this morning. I thought they'd be agreeing the next tranche of money. It shouldn't have been a problem. It's all for straightforward project work, Dodgem and Cracksman 2.'

'So what's wrong?'

'Well, I just wish I knew,' said Purkiss. 'It's the sort of thing we've done lots of times before. We've got the letter of intent from the M.o.D. We're not asking for anything unreasonable. We just can't do it on our own resources, not with times like they are at the moment. Should be a breeze, but suddenly the fucking bank's making noises about wanting some sort of management restructuring. Bloody nonsense.'

Busby leaned forward, 'What does that mean, boss? Management restructuring?'

'A bit more depth in the board structure was what they said. I'll tell you what it means. It means a bunch of outside directors, picked by the fucking bank, sitting on us, poking their noses into everything we do.'

There was a silence while they all digested the implications of that one.

'That's what they do when they don't trust people, right?' said Busby.

'You got it,' said Purkiss. 'There's someone pulling the bank's strings and I don't like it.'

'OK then, time to look at this logically,' said Donaldson. 'First the bank. Whatever's going on there, we'll have trouble trying to fight it, so the answer is to get out from under.'

'Come again?'

'I mean, if we didn't need the bank, we wouldn't have to listen to their conditions, right?'

378

'Right. I've got you so far, but how do we do it?'

'Easy. We go all out at WEPEX to sign up all the business we can. If we have contracts there, we can turn them into cash. Raise money against them somewhere else. They'll be as good as letters of credit.'

WEPEX is the annual Weapons and Electronic Systems Procurement Exhibition held at the Churston Park race-track and exhibition centre on the outskirts of Birmingham. It is where the latest in weaponry goes on show and where the big overseas orders come in. It was due to start in two days' time.

Purkiss started jotting down sums on the menu.

'It's a good approach, Martin, I'll give you that, but I just can't see it producing quite enough. There's something like seven hundred thousand quid's worth of business we can count on. There's another two hundred thou we might get if we're a bit lucky. That still leaves us short of . . . well, call it four hundred grand.'

'OK. We get the rest of it from Dodgem and Cracksman 2.'

Busby guffawed. 'Come on. We can't put those on sale. That's the next generation. The M.o.D. want them for themselves. There's no way they'll agree to exports at this stage.'

'I wasn't thinking of doing it through Bamco, Geoff. I was thinking of BFSS.'

It was the make or break moment, and every one of his senses was quivering to assess their reactions. It was just what he expected. There was a quick, doubtful look from Busby to Purkiss, and Purkiss's eyes widened. I'm bloody right, he thought. They set this up way back and it was too good to cut me in on. They've got it all tied up in some other front company, somewhere else, Isle of Man maybe? Panama? Who knows. Still, there was no point in direct challenge. Softly softly. He continued.

'I know we wouldn't normally think of it yet, but we're between a rock and a hard place, right? Either we raise the money that way or we'll have a bunch of establishment spies on the board and we're right royally fucked anyway. We'll have to hide it in the accounts, but it would bring in the bacon.'

It took the other two a long time to bite the bullet. They could see a sweet little deal going down the drain, and Busby must have known it might well be the last deal Purkiss would ever cut him in on. But there wasn't any other way, and they both knew it.

'Well, maybe,' said Purkiss. 'If we're careful. Bit tricky, though. We couldn't sell whole Dodgem units, it would stand out a bloody mile.' There was a silence into which Donaldson could have stepped with a suggestion based on the guesswork he'd done, but he didn't. He sat it out, and Purkiss took off another of his seven veils. 'I suppose we could just offer the guidance units. Come to that we could just sell the gizmo to upgrade Cracksman 1 to Cracksman 2. Wouldn't be so obvious then if anyone came sniffing.'

Busby was nodding unhappily all the while. Donaldson looked brightly at Purkiss, naïve enthusiasm all over his face.

'Good. All we need is some ideas about clients and I can start setting it up through Jersey.'

'I'll let you have a list,' said Purkiss, and his last veil dropped. 'All right,' he said decisively, writing off direct personal gain against the more pressing problem of keeping control of his company. 'Go to it. You and me will work on that, Martin. Not Jersey though, not this time. I'll think up somewhere else. Let you know.' He turned to Busby. 'Geoff, you make sure everything's smooth for WEPEX. No fuck-ups.' He sipped his drink for a moment, then a thought struck him. 'Are you satisfied all that Challis stuff has died down?'

380

'Oh, yeah,' said Busby between mouthfuls. 'No problem.'

'I heard the police had been calling you?' said Donaldson.

Busby shot him a vindictive look. 'Just routine.'

'By the way, what were you doing in France?' persisted Donaldson.

'Little bit of this, little bit of that,' said Busby aggressively.

'No, come on, Geoff,' said Purkiss. 'I was wondering too.'

'Just making sure there weren't any loose ends. It really doesn't matter, I'll tell you some other time when we haven't got all this to worry about. OK?'

Purkiss looked at him broodingly. 'If you say so, Geoff.'

Chapter Thirty-five

Thursday August 8th 1991

David was deep in paper. He'd started at one end of Duncan's filing system, Josie had started at the other. Nick was keeping them supplied with coffee. They were looking for anything at all that could be a further clue to the loan from Trebitsch Finance, hoping against hope that they might find the money had been put away somewhere where Duncan hadn't got round to squandering it. The more he searched, the more convinced David became that it wasn't like that at all, that his brother, flying as usual on a wing and a prayer, had simply concocted some sort of commercial project to justify raising extra cash, which had in fact been spent on the house.

They met in the middle of the filing cabinet, slumping in failure, and all he could do was shake his head at her. They'd looked at everything, however unlikely the subject heading.

'What else is there?'

'There's nothing else,' she said. 'There's just the in-tray, and there isn't much in that.'

David turned to it purely to avoid having to acknowledge defeat. It was a simple stack of wire baskets, marked IN, OUT, FILE and INVITES. OUT and FILE were both empty. There was a handful of bills in the IN section and a brown envelope sitting in INVITES. David took it out, just to leave no stone unturned, and was astonished to see Bamco's logo on the back flap.

'What's this?'

'No idea. It must have been there a while.'

'Yes, it has. The postmark's June 16th.'

'Have a look.'

Inside was a compliments slip, a folder marked 'WEPEX List of Exhibitors' and some sort of entry ticket. Nick came in while they were reading through it.

'Listen, David,' he said, 'today's decision day. I can't ask Gunk and Donnie to stay on for too much longer. Nothing's happened, so they're getting a bit bored with it. What are we going to do?'

'Yes, Nick, I've been thinking about that.'

'Maybe we should make a movie? Do a doco all about what we know. Lean on Glass to put it in the show. Get it all out in the open and then no one will dare do anything nasty.'

David snorted. 'Bertram wouldn't touch it with a barge-pole. Channel 4 might, or one of the ITV companies. The trouble is they're all up to here with the franchise auction. Nothing's being commissioned at the moment. Anyway, I think the time-scale's too long. It's going to take weeks to set that up, but the principle's right. It's just the medium that's wrong. We've got a short-term problem here.' He waved the leaflet in the air. 'And I think maybe, just maybe, I've found a short-term solution.'

Friday August 9th 1991

The following morning they were up with the lark, leaving Josie in the care of Gunk and Donnie, who'd agreed to another couple of days. In a box on the back seat of the Jensen was a pile of glossy brochures, the product of a long afternoon groping their way through Duncan's desktop publishing equipment. As David turned south on to the motorway, Nick pulled one out of the box and rustled through it. They had used the outside of Duncan's special folders, normally intended for pitching at new clients for his video business – vivid, glossy yellow with 'Duncan Challis' in a crimson slash down the front. Below, there was a window, and visible through that window in bold black letters, hot from Duncan's laser printer, the words DID BAMCO SELL *YOUR* SECRETS? Inside, it was short and to the point. It said:

In research conducted by TV journalists since the Gulf War it has been established that BFSS, a Channel Islands company connected to the owner of the Bamco Group, has been selling countermeasures to a wide range of British-manufactured weapons systems. In an effort to get rapid action taken to rectify this, we enclose a list, taken from Bamco's own files, of the systems involved, with a summary of the foreign countries to which details have been passed. We are taking this action because we believe the deaths of two people have already resulted directly from their connections with this affair.

It was followed by a few sheets, photocopied from the faxes they had intercepted.

Nick chortled. 'This should do it,' he said. 'How many of the companies on the list are going to be there?'

'Ten out of the twelve,' said David. 'I'll put them in the hands of the highest-ranking bloke I can find on each of their stands, then we'll get out of it a bit sharpish.' He looked at Nick. 'By the way,' he said, 'just for belt and braces, I sent one to the Ministry of Defence in last night's post.'

Nick frowned. 'I suppose, technically, bugging faxes is an offence.'

384

'Not just technically,' said David grimly. 'You get a nice big prison sentence for that sort of thing, but somehow I think that's the least of our worries.' He looked across at Nick. 'I know I've said this before, but you don't have to be there for this one.'

'Me? I'm just along for the ride. You're the one that's going in. I just wish the hell I could come in too.'

They pulled into the large car park at Churston Park at lunchtime, keeping a careful eye out all round. There were two or three hundred cars there, all the usual executive models. One thing stood out, though. There was a much higher than usual proportion of Range Rovers and their Japanese imitations. Not only that, but a surprising number of them were in metallic green.

'Look at that,' said Nick. 'It's a keeny-meany convention. They're all pretending they're still in the army. Which side does that put us on?'

'The side of the angels. I just wonder how long it will take them to realize that,' said David. He considered. 'I'm the only one who can get in. The leaflet with the ticket says there's very tight security. I'll go inside and take a look round. You hang on here and I'll come back for the folders once I've seen what's what. I'd better locate the people before I start wandering around with these under my arm.'

Nick was looking at the admission document again. 'Did you see this? It says you have to show a passport.'

'I've got it here. Lucky the invite only said D. Challis.'

He got out, suddenly feeling nervous, and walked across the grass and gravel, following the arrow marked 'Exhibitors' Entrance'. Inside the swing-doors stood two guards, a metal detector for bags and a walk-through security gate.

'Good afternoon,' he said, and passed over his invitation card. The first man consulted his list and then shook his head with a sigh. 'Well, you're down all right, Mr Challis. It's just that Bamco told us you wouldn't be coming. You've been crossed off.'

David froze inside, but put on a jovial tone of voice. 'You're kidding,' he said. 'What a cock-up. I've come two hundred miles for this. I'll soon sort them out.'

The man took a look at his passport and shrugged. 'Well, I suppose the fact you were on the list makes it all right. Give them a rocket for me, will you? They're only supposed to give us the definite no-shows. Step this way.'

The other man held up his hand. 'Before you go through, Mr Challis. Are you carrying any firearms or ammunition?'

'No, sorry, I didn't know I was supposed to.'

Wintry half-smiles, but the way was open.

He walked in through a lobby area to hear a loudspeaker intoning, 'Companies participating in the live firing and night vision exercises, please confirm to organizer's office straight away.'

The hall, at first glance, could have been hosting an exhibition of anything from plumbing supplies to model engineering. At a second glance it was quite distinctively different. Dress was a mixture of suits or well-cut flak jackets in roughly equal proportions. The people came in a limited range of types, company men of ex-military, public-school mien, boffins with zealous but childlike expression, exhibition girls with an army stamp, ranging from Sloanes for the officers to tarts for the rest, and then there were the keeny-meanies. They were everywhere, hatchet faces, cold eyes, hard bodies.

The stands themselves were extraordinary, placards couched in the weird language of deathless death. HIGH-

SAFETY AMMUNITION screamed one. Attracted by the apparent contradiction, David read the prose. *Virtually no shoot-through. Ability to penetrate woven body armour. Superb target neutralization capabilities.* Safety to whom? he wondered. Presumably the person doing the shooting.

And so on. Non-polluting lead-free bullets, targets of all ethnic types, cut-outs of Afro-headed youngsters with petrol bombs, deranged white mothers with knives, stands with rows of pistols and automatic weapons freely available for the keeny-meanies to heft in a familiar, evaluating way.

The speaker came on again. 'Gentlemen, just to remind you to sign up for the transport this afternoon to Bamco's unique ammunition demonstration. As many of you know, this will include the never-to-be-forgotten sight of Mr Spencer Purkiss being shot with his very own ammunition, and there's to be a bottle of champagne to each of you who is brave enough to volunteer for the same treatment. Coaches leave for the Bamco works at quarter past two precisely. Thank you.'

It woke him up again to the threat of recognition. He kept alert for any sign of Geoff Busby in the throng. He had put a mac on to cover the badge he had to wear, the badge that identified him as Bamco's Video Adviser. It was hot. He was looking in this rabbit warren for the stands of the companies he needed, while trying to stay well away from the aisle with the big Bamco stand. It was a tactic that should have worked. It would have done if Geoff Busby hadn't been on quite a different stand, trying out a new laser sight on their little demonstration range next to the display.

Busby recognized David at a distance, like a nightmare on two legs. Whatever he's doing here, it can't be good, he thought. He ducked out of sight until he could see his back

387

view retreating down the aisle, then he headed for the organizer's office.

David was walking slowly through the far end of the hall, putting his dossier-delivery route together in his head. He didn't want to have to answer any questions from the recipients in here, so he had sketched out a route that didn't involve any doubling back. It was just a matter of shoving the dossier into the hands of the right people and then merging into the crowd before they had a chance to react. He didn't take any notice of the approaching security guard and the man in the suit who was with him until the guard grabbed him by the arm and quietly asked him to step outside.

'Why? What are you doing?'

'You are Mr Challis?'

'I am.'

'Then please come with me, sir.'

'Look, what's the problem? Here's my badge. See?'

The other man, the one in the suit, stepped forward as people turned to watch. 'This will be a lot less embarrassing in the organizer's office, sir.'

In the office David, with a sinking heart, was confronted by the list.

'You appear not to be Mr Duncan Challis at all, sir. Your passport says you are Mr David Challis and we understand you are a journalist? I'm sorry to say that passes to WEPEX are not transferable and, in any case, journalists are not allowed entry in any circumstances.'

'I'm not here as a journalist. I'm here to represent my brother Duncan.'

'I'm afraid you'll have to leave.'

It was the bum's rush. Ignominious ejection past a group of curious onlookers. David walked back towards Nick and the car, shoulders slumped, a trail of defeat all the long way across the car park.

Nick reached over and pushed the door open for him as he approached. 'Trouble?'

'I got slung out. They took my pass.'

'How come?'

'I don't know. Someone spotted me as a journalist.'

'The perils of a famous face.'

'Well, maybe,' he said doubtfully, but he wondered.

'Then it's down to us,' said Nick. 'There's gotta be another way in.' They stared out of the windscreen at the exhibition centre, but their view was blocked as a big white van was driven across the front of the car. Their minds were so far away that they were waiting patiently for it to move, right up to the moment when Geoff Busby got out of the driver's seat, came over to the open window and stuck the silenced muzzle of what David recognized with no great satisfaction as a Welrod pistol in their faces, just like in the movies.

Chapter Thirty-six

Same day

They both wanted the journey to end and feared its ending at the same time. The van could have been designed to amplify the smell of fear. They guessed it was for carrying ammunition, a thickly armoured steel box with no ventilation and no light. In the darkness the sour smell of sweat soon filled their nostrils. The steel was smooth except for ring bolts dotted all around for securing its normal cargo. The cornering forces made them slide painfully into these projections. David could feel his knee swelling from one impact, and the pain in his scalp was wet to the touch. Nick's grunts told him the same story.

'Where do you think he's going?'

'No idea, Nick. God, I'm sorry.'

'Save it. Let's think up something.'

'Huh.'

'When it stops, let's get right to the back, then we can jump him when he opens the door.'

'Nick, there's something I should tell you. That pistol he was holding.'

'Yeah?'

'It was a Welrod. Do you know what that means?'

'No.'

'It used to be a favourite SAS weapon. Anyone who chooses a gun as unusual as that and looks like Busby at the same time has got to be ex-SAS.'

'So? Is that meant to make me go all weak at the knees?'

'It should, if you know anything at all about the SAS.'

'Well, you tell me another option, then.'

He couldn't. After nearly half an hour's painful lurching the truck slowed to a brief stop, then moved off again for only another half a minute or so before it reversed a short way to stop for good.

'Come on,' said Nick, and stiffly and painfully they moved down to the end with the doors. There was the sound of bolts being shot back, and then bright daylight, too bright. Even if their legs had been working properly, their eyes, fully dilated in the dark, were immediately disabled by the glare of sunlight. In any case Busby was standing well back.

'Don't move,' he said. 'Just listen. In a minute, when I say, you get out of the truck, walk straight ahead and go in through the door. You don't shout. You don't run. You don't do anything. There's two of you and one of me, but before you get any silly ideas, remember this. I'll only be pointing the gun at one of you. Whatever the other one might do, that's the one that gets it and that will be you, Challis. I'm on my turf. I know what I'm doing. You don't, so don't even think about it.'

They didn't. They got out, walked through the brief sunlight into a doorway, then down a sloping corridor into a dark chamber. A heavy door slammed shut behind them. Wondering, they took stock. The chamber was a cube, ten feet in each direction, and brightly lit by deeply recessed lights in its ceiling. It was lined with steel. In the wall facing them was a small panel of thick glass, also deeply recessed. Behind it was something circular that looked like a camera lens. From the left-hand wall there protruded a short, blackened steel tube. The right-hand wall had a square aperture in it, opposite the tube. The aperture was filled by more steel, a plate that looked as if it was removable or replaceable from somewhere beyond the chamber. The centre of that plate was deeply dented and discoloured. The walls of the chamber itself were scarred with little furrows of bright metal and discoloured in streaks of fawn, green and blue, with the occasional patch of sooty black. That was all there was.

They moved slowly round it, like people in a dream, trying to understand, knowing there was some deliberate and lethal purpose behind it which they could not fathom. Then there was a click and a voice, Busby's voice, came from one of the light apertures in the ceiling.

'Gentlemen,' he said in a mocking tone, 'you may be wondering why you're here. You are standing in the testing chamber for projectiles designed for use by tank main armament. Very shortly you will have the opportunity of witnessing the test of what we call a sabot round with a warhead made of depleted uranium. It will emerge from the barrel on your left and it will impact against the slab you can see to your right.'

As if with one mind David and Nick moved back to the left-hand wall, pressing themselves against it, one each side of the gun barrel, to keep out of the line of fire. There was a chuckle from the grille.

'Don't be absurd. If this round was to be used against a tank, it would penetrate the armour. The kinetic energy it releases would vaporize it and fill the inside of the tank with white-hot gas and tiny shards of metal travelling at several hundred miles an hour. Here it will not penetrate anything. To all intents and purposes you are already inside the tank turret. It will vaporize within the chamber. A sad case of over-enthusiastic investigation by two idiots who walked through the wrong door at the wrong time.' There was a brief silence, then he spoke again. 'That's all. You've caused me a lot of problems. Now I intend to cause you rather a larger one.'

David shouted. 'They'll know it was you, Busby. I've sent all the details to the M.o.D.'

'I can see your mouth moving, Mr Challis, but I'm afraid the return sound circuit is switched off. I doubt I'm missing anything. That really is all.'

The speaker fell silent. They could hear indistinct movements through it, but nothing more than that. David looked despairingly at Nick. Nick looked sombrely back at him, sat down against the wall and started to sing quietly. 'Mine eyes have seen the glory of the coming of the Lord, He is trampling out the vintage where . . .'

Each second dragged out unbearably as David tried to cope with the numbing realization that his life was about to be over. He stared at the muzzle of the gun, hypnotized by its ordinariness, wondering if his eyes would provide him with any tiniest forewarning of his death. He had wild thoughts of pushing something up it. Then the speaker made an unexpected noise over Nick's low singing.

'Nick,' he said. 'Be quiet.'

Nick looked affronted, but he stopped singing and then he heard it too.

Busby's voice, at a distance from the microphone and very distorted, said something in a startled tone. It sounded like a question. There was what could have been a short answer, even further off. There was no mistaking what came next. A loud shout, 'You bastard. You fucking bastard. Don't you . . .' Then, shockingly, a tremendous crash which had both their pulse rates going into overdrive, but it wasn't the cannon blast they'd been waiting for. Nothing in the chamber had changed. There was a second or two of silence while they just looked at each other, white-faced,

393

then a voice came though the speaker and it was a new voice, a man's voice they had never heard before.

'Challis, Listen. I am watching you through the monitor. Sit down against the wall where the door is, facing away from it. When you are in that position, the door will be unlocked. Don't look round. Don't move or it will be locked again. You must wait for five minutes before you come out. You won't be harmed so long as you wait five minutes. I see you are wearing a watch. Hold up your thumb if you agree.'

With shaking hands David and Nick both held up their thumbs. They went to the wall and collapsed against it, still staring at the gun barrel, wondering if the worst would yet happen. They heard the door latch being drawn back.

'Who are you?' David called, but there was no answer, just footsteps going away. He looked at the time on his watch.

'Why don't we just go?' whispered Nick. 'We could creep out really carefully. That way we might find out what's going on.'

'We could,' said David, thinking that, after coming so close to death, it seemed a more attractive option not to take any extra risks with his newly restored life. 'Do you really want to take the chance?'

'No, can't say I do. How much time have we had?'

'Fifteen seconds.'

'Is that all? He'll be miles away by the time it gets to five minutes.'

'I think that was probably what he had in mind.'

Nick fell silent for a bit, but time was weighing heavily on both of them and their brains were racing. 'Even when we get out, we're still . . . well, wherever we are.'

'I guess it's somewhere in the Bamco factory. We were in the truck for about the right amount of time to go through Birmingham.'

'So what do we do? Try to get clear without anyone seeing?'

'Beats me, let's see what we find when we get out of here.'

Eventually the time was up and, with great care, they moved out of the chamber and up the sloping passageway to where the open outside door was letting in sunlight. They stopped and David peered cautiously out. They were on the edge of a factory complex, some twenty yards from the long brick wall of the factory. A blue and yellow sign mounted high on the wall spelt out BAMCO. The little building surmounting the buried test chamber was on its own in a stretch of wasteland, with the high perimeter security fence another fifty yards off. There was no one in sight.

There was another door next to the one they had come out of. Nick twisted the knob and it opened. Beyond was a small lobby and a second door. It opened into a room that was clearly the observation gallery for the test chamber. There were chairs and electronic equipment, with a big video monitor on a desk, but they could see only half the desk. Slumped over it, obscuring the other half, was the body of Geoff Busby. His fingers were locked around the butt of a pistol. The muzzle was in his mouth. The back of his head was all over the wall behind.

Nick gagged. David walked over and looked down at what was left, then turned abruptly on his heel and led the way out.

'David, wait,' called Nick after him in a low voice. 'Go easy. We're not out of the woods yet. We're still in the middle of Bamco.'

David walked on, no longer afraid. A two-tone siren was coming closer. 'Something's changed,' he said. 'I can feel it. Let's go and see.'

They turned the corner to the front of the factory as an ambulance pulled in through the gate. There was a police car behind it. A coach was parked in front of the reception area and a crowd of people were coming out through the glass doors of the factory main entrance. David and Nick moved in amongst them. They were of all nationalities and they seemed excited and stunned in equal measure. Off to one side, a small Japanese man was crying. 'What happened?' David asked.

'It was not my fault,' said the man. 'I do what he say. I just do what he say. I just pull the trigger, that is all. I did not know.'

Then the police were ushering them all back inside, trying to calm people down, taking names, commandeering offices to use while they took statements. David and Nick were shoved into a tiny office by themselves, told not to move and left sitting there. Every now and then a police constable would glance at them round the door, then leave again. After half an hour they'd had enough, so they opened the door and confronted a uniformed inspector who was hurrying past.

'Whatever's going on here, we weren't inside the factory,' said David. 'Can we go?'

'Certainly not. You were told to stay in there.' He looked hard at David. 'Hold on a minute. Could I have your name?'

'My name's David Challis and I live . . .'

That was as far as he got. 'Right,' said the inspector, 'and this is Mr Nielsen?'

'Er, yes.'

'Come with me then, straight away.'

They were whisked off into a separate room. An older man in a tweed suit came in. 'You're Mr David Challis? Can you tell me exactly how you came to be here?'

396

'I can, but I'm not at all sure you'll believe it.'

'Try me. You might be amazed.'

So they did, and to their surprise the man, with a little tape recorder on the table between them, just nodded as the story went on, Nick filling in any details David left out.

At the end the man brought something out of his case. It was one of the dossiers they had prepared. 'We found your car at the exhibition. I was alerted as soon as your document arrived at the ministry this morning. We spoke to your sister-in-law and she told us where you were going.'

'Exactly who are you?'

'The sort of person that doesn't have to answer that sort of question, Mr Challis.'

'What are you going to do? Busby's dead, but Purkiss and Donaldson are still around.'

'Well, not exactly. We don't yet know where Donaldson's got to, it's true. You mean you didn't hear what's happened to Purkiss?'

'No, we didn't,' interjected Nick in an irritated voice. 'We've been stuck in a closet.'

'Well, that's what all this fuss is about. Unfortunate accident, it seems. He was doing his usual stunt for a coachload from this exhibition you went to. We're told he put on his armoured vest, sat down in the chair, invited one of them to pull the trigger, and bang! The only thing was, instead of the half-charged round they were meant to be using, it had somehow got switched for a fully charged one. Not just that, but it was their very latest high-power ammo, specially designed to deal with body armour. Dead as a doornail.'

David let his breath out with a noisy sigh.

'So, who switched it?'

The man gave a slight smile. 'I don't know. A cock-up

probably. If it wasn't for your story, I think we would assume that this man Busby had done it and then shot himself. Jealousy, I understand. He thought he was being eased out.'

'So who let us out?'

'Can't help you there either. Now, we just have to work out how to deal with you two.'

'How to deal with us? Who are you, M.I.5?'

'If you've got any doubts about my authority, we'll call in the superintendent and he can spell it out for you.'

David didn't like the edge in his voice and suddenly just wanted out. 'No. Go on,' he said.

'We have removed certain materials from your sister-in-law's house this morning. Namely, some still pictures brought back by you from France. I have to insist that you both sign these copies of the Official Secrets Act and that you acknowledge that all information which you may have come by relating to classified weaponry comes under the terms of that Act. Further, everything that has happened in connection with Bamco, including today's events, is similarly covered by the Act. You may find that a simpler version of these events appears in the press. If you reveal your knowledge of the affair to anyone else, you will be in breach of the Act.'

Back in the sunlight Nick was disgusted. 'We shouldn't have signed. They couldn't have done anything.'

'And after all we've bloody done. What say you we make the film anyway?'

'Yeah. Sod them all.'

Chapter Thirty-seven

Saturday August 10th 1991

He put the phone down. Two weeks on the Red Sea. A bit of snorkelling and a lot of sunbathing. He deserved it. He stretched luxuriously, relishing the effects of a good night's sleep, then ran his finger along the shelf next to the phone and looked at the thick dust. The buzzer went and he checked his watch, then walked to the door and lifted the flap over the peephole. Nodding, he opened the door and a gust of hot wind came in, bringing with it the exciting, noisy buzz of Tel Aviv and the spicy smell of the falafel stall on the street corner. He sniffed deeply as he smiled at his visitor.

'Oren,' cried the older man as he came in and embraced him, 'I am so sorry I was not here to greet you yesterday. I was stuck in Jerusalem. Hostage business.' He strode into the room. 'I read your final report this morning. You did very well. How is it to be back?'

'My plants are dead,' he said, waving a hand around. 'Otherwise all is well.'

'Plants. Well, worth the price. We will buy you new plants,' said the old man. 'What you did is worth all the plants in the world.'

'What's happened since?'

'It seems the British are inclined to close the file. They will say Busby killed the man Purkiss then killed himself in remorse. They will go on quietly looking for Mr Donaldson, no doubt.'

'Let them,' said Oren.

'After this, for you there will be a promotion. From planning to back-up in the affair of Dr Bull, then the executive role for Bamco. Next, I think, we will have you as project leader.'

'Is there another operation already?'

'Soon. Soon. There will always be those who don't hear our warnings. Our enemies are never short of suppliers.'

'I have two weeks' leave booked.'

'Take it. Take it. One thing, though.' He looked appraisingly at the younger man. 'In the end-phase, you took a risk.'

'No risk, really. Just a small change in timing.'

'To save the two journalists? Even a small change can have big effects if it has not been thought out. Some would say you were sentimental.'

'You know I am not a sentimentalist. If it had hazarded the operation, I would have let them die. But you know, we who should know it so well often forget that there are other people who have suffered too much,' said the man who had been Martin Donaldson.

The older man nodded slowly, then clapped the other on the shoulder. 'Will you come and share our Shabbat meal tonight?'

'I would very much like to.'

'You have not only fulfilled your assignment, you have brought the added bonus of Cracksman and Dodgem. You deserve your holiday.'

'Yes, maybe,' said the other. 'Just make sure they really work.'

Nick was pushing his luck, trying to get anyone, anywhere, to say something meaningful about what had happened at

Bamco. The papers reported that, after the tragic accident, the future of the company looked assured, with Purkiss's widow and the other family shareholders having agreed to a friendly takeover organized through the merchant bank Hazzard Mackeson. Insiders said Bamco's advanced weapons systems were of great value and would guarantee its future. However, all their Bamco fax material as well as the photos had been seized, and when Nick tried to remonstrate with the police, they politely reminded him that it couldn't have happened because if it had done, it would have involved bugging, and that would have to lead to criminal charges, wouldn't it, sir?

For Josie and David only part of the nightmare had lifted. The disappearance of the immediate danger to their lives left the dull ache of loss with no distraction and the pressing threat of the repossession of Chalice Hall. They went over and over the sums. The net worth of the estate was less than zero. The houses would take an age to sell.

They sat side by side at the desk, adding it all up, until David put down his pen with a sigh. 'If the worst comes to the worst, there's always my house. There's always space under my roof for as long as you want.'

He didn't see the look she gave him, and he still wouldn't have understood it if he had.

'There's another letter from the solicitor,' she said. 'He wants to know if we've had any luck looking for George's will yet?'

'Oh. I suppose we could go over there later on.'

'It seems he's been in touch with the bank. George lived on a fairly generous annuity, apparently provided by the Mainwaring family, to keep him going with a monthly income for life. That's stopped now, of course, but there's a

401

balance of seven thousand and a bit pounds in the bank, and something's got to be done with it.'

'All right then,' said David, getting up. 'Come on, I'll buy you lunch at the Percy Arms, then we'll go over and root around.'

Over lunch they talked mostly about George Middleton. David told her all about the diaries and what he had read in them.

'I think it's rather grand,' he said, 'the old man keeping Jackie Mainwaring's memory alive for all those years. It could so easily have all ended when he disappeared. Just another war statistic. But George Middleton cared about him. I think he really understood the agonies Jackie must have gone through. I'm sure it was a big comfort to Jackie's mother.'

'What are you going to do now?' said Josie.

'Do you know what I'd really like to do? I'd like to write a book about Jackie and George. Maybe a novel. Give up television for a bit.'

'I like that idea. Would you do it in London?'

He looked at her for some time before replying. 'Maybe I should do it up here. I could buy George's house from you, couldn't I? Get rid of the flat.'

She smiled and he felt a rush of great fondness for her.

'It's a lovely idea,' she said slowly, 'but it wouldn't help, would it? I mean, I can't think of anything nicer, but even if it paid off the finance company, there would still be the mortgage and the overdraft.'

They paid the bill and drove to the farmhouse. Before they went inside, he took her into the barn and showed her the Seafire model.

'I don't suppose anyone will finish it now.'

'Why don't you try?' she said. 'He would have liked that.'

In the house they were a little reluctant to start poking around too much. Under George Middleton's desk was an old black japanned deed-box, a small trunk really. David pulled it out.

'It's locked.'

Josie opened the desk drawer. 'There are some keys here. Try this one.'

It fitted. They knelt down on the rug and opened the lid. On top was an ancient teddy bear in a flying helmet. David, entranced, picked it up gently and stared at it. He spoke softly. 'He never goes up in the air, without his faithful teddy bear.'

'What?' said Josie, half laughing.

'This was Jackie Mainwaring's,' said David, astonished. 'It was mentioned in the squadron line book. He always flew with it.'

'Not the last time, he didn't,' said Josie. 'He couldn't have, or it wouldn't be here.'

David just stared at her. 'I'm not so sure,' he said.

Under the bear was a crisp white envelope, new-looking. They opened it. Inside was a will form, the kind you buy at stationery shops. It was very simple. It was dated just a month earlier. It left 'all my goods, chattels and money to my dear friend Mrs Joanna Challis, bereaved widow of the son of my wartime friend and colleague Bill Challis'. David gasped, and Josie said, in a strange, thick voice, 'Look at the signature.'

It was signed 'Jackie Mainwaring, more recently known as George Middleton.' Underneath was a witness signature by Michael Orde, who gave his profession as milkman.

In the trunk under it they found Jackie Mainwaring's account of his last wartime exploit. Suddenly removed from the recent turmoil into a different world, Josie sat in silence as David read it to her.

I am a coward and I can do no more about it. I am only glad my father is no longer alive to see what I have become. Yesterday I woke up in the usual pitiful state. I get so little sleep now, and I had once again to change my own sheets so no one would see what I had done. I had a slow ride south in an Anson, sitting in the second seat, to fetch a new cab. The pilot must have thought I was pretty pathetic. I had to hold my hands together to stop them shaking on take-off, even in that old tub. I could hardly talk to him.

I collected a new LIII. It felt better to be back in a Seafire. At least flying it still comes so naturally, I can do it without using that part of my brain which seems to be causing all the trouble. I suppose it's my imagination. The first forty minutes were all right, just cruising along trying not to think about anything much, then somewhere just beyond Darlington the cloud started banking up. It was getting pretty bumpy. I tried to climb over it, but there were great big thunderheads and the turbulence just got worse and worse.

I found I couldn't keep my imagination switched off. I could see the artificial horizon and the altimeter perfectly well, but all there was outside was grey murk and I kept seeing mountainsides and buildings whizzing at me out of it in my mind's eye, even though I knew there wasn't a mountain for miles and I was thousands of feet up.

In the end I panicked a bit. I never used to do that. I decided to dive, to get out through the bottom and hug the ground. Well, I did that, but what did I blasted well do but misread the altimeter. I came out of the cloud, pointing down, with three hundred knots on the clock, and there was the bloody ground, right there. I hauled back on the stick and almost took the wings off. The plane did a grand job. We shot back into the clouds like a startled racehorse, but when I looked at the panel again, the instruments were all over the place. I'd made the artificial horizon and the compass both tumble. They'd been set spinning meaninglessly by the violence of my manœuvres.

404

It took a second for it to sink in. I was worse off than ever now. I didn't know which way was up any more. I couldn't see a thing. All I had to go on was my altimeter and the air-speed indicator. Anyway, I throttled right back and tried to ease down. It was horrible. When the speed started creeping up, I would pull the stick back. Once I was clumsy and she hung on the edge of a stall for a second, but she came back without spinning.

We got down. Well, the plane got down with only a bit of help from me. We came out again through the bottom of the cloud, one wing low but in quite good order, with the best part of a thousand feet to spare. I circled, while I tried to work out where I was. There was a river that looked like the Tyne, and a bridge. Then I spotted Prudhoe Castle and that was a big relief. I turned northwest and flew along the Roman Wall for a bit. I can't really explain what happened next. Something took over. I'd had enough. Suddenly, for the first time in ages, I seemed to know what to do. I flew home up the valley of the North Tyne towards Otterburn. When I got to the house, I circled it until I saw Mother come out and stare, then I turned and came in as low and slow as I could down the valley into the old pasture by the barns. I sat in the cab for a while, watching Mother huffing and panting down the hill towards me. I thought, it's still my choice. I can just go back to the house and phone the CO, but I knew I wouldn't.

That was how it ended.

'I wonder what happened then?' asked David.

'His mother must have understood. I suppose in the confusion of war it wasn't too hard to pretend he was someone else, out here, miles from anywhere. Then they set him up with the house and money so he could stay on here after she died. It explains everything, the terms of the lease and so on. How sad. What a lonely life. No one else to love him.'

'I'm glad you were there at the end of it. I think he cared a lot for you.'

That just brought the tears to her eyes, and they clung to each other for a long time, until he kissed her on the forehead and she quietened down.

'It doesn't explain one thing,' he said. 'What happened to the plane.'

'Perhaps they took it apart.'

David shook his head. 'I wonder.'

An hour later the sweat and the splinters were forgotten. They had lugged the vast piles of planks and logs out from the end wall of the second barn, past George Middleton's little car. David couldn't think of it as Jackie Mainwaring's. It belonged to an altogether quieter person. There, revealed, was a brick wall, built right across the back of the old stone barn.

'There's no sign of a doorway or anything.' said Josie.

'There are five windows down the outside of this barn,' said David.

'So?'

'How many can you see in here?'

'Three. Oh, I see. Couldn't we get in through one of them?'

'I've tried. They've been boarded up from the inside.'

David took a hammer and a chisel and started on the mortar. It was old and soft. Soon he had opened a hole into the darkness, a foot across. Now he could pull the loose brickwork away with his hands, and in a minute or two the hole was wide enough. He crawled through and Josie passed him a torch. He stood up, but with a bang and a yell his head came up against something hard.

'Damn,' he said, and shone the torch up as she crawled

through and joined him. Then they were both completely silent. Towering over them in the gloom was a rising metal ellipse of pale blue paint, the underside of the folded wing of a Supermarine Seafire LIII. The plane had been man-handled sideways so it filled the width of the barn. How many people had it taken to do that? How many loyal estate workers had shared the Mainwarings' secret? The torchlight showed how, without the special struts to hand, the wings had been propped up by crude wooden beams. The tyres were perished and flat, the blue and grey paint peeling. The exposed aluminium underneath had the dusty look of oxide to it. There was a faint smell of old oil.

They stood in silence as if in a temple. 'It's the only one of its type there is, Josie,' said David. 'All the others have gone.'

Josie reached up and touched the rounded leading edge of the wing-root. 'It's not ours, though, is it?' she said practically. 'We'll have to tell the Navy or something. It must still belong to them, really.'

'Mmm, I suppose that's right.' They walked slowly round, ducking under the engine cowling, and he shone the torch beam into the gap between the tailplane and the back wall of the barn. 'There's something else in here.'

They squirmed under the far wing-root to get to it. There wasn't much space. Filling the small gap was a towering shape under an ancient tarpaulin, which fell to pieces as they tried to pull it off. But David knew what the shape was even before he saw the old green paint and the brass showing through the thin, often-polished chrome of the radiator, with the supercharger protruding below. The Bentley. Jackie's old bus. A hundred quid's worth of car in his day. Maybe a million now. One of the world's most desirable vehicles.

They stared at the dusty green monster and the plane above it for a long time, each thinking parallel thoughts of the things war could do to a man, then David broke the silence. 'George Middleton's last act of atonement for Jackie Mainwaring, Josie. He's given you your house back.'

They gazed at it in the yellow torch beam, both thinking how much Jackie must have longed to get it out into the full light of day again. He put his arms round her and she eased into his shoulder.

'David?'

'Yes, love?'

She chose her words carefully. 'If you really meant what you said about how there was space for me under your roof . . .'

'I meant it.'

'Then we could keep Jackie's car, couldn't we?'